MECCA

MECCA

SUSAN STRAIGHT

FARRAR, STRAUS AND GIROUX
NEW YORK

Farrar, Straus and Giroux
120 Broadway, New York 10271

Several of these chapters previously appeared, in different form,
in the following publications: *ESPN Magazine* ("Angel Wings"),
Granta ("The Lyrids, the Eta Aquariids, the Perseids" as "The Perseids"), *Alta* ("Ribs,
Muscle, Bone"), *Orange County Noir* ("Bee Canyon" as "The Phantom of Bee Canyon"),
and *Black Clock* ("San Luis Rey" as "Archaeology," and "Todos Mrs. Bunny").

Library of Congress Cataloging-in-Publication Data
Names: Straight, Susan, author.
Title: Mecca / Susan Straight.
Description: First edition. | New York : Farrar, Straus and Giroux, 2022. |
    Summary: "A California epic following several native, diverse Californians
    grasping for air in a world that continues to marginalize them"— Provided
    by publisher.
Identifiers: LCCN 2021049647 | ISBN 9780374604516 (hardcover)
Classification: LCC PS3569.T6795 M43 2022 | DDC 813/.54—dc23
LC record available at https://lccn.loc.gov/2021049647

Designed by Gretchen Achilles

www.fsgbooks.com
www.twitter.com/fsgbooks • www.facebook.com/fsgbooks

1   3   5   7   9   10   8   6   4   2

For all the Californios, the Californias, for my home and my people, every river and freeway, canyon and mountain, every dirt road and hidden trail, every classic 1964 Impala and 1976 Chevy Cheyenne truck. For all my childhood friends and the soul mates I just met, no matter where you are. For my family of hundreds from Rubidoux to San Bernardino, Riverside to Sacramento, Los Angeles to Albany, Ontario to Echo Park, Anaheim to Los Feliz, Corona to Calexico. For everyone I love in this state, and this nation, and for everyone who loved me back.

Truly this book is in memory of my brother, Jeff. When confronted with hatred or violence, he used to say: *I don't get that station, man.* His inner radio was all about oranges, dogs, and trucks. We always made up life on our own. I miss him every day.

CONTENTS

PART I

FUEGO CANYON

THE SANTA ANA RIVER BETWEEN
YORBA LINDA AND CORONA

The wind started up at three a.m., the same way it had for hundreds of years, the same way I used to hear the blowing so hard around our little house in the canyon that the loose windowsills sounded like harmonicas. The old metal weather stripping played like the gods pressed their mouths around the screens in the living room, where I slept when I was growing up. After I got off work this morning, the wind took a break, and I was knocked out for a few hours, waking up to hear Rose Sotelo's radio next door playing ranchera music, tubas and trumpets thumping against the stucco, her canaries worried in their little songs.

But now that I was back on shift, the Harley was pushing hard against the biggest gusts, the Santa Anas blowing crazier than ever, the way they did in the afternoons. Fierce from the nap. Brazilian pepper trees, the ones that grew in every vacant lot or frontage road area along the 91 and the 55 freeways, had those long branches like ferns or seaweed, and when the wind blew them sideways like skirts I could see homeless encampments under a lot of the trees.

A Thursday in October. Santa Ana winds, ninety-four degrees. Fire weather. People were three layers of pissed off. Everyone hated Thursday. Wednesday was hump day, but Thursday was when people drove like they wanted to kill each other. Today everyone was thinking of Halloween—the women wondering what sexy costume to wear for parties now that grown-ups had taken over the holiday, the men pissed that the Dodgers had lost even though they were supposed to be the Boys of October, and now the 2019 baseball season was over. The kids already tired as shit of school and practice. Then the wind. Every few minutes, dust and trash flew across the lanes.

But fall winds always made me think of my mother, holding me tight in the old redwood chair my father had tied to the porch railing, up in Fuego Canyon, while the Santa Anas blew in the black night when they always started. My first memory—her talking to me before dawn, gusts so strong it felt like our house would go rolling down the canyon like a tumbleweed, the horses snorting in the barn, and my father down in the orange groves, making sure the trees didn't dry out. "Nothing else is for sure but the wind," she'd say while the eucalyptus leaves and bark flew past us. "We might not get rain, mijo. For a whole year. But we always get the Santanas." My mother loved the wind, but she knew the flames would follow. And it wasn't just that she was watching for fire—she would hold me tight and say, "We're gonna look out for smoke, but right now, it's like we're in the ocean. Look at this, Johnny."

Today I was looking at one box truck that had blown over on an exit ramp near Corona, an overturned big rig up near the Chino Hills, and downed branches on most of the surface streets. The famous wind named for right here, where I drove every day, the Santa

Ana Canyon carved out by the river through mountains all along southern California. Hot as hell under my helmet. I kicked up the motorcycle and moved down the fast lane past the Katella exit. The old way to get to Disneyland. The Harley humming under me in the lane, and I never stopped thinking of it like a horse. Almost twenty years on the job and I still tensed up my right thigh when I was shifting the bike to change lanes—like my father taught me on my first horse when I was eight. "Let Mano feel where you want him to go. You have to love him that much and he has to love you, so he moves and you didn't even open your mouth." I was thirty-nine years old now and I saw my father almost every day—if I rode up to the ranch today for dinner, he'd laugh with the Vargas brothers who worked the cattle with him, watching the big cloud of dust the motorcycle would leave near the barn, and say, "Elegiré un palomino cualquier día. Preferiría cultivar heno que comprar gasolina."

But under his laughter his eyes would be serious, if I went into the barn to check a dent in the body from where a rock had hit me when I pulled someone over to the shoulder, or to see if a tire seemed low, like someone had tried to put a nail in there while I was getting coffee. We took care of our own patrol bikes, washed them and kept everything running. My father raised me to know we could die on a horse, a tractor, in a 1964 Chevy Impala if someone shot at the car, and definitely, I could die on that California Highway Patrol motorcycle, since nobody in the world was happy to see me ride up unless they'd been in an accident and were scared of dying if I didn't get them out of the car.

I had gotten three people that might have died out of their cars, in my time. I had crouched beside three people who died just before I got there. I never knew my own grandparents, but my friend Grief Embers told me his grandmother used to say if you lived where you were born, and you got to fifty, you saw every few miles the place where a soul you'd known left this world.

Back in 2002, when I was on my first solo patrols, I worked graveyard shift. Even the words made me nervous. That summer, in Santiago Canyon, I found the body of a young Cambodian girl, only twenty, whose car had hit a deer leaping across the toll road at three a.m. She and the deer lay fifty feet apart. The old Volkswagen Bug her surfer friends had restored had flown off the freeway and landed in the arroyo, and she was ejected. I shined the flashlight into her face and almost passed out. Her eyes. I put my fingers on her neck. Nothing. I called in the accident, and I sat next to the girl. The deer was making terrible noises from the brush. I knew it had managed to crawl a ways. And I was afraid to shoot it with my service weapon until my sergeant got there. We were way up in the mountains between Anaheim and Irvine. The sage and brittlebush smelled peppery where the car had crushed them. The blood left her with no sound.

She had a necklace made of dimes with holes punched in them, braided with red and gold embroidery thread. My mother had coils of those threads in her sewing box. When I went to notify the girl's father, Samana Som, at the apartment where he lived next to his doughnut shop in Santa Ana, he sat down on the two cement steps. Put his head down, put his hands inside his black hair like two starfish. That's what I remember. He sat like that for what seemed like forever, but was really about one minute. I know. That's how I got through every shift. Ten seconds. Thirty seconds, to let someone pick their words to me. One minute was forever, for humans. It meant pain or fear or calculation.

He lifted his head and said, "She have a necklace. You don't let someone take?"

"Dimes?" I said. "I'll make sure you get it."

"She grandmother make that when we come from Cambodia. We come from the killing field. That dime for break fever, and my daughter, she have fever all the time when she small. She wear that every day good luck." He looked up at me. His eyes the same black as my own father's. He said, "She grow up in the shop, always have to work, and now she want be a surfer, so we get up the same time. Two a.m. I start the doughnut and she surf for four hour and she come back to work."

So every single day, every single dime I ever saw, every time I drove past Santiago Canyon on patrol, where people were flying down the toll road never looking at the deep ravines filled with sage and brittlebush, I thought about that deer leaping up out of the canyon, and that girl whose grandmother came from a place where no deer lived, where Samana Som had told me a story about that grandmother surviving a tiger attack in the jungle, the tiger crouching on a branch above her when she was a girl walking down a path to get water for her own grandmother. I saw that whole thing, the coins around her throat, every fucking day every time I drove by a doughnut shop, in the time it takes our brains to tell us an entire story.

Two seconds?

Then I'd light up a brand-new Mercedes S-Class, going eighty-five in the second lane, weaving around people, someone coming from the beach back toward the real world in a hurry, the freeway something to complain about.

I drove past countless canyons every day. Black Star, Santiago, Silverado, Coal, Gypsum. Hundreds of miles of strip malls, housing tracts, Disneyland, and Knott's Berry Farm. But my dad's words were always in my head—*Johnny, there's bones buried in every canyon in California. Algo muerto. Vacas, linces, perros. Coyotes, conejos, chavalos.*

Then he always stopped. Took out his bandanna and wiped his forehead. Thought about the ranch cemetery further up the canyon. Where my mother was buried, in a metal casket that had been invisible under roses and lilies and bougainvillea blossoms. The next plot held two baby girls who had lived only hours. My sisters.

Then my father would say, *Johnny. Don't end as bones. Cause you're all I got.*

And every day, when I rode past Bee Canyon, I thought about the human I buried there, back when I was twenty. I'd never told anyone what happened in Bee Canyon. Not even my father, who might be the only one who would understand.

For the last fifteen years, I'd always worked second shift. Started at two p.m. Now I lit up a 2019 Tesla going in and out of the carpool lane like the 91 freeway was his own personal video game, like at 2:42 p.m. there was no way he shouldn't be able to drive like Formula One. Arne Johansson. Thirty-two. Yorba Linda. Told me, "Hey, Officer, uh, Frias? Is that how you say it?"

I let him think about that. Then I said, "Yup."

He got reassured that I sounded California. "Yeah, no, sure, I meant, I work at Digitech. Come on, man, I'm late for a meeting in Palm Springs." His fingers so perfect and white they looked like Pillsbury Doughboy on the black window frame, just resting there. He typed on a keyboard all day. He wore a black knit shirt like Tour de France. His meeting was on some mountain or desert.

"Yeah. I'll write this up really fast then," I said.

Then he went on his merry way, as my first partner Melt Olson used to say, when he was training me. I got back on the bike. Melt would hate that Tesla on general principles. But he'd really hate how boring the car looked.

I lit up two young guys in a lowered tricked-out 2016 black

Honda Civic trying to go eighty in the third lane, around the trucks carrying the millions of things people ordered online and then sent back. Binh Thanh Nguyen. Twenty-one. City of Westminster. He didn't tell me shit. He looked out the windshield. He took the ticket in silence and his friend said something very softly in Vietnamese and they waited until I got back on my bike. Then he pulled out into traffic and went seventy-two instead of eighty. Acceptable.

I had to light up a mom in a white 2008 Suburban for going in and out of the carpool lane. Janine Hughes. Thirty-six. Fullerton. Two car seats empty in the back, and she started crying, telling me she was late to pick up her kids from after-school care because her boss kept her an hour extra.

"Where do you work?" I said. She was heading west—home—so I figured San Bernardino.

"The Skechers warehouse in Moreno Valley," she said, tears going down her face. She wasn't looking at me. She was terrified of me. Of the $341 minimum carpool violation. She looked at the sky ahead of us, the wind tearing leaves off the cottonwood trees near the Green River Golf course. Leaves swirling past my boots like schools of fish on the road shoulder.

And even after this long working CHP, I always thought, yeah, I can do one thing today. Even if Janine is lying through her teeth. I stood there. Lying through your teeth. When I was twenty and heard that for the first time I thought, where else would you lie from? You can't hide your lying eyes. That old Eagles song. And your smile is a thin disguise. The guy who sold me my first motorcycle loved the Eagles. He gave me a 1973 Indian for $300.

Janine Hughes looked up. Because I'd been quiet for ten seconds, she thought I was fucking with her. Normally I would be.

People hate ten seconds of silence. Melt Olson taught me that the first week on patrol.

I was sweating under the helmet. You never got used to that—your whole skull felt like a cave dripping plink plink plink down your back into the uniform. Long-sleeved wool-blend shirt. People thought we were cyborgs and they forgot we sweated and then some asshole would say, "Wow, that uniform must be hot, and those boots, right?"

I wasn't giving Janine Hughes ten seconds to let her get nervous—she was already nervous—and I hoped she wouldn't say some stupid shit. I was only moving my sunglasses off my face so that sweat could evaporate. And so she wouldn't be staring at herself in the reflection—her mascara collecting under her eyes while she was crying.

I said, "Just a warning to remember to enter and exit the car-pool lanes only where there's a broken line. Not a double yellow."

She said, "What?"

I handed her the warning citation and said, "Yeah. Watch yourself out there, ma'am."

She said, "Ma'am?" Her eyes narrowed. "I'm thirty-six."

She was the kind of woman who got embarrassed when someone was nice to her and she had expected shit. Every day, I met people like that—even if I hauled them out from behind an airbag, or pushed them out of the way of an oncoming car.

I said, "Well, you have kids."

She said, "Don't you? Sir?" Her mascara had smeared so black on her cheeks she was like a quarterback on game day.

"No," I said.

She sniffled and said, "Sorry. I figured you must have kids. You're married?"

"No," I said.

"Me neither. It's so hard." She didn't say it like flirting. She just said it.

There's something very wrong with a guy who's never been married, though. When your friends set you up for years, at a barbecue or a bar or birthday party, when three or four women a week say, *You see my number right there. Nobody has a home phone now so you know I'll answer if you call. Don't text me anything you can't back up, baby, and don't be surprised to see me different. You know. When I text you back something good.*

She looked up at my glasses. At herself. "Thank you. Thank you."

I said, "Drive safe, Ms. Hughes."

She drove away like my favorite word I'd learned from Melt. *Chastened.* He said it was all about guilt and confession and penance. For about ten miles. Maybe twelve.

I got back on the bike, drove for a long time herding everyone. Scaring them into slowing down. Just like the steers up at the ranch. Moving a group of animals by slanting behind them at their flanks. California freeways were all about the right rear tires and the rearview mirrors and me watching about forty things at the same time. No different from the ranch, except that if someone wanted to shoot me, or suddenly swerve and take me out, I'd be dead faster and more thoroughly than if a bull or an aggressive yearling calf decided to turn on me and my horse, Mano.

You don't have kids? Every time I'd been with a woman for a few months, eventually the idea of kids came up. I couldn't tell them about the girl in the canyon, her father's eyes. I saw Samana Som every Tuesday, when I bought doughnuts, when we talked for a few minutes about his life. She had been his only child. Chhoua Som. When I left the pink box of two dozen at the Santa Ana Division where I worked, nobody rolled their eyes, because they all

remembered Chhoua Som. Our dispatchers at the 675 were mothers, and most of the guys I worked with had kids. But there were
a few of us who I know felt like I did. Keep to yourself, and you'll
have fewer people to lose.

Every week I took doughnuts to my father and the Vargas
brothers on the ranch, too. Three men alone in a canyon, with
me as the only kid all those years, and now I was almost forty. No
one else to carry on with the cattle and horses, and I was a cop.
"Keeping strangers safe, people who don't give a shit about him,"
as Ramón Vargas said one night, when he thought I wouldn't hear
them talking about me in the barn.

I lit up a 1978 Cadillac Eldorado near Tustin. Original white with
rag top. On the shoulder, I walked up to the passenger-side window and motioned for the driver to roll it down. An older man. Of
course. He scooped the air trying to tell me to come around to his
side. "I can't hear you!" he yelled.

Shit. We were never supposed to lean in the driver side now. I
figured the old man wouldn't shoot me. Pale blue golf shirt, his
arm so covered with brown spots from sun he looked like a pinto
horse, and his hair pure shiny silver combed straight back from his
forehead. He said, "Holy cow, officer, why'd you pull me over?"
and everything came back to me, like it was my first months on
patrol.

I always wanted to speak perfect American. Every time I
stopped a driver, I wanted to say exactly the right sentences and
mix in exactly the right weird words for whatever I could see about
the person, so they wouldn't get to say, "Officer *Frias*? What the
hell. *You're* pulling me over? You sure you're a citizen?"

Because I was moreno, and I was in the sun all afternoon, and my Ray-Bans were black, and my boots were black, and they were pissed. They didn't want to see a face like mine. They didn't say the same things to Raymond Ayala or Frank Orta, who worked patrol, too, because they had green eyes and light skin. Güeros. They said different things to Viet Nguyen and Justin Pham—whose parents were born in Vietnam. They said plenty of crap to Odell Roberts, who was fifty-two and had gotten shit for being a Black officer in Orange County for years.

But now, after three years of MAGA, some asshats said, "You know this is an S-Class Mercedes, right? Maybe I need to see your ID, make sure you're not a bad hombre yourself."

They didn't have to call me a wetback now. They could say what the leader of the free world said. I knew every fucking make and model of car—American, German, British and Italian, Korean and Japanese—because I studied car magazines, because I loved cars. I spoke better American than they did because I listened. They never listened.

Holy cow was one of the first ones I learned, back in 1999. Hardly anybody said it now. Only someone like this guy. "Your right brake light is out, sir," I said. "Can I see your license and registration?"

"Well, if that's all you can think up." But then he grinned, his teeth full of those old metal fillings in the back. "You can bet your Sunday socks I'm the only person on the road would use my turn signals anyway. But I feel safe in this big metal boat. They don't make cars like this anymore. If you get hit in a Hyundai, you bought the farm."

Bought the farm. Dead.

"Here you go." John Robinson. Seventy-two. La Habra. I wrote the fix-it ticket and he said, "This'll give me an excuse to get out of the house tomorrow and see my friend Bum. He's been working on this car for forty years." He squinted at me. "I'll bet you don't know anyone named Bum."

"I do," I said. "My first patrol partner has a brother named Bum. His name is Melt."

Robinson grinned again. "Well, I'll be." And I filed that one away, too. *I'll be what?* Robinson said, "Okay, young man."

I said, "I'm fixing my dad's '76 Chevy Cheyenne every weekend. So good luck."

And I waited for him to say something about Melt Olson. About cars. About fathers. But he lifted his hand how older people did, and moved the Eldorado forward slowly on the shoulder, and I stepped back.

I got back on the bike. I remembered being twenty, trying to figure out all the variations. *Holy cow.* Never horse or dog or chicken. *Holy smokes.* Never fire or flame. *Holy mackerel.* Never trout or salmon or sardine. *Holy moly.* Whatever the hell that was. Roly-poly was a pill bug.

Holy shit. But never any other bodily function. Never holy pee.

Who thought up all this stuff the first time? Where did it come from? I used to ask my best friend Manny Delgado what he thought, and he said, "Homes, I think you're fuckin loco in the cabeza, man. Who thought up tostilocos and the garbage burrito? I always wondered, do they have tostilocos in Mexico? Cause we still never been there."

I kept thinking about my mother, while I drove the 91 in the almost-stopped traffic, some of the worst congestion in America. From Anaheim, where she took me and Manny one time to Disneyland, with free tickets she got from someone at the citrus packing plant, to Placentia, where she used to stand sorting the oranges into boxes. I drove through Santa Ana and Tustin, dipping in and out of the first and second lanes between cars, watching for people tossing cigarettes into the wind, people drifting. Most of them were speeding, most of them were texting. I could pull over a car every ten seconds and it wouldn't mean shit. I went through clouds of vape rolling out of open windows, smelling way too sweet, like bubble gum or fruit. Made me feel sick if I got a big mouthful.

And I kept thinking about Melt Olson. I had to go see him one day, out in La Habra. He'd retired four years ago, and we always said we'd keep in touch. Like guys, we didn't. He and my father were the same age, sixty-two.

When I graduated from the academy, I was twenty-one, and they assigned me to a patrol car. Melt was my training officer. He'd been on the road for twenty-five years. It was 1999. I remember keeping track of the days on my calendar, hanging on the wall in the apartment Manny Delgado and I rented in Corona.

Back then I worked morning shift with Olson, so I left at five a.m. Sometimes Manny had talked his girl Magdalena into lying to her parents and spending the night. Once I heard her talking in her sleep when I was heading quiet out the door. She said, "Nopalitos. No más, no más."

Lena was the oldest of eleven kids, born in Buttonwillow. She told me her mom used to make her clean the spines off the nopales and cut them up for dinner. They survived on homemade tortillas, nopales, and one piece of chicken shredded into the cactus. Lena said there would always be one little red spine stuck in her finger and she couldn't find it, and it would hurt all night.

Manny and I were lucky, we knew. We had meat every day, papas and eggs, and oranges. In summer we had the corn my mother grew, elotes dripping with butter and chile. Back in 1999, when I got into the Santa Ana station, I opened my locker, put on my uniform and boots, and I was thinking about Lena's fingers. It was the tenth day, when we were driving down the 91 through Anaheim, and Melt Olson said, "Your dad Mexican?"

I'd been waiting for that. Olson hadn't been talking much. I said, "He was born in Chino. Then they moved to Placentia. Right there." I pointed to the hills above Placentia, where it used to be orange groves, and now was thousands of houses.

"La Jolla Camp?" he said.

I was surprised. "Yeah, that was the old ranch camp."

He nodded. He was a short thin dude, but his arms were all ropy muscle, and he had no belly. He had a mustache like an upside-down brown staple. He said, "My dad come from north Texas. The dust bowl. We were Okies and we weren't even from fuckin Oklahoma. We come out here to La Habra and he was a ranch foreman. Valencias."

So I said, "I grew up in Fuego Canyon. Valencias and navels. Cattle up in the hills."

He nodded again. He said, "I'm watchin how people talk to you, when we pull em over. You let them say their shit. Then they can hear how stupid they sound, but you didn't point it out. Pisses them off, so watch their hands and not their mouth. Watch their legs. See if they're jumpy. If it's a woman, she's not gonna shoot us. She'd try to flirt out of the ticket with me, but with you . . . we'll see." Then he grinned. "If she speaks Spanish, I'll only know half the words, so you can flirt back as long as you keep a straight face."

He was watching me drive. I hated the patrol car. The Dodge Charger. I wanted to be on the motorcycle, but I had to ride patrol with Olson for at least a year. Then I might get the Harley bike. Back in the day, CHP used the Indian and the BMW. But by the time I got in, it was the Harley.

Melt said, "Okies and Mexicans. They never get it out of their minds. California thinks they're the most liberal and they fuckin love everybody. But they'll ask you where you were born just like people do in a small town in Texas. Same old shit."

Then we were driving and he said, "Shit on a shingle. You ever eat that?"

I was surprised. "What? What's that?"

"Whatever kinda cheap canned meat you got from the government, and your mom mixed it with some white gravy and plopped it on bread. Wonder bread."

White gravy? I'd thought. *What the hell?*

I was watching a new black Mercedes weaving in and out of the carpool lane ahead of us. "No. I never ate that. My mom made tortillas every day when I was little. And we always had beef cause of the cattle. Then my dad would make breakfast and lunch. Put six tortillas on the grill, scrambled eggs and potatoes and shredded beef. Cheese and red sauce. Wrap them in foil and we put them in the dashboard of his truck. They'd be hot for hours in the sun. We were lucky."

"Who's we?"

"Just me and my dad."

"No brothers and sisters?"

I shook my head. I moved on the Mercedes and hit the lights.

Melt said, "Yeah. I only eat Mexican food now. But sometimes I miss shit on a shingle. There were ten of us. We fought for every piece of bread." He pointed. "I hate pullin them over in the carpool lane and I ain't ready to die today. I got an annuity about as tiny as a baby turtle. Get him over to the shoulder. Remember what I told you."

Annuity. I had no idea what that was, back then. But every day, I remembered what Melt said about watching their hands and legs, their knees and thighs, to see if they were gonna mash down on the gas and run, their fingers on the wheel. Not their mouths and all the shit that came out when they hated me.

Now it was 4:27 and I was heading past Yorba Linda, toward the canyons where I grew up. Every single damn day I was on shift I drove past home, looked up at the five canyons. Even after thirty-one years, every time the Santa Anas blew, I saw my mother so clearly I felt like a kid. The backs of her knees, when I was so small I held on to her legs while she made burritos, standing at the stove. She wore dresses, sandals or slippers or boots, but there were three seams at the back of her knees. Like someone sewed her legs together, and that scared the hell out of me. I used to try and twist my legs up to see if I had them, too. I had never seen my father's legs in my life.

My mother could help my father cut up a dead orange tree, she could skin a rabbit and put it in a sauce, braid ribbons into her hair, and she knew the words for every flower and tree in these canyons. She had lived her whole life in Fuego Canyon. Back when I was five, we went to the beach and some asshole told her to go back to Mexico. Mami lifted her chin and looked down at this big dude like she was two feet taller than he was, and she said, "My grandmother's grandmother came from Mexico in 1774. But I never been there. You go down to Cabo for spring break? Next time, you stay there."

Now I headed east, and got off on Gypsum Canyon Road. The wind made me thirsty a lot faster, and I'd had a bottle of water at the division during our shift briefing. Usually I'd get through my first three hours fine before I stopped to see Ali Sadaat for coffee, but not today. I pulled into the Circle K, and parked the Harley near the entrance. Then the wind shoved down the canyon and blew the hair sideways on two women who were just getting out the glass door, wearing scrubs and clutching insulated mugs with Mickey and Minnie Mouse holding gloves. Long black hair whipping around the women's faces and wrapping their necks. Like they were the ones flying. I grabbed the heavy door.

"¡Ay, mierda!" one of them said. "¡Pinches Santanas!"

The other one laughed. She put her mug down between her feet in those green booties and said, "You're cussing at a weather pattern that's existed for centuries, Nelda." She grabbed her friend's shoulders and raked back all the hair off her face and neck and made three twists like magic and slid one of the ruffled things off her wrist.

Scrunchie. Leti called it a scrunchie. Hers were silk.

The woman named Nelda had a face now. Soft and round and her eyes tiny and black, her eyebrows drawn on heavy. I said, "Ladies." They looked at my helmet, my gloves, my boots. They had no idea who I was. And when they ran toward a van with Alta Vista Assisted Living Community painted on the side, I knew so many things about them—they spent their days taking care of other people's parents, they loved Disneyland, and they had known each other forever. The other one wrapped up her own hair now—she kept her eyes on me, and smiled.

Ali was sweeping—the floor near the entrance was littered with tiny leaves from the pepper trees. Dried slivers of palm frond. Receipts he'd just handed to someone. He looked up and said, "You're early, man. You okay?" He was huge, six-three, a bear with slumped shoulders and big flat feet, giant brown eyes and thick brows and beard. I was glad there wasn't anyone in the store for this moment—I went toward the back, to the employee restroom Ali always let me use. Nobody wanted to stand and unzip at Circle K when a cop with a gun walked in.

When I came back out, Ali had gone behind the counter and poured me coffee from the pot we shared five evenings a week. He was born in Afghanistan, but his parents came to California when he was three. His father bought the store when Ali was seventeen; Ali had gone to college for two years, but then his dad had a heart attack. Ali kept the store going, alone, for a year, until his father was recovered. Now he worked swing shift, just like me, but he did twelve hours, and his father did the other twelve. Ali made Turkish coffee that tasted like nothing else; only my father's Café Bustelo was better. He handed me a go-cup and sat on his tall stool, watching the trash blow in furious circles around the parking lot.

I took the first sip. "You got tomorrow off? You have how many dates?"

"Very funny," Ali said. He would turn thirty-nine in a month. His mother was determined to get him married this year. He had three sisters, all younger, and they were married with kids.

Ali had wanted to move to Palm Springs since he was a kid; he had wanted to be an architect, loved mid-century architecture, all the clean lines and minimal design. He had a magazine open on the counter right now, a house on a cliff, solid wall of windows. His parents' house in Fullerton was huge, dark, and crowded with traditional Afghan furniture and rugs and paintings. And children.

"What about you?" he said. "Did Leti come see you?"

I took another swallow. "Yup."

He shook his head. Sometimes I couldn't believe this guy I met ten years ago—when he and his father traded shifts—was who I told about women. But we had this space where I usually stood after nine p.m., when I was tired as hell and ready to be done, and he was just heading into the long night, and we started talking about our fathers.

I said, "She stayed two days. She's moving up to Stanford. Going to law school."

"Lucky for her," he said, putting his head down a little, so I could see silver hairs already coming at the top of his head. "Reinvention. She's what—thirty-five?"

I wiped my face with one of the napkins near the hot dogs and taquitos. "Yeah," I said. "It's cool." There was no way to explain that part to Ali, what Leti had said. And this wasn't my twenty-minute break. I put my helmet back on and slid a five onto the counter. "See you at nine," I said.

I headed west again, toward the Orange Crush, where the Golden State Freeway, the Garden Grove Freeway, and the Pomona Freeway meet—half a million cars get tangled up there every day. Out of Santa Ana Division, we rode 225 miles of freeway on patrol, unless we got a pursuit, and then we might go all the way to the desert, or through LA, or down toward San Diego, until the vehicle pulled over. I got on the Riverside Freeway, the 91, and moved through the stalled traffic slowly, steering the Harley down the line between the carpool lanes and the fast lane—the eight-foot-wide channel I navigated every day—just like when my father taught me to ride his big horse Jefa through a streambed or ravine with only a few feet on each side of her belly, away from tumbleweeds or nopales.

Swing shift was the worst, with the rush-hour traffic. By this time, I usually had to work at least two fender benders, but not tonight. After eight, until my shift ended at ten p.m., I'd ride faster, catching drivers who'd waited out rush hour at the bar with beer or margaritas, or the landscapers and contractors who were so tired they forgot to tie down a mower or ladder that fell into lanes, or the idiots coming back from the beach or heading to the desert. You'd be surprised how much having surfboards or racing bikes or camping gear stowed on the roof makes people think their time is more valuable than anyone else's—especially when they're checking their Instagram.

That was when something careless would get someone killed. A cooler flying off into the fast lane and somebody swerving to avoid it. A ladder bouncing one too many times and breaking the frayed old rope a landscaper who made shit money had tied on there—and the metal ladder hitting a windshield. I'd never forget the night four teenagers hadn't tied down their expensive surfboards, were heading for night surfing at Huntington Beach, and all four boards went sliding across the lanes. It was 9:40, and I was heading back to the division, but I saw shadows running across the freeway—the fucking kids trying to retrieve their boards. I had to call for two patrol cars to slow the traffic or the kids would have gotten hit. They were so high they laughed the whole time.

Every day, even a windy hot Thursday, I'd wait for my father and mother's favorite time of day. No matter the weather or what had happened on the ranch. Ocaso. The blue edges of new dark while the sky figured out how it would turn the world around this evening. This night, different every single time. Then sunset.

Most days, on my lunch break at six or six thirty, I'd drive up into Fuego Canyon to check on my father and the Vargas brothers. Eat a quick meal, meat and papas and tortillas—beer for them, and my father made fresh coffee for me.

Today, with the wind, I wanted to pass by the canyons every hour or so—in case of fire. I got off the freeway near Box Canyon, looked out at the Santa Ana River, the tall arundo cane and eucalyptus trees that could go up like torches. Homeless camps were full of wood fires, and many times, propane tanks. Kids riding dirt bikes would scatter sparks. On the few ranches left around here, tractors or brush clearing could start a fire when a blade hit a rock. A gust blew the Harley, where I was parked at the edge of the frontage road that led to where the old Bryant Ranch used to be. It was now hundreds of tract homes and parkways and strip malls. A line of cars exited behind me.

This canyon was like all the others in southern California, all the places that were wild when my mom's people got here before this was a state, all the places where the Tongva and Cahuilla and Serrano people knew each canyon and mountain like I did—now filled up with housing tracts and shopping centers. Except canyons or foothills or rivers or arroyos nobody could level. I took off my helmet. The wind shoved my sunglasses into my forehead. I kept thinking about what the Cadillac driver said today—the older guy. Same as Festus used to say on *Gunsmoke*. *You can bet your Sunday socks*. I didn't have Sunday socks, but if I did, and my mother was still alive, I'd bet she would be sitting up tonight waiting for the spark, and the flames.

"Chispa," she used to whisper, when I was in that wooden chair with her, the wind tearing past us. "So little. But then fuego. So easy to start. You just have to blow."

Five canyons between the Santa Ana River and the mountains that separated Orange County from Chino. Every canyon had a name, my father taught me, when I was learning to ride Mano, and we went down the trails between the river, the railroad tracks, and the base of the hills. At the end of each ravine, a white sandy place where water and stones poured down the mountains after a storm. From the west, Box Canyon and Bee Canyon. From the east, Gypsum Canyon and Coal Canyon. And in the middle, we lived two miles up a dirt ranch road into the hills, on Anza Ranch, in Fuego Canyon. Named for Fire.

He taught me three things to survive living in a canyon: They always burned, eventually. They always flooded, as even an inch or two of rain would gather in the arroyos and rush into the canyons as murderous torrents. The third—that was the bones.

My father showed me and Manny Delgado how to get home to Fuego if we got lost when we hunted rabbits, or if we had to find a stray calf, or chase off coyotes. He showed us to how to look for rain clouds, and when not to be up in the ravines because they'd flood or burn.

Manny and I grew up together, since we were three, when his parents got here from Jalisco. All those years, we were gonna run a custom car shop. Restore Impalas, 1959–64, and Chevy trucks, the old Apache from 1958–59. When we were sixteen, we restored a 1959 Cadillac with the fins—a Batmobile. Now he ran the shop with his dad, in Fontana. He and Lena got married in 2002. She was manager at a KFC in San Bernardino.

All my friends and cousins were married, had kids. Everyone except me. And Leti had packed up for good two days ago.

Before I put on my helmet and got back on the road, I looked at Fuego Canyon, across the riverbed. The faint pink of old fire retardant high up on the mountains above, from five years ago. The water tank my father taught us to use as compass center— Anza Ranch water, for the cattle we ran up in the hills. And below that, down the dark line of trees like a vein of green, that lined the ranch road, there was a scarlet only I would know to look for. My mother's bougainvillea vine, thirty years old now, and my father never stopped it from growing for hundreds of feet, blooming in red waves all over the canyon.

Then I looked at Bee Canyon, about a mile east. When I was twenty, I'd killed a man in Bee Canyon, and his bones were buried there. Every time there was a flood, I worried that his skeleton would wash down into the river and catch on the rocks or circle around in some fucking eddy, where a bike rider or homeless person would see it and call somebody. I always hoped he'd washed all the way down the Santa Ana, into the Newport Channel, and out to the Pacific Ocean, one bone at a time.

I had never told anyone what happened that day. Not Manny, who knew every damn thing about me; not the other guys we used to ride with, Bobby Carter and Grief Embers. All four of us had gone to the academy up in Sacramento for CHP, but I was the only one who made it through training and got a badge. I'd been on patrol barely six months when I shot the man, with my service weapon.

I'd never told my father. Not the priest at Our Lady of Perpetual Help. Never confessed my crime to anyone.

Only two people saw me shoot, and only one knew he was buried. That man was a phantom, a ghost, and he died five years ago himself, in a mental hospital.

The wind ripped down the arroyos now, pushing me against the bike. My uniform boots brown with dust. Chispa—one spark, from a mower or fallen power line or tossed cigarette butt. Fuego.

Every time there was a wildfire, I hoped it wouldn't burn deep into Bee Canyon, because if his skeleton wasn't gone, and the Sikorsky helicopters dropped water in that ravine, they might finally wash him out of the grave I dug with a pick—all I had—and the rocks I laid on top to keep him there.

BEE CANYON

I'm not done with you, little Bunny, he said to her. The woman was on all fours, her legs covered with blood and bruises, her long flowery skirt crushed up around her waist. Like the tutu on a cartoon elephant. Her nose was broken and the blood was spooling out into the sand like a tether, holding her there, like the blood was a rope and she couldn't move, while he came for me. *You don't even know how to shoot that, Fritos,* he said, reaching for me like he was John Wayne, like I was some scared little kid.

I want to think it was self-defense. But I wasn't just scared he'd kill me, and her. I hated him. Every part of him. The blond hair on his chest, her long reddish hair caught in his metal watchband like strands of a tail. His mouth that never stopped talking.

The freeway phantom watched us, hidden up in the rocks. I didn't know it was the phantom at the time. Everyone in CHP had been searching for him, back in 1999. But no one had ever seen him, until I did that day.

★   ★   ★

It had been my day off. I didn't go up to Bee Canyon that day to shoot gophers, even though it was a bad year for them and my father and I had been taking them out when we could, with the .22 rifles, sitting on the old metal folding chairs in the lemon grove waiting for their heads to pop up. I could shoot a gopher from thirty feet away while the animal hesitated, looked around, waiting for footsteps, for the smallest tremble of the earth. But I was having trouble with the service revolver.

I'd been CHP for five months and two weeks and three days. I'd come to the ranch that Monday to help my father take out two dead Meyer lemon trees. Gophers had killed seven trees so far. My dad said that his father used to joke about eating rabbits, quail, doves, but never gopher, and we both laughed. By the time we pulled out the stumps, I was covered with sweat and dirt and crumbled roots. We chainsawed the trees for firewood, and I stacked the green wood on the west side of the barn so it could dry out.

I told my father I was having trouble with the gun. A Smith & Wesson .40-caliber police-issued service revolver. No one up at the ranch had a handgun. We had rifles and shotguns. Mrs. Dottie Anza, who owned the land, had some old musket from the 1800s up at her house, hanging on the wall. Her grandfather's gun, from Spain. No one had touched it in decades.

The Anza land had fifty acres of citrus, just past the Santa Ana River, then the dry Fuego Creek and stone bridge. Then our barn and the ranch camp houses. Another mile up the ranch road was the original adobe house built in 1849, by the first Anza to get this land from Mexico. Since 1942, the only one lived there was Mrs. Dorotea Juana Antonio de Anza, who everyone called Dottie. She had never married, but my father and the others called her señora. She was about seventy back then, in 1999. Past her house were the horse corrals, the big stone barn, and the six hundred acres where we ran the cattle.

I had been shooting a .22 rifle all my life, my dad had his rifle, and the Vargas brothers had two rifles and a shotgun, for coyotes, bobcats, snakes. None of us shot handguns. It was the second Monday in August. Around four, we would make coffee, like we had always done in summer. We took the quad runner from the groves back up the ranch road. My father parked the four-wheeler by our barn, where we kept the tractor, the tools and fertilizer, and old smudge pots. The Vargas brothers had already ridden down from the cattle, and their horses were tied to the rail, eating apples.

There were two rows of five wooden houses, built back in 1905, framing painted white, each with a board porch and railing across the front. Ours was the first house, almost hidden by the huge bougainvillea vine that covered part of the roof and all of the porch. The Vargas brothers lived in the house across from my father. All the others were empty by then, boarded up blind. When Manny came to hang out with me in Fuego Canyon, he always sat for a while on the steps of his old porch—the third house down.

"I'll make your coffee," I told my father, and he washed up at the kitchen sink. Every afternoon, he'd make a fresh pot in his old Pyrex glass pot. He and Ramón and Sergio Vargas would drink coffee and watch an hour of *Gunsmoke* on their favorite channel that showed old Westerns. They kept the television out under the ramada, the wood structure we covered with new palm fronds every spring. The long orange extension cord went into the kitchen window. It was too hot in the house to watch TV until the end of October, and then my father would put it back in his bedroom.

When he went outside, I washed my face, got the sawdust out of my ears, and combed my hair again. It was short, for the job, but I hated looking military when Manny and I went to a bar or a lowrider show, so I kept the top long enough to brush back with Tres Flores pomade.

The kitchen was my mother's small dance of efficient. Four-burner stove from Sears. Old Frigidaire next to that. Cast-iron sink. About three feet of wood counter my father kept sanded and polished. She used to turn circles like ballet, she said when I was little. "A ballet girl would probably get dizzy in here and fall down, Johnny. You better stay out of my way!"

She made tortillas every morning, on the old cast-iron comal that used to belong to her mother. Stacks of tortillas that we all ate for the rest of the day. For years, after she died, my father kept the last bag of harina in the wooden cupboard, until moths got inside. Now I brought bags of handmade tortillas from Mercado Banderilla on Wednesdays and Sundays.

The smell of coffee always seemed to fill the three rooms. I glanced inside my parents' room, with their wedding portrait on the wall, the dresser neat with my dad's combs and Tres Flores by the circle mirror, the bed made tight. The tiny bathroom had been added on the side of the house in 1950, when they finally got rid of the outhouses. For a few minutes, I sat on the couch in the living room. My bed. Just under the front window, and every morning before dawn I used to wake up because all the sparrows that lived in the bougainvillea started chirping. Hundreds of them.

I looked at the hot August light pouring through the flowers that day. From the west. I remembered in winter 1987 how the crows and my mother kept me awake. The temperature dropped to twenty-seven degrees, three nights in a row, and we stayed up trying to keep the oranges from freezing, which ruined the juice. My father even turned water on some of the trees—the fruit froze at thirty-two, but the juice would stay sweeter than at dry twenty-seven. I woke up on a blanket under fantastical icicles dangling from the leaves and oranges, and my mother was asleep in the truck bed, sitting up, wrapped in her coat and blankets.

Two days after that, the crows started their raspy craws in the blind foggy morning, and my mother coughed for hours. She had pneumonia.

The altar had never changed since she died. It was a wooden shelf my father built for the wall near his recliner chair. A picture of my mother at a party when she was young, maybe twenty, her hair blown out big in curls away from her face, her lipstick red, her eyes black and shiny as fresh-charred wood, a silver underneath. My father put fresh roses or wildflowers every day on the altar, left the veladora of Our Lady of Guadalupe lit all night, no matter how many times I told him it was dangerous.

The flame was little now, inside the glass, swimming in pink wax. A golden grain of rice. Shivering.

That spring, she still coughed all night, and the coyotes would chatter at the edges of the camp, and the mockingbirds would fight with their songs, and I lay on the couch awake. I nodded off in school. It was fourth grade. When I got home, I slept on my dad's cot in the barn.

The weathered redwood chair my father had tied to the porch post for her, for me, for the wind, fell apart a few years ago.

That day we took out the lemon trees, I brought four cups of coffee out to the ramada. My father was only thirty-nine, but his shoulders were wrecked, full of loose cartilage. He said, "Listen," and he moved his shoulders; the popping was so loud he laughed and said, "Like that cereal you and Manny always wanted."

We always begged for Rice Krispies. We had warm tortillas for breakfast, lunch, and dinner. Same as my mother and father had grown up eating.

The Vargas brothers were fifty-two. Twins. They were born here in Anza Camp, and they would never live anywhere else. Sergio was half-asleep, Stetson hat over his face like a vaquero, slumped in his big wicker chair Manny and I had found at a yard sale. Ramón took his coffee and said to me, "¿Qué pasó? ¿Una chica y te arañó?"

My right forearm was cut up, just scabbing over. "No girl got me. The freeway phantom," I said. "He busted someone's window and I had to get her out." A middle-aged woman, she'd been screaming, sitting straight up in the Toyota Corolla, a few miles west near Green River Road. For months, some guy had been throwing rocks from the freeway shoulder, from the oleander bushes near the exits, even from the overpasses at night. The newspapers called him the freeway phantom, said he must be a disturbed veteran with PTSD, living in the river bottom. They'd found a crude bridge made of vines.

"The CHP is bringing in a tracker," I said. "They're putting together a search party. He's gonna kill someone."

Sergio said from under his hat, "I seen him. Ocaso. Una sombra. I was on the tractor. Es que los tumbleweed."

Ramón said, "I seen him, too. En la noche. I hear him in the stock tank, es que a bath in there."

My father said, "Rafael, the cook at the golf course, he told me el fantasma es un negrito. Moreno or negro. Travieso pero no peligroso. He took food from the dumpster in the back." My father sat on the wooden bench where he repaired tractor parts and sharpened pruning shears. His hands and mine still stained with black rime from the citrus. "Como mocoso, throwing rocks."

Sergio said, "He makes little piles. Las piedras en los cañones. But Johnny, no policía up here, tú sabes."

I knew. Everything about the way we lived in the canyon was illegal. Nobody really knew we were still up here, and Mrs. Dottie wanted to keep it that way. People kept telling my father she would have to sell the land if the county sent code enforcement.

She had almost a thousand acres. "Look at all those new houses," my father said. "Carbon Canyon, Bryant Canyon. They'll bulldoze all this down. The place will be full of people instead of cows."

"Pero now Johnny's a cop," Sergio said.

I finished my coffee, and took out my service revolver. Ramón Vargas looked at it warily. I said, "It's not what you think. CHP is tickets. Accidents. And I don't have cop friends who are gonna come up here."

I hadn't told him or Manny about what I'd already seen, in six months. The woman two nights ago with her lap full of glass, cuts on her arm. The rock at her feet. Last month, the teenaged boy we pulled out of a Celica, his face covered with so much blood it looked worse than any horror movie, and Melt Olson saying, *Calm down, Frías, breathe, don't let him see you doing that, come on, he's the one hurt, quit that shit, look, it's two cuts on his forehead, that's why so much blood, didn't you know the head bleeds that much, good thing you don't have a kid yet, or you'd have a fuckin heart attack, look, see the cut? Now call it in.*

I turned the Smith & Wesson over in my hand. Heavy, slick polished. Didn't feel like my gun. "It's the shooting range, at the academy," I said. "We have to practice and get certified every year. I want to get the highest score. I know I can shoot better than any of them, but the kick on this thing is weird."

My father held out his hand, and I put the gun there. He checked out the trigger, the barrel, and gave it back, like it smelled bad. I said, "The target makes me focus a different way than when we're sighting something out here. There's three gabachos keep messing with me at the range. Their favorite word is wetback. Go back to a hoe if you can't handle a gun." The anger rose up in my chest, every time I thought about Michael Miller Jr. and his friends. I didn't tell my father what else they said: *You missed, you're dead,*

your Mexican gangbanger friends just killed you in a drive-by! You don't
have what it takes. Homeboy.

"I want to tell them I'm not used to shooting something
that ain't alive. But I can't say shit. One of them, his father is the
sergeant."

"You been shooting all your life," my father said. "A gun's a
gun. Go up there in Bee Canyon and find something to aim at.
Nobody's ever up there now that old man is gone. But I got asada
con papas in two hours."

I put my T-shirt back on, even though my skin was sticky, and
then my shoulder holster. I grabbed a flannel shirt to cover the holster, started walking from the ranch through the narrow trail in the
brush that Manny and I used to take when we were kids. I missed
riding my horse, Mano, but I wanted to walk today, take time to
think about this gun. How during the academy I was the highest
percentage at the range, but now on patrol, I was nervous.

The brittlebush and wild mustard were skeletal and gold by
now, and baby grasshoppers jumped away from my work boots.
Our old trail was pretty overgrown, at the base of the mountains.
Plenty of people rode dirt bikes and four-wheelers off Coal Canyon
Road and onto the railroad right-of-way or the frontage roads,
when they thought nobody would see. Lots of homeless people
had made camps in the trees and brush between the freeway and
the Santa Ana River. But up here at the edge of the steep flanks of
the Chino Hills, there were only two access roads. Our ranch, and
Bee Canyon, where there was still a long dirt road. An old man
used to live up that canyon, in a shack, tending to his bee boxes. My
dad and the Vargas brothers remember trading him orange blossom honey in a pail, back in the 1970s, for steaks and ribs.

I walked a mile from Fuego Canyon to Bee Canyon. Every
twenty yards or so, a deep rough cleft where rainfall had started a

new cut in the flanks of granite and clay. My father said the world was just one big irrigation system. High and low was all that mattered, every rainfall first a narrow stream down the side of a mountain, then a creek, then an arroyo, finally a canyon big enough for men.

"And women, cabrón," my mother called from the stove. "Because everybody knows who runs the show." I walked through the brush, lizards and small birds scrambling from my boots.

The water fell, the water moved, the water shaped the earth, and we meant nothing.

I met Sergeant Miller after the first recruitment meeting for the CHP academy. Four of my friends took the test together with me. But none of them knew I aced it. Miller took me to a separate room and asked me a bunch of questions. He thought I had cheated. He said, "Frías. You're from Santa Ana High. What are you—Mexican? Guatemalan?"

I wanted to tell him that I bet his father ground wheat into flour back in the day. If he was even from America since the beginning. My teacher in seventh grade, Mr. Wheelwright, told us about the names: Carters were the men who drove the wagons, Millers ground the grains, Shoemaker was easy, Smith was from blacksmiths or silversmiths. Wheelwright was what it sounded like, he told us. His own grandfather fixed wheels on wagons, back in Iowa.

"American, sir. I was born in Santa Ana."

"Your parents come from Mexico? Crossed the border? Wetbacks?"

"American, sir. My dad was born in Chino. His grandparents came from Jalisco in 1889, but his parents were born in Placentia. In 1903." In the wooden shacks built for pickers. With ditches for bathtubs. With outhouses. My grandfather was born in a horse barn. Like Jesus. But his name was Enrique. Which wasn't hard. Henry, to the sergeant, if I wanted to tell him. But I didn't want to.

"And your mom?"

I kept my face like a mask. "My mom's people were Spanish and Yuma. They came with the priest Garcés and the explorer Juan Bautista de Anza in 1774. The first Spanish to come to California, they had Yuma Indian guides."

"Yeah, but they came up from Mexico."

People like him always said up and down. They came *up* from Mexico. I'm never going *down* there. For their parents it was, They came *across* from Ireland. England. Germany. On a boat.

I said, "So did Father Serra. The one from all the famous missions. After he came *across* from Spain."

His face didn't change. He looked down at my test.

I got nervous and said, "My great-great-grandmother's sister married a Lugo. Like, the Lugos that owned everything back then. They had twenty thousand acres of Orange County."

He looked up. "I don't give a shit. I'm from LaGrange, Indiana. Where they used to have Indian trouble and then they didn't. My grandparents made sure of that."

"Yes, sir." *Gunsmoke.* Sergeant Miller was Dodge City all the way. His grandfather was the miller. They ground up the wheat. Maybe. Maybe they just killed people.

He was sitting across from me at his desk. He stabbed his big finger at the test. "How the hell did you score this high?"

I wanted to say I grew up picking oranges and moving cattle, and I had no brothers and sisters. After Manny and his parents moved to San Bernardino, there was no one for me to talk to except myself. After school, I'd work in the oranges and my father would be five rows over, and I had until dark to think about every word and every math problem and every element on the chemistry chart. When we rode up into the hills to separate the yearling steers, I had hours to memorize every form of rock—igneous, sedimentary, volcanic—along the trails.

I knew every animal and every plant and every kind of weather because I lived in the canyon, and that didn't have shit to do with school. I was great at tests.

So the CHP test was easy. I scored 100 percent. "Your friends barely passed," he said. "What the fuck happened here? How did you cheat?"

I wanted to say I got 100 percent on my driver's test the day I turned sixteen because that shit was easy, too. Left-turn lanes? Merge and yield? Double yellow lines? Way easier than riding up into a box canyon hoping a coyote hadn't killed a lost calf.

I wanted to say I got 100 percent on almost every test I ever took in high school, but nobody gave a damn because I lived in a worker camp. I loved having a motorcycle now, cruising out to the desert on the Indian, with Manny and his friends on the Harleys, and as long as we avoided the guys who were actually motorcycle gangs that wanted to kill us—Mongols and Hells Angels and whoever else—there was nothing better than riding. I figured if we got to cruise the CHP bikes all day on the freeways, and give out some tickets to assholes, and barbecue at night with some Tecate beer, I'd be happy. I thought Manny and me would stay in our apartment in Corona, if he didn't get married to Lena right away. We were twenty miles from his dad, ten miles from mine. I didn't want to stay with my father in Fuego Canyon because he was the saddest man in the world since my mother was gone.

I knew how to talk to dudes like Sergeant Miller. All the teachers and coaches and cops and doctors that looked at my forehead and my left cheek and said, "Got in a knife fight, huh? You in a gang, son?" The white line on my skin like somebody drew with

Wite-Out on my cheekbone. Two inches. That wasn't long on a measuring tape but it was a lot on my face. We were picking Meyer lemons when I was ten, and the ladder broke, and I fell through the branches. People forget citrus trees have big thorns.

My forehead had a thicker scar—like a little Nike swoosh. From when Manny and I got jumped by some white kids in Yorba Linda when we were twelve, at a park. We all had rocks. One of the gabachos must have been a good center fielder, because he got me at distance. Foreheads bleed like crazy, but that cut didn't even hurt. Butterfly was the name of the bandages the nurse put on at the clinic. Easy to remember that. Not moth or dragonfly.

I told Miller, "I studied really hard for days. But I guess I just got lucky. Sir."

I walked a couple miles along the railroad right-of-way, along the hills. I saw the bridge made out of vines and cable over the arroyo that led down to the Santa Ana River, the photo that had been in the newspaper, when they wrote another story about the freeway phantom. People speculated that he was old, a Vietnam vet, or younger, a Marine who'd served in Grenada or Afghanistan, living rough, pissed at the world and throwing rocks at cars.

But my dad and the Vargas brothers had seen shadows. A short Black guy. I kept an eye out for piles of stones, for signs of a camp, but nothing. When I got to the mouth of Bee Canyon, where there was a wide sandy clearing, there was a pile of tall Coors cans. Dirt bikers and teenagers came up here to drink beer and smoke weed. There was shade under a pepper tree, and a trail widened by wheels that led up into the canyon. I figured I'd get up there far enough so no one would hear me and set the Coors cans on a rock.

They were old and faded, perfect to shoot. I stuck four fingers on each hand into four sharp tab holes and kept walking. Past the clearing, behind a huge boulder covered with graffiti, a car was parked in the dirt. Not what you'd expect. A classic Karmann Ghia, 1974 convertible. Manny and I had seen a few of them. Loud as shit, he said. Maybe the driver had gone toward the river. No laughter or radio from the canyon.

I went up the trail between the bluffs, about a hundred yards. Then I heard a slap. A crack of hand on face. Cheek skin sounds more hollow and loud than when a palm hits a shoulder. Somebody was fighting, but not punching.

Then I heard huffing, from up higher somewhere. *Huh, huh, huh.* Breath like a hammer. Like a kid trying not to cry out. *Huh, huh, huh.*

A man said, flat and hard, "What the fuck! What the fuck you lookin at? What's a nigger doing up here in Orange County?"

I dropped the cans in the sand. But I kept walking, quiet and slow, up past a flat section of sand near the deep scour where the rainwater poured down, and then around another huge granite boulder.

A white guy with long dark blond hair hanging down his bare back was straddling a girl. She was on all fours. He shoved into her two more times, three, four. Hard. Holding her head up by the hair. But he was looking up the canyon. He hadn't seen me. Then he pushed up off her. He knocked her over onto her back.

She looked dead. Laid out flat, to the sky. Dried blood dark under her nose. Flowery skirt hiked up around her waist, her legs open, blood there, too. Her feet black on the soles. She didn't move.

The guy was standing up now, casual about his dick, and there was blood all over his jeans. Not his blood. He wasn't in pain. He took his time adjusting himself. He was looking up the canyon, to where the sounds had come from. Who was he talking to? "I'm gonna fuckin kill you, freak," he shouted at the rocks.

He hunched over, zipped up his jeans, the muscles in his back jerking like snakes, and then turned and saw me.

"What the hell?" he said.

My CHP voice came out before I could think. "Sir, I need you to tell me what's going on here."

"You speak English?"

My face burned. "Sir, is this—"

"You that nigger's brother? Shit. You're dark enough. He was right up there. Watching. Fuckin freak."

"What's wrong with the young lady?" I hadn't moved. My boots were sinking into the sand.

"Young lady? Why you talking like you're on TV?"

"I'm law enforcement, sir."

"No, you're not. Pedro."

"Is she okay?"

He laughed. "She's a rich little bunny. She was supposed to do a Slow Ride. Take it easy. But the stupid chick OD'd. Couldn't handle the trip. Couldn't handle the ride, man. Like it's your fuckin business. Wetback." He pushed his hair behind his ears and started walking toward me. He must have been about thirty-five. His skin lined around his eyes like birds had clawed him deep.

Was he the real phantom? Shit. Was he the vet who'd built the bridge?

The girl hadn't moved. What if she was dead? I made my voice louder. "I need you to turn around and walk over to that rock and put your hands on the rock." I didn't have handcuffs. I had baling wire in my pocket.

"I need you to turn around and head back to Mexico."

"Sir."

I didn't move. There was no sound except his bare feet on the sand. Like dry masa.

"Sir." He was close enough that I could see his eyes were green.

People said the phantom was a guy who still wanted to live in the jungle. Maybe if I brought up the war, he'd know I respected him.

"Are you a veteran, sir?"

"Fuck war. I don't need to be a fuckin vet to kill somebody."

He was about ten feet from me now. Kill her? Kill me?

Then the girl made a noise. She coughed. Her throat rasped like it was full of sand. He grinned at me and said, "You just get here from Tijuana? You swum all the way up that river and this is where you made it?"

I looked past him. The girl raised up on one elbow and tried to pull down her skirt. She got to her knees, scrabbled against the boulder, stood up, and swayed. I saw her left hand on the rock—missing the end of her middle finger. He turned back fast and covered the ground. He said, "I'm not done with you. Rich little bunny."

He drew back his arm and punched her in the face. Like she was a man. The sound of her nose breaking. A popping. Then an animal moan—like a coyote, full in the throat—but not her. From above us. A kid hiding there. He moaned again, like he couldn't stand it when the girl fell.

I pulled my service revolver from the shoulder holster under my shirt. Silence now above us. The girl lay still. Small breath in her throat like a saw blade in wet wood. Then nothing. She could drown from the blood in her nose.

He wouldn't shut up. He kept talking as he came back toward me. "What the fuck are you gonna do with that? Fuckin wetback.

You steal that from a cowboy? From an American?" He grinned and sang, "Ay yi yi yi—you are the Frito Bandito."

He was three feet away. Reached down and took a knife from an ankle holster. His jeans smelled like when we butchered in fall. Buck knife. He held it loose and casual, swinging it gently. He knew how.

I was Mexican. Off-duty. He was a criminal. Scumbag. Rapist. But he was white.

He came slowly forward. A turquoise ring on his finger. "You better give that gun to somebody who knows how to use it, chico."

My mother used to call me chavalito. When I came in at night smelling of the river.

I shot him in the chest like he was a silhouette at the range. But he didn't move sideways. He fell straight back. Then silence.

The girl pushed up again, on all fours, like a new calf. She crouched and swayed and stared at my face, squinting, her long red-brown hair touching the sand. Her eyes. One blue and one half-green. Blood running like a lariat from her nose, running down into the sand. I went over to the guy and stared at the hole in his chest. About five inches below his left collarbone. The blood running down his ribs. Different blood. Darker.

Heart blood. Lung blood.

I looked up to say, "Miss, I'm gonna call—" But she was crawling sideways past me. Then pulling herself up against the boulder again. Arm over her nose and mouth. She bumped around the rock and started to run.

Five flies landed on his chest. Checking it for taste. The knife was in the sand. Glinting dull in the late sun.

Then the car started up at the bottom of the canyon. Karmann Ghia engine, loud rattle and whine. The tires popped over the gravel like firecrackers.

She was gone. The victim. The witness. I would lose my job over this asshole. I would go to prison.

His shoulder was sweaty and hot. I grasped it to see if the bullet had gone through. It had. Went into the soft sand that smelled of animal waste and creosote roots. I put the shoulder back down. I didn't look at the open mouth. I didn't have time to go back to the ranch for a shovel. I found a dead branch and started trying to dig in the damp sand where the water had pooled long ago. *Deep enough to keep him from coyotes* was all I thought.

A scraping above me, and granite pebbles falling. Up on the ridge, in the thick brush.

He had a stuffed dog under his arm. A brown dog with floppy ears and a red collar. He was a short Black guy, leaning on a shelter made of arrowweed, and he was crying. Maybe five foot five, with a real thin beard around his chin, and his dog was missing an eye. His hair gold with dust and his shirt in rags. I got my gun out. I waited to see what he would do. If he looked at my face and shouted out what he'd seen me do.

The woman had run—she didn't know whether the guy was dead or alive.

The phantom made that huffing sound again. The sound you make when you're a boy and you've been keeping that cry in for a long time. How long had he seen the rape going on?

He bent forward. The phantom. A pick slid down the steep hillside and landed a few feet away from me. Homemade. Metal wired to a piece of crudely sanded wood. Like someone had thrown an anchor overboard.

All these years, when I'd pulled people over and they said the things they said to me, I still counted to five, like Melt had told me. Slow five. And you'd be shocked, but five fucking seconds was a lifetime for people to hear quiet after they talked.

Manny and I had spoken Spanish first, with our parents, with the Vargas brothers and the other people in the canyon. In kindergarten, Manny and I started learning English, and by junior high, we could go back and forth like most kids we knew, between teachers and coaches, friends and parents. But in my head, I had to forever learn a third language: American.

And now there was a whole generation of new American. Nobody *toked*. They *baked*. Wake and bake. Drive high as hell, and text, and I could follow them while they wove slowly in the middle lane, as conspicuous as the old drunk men of my rookie years.

Today I threaded through the heavy traffic toward Fullerton. Pull him over, Melt Olson used to say, and the physical action was the opposite, especially on the motorcycle. We pushed the cars over. Like when I rode with my father, moving the cattle, watching him ahead of me, his palomino mare Jefa nudging the calves over with her body. On the motorcycle, I was cutting out a car from the herd.

But it was pull him over. Pull out that ticket. Better not have to pull your gun.

In the triplex in Santa Ana where I'd lived since Manny and Lena got married in 2002, a stucco building where I had a garage for my patrol bike and the Cheyenne, I still had the notebooks I'd started in 1999, my first months on patrol. Notebooks with lists of words and phrases and sentences organized by whatever made sense. My first year of patrol, I was obsessed with how people talked to me, and what I should say back. Most of the time, I didn't say anything. That worked, because if I was quiet, the stupid ones incriminated themselves straight up like they couldn't help it.

You pulling me over? The smell of beer or alcohol stunk up their breath and made its way through the air rushing out the heater or air conditioner to me, at the driver window, where we always stood back then. *You think I'm hammered/tanked/looped/smashed/three sheets to the wind/tied a load on/full tilt/tipsy/knockered/pie-eyed?*

Shit, bro, you pullin me over? What if I swallowed the roach? You gonna search me for a joint? You think I'm baked/faded/lit/buzzed/fucked up?

You think I'm way too happy? Cause cops are never fuckin happy, man. Look at you. Asshole. You never been happy a day in your life. You need to get laid/fucked/blown/drunk/high/cooled out.

Melt was right. I just listened. Walked back to run their plates. Came up to the window with their citations or with the Breathalyzer.

Let's get down to brass tacks/the nitty gritty/the real deal. The tailpipe is jury-rigged, I know that. Let's take a stab at this. My dad's car is Mickey Mouse and I didn't know the blinker was broken. Hey, chop chop if you're gonna write a ticket! I got places to go and people to see.

Man, I'm not drunk, I only had four beers. That ain't shit for a guy my size. I been roofin all day!

Honey, if you pulled me over because you wanted my number, you're out of luck. I never sleep with cops. Only firemen.

What? You know I was just using the carpool lane to pass that fuckin truck.

They got angry.

You hate red cars? Trucks? Beemers? Women? White dudes? People with money? You sure you're not blind behind them shades? You need to fill your quota?

And then it came. *You can't talk? You speak English or you a special cop just for Latinos? How are you gonna give me a ticket? I was drivin slower than a fly in molasses. Slower than a Mexican when you ask him to work. That slow, hombre. Slower than that. What's your name? Frias? Fritos?*

But I had a gun. And everything in America went back to *Gunsmoke*.

Today I kept thinking of Janine Hughes and the thick mascara smudging under her eyes. My dad didn't like *The Big Valley* or *Bonanza* as much, even though there were more horses and steers. But *Gunsmoke*—he loved it and hated it. Matt Dillon was the law. Incorruptible, unwavering. He liked that part, how Dillon just did his job. But all the brown characters—Mexicans, Arapaho, Comanche, even Burt Reynolds, who was supposed to be half Comanche—they were white dudes with brown paint, and their accents were ridiculous.

"The women are worse!" my mother used to say, going outside to trim the bougainvillea, ocaso, when the birds were talking to each other before night, making these soft little sounds she loved. "Amazing they had false eyelashes and Aqua Net back then. Pues, they cry and cry pero all that makeup stays perfect."

"No one cares about that," my father would say. "Just who pulls the gun first. In Dodge City."

Hurry up and write that ticket. It's time to for me to get the hell out of Dodge. You think this is high noon? You think you got a six-shooter there on your fuckin hip?

I had written four citations in forty minutes on the 91. No speeding—the traffic was shit. The wind had everyone on edge, and two guys had gone out on the shoulder to pass, and two zigzagged in and out of the carpool lane, one knocking down a pylon. I was in Fullerton when Manny called me. "Hey, can you meet me at your house in half an hour? Just for five minutes, mano. I know you don't get breaks. But I really need those rims for the Impala from your garage. Five minutes."

"Lucky I'm not on the toll road, bro," I told him. "You better hope nobody has an accident real quick."

It only took me fifteen minutes to get home. I took the 5 past Disneyland, hoping dispatch wouldn't call with a collision, hoping no one would do something egregious—my friend Justin Pham's favorite word. I headed down Bristol. I lived on Jacaranda Court. The triplex was three two-bedroom houses, mine in the middle. Rose Sotelo's was painted pink, mine was light green, and Albert Chagolla's was bright Dodger blue. We each had our own garage, and I parked the Harley in front of mine.

Albert was standing on a ladder in his truck bed that was propped against the wooden eaves of his place, hanging up ghosts and skeletons all along the front. His two teenage sons were in the cab, grinning wide. They were learning to drive, moving forward three feet or so every time he got down off the ladder and whistled.

When he saw me, Albert said, "Whappen, Casanova? She left?"

I took off my helmet and said, "Shut up, man." But I couldn't be mad at him. It was pretty funny, that last hour before Leti took off.

I rolled up the old metal garage door and stood there for a few seconds. Leti. She had left a box of books for me, and the six plates we bought together at Azteca Pottery sat on the red Craftsman tool chest my dad had bought me for my twenty-fifth birthday. She said someday we would have a dinner party, when we got married.

What happened was crazy. I took a history class at Santa Ana College, when I was getting my AA degree. I was twenty-eight then. And Leti was the lecturer. She was twenty-four. She had just graduated from Stanford, she was teaching summer school, working on her master's degree in history at UCLA. Her thesis was about *Mendez v. Westminster*, about the Mexican parents who started desegregation way back in 1947. Leticia Espinoza, sitting up there showing us slides of people who looked like my grandparents I'd never met, women with their hair up in shiny rolls and men with sharp mustaches, grown up in labor camps and wanting better for their kids.

We hung out after class twice. We had coffee four times. We had dinner once, at the taquería near my house. Leti was an only child, too, but her parents were rich. Her father was born in Morelia, Michoacán, a lawyer, and she grew up in Downey—the Mexican Beverly Hills. She was still living with them when she taught at Santa Ana, and then her father got her an apartment in Westwood. I only went there two or three times—it took forever to get there, on my day off, and I hated walking around that part of LA. I looked like a cop no matter what. She said I stood in stance when we were waiting in line for a movie.

She came to my place, a lot. She would stay for a week at a time, then go Sunday to her parents for dinner and her huge familia. But I wouldn't go. And I only took her once to the rancho. She acted like she loved the barn, the viejos and my father, and our house. But my dad said, "She never saw this much dirt in her life. She would never last here, mijo. You better move there to LA. With her."

Now I heard Manny's loud Dodge Ram pickup engine turning the corner. I opened the flap of the box with the plates. They were dark blue with gold rims and tiny green nopales in clay arranged on the edges in three places. We used the plates for us. It was hella nice to come home to someone at midnight who made coffee and warmed up chicken and rice, and watched TV with me for two hours until I could sleep. She made me watch movies I'd never seen—my favorite was an Italian director, Pasolini, and his Rome, where so many guys looked like my father and his friends. But then

Leti's dad called me one day. He told me to meet him at his office, in Downey. I went before my shift. He was old-school, and he sat there at his big shiny desk with the bookshelves behind him, saying, "She needs better than you. A cop. You're gonna break her heart. Or shoot somebody and then you'll go to prison. Because you're Mexican first. Then policia."

Really, I had overhead him and Leti's mother talking to her one day, on her laptop, when I was just waking up for my shift. She was in the kitchen, but I could hear. "No, amor, está muy prieto prieto," her mother said. "You have to think about your kids, mija, if they come out moreno and they don't even look like you. How hard it would be, you know how people are."

I knew how her mother was.

We broke up and got back together five times, in all these years. And two days ago, that was the last time. She cried on my little patio here, where I kept all the tools Manny and I had used to restore the Cheyenne truck, and the old Indian motorcycle beside it. She said something different from her pops. "If I become a lawyer, I'm gonna defend our people, Johnny. And you'd always be on the other side. You'd have to pick. Gente, or cop." She put her head on my neck. She was sitting on my lap, in the old barber chair Manny had brought here years ago. She whispered, "And somebody could shoot you. I can't live like that."

Manny pulled up the driveway. When he cut off his engine, Rose Sotelo's birds filled the silence for a moment before another gust of wind shook the skeletons hanging from Albert's roof. He waited for the wind to subside. Then Albert whistled, and the boys moved the truck forward, and he climbed back up the ladder, long white-checked shorts all the way to his thick white socks, no shirt, his giant Virgen de Guadalupe tattoo covering his back, and his arms covered with images of his wife, with her hair long and a Dodgers cap on her head. His chest with the names of his friends and family he'd lost already. When he was at the top of the ladder, holding another skeleton, he turned to look down on me, and said, "For reals, though, homes, sorry I scared her."

Leti and I had been in bed, arguing, and she kept hearing the whistles, and she thought some weird bird had shown up. She lifted up and threw open the bedroom curtain, and there was Albert, up in the air, and his sons, who were never allowed in the front seat of his big truck. She was only wearing a black bra. Albert had dropped the calavera and leaned sideways, and had to grab the roof. Leti screamed, and he laughed like hell. "You can't live here forever," she said to me, slamming into the bathroom.

"She said you were calcified, bro," Manny said now, walking up the driveway with his short legs swinging out like they did, his long torso and wide belly in the T-shirt, his own long black shorts. "Albert told me. I came by before."

"My life was calcified. Better than ossified," I said, trying to make a joke. "That means I'm bones." But then I bent to get the stack of four rims for the 1964 Impala. Bones. I could never tell Leti about the body in Bee Canyon. Every time she said she was scared I'd die, I thought about all the secrets I'd never be willing to tell her. What she'd told me last week was that she'd gotten into law school. At Stanford. She was moving to Palo Alto.

Albert came down the ladder. His wife stuck her head out the kitchen window and said, "That's enough calaveras, pendejo, the wind is gonna blow you half a mile. Anthony, Alex, get out of the truck. Get in here and do your homework."

Manny said, "You comin out to my house for Halloween, bro? Lena's making birria."

I handed him the key to the garage. I didn't want him feeling sorry for me. "That was my ten-minute break." I got back on the Harley and headed toward the freeway.

I looked under his body, carefully, and all around the wet sand for twenty feet each way, pushing the phantom's pick through the edges of the brush, but I never found the single bullet that went through the man's chest. Exit hole. Either the .40-caliber missed his ribs, or nicked one. I knew that if he washed out into the open, that winter of 1999 if it rained hard, or if his skeleton was uncovered even years later, there could be evidence that he was shot.

The phantom never put his head back out. He had stopped crying. Either he waited in silence, or he'd melted back into the brush somewhere else.

When I was finished digging the hole, I knew to check for a wallet, keys, anything. I had to slide my hand into the bloodied jeans pockets at his groin, heavy with the smell of sex and shit. I threw up three times in the brush, and I covered that with sand, too, and rocks. Nothing in his pockets. ID must have been in the Karmann Ghia.

I rolled him into the trench. Matt Dillon had buried hundreds of men in graves he dug in the hills, on the prairie, and he'd always left a big mound of dirt. But in reality the body didn't displace that much earth. I pushed the sand back over him, and dropped in rocks, and then more sand. Coyotes, bobcats, raccoons, and rats, even feral dogs and cats would smell food if I didn't do it right.

I filled the hole, leveled it off. Still, a real flood would uncover him. I rolled a few larger stones with the pick, and then carried the other boulders like I had all my life, making walls on the ranch.

Seventeen stones, for no reason. I brushed everything away with creosote branches.

I leaned against the boulder where she had steadied herself, the blood dried now, and on the ground I saw her wallet.

A cream leather wallet. Chanel. She wasn't poor. She had three credit cards—Bunny Goldman. Four twenties, two tens, and eight ones. Two driver's licenses. One from 1997. Bunny Angela Gunnarson. An address on Catalina Avenue, in Hollywood. One from 1999. Bunny Angela Goldman. An address on Dundee Drive, in Los Angeles.

I waited about six months before I went. I told Manny I'd met a girl, asked him if I could borrow the Mercury Cougar he'd restored.

I went to the apartment building on Catalina first because I figured nobody would notice me in Hollywood. One of those old blue stucco shoeboxes from the 1950s set horizontal along the street with a staircase on each side. The EXCELSIOR in wrought-iron letters on the wall. Oleander bushes for a dark fence against the street. I sat there for a long time.

I climbed up the pebbly stairs and knocked on number 8. If she answered, I would just tell her that she didn't have to worry about the guy. He was taken care of. That's it. I had thought about it every day, what I would say.

A blond woman wearing a fancy robe answered. She said something in Russian. She slammed the door.

On my way down, a voice called from number 1. Open door, the apartment under the stairs. "I'm the manager, hon," she said. She sat in a recliner with her shoulder to the doorframe, where she could watch everything. A woman in her sixties, built so strange, flat and wide like a giant rag doll, wearing a housedress. "What are you doing at number eight?"

I kept my voice citizen. "Just found something that belonged to Bunny Gunnarson."

She kept her eyes and mouth tight. Black drawn-on eyebrows, dark lines drawn around her lipstick. She said, "She doesn't need to deal with men like you now. She married up. She's rich now, and she's gone. So you just get back in your crappy old car before I call the cops."

I said, "Ma'am." Just to fuck with her.

I drove to a 7-Eleven and got coffee. I got out my old Thomas Guide. Sunset Boulevard up to Los Feliz. Dundee Drive.

It was up in the hills above Vermont. I always wondered who named that neighborhood Los Feliz. The Happy. The street was so narrow I had to drive up past the address, a Mercedes on my ass so I couldn't stop. A big gate. Hedges all along the street. I went up to the top, found a place to turn around, and cruised back down. All the houses big, hidden behind hedges or gates. I parked in a shallow turnout buried in bamboo, looking across the street at the house. A long driveway lined with those big Italian cypress trees. No blue Karmann Ghia visible, but they'd have a big garage. MORRIS GOLDMAN on the fancy white mailbox like rich people had.

I stared at her driver's license. What was she doing in Bee Canyon? She hadn't looked rich. That hippie flowered skirt. In her license photo, her hair was very blond, piled high in a bun, and two slices of hair dangling down along the sides of her face. She was twenty-nine years old. She had on a ton of makeup. Cat-slanted eyeliner and a lot of lipstick. How was her nose?

Red lights behind me. Private security. He came toward the

Cougar and I started it up and took off down the street. I didn't want him to ask for ID, call me illegal, or tell me nobody needed gardening work today.

I went back to Los Feliz twice a year or so, if I had to go to LA for a docket, DUI, or a felony charge. I'd leave the downtown courthouse, drive up toward Dodger Stadium, where my dad's friend Luis Padilla used to live in Chavez Ravine before everyone got kicked out when they built Dodger Stadium. Luis ran a boxing gym in East LA after that, and he taught me how to fight. If the guy in the canyon hadn't pulled the knife, I would have tossed the gun behind me and taken him on.

I would be wearing my dress uniform, driving the Harley, when I went up to Dundee Drive, and I'd stop at the gate, knowing any cars would go around me. I rang the doorbell on the gatepost, but no one ever answered. Once, though, I had gone up the street to turn around, and when I came back down, a white Cadillac Eldorado shot out of the gate and swerved down the street. Leadfoot, Melt would say. The heavy car motored down the tunnel of trees and flowers and by the time I got down to Vermont, the driver was gone.

CHISPA

SANTA ANA RIVER AND 91 FREEWAY

I drove about fourteen thousand miles a year on the Harley. Every day, I remembered what Melt told me: give someone ten seconds to make up their mind, watch their hands on the wheel, watch the sides of their faces, the trash on their seats. The gun under the seat, or in the glove box. Never any gloves in the glove box.

Now it was 2019. I was waiting for someone to shoot me when I pulled them over. Every time I got off the bike and walked to the passenger side, because we never went to the driver side now, I thought there might be a .357 or a .45 pointed at me through the open window. A rifle from the back seat. A CHP deputy had pulled over an ex-con near Moreno Valley last month, and the guy's truck was full of rifles. We all went to the funeral. Hundreds of us riding behind his coffin.

It was 6:07 p.m. I was thinking about lunch break. The wind had kept on today, still blustering hard as hell. I always liked that word. Bluster. The Santa Anas had a way of shifting from constant blowing to sudden gusts, like the cartoon pictures of a big god with his mouth puffed up. A long minute where you felt sustained force, the sound like cloth whipping past your ears. I always thought it was a goddess snapping a dish towel close to our necks so we'd jump.

Like my mother did to me and Manny.

Then a few minutes of quiet.

I was threading through the Thursday hell, people pissed and late, on their phones and arguing or laughing, checking their hair and their Instagram and their rearview hoping they weren't going to see me. The blue lights.

Especially at dusk. I always thought my mother would have loved to see the blue lights if I brought the motorcycle up the canyon road, and she knew it wasn't about trouble, just me, coming home to hang out. Blue like nothing else. Her favorite blue—the flame when it changes over to deep sapphire when we cooked over the fire in the yard.

I had to work a collision near Green River Road, where there were always distracted drivers. A young woman with her head down on the steering wheel. Red 2018 Audi. Nice car. Back crumpled. I said, "Miss, are you injured? Do you need me to call an ambulance?" She lifted her face and looked at me. Trying so hard not to cry. Her beauty caught me off guard. A lot of makeup, glitter on her eyelids, her brows dark, lipstick bright pink against her dark skin. Her hair an explosion of black curls with tiny flowers tied inside. On the seat beside her was a pair of maroon cowboy boots.

"I can't believe he hit me," she said, hiccupping. "I don't want to mess up my face. I was on my way to a video shoot. Shit. He hit me. I can't be late."

"But you're okay?" I looked closely at her face—her posture.

"I'm late," she said again. "Please. Hurry."

She'd been rear-ended by a white work truck, a 2006 Ford F-150. Rich Porter. Forty-eight. Lake Elsinore. "Is it Richard?" I said, holding the license.

"Nope," he said. "They named me Rich. Ironic, right?" White guy with a goatee, pissed, staring straight ahead. "She stopped suddenly. Accident's her fault. Probably trying to get a payout."

They hadn't been going that fast. His bumper had old dents, traced with rust, and two new ones, paint still flaking. Her phone had been in a dash holder. His was on the seat, face down. I said, "It's not an accident. It's a collision. An accident means you couldn't have avoided this. You could have avoided this by not having a six-pack of Michelob Ultra on the floor."

"Unopened."

"Okay." I called in both plates, standing behind the truck, hoping neither would take off. He had no DUI priors. I asked for backup and within two minutes saw a patrol car coming up through the traffic, trying to get people out of the way. Justin Pham and Evan Sims. They parked behind Rich.

I went back up to the girl for her license and insurance. Esme Portillo. Her boots were exactly like my mother's. "I'm supposed to make it to Coachella," she said. "That's where the shoot is. For a preview for next year's festival. Please. Please make him go away fast."

I took my break when the paperwork was done and Rich had told us he wasn't drinking but texting some woman and looked up late. Esme went east, toward Coachella.

I went east for another two miles, got off on Lincoln in Corona, where Manny and I used to have our apartment, and got some coffee at an Arco. I kept seeing the cowgirl boots. Just like my mother's. When the wind blew hard like this, sometime she'd say, "We better sleep in our boots, Johnny. In case we have to run."

She was buried in her boots.

We'd be sitting in that redwood chair, tied to the porch post, and she'd say to me that the wind came before the people. Her abuela told her that. *We can't complain about wind, because we're not special. ¿Entiendes? Zorros, leones de montaña, coyotes. We're the two-leg animals. Us and the birds.*

The whole world would be moving around us, and the chair stayed still. *I love it. I can't help myself. You know how when your papi takes you in the truck up to see the cattle? Then you and the truck are moving and everything else is standing still. Pero look, just you and me out here. I got you. You can't move. Mira, like we're underwater. Under the sea. Under the waves. Like—what is it? The damn thing. In your classroom. The glass case full of water and the little fish are going through the fake castle. And you blow on the top. To make the waves.*

I must have been six. I said, "Aquarium."

Sí. Pues, we're in the aquarium.

The eucalyptus trees had white bark trunks, like giant bones, and the long silver branches blew sideways like the hair of old women. The wind gusted hard every few minutes, and the windows inside our house hummed. We slept in our boots.

The rope knots around the porch post were melted together like bark. When the next big gust came blowing down the canyon, she crossed her arms over my chest. Like a gun belt holding me close. Like in the picture up at the Anza ranch house, the historic painting of her people who came here before California was called California. Before America was called America. The man she showed me was a Spanish soldier, and he married a Yuma girl, in Baja, Mexico, just when they got on the road. Their baby was born in the mountains of San Jacinto, two days before they crossed the Santa Ana River.

Anza was the one who named the river Santa Ana. Even though these winds started way out in the desert of Nevada, they got named Santa Ana, too.

When I was little, and we were at a store in Yorba Linda or Fullerton, and someone would say, "Go back to Mexico!" or call us "fucking illegal aliens," my mother would say, "Mi gente estaba aquí antes que tu gente." *My people were here before your people.* When their faces twisted up in anger, she'd do that thing women do—put her eyes on the other human's forehead and then drop her look all the way down the body to the shoes—raking the person. Like evaluating an old horse. Then she'd suck her teeth, grab my shoulder, and we'd walk away.

I was always afraid someone would punch her in the back of the head, but nobody ever touched my mother. Those Sundays, she'd worn print dresses to her knees and her favorite maroon leather tooled cowboy boots. My mother hated the way jeans cut into her waist, and she always said she could work harder in a dress. Esme, today—the flowery dress, the flowers in her hair, the leather flat-top hat, and boots on the Audi seat—that's expensive fashion now, according to Leti. "Boho Festival," she says, rolling her eyes. "Three-hundred-dollar dresses from Free People. Two-hundred-dollar hats."

My mother only wore stockings and heels to church. We went to Our Lady of the Sacrament, in Santa Ana, since that was the church of my father's cousin Iris Valdez. I'd sit with her son Tony, because we were the same age, but he never talked much to me

except to make fun of my boots and hat. He wore Converse and an Angels cap.

We lived in mud all winter and dust all summer. Manny and I went barefoot when we could, and we had Converse for school, but our first shoes were little boots, bought in Santa Ana by the Vargas brothers.

My father had work boots, and fancy tooled vaquero boots, from Zapatería Jalisco in Santa Ana. Jalisco style, even though he'd never been to Mexico, either. His father's father was from the mountains of Jalisco, and he was brought to California in 1889, when he was seven. The ranchers brought forty-two vaqueros from Jalisco. Asked them to come.

My father was born in Chino, where the big dairies were, and he lived there until his parents moved to Placentia. When we'd go to the feed store in Corona and some asshole told him to go back to Mexico, called him a wetback, my father always did the same thing: he just stared at them, from under his hat, and then he spit his chewing tobacco into the neck of his Tecate beer bottle, slow and careful. Like some cowboy on *Gunsmoke*. He didn't say shit—like a vaquero.

Back in the truck, he'd say to me, "Stupid cabrón. Thinks he's the Marlboro Man. Probably can't even ride a horse."

I got back on the 91 and headed west. I hadn't gone more than five miles when I saw the spark.

Chispa.

The dragging muffler on a 1999 Ford Ranger truck, one of those little white pickups you always see some old guy or struggling landscaper driving, loaded down with junk in the back. This one had the bed full of scrap metal—shit, he had aluminum

benches that looked like bleachers sticking out. Spools of copper wire. Had to be a meth head stealing metal to sell.

He was in the slow lane, but a gap had opened up and he gunned toward it, and the muffler sent sparks into the dry brush on the shoulder. I was about five cars behind him. I saw the smoke rising thin and black right then—like a string up to the sky. The wind took that smoke and smeared it fast, and then the next few bushes caught like explosions. Old tumbleweeds.

He knew, the driver. And he didn't stop. There was only one exit past Green River Road, before Gypsum Canyon Road. He skidded off into the little parking area for the bike trail, along the river, and then the pendejo headed down Coal Canyon Road, the narrow asphalt frontage road along the riverbed.

He was sparking fires every twenty or thirty feet with the fucking muffler. The wind was taking the sparks in circles and then flames burst up into the old eucalyptus bark like god blowing on his campfire. Now the truck headed toward the canyons and the hills. Shit.

I lit up and swerved onto the shoulder. I could take the Harley down the bike trail and back to Coal Canyon. I went slow until the frontage road, accelerated, and got behind him. Then another truck came toward us on Coal Canyon and cut him off. I got off the Harley, put my hand on my gun. The driver had a damn fire hydrant in the Ranger truck bed. Definitely a speed freak who needed money fast. A tall skinny white guy with a bandanna around his neck jumped out. I pulled out my gun, but he didn't even look at me. He had a fire extinguisher.

At least he'd stolen one of those. He started foaming up the nearest fire, throwing down like he'd put out a lot of flames before. I holstered my gun, tapped out his plates fast, and called in

the fire to dispatch. "I'm just off Coal Canyon. Already multiple fires. Send everyone," I told Diane, the dispatcher. We had a drink sometimes—she had freckles and four-colored hair always swirled perfect. She said, "Well, shit, we knew today would end up like this."

I heard someone yelling, "Hey, man, you can't leave!"

A plume of dirt in my face. The meth head had gotten back into the Ranger and burned out heading east on the frontage road—back toward the freeway.

But the other white truck was still there. A big 2010 Chevy Silverado. Blue Diamond Pool Cleaning, the decal said. Bill Densmore. Norco, CA. The truck bed full of pool cleaning equipment, hoses, and buckets of chemicals. He came running toward me with two extinguishers. He shouted, "You call it in?"

I shouted back, "Yeah." We sprayed white foam onto the flames, and the wind blew it right back at us. The flames leapt ahead. We were useless. The fire headed fast into the vegetation on the banks of the Santa Ana River, and the eucalyptus, pepper trees, palms, and sycamores exploded like bombs were falling.

We were between Bee Canyon and Fuego Canyon. My father, always vigilant, would already see the smoke and flames. I shouted at Densmore to get out of there, waited till he got back into his truck, and made a U-turn. I followed him back to the railroad tracks, and he went toward the new housing tract.

Three helicopters were already overhead—OCPD, maybe two news choppers. And the red lights coming behind me while I drove to the ranch. On the radio, I heard the brethren of my job. Yorba Linda Fire, Santa Ana Fire, Corona Fire. I heard CHP from Riverside, Darren Fredow and Rob Jekel, they said, "Frías—that's your dad's place, right? We're in Corona, man, we'll be there fast."

I speed-dialed Manny. "Mano," I said, my voice tearing off into the wind.

He said, "Johnny?"

I shouted, "The riverbed's on fire. Bring Bobby and Grief, man. Get on the bikes and come the back way. The viejos are gonna need some help this time."

COACHELLA

The white cards that said DO NOT hung from the doors of number 11 and number 12. Ximena walked down the shady red-tiled sidewalk that connected the cottages at Seven Palms: A Desert Medi-Spa Experience, listening for women's voices. The white wrought-iron tables in front of number 9 and number 10 held trays of food, delicate white plates covered with silver domes. She lifted the domes. Untouched lunches. The first thing Ximena did every afternoon was collect the trays, put them on the food cart, and take them back to the kitchen. That way señora Luz could never accuse her of eating anything.

Ximena would never touch the eggs or pale fish or lettuce on those plates. She had chilaquiles in a plastic container. GladWare. In her locker. Glad. Happy. Blue lid.

Seven Palms was like a village where only twelve women lived, she told her cousin Fidelia at night. Each apartment was separate, one bedroom, living room, and big bathroom, white stucco walls

and red-tile roofs. "Cottages," Fidelia read on a brochure Ximena
brought home from the trash. Fidelia rolled her eyes. "Not apartments. That's for poor people. Cottages are, like—English. Like
this." On her laptop, she showed Ximena pretty little houses with
black straw roofs sitting in green fields. "Americans love English shit."

Ximena had worked here for three months. The medi-spa
building, with the doctor rooms, was like a church at the center of
the village, surrounded by rose gardens and climbing vines. The
laundry/maintenance building was hidden by walls of tall hedges.
Bougainvillea that Rodolfo clipped every three weeks by hand, to
keep the red blossoms constant. Two lines of cottages slanted out
like rays, connected by red-tiled sidewalks shaded from wooden
structures also covered with vines, so that no sun would touch the
women. There were hedges between each cottage for privacy, because some of the women were famous. And the air-conditioning
was on so high everywhere that the whole place felt to Ximena as
if it would lift off, humming into the sky.

Every day except Sunday, Ximena cleaned numbers 7 through
12. Señora Luz held the clipboard and told Ximena which of the
cottages were empty, which needed extra service, and which
women had complained if she knocked or entered, or if she made
too much noise. For two days, DO NOT had hung on number 12,
the last cottage. When she listened at the window, Ximena had
heard a lone loud cricket inside, screeching in rhythm, even in the
daytime. Crickets got confused in the dark, and the shades were
pulled tightly on television voices and the roar of air-conditioning.

Now she dumped the wet towels from number 9 into her laundry cart. Today was Friday. Since Tuesday, number 9's thick white
cotton had been marked with the particular pink of blood light-
ened by bathwater. Sometimes the towels had maroon markings

of pure dried blood. Sometimes just a trace. Number 9 had been a pupa in the bed, sleeping in the humming cool darkness. Now she was gone. She had only been lips, eyes, cheeks, chin, and neck. Not boobs.

The finished women left by eleven a.m. The new women came after three or four, when their surgeries were done. Some of them didn't care while Ximena moved about. They lay in bed watching television, holding their phones, talking on Bluetooth with things inserted into their ears or tiny white capsules near their puffy lips.

She looked at her work list. The first thing señora Luz had said to Ximena back in April, when Rodolfo brought Ximena and Elpidia to Seven Palms: "¡Dime los números! En inglés."

Elpidia bit her lip.

Luz had rolled her eyes and said to Ximena, "You. ¡Cuenta! Hasta veinte. Cada cabaña tiene un número."

Señora Luz had cheeks pale as boiled corn. She spoke no Mixtec. She ran the housekeeping crews, and her husband ran the maintenance crews. Luz said to Rodolfo, who'd brought them, "You! Rodolfo! ¿Dónde está el otro? Emiliano dijo—" She looked at her notepad. "Esteban."

Ximena kept her face still. She imagined her skull filled with sand so she wouldn't cry at the name of her brother.

Rodolfo said, "Solo dos."

Luz stared hard into Ximena's face. At her hair. "Todos Oaxaqueños." She'd sighed. "Todos indios. You. ¡Cuenta! Twenty."

Ximena counted, Elpidia breathing hard beside her. They had spent ten days recovering after they had crossed, eating and sleeping in the Prowler, but also learning from Fidelia everything they could. Numbers, names of people who worked at Seven Palms, some words in Spanish and English. Elpidia remembered nothing.

Now, every morning, Luz put their numbers on washable cards she attached to the carts, next to the keys. The keys themselves were locked to the cart by Luz, so no one could take home a key and copy it and come back here at night to steal.

Ximena heard the rubber whisper of tires. A woman in a wheelchair. She sat with her head thrown back, eyes only covered with bandages. The nurse was Ellen. She warned Ximena away with her lifted chin. A wedge of thick blond hair, like a curled broom edge, peeked out from the turban over the woman's head. They went inside number 8. The DO NOT sign trembled when the door shut.

Elpidia came down the other walkway from her cottages, numbers 1 through 6. "Four towels," Elpidia said in Mixtec. "Luz gave me not enough. I will finish early and come help you."

The towels were thick blurry stacks. Ximena said, "Do not," and laughed. But she added, "She won't like it."

Elpidia took four towels, then slipped her hand into Ximena's apron pocket. One saladito. She grinned and said in English, "Do. You do."

Suddenly Luz. Her black heels striking the tiles. Clipboard in her hand. She had sold Ximena and Elpidia their rubber-soled lace-up white shoes. Twenty-seven dollars for their foot silence.

Luz always knew when they stopped working and started talking, as if a fly winged directly to her cubicle near the laundry room to tell her. "¿Tesoro?" she said softly, frowning at Ximena's hand buried in her pocket, holding the saladitos.

Tesoro. Treasure. Luz had warned them. Take nothing. Ever.

Ximena held out one saladito. The salted dried plum like a wizened red stone in her palm. Luz shook her head, then looked into the laundry cart for discarded bras and shirts. None. She pointed at number 9.

"Ándale," she said, her Spanish enunciated, crisp, and angry as always. "You're behind. You have to start the laundry."

Wash—the English. What Ellen and the other American nurses said. Put this in the wash. But also, wash down this floor. Clean. Limpie, in Spanish. Sandoo, in Mixtec. But wash, like laundry, was different.

Ximena was memorizing the three words for each task, or flower, or food. Her cousin Fidelia, who was only sixteen, said to her most nights in the trailer, "You can't go to high school, you're eighteen now, right? We have to get you to speak Spanish and English. Then you can try for, like, technical school. Community college."

HOUSEKEEPING was embroidered on the pocket of Ximena's uniform. Keep the house. Clean the room. Wash the towels. Iron the sheets.

Iron was an element on Fidelia's chemistry chart, and also a component in her geology textbook. Fidelia had been born here, in Coachella. She didn't mind Ximena. She had no patience with Elpidia. "Elpidia thinks the whole world is gonna exist in one male body."

There were no names on the uniforms for Housekeeping. No one should know your name. The doctors wore pale green uniforms. The nurses and therapists wore apricot uniforms. Señora Luz and her husband wore pale blue. Rodolfo and the landscapers wore dark blue. Housekeeping wore white. Ximena's uniform blouse was huge. The last woman who wore it had been big. She had been fired for stealing towels, sheets, and vases, Luz said. She was in jail.

Ximena heard Rodolfo singing in the distance, holding the stick like a wand, the plastic hump on his back filled with liquid. Ants. Hormigas. Kill the ants.

She stood beside the flower beds along the edge of the red tile, listening to Elpidia's cart. Hummingbird in the big white flower. Hibiscus. The dart of beak past her.

Ncho'o. Chuparrosa. Hummingbird. She could have flown all the way from the border to here. Iso. Conejo. Rabbit. They crept out at dusk near the water tank where the weeds grew. Va'u. Coyote.

Coyote. The sound. The breathing.

In Oaxaca, in San Cristóbal, the world had three layers. Her grandmother had taught her and Estaban this when they were small, after their mother had left. Ximena was five, Esteban three. No one had known their father—he was a man from Oaxaca City, miles away, who had met their mother when she went there to work at a market. Her mother had left for California with him, and she said she'd return for the children in a year, but she never came back.

"There are the humans, the clouds, and the spirits who live between." Her grandmother said this while they were carrying firewood down from the mountain. "They are watching us in the trees just now, because we are leaving too late. Look—the clouds are moving down, dark. The spirits are waiting to take something. Right there. By the stream. They live near water, in the branches that hang down close, waiting for you to be careless."

Ximena had moved the wood on her head. She was maybe seven when her grandmother said this the first time. She said it again when Ximena and Esteban were leaving, too. For California.

"You can't ignore any of the three or you'll die. Like your mother. Look where they finally found her." Her grandmother hadn't said it with anger, but calm and certainty. Her three sons had been gone for thirty years. Her daughter was dead.

She'd told Ximena to remember. "You are Ñuu Savi. People of the rain."

But there was no rain here. No fog. No clouds. The sun alone from the morning when it rose until it went down.

Eight days from Oaxaca to Mexicali on buses and then two different vans to get here. Uncountable hours to walk and crawl. Then the wide canal.

Eight days in complete darkness, with only water and tortillas, in the garage somewhere in the desert, waiting for her uncle to pay. Only the penlight in her eyes, to see whether she was still alive, and then the hand grasping her hair and pulling forward.

In California, everything had three layers as well, which had surprised Ximena these last four months. At Seven Palms, there were the male doctors, who cut and abraded and altered the bodies; the American women—nurses and therapists and stylists—who touched the bodies for the days afterward; and the Mexicans who touched everything else. When she tried to explain it to her cousin, at night in the trailer, Fidelia gave her the terrible sideways frown of condescension. *Strata*, Fidelia said. There are never only three layers. Use *strata*. Look. She opened a book. "Geology. Look at how many layers are under the dirt. Way more than three." Fidelia's words were precise and beautiful and exhausting, late at night at the small white table which turned into Ximena's bed, in the trailer named Prowler. At night, while everyone else was asleep, only Fidelia and Ximena sitting at the table.

"Abuela says three," Ximena whispered.

Fidelia had never been to Mexico. "Yeah. But Abuela never left Oaxaca," she said, her voice dry as ever, not even looking up from what she was writing. "You sound like a vieja. Like you're seventy."

Inside the maintenance building, there were Luz and her

husband, Martín from Sinaloa. They lived in the small stucco house just outside the front gate of Seven Palms. Rodolfo said they rarely left the place. Then the three people who drove in from Coachella: José and Guillermo, born in Mexicali, who worked on all the machines and pipes in the buildings. Antonia, who cleaned the medical areas of waste and blood and chemicals, and sterilized all the instruments. Then the landscapers and housekeepers, from Oaxaca.

Three languages. Each word had to be repeated in Ximena's head. Agua. Water. Nducha. Pelo. Hair. Ixi. Only one word was always the same; Luz never said it in Spanish, only English. *Ice.* More ice! Bring five bags of ice. Hurry up. You want me to call ICE? Check the machine for ice. Crush. Not chip! You get lazy, I will call ICE tonight and you will be gone tomorrow morning. Don't make me do it.

Where do you live?! That is what Uncle Emiliano said ICE would shout if they came, or if they stopped Rodolfo's truck on the highway. *Where were you born? Hurry up! You should know. Where's your ID? ID ID ID!*

Ximena and Elpidia were to say calmly, *Mecca,* to every question or shout, and to pull out their ID cards, which they had gotten from their uncle. *We live in Mecca. We were born in Mecca.* This word, not Spanish or English. Fidelia said it was one of the most holy places in the world; she showed it to Ximena on the laptop, millions of people walking there to Saudi Arabia. Holy. Hole. Whole.

The plan as explained by Uncle Emiliano and Rodolfo was precise and had to be followed immediately. Stay in the truck, as if you belong there; do not get out; do not smile, and do not cry or they will certainly take you. Say *I was born in Mecca. I live here all my life.*

Show them the card. Look straight ahead at the place where the sky meets the earth. Keep your lips over your teeth.

She always began with the flowers. Five dead carnations in the small vase on the dresser inside number 9. Flores. Ita. Señora Luz counted the white carnations and roses every morning, and the thick towels. The soaps. Every single thing stocked on their carts. She checked their carts and uniform pockets every night, to make sure they hadn't stolen anything. Everything could be sold at the swap meet in Indio—robes, towels, magazines, wineglasses, bras, and flowers. Last year, a girl had stolen entire buckets of yellow roses and white carnations from the maintenance building; during the Coachella music festival in April, she sold every flower to rich güeras. That girl was born in Indio, Rodolfo said. She had laughed at Luz. Luz couldn't call ICE on her.

Ximena dropped the brown shriveled blooms into the trash bag that hung from the cart and plucked new ones from the bucket. White: flowers, towels, sheets, robes, washcloths, bandages, bedspreads.

The bedroom door was open. Voices. Anita, the facialist.

Ximena said, "Housekeeping," at the doorway to the bedroom, without looking inside.

She vacuumed the pale blue carpet in the small living room, vacuumed the couch and white wooden blinds because every day Luz checked for dust and hair, and ran her cleaning cloth over the television, the end tables, the coffee table. Then the bathroom: three dead carnations in the small gold bathroom vase. Medications, lotions, makeup, and washcloths covered the white tile counter below the mirror. Pinkblood-stained tissues filled the wastebasket, pinkblood towels in the bathtub. When she took towels to the cart, señora Luz stood in the corridor. "Ximena. Pelo."

Her heavy footsteps, her black pumps, went back toward the other wing.

Ximena knelt by the bathtub. Luz checked constantly for stray hair. Ximena lifted the circular net of blond hair gathered on the drain. Like a tiny fishing net, with small holes where the water had drained through the fine strands. Pelo. Hair. Ixi.

Finally, she looked at the women in the bedroom. As she brought the flowers inside, and new pillowcases, Anita shook her head and motioned toward the dresser. Anita was working on the face above the bandages of the boobs. The television was on. Ximena was dizzy with all the sounds. Anita, a pale American woman with an apricot uniform moving the skin of temples and cheeks and throat, tapping lightly above the eyebrows, her long fingers in perfect unison while her own eyes watched the television; the closed eyes and slightly open mouth of the older woman lying flat on the special bed. The room loud with the humming of machines. All these humans, the ice and towels, cold air and water, to rearrange the thin skin around her eyes, along her jaw, covering her cheekbones, the soft plumped lips. The new breasts could not yet be touched. They were only two days old.

Anita might have been the age of Ximena's abuela. Anita's forehead shiny and tight, but her throat ringed by twenty or thirty lines like delicate necklaces, her chest marked by pale sequins. Abuela's face was two smooth mounds of brown cheek, black eyes squinted to gleam, but her throat and chest unmarked and golden. Her grandmother was so small as to fit under the arm of Esteban, the night before they left.

Her grandmother had given birth to six children. Two daughters died as babies, of fever. Three sons went north to California.

Emiliano, Epifanio, and Eufemio. And Josefina. The last child. Ximena's mother.

Today was October 22. Blistering, shimmering heat. One hundred five degrees. The women all needed ice for the swelling. She checked the special white freezer near the front door. Two bags half gone of the ice crushed fine. One bag gone of the ice chips. Both bags gone from the bag with cubes, for drinks. Ximena took the bags outside, as she'd been told, and layered the crushed ice like snow around the base of the small palms lining the walkway. Water was the most expensive thing here in the desert.

Now Rodolfo was clipping the grass by hand around the flower beds. The men couldn't use blowers. The women slept all day.

There were always bras in the trash. New bras in bags beside the bed.

Elpidia had moved down to number 6. Her last one. She waved, leaning on her cart. Elpidia's head had ached for days from the heat. Maybe she needed salt, Fidelia said. Maybe low blood pressure. Every day, Ximena braided Elpidia's long hair tightly, and then Elpidia did the same for her. Elpidia's cheeks were heavy and her eyes huge and shadowed.

Ximena went back for the vacuum. In the garage, outside Calexico, the coyote had flashed the penlight into Elpidia's face, too, but she had not been taken. Elpidia had never said anything to Ximena about those five nights.

Blond hairs had collected like intricate lace on the brush of the vacuum attachment. This woman had lost so much hair in three days. Ximena emptied the hair into the trash can, onto tissues and wipes and a beige bra, with blurred seams of age.

How did they know exactly what size of new bra to buy? Did they order new breasts by number as well? Boobs. They couldn't walk out of Seven Palms without a bra, with new breasts so large they should never hang free. Ximena felt dizzy now, her mouth filled with saliva, and she put another saladito on her tongue.

She had two white bras, bought at the Indio swap meet. Back in June, Ximena's breasts had swollen to twice their normal size. Her tía Inez had said it was good cooking in Mecca, but Fidelia had watched Ximena. She'd seen Ximena throwing up in the oleander bushes behind the trailer.

Now Ximena steadied herself on the cart, the heat rushing around her. Skull and fingers. Nostrils. Knees.

She pushed herself off the cart handle, went back inside number 9 to make sure the blinds were closed tightly, and closed the door. The first day, Luz warned her sternly about no light. "No sun. Never," she had said.

Nicandyi. Sol. Sun.

The women often checked out at night. Ximena figured they didn't like to see each other.

In front of number 10, she took a drink of water from the plastic bottle with her name on it, next to the cleaning bottles and the white hand towel she used each day to wipe her own face. She would have to head to the laundry room soon, and begin a load of towels.

Inside number 10, there was an empty plate on the coffee table. The women hardly ate for the first two days. Food was delivered with a quiet knock, after the medi-spa kitchen had called ahead. If the DO NOT sign was hung, food was left outside the door. Liquid only past the new lips.

It was almost four now. Ximena brought the soiled robe for the other laundry bag. Elpidia was rummaging through the cleaning bottles on the cart, her own cart behind Ximena's. Most of the time, they were not allowed to work adjacent rooms. Señora Luz said it made them slow. Elpidia loved to talk and laugh. But now Elpidia said, "I don't care. I do eleven. You do twelve. Rodolfo says his friend Carlos from the big hotel is bringing chickens tonight. Friday! We can make a sauce. As long as Fidelia doesn't help."

Fidelia refused to cook anything. She ate flour tortillas heated on the stove burner and rolled into easy snacks while she studied for hours. Everyone said Inez spoiled her. She was the surprise daughter of Uncle Emiliano and Inez, had come late in their lives. Their four sons had married and lived in Oasis and Bombay Beach. They worked dates, beets, and carrots with Emiliano's crew.

Inez said Fidelia would go to college, in Los Angeles. She didn't make her cook. And Ximena would rather sit with Fidelia in the Prowler, looking at the books, than outside with the other women near the grills and picnic tables. Fidelia showed her science books. The earth had its own skin, and the strata underneath. The human body had skin, and the strata underneath. Sheath of woven muscle, purple glisten of tubes, yellow fat. *Subcutaneous*. Ximena looked at the bloody towels in number 10. Fidelia said, "Subcutaneous fat is what they pull out of their thighs. I heard they inject it somewhere else like their cheeks." She laughed. "Try saying it."

Fidelia went to Desert Mirage High School. She said, "Yeah, if you guys went to Desert Mirage, Elpidia would be the annoying pretty cheerleader. You'd be the nerd. Like me."

She needed to start the first load of laundry. Into the massive industrial washer, she loaded towels and sheets. Smells of perfume, lotion, blood, urine, salt, and bleach mixing so strong she imagined she could see a cloud rising from the dark well.

Then she went back for the last cottage. At number 11, she left one saladito on Elpidia's cart, beside the water bottle. The salt on the dried plum sparkled in the fading sunlight. Elpidia would never buy them, but she wanted them all day. The salt stung her teeth, she said, the way she liked in the long last hour of work.

At number 12, Ximena looked out into the desert beyond the grass and hedges and the golden cement block wall around Seven Palms. The Santa Rosa Mountains rose in purple folds in the distance. Dusk was early in the massive shadows. She listened at number 12 for that one confused cricket, shrilling inside this cottage for the last two days, fooled by the dark rooms into night song.

Even the crickets were not the same here. Heads too large, antennae too long, wandering around the spa grounds knowing no one would eat them. Not the same as grasshoppers. Ximena and Esteban had collected grasshoppers and crickets in stubbled cornfields for their grandmother, who roasted them, dusted them with chile, and heaped them in a palm basket for market. Chapulines. She closed her eyes. She saw her brother bent down, his hand leaping onto the grasshoppers. She saw his head above the black slide of water at the border.

She touched the small sign, dangled on its ribbon like the scapular around Esteban's neck when they were small. Luz said DO NOT meant the woman wanted nothing. Dirty sheets, dirty dishes— they didn't care. They didn't want anyone to see their black eyes, their skin etched raw as butchered meat, their noses swollen like gourds.

And Luz was behind her now. "Are you sleeping?" she hissed.

"Do not," Ximena said, pointing at number 12.

Luz fluttered her fingers in the way that meant, Gone. Flown. A butterfly returned home. "Empty," she said. She looked at her watch and walked away.

Ximena used her key. Stale frigid air rushed out. The room black. She waited cautiously, for her eyes to adjust. For a woman's voice. The air conditioner blew hard. Set on High. The television murmured. How had this woman slept through the cricket and television? The young red-haired woman, she remembered.

She had seen the woman checking in three days ago. Ximena had been collecting linens from the medical building. Most women had blond hair or silvery hair, as if ashes had been painted onto the strands. But number 12's hair was reddish-gold. Thin and long as silk fringe against her neck. Her cheek, turned away, splashed with freckles like a gathering of gold flakes. A tattoo on her shoulder blade. A striped bee, smiling, and the top two legs held up, wearing boxing gloves. On the other shoulder, a girl rabbit wearing a red dress, her tall ears cocked forward as if listening.

It was hard to tell how old she was. Big sunglasses like all of them. She carried a big soft pink bag, unzipped partway. Rodolfo and the other men carried the larger suitcases on their golf cart, to the rooms, but the woman kept this bag on her arm. Her legs were so pale that blue strings of blood laced the backs of her knees.

Luz had said number 12 was only eyes and lips. She rolled her eyes and said number 12 had gotten new boobs here late last year. "From LA," Luz said. "LA women are never finished."

Ximena turned on the lights, waited cautiously in case someone shouted. She smelled something sweet and musky, and something terrible. Old shit. She gagged a little—that didn't happen often. In the living room trash basket, tissues smudged with pink lipstick, beige makeup, and black mascara like oil. One bra. Black silky material. Stiff somehow, and the smell of curdled milk. And two dirty diapers.

Ximena opened the bedroom door. The baby lay on the center of the big bed. On her back. A girl. Slanted to the left, as if she had kicked for a long time. The white spread dimpled around her feet.

She was not old enough to turn over but she was not a newborn. Ximena bent toward her. Maybe six weeks old. Hair sparse and red, fine on her skull. Her eyes were closed. Sunken like dimples. Pale pink dress, with lace at the collar and hem, and thin legs, gray. Pink booties on her feet. Her face was tight and pinched, her nose a tiny white knuckle poking through her skin.

The salted plum leapt and wriggled in Ximena's mouth, swollen from her saliva. She spit it into her hand and ran to the bathroom. She threw up in the sink.

Never leave your own liquids in a room, Luz always said. I will know. Ximena rinsed her mouth again and again, cleaned the basin once more, and wiped it dry with a towel.

She went to the bed. She had seen dead babies before, this size, at home. They had died of diarrhea. They had this shrunken face. Old woman bones showing through their baby skin. Her grandmother said that was the woman they would have become.

Number 12 had left the baby here. The pink bag was on the floor near the bed. Ximena's whole body shook now, in the freezing cold.

The baby that slid from her in the date palms last month had a face blurred. Fidelia said the word for a baby not yet a human was embryo. But at three months and two weeks, the baby had been curled, legs and arms bent to the chest, where its pulsing heart was supposed to beat. The intricate mesh of blood visible behind the parchment skull.

Ximena slid her fingers across the bedspread. This baby girl's fingers were dry as cinnamon sticks. The fingernails translucent like husks from washed corn. She put her finger to the disposable diaper. Dry and small as a white fist under the dress. But then the baby made a sound. Not even a raspy cry. A trill from her throat. Ximena fell to her knees. She had not entered this room for two days. The baby had cried for her. For someone. Maybe she had heard Ximena and Elpidia outside the window.

Elpidia and Luz. They would come any moment. She closed the front door silently.

She pushed one hand under the heavy small head. Lifted the baby like a doll with no stuffing. If she gave the baby to Luz, Luz would scream at her, accuse her of hiding this baby, run to the doctors. The doctors would inspect the baby with their soft ringed fingers. Either they would find the baby's mother, who didn't want her, or they would give the baby away.

They would call ICE on Ximena.

A bee and a rabbit. Tattooed on the girl's shoulders. This pink bag.

What if the baby died, right when she handed her to Luz? Luz might call the police. Or she might not. She might throw the baby away, so they wouldn't get in trouble. Rodolfo said sometimes he burned bags with the parts of bodies they took away. But Luz would definitely get rid of Ximena, and probably Elpidia, too.

She didn't touch the pink bag. Left-behind bags and suitcases and purses went to Luz. She sold them. This bag smelled of baby. Did Luz know that smell? Did Luz have children?

Ximena laid the baby on a large towel in the bathroom. The legs shook twice in spasm. She inclined the head and put drops of water on her forefinger, and slid them into the tiny slot of mouth. Five drops of water. The lips moved. Three more drops of water. The lips touched each other, and then her finger.

Ximena trembled, picking up the baby. Her own milk had never come in, though her breasts had stayed bigger, even now. The breathing was faint in her ear.

She went to the door. She folded the towel into a bundle, keeping a slot open near the tiny face, for air. Outside, the heat was bronze. She took two steps to her cart, put the towel into the laundry bag, lay wet towels from previous rooms around it. If the baby cried, Ximena was in trouble.

Elpidia's cart was gone from number 11. She had to be in the medical building to collect the last linens from surgery. The second laundry.

Ximena went back inside, keeping the door propped open. She vacuumed fast for only a few minutes. On the dresser, next to the dead carnations, there was a note. Neat handwriting on the small pad with golden fronds in raised design. Ximena slid the whole pad into her bra. When she emptied the trash, under six empty cans of Diet Pepsi was an orange medication bottle. And a tiny embroidered pouch. Ximena put both into the other cup of her bra.

She was shaking harder. The bundle made no sound while she wheeled the cart toward the laundry room, across the glimmering heat of the gardens. The wheels bumped on the flagstone path to maintenance. The baby could be slipping away into death right now. At the blue dumpster, she lifted the black plastic bag full of hair and tissue and lipstick and bras, let it fall into the cavern.

She took the blue canvas jacket from Rodolfo's golf cart, parked near the back entrance to maintenance. The jacket smelled of Uncle Emiliano's cigarettes. He had come to get her and Elpidia at the house in the desert outside Calexico. He paid five thousand dollars for each of them. Ximena—his sister's child. Elpidia—his wife's great-niece.

It was five p.m. The western sky was dark blue at the edges of the seven palms near the entrance. She lifted the towel-shrouded baby and stepped into the maintenance bathroom, behind the booming whirl of the dryers.

The baby's eyes were open. The left was green, clear as beer bottle glass. But the right eye—it was half-blue. Like a strange marble.

The mouth was open halfway, a tiny slit working as if for a nipple. Fidelia said Coke was bad for humans. Strong enough to clean the car battery. But it was all Ximena had to drip into the baby's mouth, and the lips fastened onto her finger. Soft. But deliberate.

What would Luz do with this baby? "Our clients are famous," she always said. "We say two words. Protect. Privacy. Dilo! No phones for you here."

Ximena unbuttoned her uniform shirt. It was very big, but the towel was too bulky. She took two pillowcases, hot from the dryer, and wrapped the small body. The dress new and stiff. She put the bundle inside her shirt and rebuttoned her uniform, put Rodolfo's jacket on, and zipped it up to her throat.

Rodolfo smelled like cut grass and gasoline. In the front seat of the truck, beside him, Elpidia laughed at everything he said, in English, like a woman. "Kill the ants! Kill the spiders. The crickets. The wasps! Oh, my God!"

Elpidia bent over laughing.

Ximena was pressed against the window. She remembered helping him spray poison onto the crickets, breathing in the sweet thick mist. Rodolfo poked at the sleeve of his jacket and said, "You have fever?"

She nodded. "I'm cold."

He said, "One hundred six today. Inside cold, outside hot, inside cold. Maybe you have flu."

It only took ten minutes to drive from Seven Palms to Thermal. Harrison and 66th Avenue. The streets were all named for American presidents or given numbers. "You have to know exactly where you are all the time," Fidelia said, bent over the notebook she had given Ximena. "Here's the grid of avenues. If ICE comes and you have to hide, you have to be able to get back here. What if they take Rodolfo and you have to walk?" Fidelia had looked up, her long braid dangling onto the little white table. "You have the uniform. You have to be able to wait for a few hours in the bushes, then buy something in a bag and then just look like you're walking home. Like you belong here. You can't hide in the desert."

Rodolfo pulled into the parking lot of the AmeriGas market. "Carlos is bringing five chickens, Ximena. Fill up the tank." The small white propane tank, like a rocket, was in the truck bed. There was a line of women holding tanks, laughing and gossiping near the big white tank on the wooden platform. Friday night. Everyone cooking. One woman held a clear plastic bag of whole tilapia, a school of fish frozen in the air beside her thigh.

Ximena leaned against the window and said, "I can't."

Elpidia took the tank. "Lazy!"

The truck went down 66th Avenue for five more miles, until Fillmore. Another president. Then the wheels jostled off the asphalt and headed down a dirt road where the sign read TORRES MARTINEZ INDIAN RESERVATION—TRIBAL LAND.

In the distance was a windbreak of gray-green tamarisk trees, and two narrow lanes behind a long black iron gate. Two rows of old silver mailboxes outside the gate. On the right were six mailboxes sitting on a wooden fence. They all had MARTINEZ painted on the sides. Uncle Emiliano leased his land from Sofelia Martinez, Fidelia said, and her people were Cahuilla. They had lived on this land for a thousand years, when the whole valley was a lake.

On the left, twelve mailboxes. A sign that said RANCHO PALOMITAS. Since Trump, Uncle Emiliano had a man stationed always, just behind the gate, watching for ICE. Fernando was dozing in his black Silverado truck. Rodolfo said he would have a Chevy Silverado one day. He honked, and the bundle inside Ximena's shirt leapt once.

Fernando worked nights at the polo grounds in Indio, at the stables, watching the horses; he kept watch at the rancho in the day. He unlocked the gate. The truck jerked toward the left lane, and the baby startled against Ximena's breastbone. She felt it—a separate movement. A squirming of shoulder.

In the wide clearing, Uncle Emiliano's trailer was first. A pale green single-wide mobile home, where Inez looked out the big front window at them coming down the lane. Below her window was an altar to la Virgen de la Soledad, black gown and plastic flowers dusty from summer. Emiliano's green truck was gone. They were working late in the beets.

Behind her uncle's mobile home was a small travel trailer, parked just at the edge of the palm trunks. The Prowler. Her clothes and Elpidia's hung on the line strung from the hitch to a lemon tree between the trailers.

Rodolfo stopped there, and they got out. He lived halfway down the lane, in a blue mobile home he shared with three other men. The dust rose from his tires.

Ximena walked awkwardly, holding the top of the zipper with one hand, her purse with the other. What if the baby cried? She'd been silent all this time. What if this was the moment the baby chose to leave the world? What if the Coke had killed her?

"I feel sick tonight," she said. Elpidia cocked her head, studying her while they walked toward the Prowler. Did she think Ximena had stolen clothes? People in the rancho noticed everything—new sunglasses, new shoes, extra beer.

There was nowhere to hide in the Prowler. The two of them slept together on the tiny double bed; the bathroom was barely big enough to turn around in.

Elpidia disappeared inside the trailer. Uncle Emiliano said it was named for a jungle cat. The baby was not heavy at all. A tremble of nausea came over her, and she held on to the hitch of the Prowler. Rodolfo came to scrub the grill near the faucet, singing, "Kill the ants, kill the ants, baby, baby."

An older man named Julio who was always angry said, "Shut up. Better than killing five hundred chickens a day in Nebraska. I killed five hundred chickens a day."

"I killed several million ants today. But we will eat only five chickens tonight," Rodolfo said calmly. He turned on the radio kept at the long wooden table. Tubas and trumpets. A man singing about Zacatecas.

Ximena felt movement in the small bundle nestled between her breasts. She walked behind the Prowler to sit on the white plastic chair near the clothesline, where no one could see her. She unbuttoned the jacket, unbuttoned the uniform shirt. The edge of gold embroidery on the pillowcase. The skull. Pink scalp. Pale red hair like chick feathers. The lips moving as if the baby were telling herself secrets.

No. A finger. A nipple. She needed something in her mouth.

Ximena looked at the back of her uncle's trailer. Two windows—Fidelia's bedroom window with slats of glass, the bright purple cloth she called satin. Silence. Fidelia would be wearing her white headphones, listening to her music. Her father hated the headphones—she wasn't allowed to wear them when he was home.

Even after five months here, Ximena was nervous around Uncle Emiliano. He was forty-five years old, her abuela's eldest son. He leased this land twenty years ago. Fidelia said he told her after he crossed, he hadn't slept for five years. He worked fields in the day and the tilapia farm at night. He saved enough to buy his mobile home and two others. Then people brought their own trailers to live here. All Oaxaqueños. All Mixtecos.

But he was a son. He called Abuela every Wednesday and Sunday. And he had not told her yet what happened to Esteban. Gone. Just like that. No body. No chance to mourn. Nothing of his to keep by her bed. Her uncle couldn't say it yet to Abuela, and Ximena wasn't even sure he believed her. He had come to the garage out in the desert near Calexico, and no Esteban. His eyes hard on Ximena when she was finally in the truck. And she could never tell him what had happened to her in the shed, somewhere she had never seen, through the blindfold.

Esteban hadn't wanted to leave Mexico. But he had to come with Ximena and Elpidia. To protect them.

Abuela was alone now, with her friend doña Patricia to stay with her. Every Saturday, when Luz handed her cash, Ximena gave it to her uncle—$400—and he gave her $50 back. The rest was sent to her grandmother.

Ximena felt the heat on her legs. The music was faint and the accordion threaded through the air. With the warmth of the baby, she closed her eyes. Imagined her mother sitting like this. The smell of woodsmoke and cinnamon and coffee. She remembered that smell of her mother. And a pink rose on her mother's elbow. She thought that was her imagination, too, until she asked her grandmother once, long after her mother was gone. "A pop," Abuela made the sound with her lips. "A piece of ember flew from the fire and burned her. Right there. When she was little. Like you."

The young woman with the bee and the rabbit on her shoulders. She had dressed this baby in pink, a dress smelling of new. She had closed the door to number 12. Thinking what?

Ximena took a clean T-shirt from the clothesline. She always hung the socks near the ground, the shirts higher up. She had to show the note to Fidelia.

Inside the back bedroom of the green mobile home, her tía Inez didn't seem surprised at all when Ximena handed her a baby. She dropped the pillowcases on the floor and grabbed a crocheted afghan from her bed, held the baby in her arms as if any other infant, and said, "Where is the milk?"

The eyes were open. The mouth moved, and two fingers detached themselves from the fist of the right hand. Ximena thought, The pillowcases were hot. I was hot. The baby's cheeks were red now. She was not freezing.

Fidelia came into the room. "What the hell! Ximena! A *white* baby?"

"Where is the milk?" Inez said again.

The small refrigerator in number 12. Ximena hadn't even looked inside, or cleaned it. She shook her head. She sat down on the floor, dizzy.

Inez said, "Fidelia. Go down to Enedina's. She has formula. Tell her we found a baby kitten and we are trying to keep it alive. We need a small bottle." Her voice was calm. "Smile. Hurry."

Inez made Ximena lie down on her bed. When Fidelia brought the formula, Inez fed the baby in the bedroom. Everyone else was gathered at the wooden tables near the end of the lane, cooking and playing music. The baby made no sound, sucking gently on the nipple.

Fidelia sat beside Ximena on the bed, reading the note. She turned it over, then looked at Ximena. She said in Mixtec, to her mother, "This is gabacha crazy." Then she read the English, to Ximena: *Dear Don. You lied. You said Enhancement will change your life. You said these are the most beautiful breasts you ever created. I called you seventeen times. These DDs don't work. You're a doctor. You're loaded. You feed her. She's yours.*

Fidelia handed back the notepad as if it had burned her fingers. "Enhancement, that must be a surgery. Breasts. DDs aren't even that big. Like—Enedina's boobs. Not big like—Instagram."

Ximena looked at the baby's tiny feet. "Loaded."

"That means he has money."

The baby cried, twice, in the arms of Inez. Rasp rasp. Not a cricket now but a kitten. Inez did something and then there was silence. Ximena knew she could never explain the sound of the cricket, desperate, behind the curtains. They'd never been to Seven Palms. She couldn't explain the woman. Not why she took the baby.

She had touched that cold hand and thought of her own baby—hot and wet in her palms.

Fidelia said, "Two girls at school already got their lips done with Botox and they said when they turn eighteen they get boobs. Twins." Fidelia glanced at her mother. "The doctor has to, like, move the nipples." She looked again at the notepad. "So this girl says the rich Dr. Don is the father."

Uncle Emiliano came inside the silent, dark trailer. In the bedroom, while Inez spoke, he said nothing at all to Ximena. He studied the baby with his face unmoving.

She imagined her uncle's brain. Like in Fidelia's textbooks—synapses, neurons, pathways like tree roots moving through the skull. Braised cow tongues and brains in tacos at the market—lengua y cabeza. The brain of the baby small as an orange, but already full of darkness and cold and silence. The air conditioner roaring. Throat rasping and rasping.

The baby would never remember the smell of Ximena, the bleach of the pillowcases, the sound of Inez murmuring, or the feel of Emiliano wrapping her in a plain brown towel from the bathroom, because the pillowcases were stitched with Seven Palms in gold thread and they would have to bury those somewhere. Inez carried the baby in her arms out of the trailer, but she also held a sports bag with soccer balls stitched on the sides. Emiliano turned the truck around and they left in the dark, near ten p.m.

Fidelia wouldn't look at her. She went to her small bedroom and shut the door. Ximena took the two pillowcases. She took the lighter from the kitchen table. She headed out of the rancho, into the ghostly date palm garden. The narrow furrows of hot sand were dry. Uncle Emiliano said there was drought ten years ago, and Sofelia Martinez couldn't afford the water, so she let this area die. The palms were tall gray candles with fronds collapsed.

Luz. If the baby belonged to this Dr. Don, how would he have found it? Did the bee tattoo woman expect Luz to read the note and take the baby to this doctor and say, "Here is your child"? What happened to fake breasts when they filled with milk?

Ximena walked toward the center of the date garden. Full moon. Rustling of night birds in the palm bark. She looked up and down the rows until she found the old cement irrigation tower, like a castle with a wooden ladder attached to the side.

Last month she had held her baby in her left hand. She had held the ladder with her right. Terrified. But she was not bleeding now. She held only pillowcases. She climbed to the top, and lifted the wooden cover, splintered and silver, hinged into half. She lifted one knee over the edge of the hollow tower, then the other, and went down the metal rungs inside.

At the bottom, the sand was cool and dry. The candles had melted into discs of pink and blue, but the plastic flowers were bright in the lighter flame. She had not known whether girl or boy. She'd held the tiny head. Fingers like uncooked rice. Three months and two weeks after Calexico. In the dark garage, five times the coyote found her with the penlight. He unlocked the ankle chain and took her outside, to a shed at the edge of the property.

He spoke some Mixtec words. He did not hit her in the face. He hit her once, at the top of her ribs, and took her breath away. Then he grabbed her hair again, and pushed her down. "They want American babies," he hissed behind her, at the back of her ear, shoving her face into the buttons of the mattress. "I have given them thirty-eight American babies. Now thirty-nine." His gold chain dangled near her temple. His bony fingers held the back of her neck so hard she had bruises under her ears.

If someone had told her a baby that small would have fingers, she would not have believed it.

She had cleaned six rooms that day, and then helped Rodolfo spray insecticide onto a long hedge of bougainvillea. Crimson blooms with tiny white stars inside. That night, pain invaded her back, then her hips, like hot wire. She left the Prowler and walked into the grove. A rush of liquid filled her sweatpants, and then a baby slid into her underwear.

Here at the bottom of the irrigation tower, the sand was soft. She'd been able to dig the hole with a rusty axe-head dropped into the tank. Now she laid the pillowcases on the earth, the gold thread of Seven Palms glistening in the flame of the lighter. She said a prayer for the baby.

It wasn't until she was climbing back up to the night sky that she realized there was no name on the note of the baby girl she had carried today. The bee tattoo girl had not given her daughter that.

When she returned, walking behind the row of trailers to avoid the last people at the grill, Elpidia and Rodolfo and the others playing music and laughing, Uncle Emiliano's truck was back. The light was on in his bedroom.

Ximena opened the door of the Prowler, expecting to be alone. But Fidelia sat at the small white table, in pajamas. Ximena washed her hands at the metal sink, and then sat on the other scratchy plaid cushion across from her cousin.

Ximena said in Mixtec, "Will you really cut off your hair when you go to college?"

Fidelia said, "Really? Seriously?" Ximena knew those words. Fidelia said them all the time to her and Elpidia. Her voice low and cut with disgust. Now she said in English, "You want to hang out and pretend you didn't just take a chance on some weird criminal baby? My mother could have gotten arrested."

Ximena thought about the strata of Fidelia, what she knew so far. The first layer was always angry. Then mildly superior, because she was younger than Ximena but she needed to win. The third layer was always curious. Ximena said nothing.

Fidelia took a big breath. "Elpidia met the love of her life tonight. Like some Hallmark movie. Carlos. He works at the Hilton. They're kissing off in the trees. I bet she thinks they'll get married."

Ximena said carefully, "Next week. A ring."

Fidelia rolled her eyes and smiled a little.

Ximena looked at Fidelia's notebooks. Pages and pages with sentences rewritten into Spanish and Mixtec. Stars and words in the margins. She went to the school library for internet, or sat in the parking lot of a hotel. Ximena said, "I have to go to sleep. Get up so I can move the table." Every night, she lifted the table off the metal pipe and laid it in the channel of space to support the cushions where she and Elpidia slept.

Fidelia didn't move. She said, "But why would you steal a white baby? Are you insane? What's wrong with you?"

"Where did they take her?"

"There are cameras everywhere in America. They say you can leave a baby at the fire station, but they have cameras, too. Mami said the hospital in Indio, on a Friday night everyone's there with emergencies. She was just an abuela visiting someone. She carried the baby down a hallway and nobody said anything. She left the bag on a chair right next to some nurse desk. She put her rebozo over her head." Fidelia sighed. "She's so fucking smart. She probably looked like a ghost and they couldn't see her face. She left the note in the bag. The cops will have the Seven Palms logo. Dr. Don. They have DNA tests. They'll find him."

"Wait," Ximena said. She had put the things from her bra into her purse. The small embroidered pouch. Three ID cards inside. Barbara Angel Goldman. Angel Gold. Angel Smith. The young woman had red hair, blond hair, and black hair—different for each card. Different lipstick and brows, too.

The medication bottle. Barbara Angel Goldman.

"Percocet. The mom was probably high." Fidelia pointed at a smear of rust on the back of Ximena's arm. "Where'd you go?"

Ximena shrugged.

Then Fidelia said, "You had a baby. Last month."

Ximena shook her head.

"I saw you throwing up. I smelled blood." She lifted Ximena's left hand. There was rust from the ladder under her fingernails. "Is that blood?"

Ximena thought for a moment. "Iron." She took back her hand. "You're not a doctor."

"Not yet. Maybe I'll be a lawyer instead." Then she said, "Can I stay here and study for a little longer? I don't want to go back home yet."

Ximena put the pouch and pill bottle back into her purse, and washed her hands. She sat across from Fidelia and opened the notebook Fidelia had bought for her at Rite Aid. Page 8. Home.

Mobile home. Motor home. Trailer. Tent trailer. RV.

House. Mansion. Cottage. Castle. Barn. Hotel. Motel. Apartment. Studio. Duplex. Triplex.

Page 3. Fidelia had printed out a map of the desert and taped it onto the page. Coachella was from conchilla. A tiny shell that used to be in this lake. Mecca was a holy place. Oasis. Thermal. Indio. Salton Sea. Calexico. Mexicali. The canal between the countries.

Esteban.

She curled up onto the narrow cushion across from Fidelia, the table just above her cheek, and put a pillow over her eyes, to block the light above. She heard the sound of the pink highlighter pen, and fell asleep thinking that her cousin was leaving pink snail trails all over the pages.

On Saturdays, they received their pay from Luz, in cash, at five p.m. At three, Ximena walked with her cart to the medical building. She hated the smells, the moaning she heard sometimes from rooms. She wheeled the cart to the front reception desk and Nicolle, the young blond woman who worked there, glanced at her and then back to her phone.

On the wall in the reception area, there were five photographs of doctors. Ximena had never looked at the photos before. Three old men. Two younger men. Don. Dr. Don Sanderson. Dark brown hair combed off his forehead in ridges, teeth white and rectangular as the small refrigerators in each cottage.

"Ximena," señora Luz hissed at her shoulder. Her fingers grasped Ximena's elbow hard. "You are looking for tesoro here, too?"

Outside, Luz shoved her hands into the pockets of Ximena's uniform shirt. Empty. "Entiende," she said viciously. "I know. Pillowcases. Towels. Drugs. Did you think I would not know?"

Ximena twisted away and headed toward the cottages. She wouldn't act afraid. Luz knew nothing. One more cottage today. Elpidia's cart was outside number 6. Ximena was on her knees by the bathtub in number 11, taking the net of hair from the drain, when she heard the whistle.

Eight notes. Mockingbird. Rodolfo said it was his favorite bird in California. It could imitate any sound. But it only sang at night. If she heard this song during the day, it was Rodolfo whistling, and she had to run.

She walked quickly outside, the moisture on her knees drying, and headed down the corridor. Elpidia's face was dreamy and flushed, from vacuuming. She had not heard. Ximena grabbed her arm and said, "ICE."

They ran behind number 12, to the space between hedges where Rodolfo kept his truck. He was inside the truck, the engine was on, and they slid under the green tarp where fertilizer and shovels were hidden from sight of guests. Rodolfo accelerated through the open back gate and onto the dirt road behind Seven Palms. Then Ximena felt asphalt smoother under the tires. He drove fast. Elpidia was crying.

Uncle Emiliano had told them if ICE came, do not drive toward the rancho, but immediately get on the 10 freeway. Rodolfo would drive fifty-seven miles, to Exit 42. The truck didn't stop until they got out in a parking lot. A Shell gas station. In a place called Calimesa.

Elpidia was gasping for cool air. When Ximena staggered against the gas pump, Elpidia hit her on the back, the shoulders. "I'll never see him again! I just met Carlos last night and you took me away from him! I hate you! What did you steal!?"

Ximena caught Elpidia's small fists and crushed hard. "Stop. Someone will call the police. Your blood is low. Like Fidelia says. You need salt. Tell Rodolfo to buy cacahuetes. Saladitos. Your favorite."

Rodolfo called Uncle Emiliano on his go-phone. He would have to get a new phone in Los Angeles. All phones could be tracked. When he was finished talking, Rodolfo bent into the truck bed and smashed the phone with a shovel. Then he put it into the empty bag from the peanuts, and threw it into the big dumpster behind the Shell.

They rode in the front seat the rest of the way to Los Angeles. Rodolfo said, "I worked there for thirteen months. Now we cannot go back to Mecca for six months. Maybe a year. Even to visit." When they came out of the mountains, Ximena could see a tall plume of smoke like a black tower rising from the west, and the wind flattened it, blew it sideways. It turned white, then black, white, then black. Reached across the sky. A big fire.

Rodolfo said, "Whatever you stole, Ximena, we don't even have it now."

Elpidia hit Ximena's shoulder again. They were both covered in fertilizer dust. Tears had run down Elpidia's cheeks and into the collar of her uniform. "We didn't get paid," she cried. "Luz gets to keep our money."

Luz. She had said pillowcases. Towels. Drugs—the medication bottles. Empty. Nothing about a baby. Luz didn't know about the baby.

"Luz is a fucking cabrona," Rodolfo said.

Ximena stared out the window at the golden flanks of mountain. Calimesa. She could read this now. She didn't care about the money. But she was leaving Fidelia. The notebooks her cousin had made for her, with drawings everywhere for each word, the five colors of gel pen. "Gel pens are my life," Fidelia said. Coffee in a thermos from Inez. Galletas.

Calimesa. Calexico. Where everything she brought from San Cristóbal was buried somewhere, by the coyote. No trail back to him. Ximena imagined the pit in the hot sand, far past the place she had been taken at night. Filled with her huipil, embroidered by her grandmother. Her photos. Her bible. Buried with maybe the bodies of pollos whose people never paid, never came for them. Dry hot sand. What had Fidelia said? "Mummies. The sand here is like Egypt. People turn into mummies in the desert."

Her baby buried in her T-shirt. She had walked back in her bra, circling around the rancho, crouching down to enter the Prowler.

"What did you steal?" Rodolfo said again.

"Nothing. She was lying. She hated us." Ximena stared out the windshield.

"She didn't hate me," he said. "Now I have no phone. No nothing. Until Uncle Emiliano gets me one. If he does."

Rodolfo turned on the radio. He found ranchera music. A man's voice chanted, Noventa y siete punto cinco. She closed her eyes. Ninety. Seven. Point. Five. She would miss her yellow shirt from the swap meet in Indio. Sleeveless. With mesh at the collarbones. Fidelia might take that off the clothesline. Maybe bring it to her one day. To Hollywood. And the two notebooks.

After miles of houses and shopping malls, they entered steep hills and canyons near Los Angeles. Ximena squinted at the signs, looking for the 101 freeway to Hollywood.

No phone, no Google maps. Rodolfo had memorized the route to Uncle Epifanio's house. Exit Sunset Boulevard. Turn left. Drive eleven miles. He stopped carefully at the red lights. A shop for wigs. Fake hair. Then a botánica. Esperanza y Caridad.

Rodolfo said, "If we live at Uncle Epifanio's, he said you work in a hotel in Hollywood. LA guys for you, Elpidia. You can forget Carlos. LA guys have more money."

In the distance, the same red bougainvillea as Seven Palms dangled off the banks beside the freeway. Women would need nets of hair lifted from their bathtub drains. Ximena would pay back Elpidia and Rodolfo. She pulled her purse from under the truck seat, and opened it just slightly. She knew her wallet held $4.89. Then she saw the orange bottle. The label. Barbara Angel Goldman. 8989 Dundee Drive, Los Angeles, California, 90027. The smoke reached across the sky now, like a dark river flowing toward them. The back window of the car in front of them was filled with small plush animals, crowded together, faded from the sun.

ANZA CROSSING

THE SANTA ANA RIVER

When my father saw the wildfire smoke, he and the Vargas brothers would head first to the cattle and horses, and then to Mrs. Dottie's old adobe mansion up the canyon. Those were the money, and the history. Mrs. Dottie was alone up there with her caretaker, Ruby. I rode into the wind shifting around now like it did in the afternoon—the smoke flattening and swirling around the bike.

The fire had torn across the riverbed, but the wind was still mostly gusting from the east, down the canyons, blowing the flames back toward the freeway. When I called it in, Justin Pham, Rob Jekel, and Evan Sims had shown up in three CHP units, blocking off Coal Canyon Road and Gypsum Canyon Road, and monitoring the smoke on the freeway lanes.

Fucking meth head and his dragging muffler. He was probably halfway to wherever he could sell his scrap metal now.

The minute the wind shifted and swirled west, it sent embers and torn blazing branches toward us, toward Fuego Canyon. It would be half an hour at most until the fire burned to the entrance of the ranch.

The first two engine crews from OC Fire went up the ranch road ahead of me, tearing half the branches off the pomegranate trees Mrs. Dottie Anza had planted sixty years ago, a tunnel of trees that went a whole mile. Somebody had written about them, years ago, for a magazine. That was the last time Mrs. Dottie let anybody up here—she didn't want strangers or the county to pressure her to sell the hundreds of acres for development, or add it to the nature preserve. She sure as hell wouldn't want anyone to see the old ranch housing—not up to any code, and all ancient wood construction.

The engines blew past the citrus groves. I smelled the water. My father had turned on the irrigation, streams pouring out of the cement cisterns into the furrows between rows, sliding like red blood in the reflection from the smoke above us now. I heard the first air support from Cal Fire, helicopters above me. They'd be dropping water and retardant on the riverbed. After that they'd start a break around the eastern flank of the ranch, I figured. I gunned the Harley up the last section of the dirt road. Dust from the fire crews like a wall in front of me. They'd head to the top of the canyon. The eucalyptus windbreak rose up in front of me, and I turned into the narrow lane that led to the camp.

My father and the Vargas brothers were in the barn, saddling the horses. Jefa, my father's palomino mare, tossed her head at the Harley, and I parked it facing the road in case shit got bad fast. My father yelled, "¿Qué onda? You got here fast."

"I was patrolling near Coal Canyon! I saw the cabrón who started it," I shouted back. I started uncoiling the big hose we kept hanging on the side of the barn. Our barn was for the tractors, machinery, and tools—the big barn up by Mrs. Dottie was for the cattle, the feed and supplies, and Mrs. Dottie's two horses.

My father wore his black Stetson, his old blue-and-red flannel shirt, and his jeans and boots were wet, rimmed with fresh mud. I knew he'd gone down to the citrus, stood in the cascading water for a minute, and then come back here on the quad. The four-wheeler was still ticking hot. My father got up onto his horse and said to her neck, "Cálmate, cálmate, Jefa."

Ramón Vargas lifted his chin at me and said, "Mijo." He and Sergio were seventy-two years old this year. They were short men, with bowed legs in their black boots, their chests and arms the most powerful things I'd ever known when I was a kid. I'd seen Ramón pick up a yearling steer and throw it five feet after it knocked down his brother, and they roped the legs within seconds. They liked to watch pro rodeo on their old TV in the barn and make fun of the young cowboys. They'd taught me to braid rawhide into reatas, to rope anything that moved. Now Sergio said, "¡Johnny, no puedes estar aquí!" He swung up onto his black gelding, Manito, and Ramón got up onto his palomino gelding with the black forelegs and white blaze down his nose, Rayo.

The three of them circled the ranch camp for a moment, looking at the houses and the ramada, where the layers of last spring's palm fronds had become incendiary devices. One ember and this whole place would go up like an explosion. My father said, "Mijo. Veinte minutos. Then I'm looking for you. You better be—" He lifted his chin toward the top of the canyon. At the big barn, if the fire threatened the canyon, they'd load the horses onto the big stock trailers, open the gates on the cattle they'd kept in the corrals, and head out onto the fire roads toward the west.

Ramón snorted. He said, "¿Qué es? Tú sabes, you eat our dust on that." He grinned at the Harley, and they took off up the ranch road.

The air support droned overhead. The big stand of eucalyptus, probably eighty years old, with bark shedding in menthol-scented piles along the eastern edge of our camp, was the worst threat. But I knew within half an hour, Manny, Bobby, and Grief would navigate the freeway and the back road all along the railroad tracks from Riverside to here, on the bikes, and help me out.

I dragged the big hose off the barn wall, turned the circular faucet, and stood up on the hitching post to train the water on the roof of my dad's house first. The front porch, all the bougainvillea. The huge flock of sparrows that lived in the carport burst out ahead of the water, wheeling around the yard for one moment and then taking off west. My mother was watching.

My dad's roof was tin now. The water drummed. I dragged the hose across the dirt lane to the Vargas brothers' two houses. Tin, too. We'd taken off the wood shakes ten years ago. I couldn't believe I'd seen Manny Delgado this morning, when I stood with the stream of water blowing into my face, looking at his dad's old place, empty twenty years now. The two old oil barrels where me and Manny used to collect beer cans and glass bottles for recycling. He liked to throw his Modelo bottles in there when he came to visit, and his son Manny Three found it hilarious to think we trucked all that down to the recycling plant for baseball money.

Shit. They better get here soon. The ashes had just started making their way to me, rocking like snowflakes down to the ground. We kept the brush cut to a wide perimeter around the ranch camp and the barn. The smoke went thick above me, from the riverbed, black and heavy, then white when Cal Fire hit it with the water, then black, then white. I moved with the hose back to the barn now. The old Massey Ferguson tractor, the plows and cultivators. A hundred years of tools and leather and saddles and the old wooden chairs worn to mirrors where our asses had sat while we oiled up boots and gear.

"Two hundred bucks!" Manny had said, when we first found out how much the CHP regulation boots cost. "And the pinche shirt is one-fifty?"

My boots were getting seriously fucked up. The CHP breeches and my long-sleeved shirt were wool/poly blend. I always wore long sleeves—since the phantom and the broken car window, since I'd been cut by a flying piece of tin from a contractor truck I followed for speeding years ago. Mud and ashes all over me. The dry-cleaning bill would be a bitch. It would take me hours to get my boots in shape again. But while I stood there in the smoke and wind, I kept seeing my mother's boots. My dad cleaning them the last time, so she could wear them in her coffin.

The only place really overgrown, that might burn today, was half a mile into the canyon and down a long dirt road to the east. The ranch cemetery. There was nothing I could do about that. Everyone we loved there was safe.

My mother wasn't afraid during the only big fire we had, that night when I was six. She said my father and the other men on the ranch would fight just like her own grandfather and his primos used to fight fires decades ago. They had the big water tank at the top of the canyon, and down here we had the irrigation tanks and the river. I remember that night; my father ran the water in the groves but in the moonlight, the furrows were filled with silver. The trees were drinking, I thought, and they would piss on the flames.

My father and Manuel Delgado, Louie Zaragoza and his sons,

and the Vargas brothers saved Mrs. Dottie's house back then. The long adobe mansion, painted white, where the hallway floor was black wood and we used to go only twice a year, on Christmas Eve and Memorial Day, to get presents from the old lady when I was a kid.

My mother was never afraid of the heat. It was the cold she hated. Frost and stillness. The cold killed her.

During that bad freeze, when I was nine, we spent four nights in the groves, picking fruit early before the ice could suck the sweetness out of the oranges. Back in the day, my father had smudge pots filled with kerosene, and when he lit them, the sooty smoke would settle on the trees and keep them from frost damage. But smudging was against the law now. We built small campfires on the grove roads and picked, all the families in the camp, loading the canvas bags. Manny and I picked from the bottom of the trees and dragged the bags to the flatbed truck beside my mother and Mrs. Delgado.

My mother caught a chill deep in her lungs. She stayed in bed for two days and drank tisanas Manny's mother mixed up, lemongrass and hibiscus. But then we'd lost money, because of the freeze, so on Monday she and Mrs. Delgado went to work in the packing house down in Placentia. And she said it was colder in there than out in the trees at night. Like ice was frosting her bones, she said. They stood on the cement floor for hours, and the chilled storage rooms sent gusts around their legs. After a month there, my mother came home one Friday and went to bed. Her cough got deeper and deeper. She was burning up. Her face was red underneath the brown. I watched her from the doorway. How could she be so cold and shiver, and then turn fever hot?

I would wake on the couch at dawn, hearing the crows caw in

the fog, and my mother's coughs sounded like those birds were caught inside her.

Pneumonia. She'd had it five times already by then. By the time my father took her to the emergency room, she was unconscious. The doctor showed him the X-rays of her lungs—full of holes and scars from old pneumonias.

My father said he wouldn't bury her down in Santa Ana because back in the day, the white ranchers didn't let Mexicans bury their dead in the city cemetery. No Mexicans, Chinese, Japanese, Black, or Indian bodies next to the dead white people. My fifth-grade teacher—Mrs. Morita—was Japanese American. Her parents were born in Anaheim, right near where Disneyland is. She told us that her people couldn't be buried in the Fullerton cemetery after they came back from being imprisoned in Camp Manzanar during World War II.

But really my father wouldn't let my mother leave him. He wouldn't let her leave the canyon. He said she'd wanted to be buried next to my two baby sisters, who had died hours after they were born. Carmen and Gloria.

Up at the Anza mansion, there was the original adobe chapel about two hundred yards from Mrs. Dottie's house, and next to that, the Anza family cemetery, from 1774. But that was for her people. The ones they called Spanish. She was the only one left. She had the priest, Father Mulcahy, who was eighty-five himself. Father went to Mrs. Dottie's living room every Sunday to give her the sacrament. But he loved us, too. And he was sitting on a chair in my mother's hospital room, touching her forehead, when she died.

The ranch cemetery was for the rest of us. Indians and Mexicans. There had been sixty-two people buried since 1774. It was up a long narrow lane, in a clearing with oak trees and one sycamore. My mother's coffin was beautiful. Blue metal, baby blue satin lining. She had a pillow. Her fingers held a rosary with pearls. The old priest led just the ten of us to the cemetery. She was carried by my father, Manuel Delgado, Ramón and Sergio Vargas, and my cousin Tony's dad, Mr. Valdez. I was too young to hold the coffin, they thought. So Manny's uncle held that front corner, and I walked beside him close enough to smell the Tres Flores shining in his hair.

Ramón and Sergio, those strong men with their hands big as skillets from working cattle all their lives, they cried. My mother had cooked for them for twenty years, since their own mother died. Señora Vargas was here. But by the time my mother died, no one had been buried in the ranch cemetery since señora Vargas. The old wooden crosses had fallen apart from termites. Their mother's grave, and my mother's mother, and her mother, were disappearing.

My father went to Mrs. Dottie. She told him she didn't have the money for marble markers, and said my father should leave the place alone, because she didn't want anyone from the county poking around. They'd see how old the camp was, they'd make her sell the thousand acres, leave for the city below, and bulldoze our houses.

That's what she always said, he told me.

A week later, we drove to San Bernardino, filled up the truck with white round rocks near my father's friend Bobby Carter Sr.'s house, where all the stones washed down from the mountains into the Santa Ana River. We spent all our Sundays outlining the graves with the white stones. When dusk fell, it looked like some god had dropped creepy glow-in-the-dark bracelets on the ground.

My father wanted headstones. Names and dates. The first people had been buried in 1775. Sebastián Tavares and his wife, Juanita.

Yuma people from Baja, the guides for Anza with my mother's people.

For weeks, when he had free time, my father took me up into the hills and we marked granite boulders for headstones. We dug them out, hauled them with chains behind the truck, and took them to the barn. My father went down to Santa Ana and got Diego Silvera to shape them. He'd been a master stonecutter in Mexico City, where he'd worked only on churches. He was like a short, fat god of frogs, I always thought, the way he sat on a low stool with his big knees on each side and hit the rocks with his chisel and hammer.

He'd moved to Santa Ana to live with his daughter. He stayed up here in the canyon for two weeks, eating with us, sleeping in the house next to the Vargas brothers' place. All day he chiseled the boulders into rough rectangles and then with an electric sander hooked to our generator, he polished a rectangular space for us to paint on the names and dates. Then my father and Manuel dragged the stones up a wooden plank into the trucks. At the cemetery, they placed them on the ground where the wooden crosses used to be.

My father traded Silvera's work for two steers, because Silvera had a huge freezer in Santa Ana. He wanted enough meat to last six months—he was always prepared for the earthquake he expected each day. Mexico City taught him that.

Mrs. Dottie wouldn't miss those two young steers. My father gave her the count every month, how many cattle she had running up in the hills, but she only went out to see them twice a year, with my father and her lawyer. The lawyer's Mercedes wouldn't make it up the ranch roads, so she made him ride in my father's truck with her. She had a small pad of paper and a pen. She was seventy then, in 1989, but she could see, and count, and she knew the difference between black baldy steers and the few longhorns that had been in the canyon since someone brought her a bull from Texas in 1942. But she didn't know if my father took two yearlings to the barn and shot them with his rifle.

It was the only time in my life he had taken an animal without telling her.

He aimed at the right place on their heads. Then he and his friend Bobby Carter Sr., who was a master meatcutter from San Bernardino, went to work. Steaks, ribs, lengua, cabeza. Asada. Tenderloin. Tripas for menudo.

The lockers they put the meat in looked like coffins to me, on the back of my dad's truck going down the canyon to take the meat to Silvera.

In the last twenty minutes, the flames had chewed through the arundo cane and palm trees along the river bottom. I knew because the windstorm had shifted, sounded like a licking god, a rumble, and each explosion when flames hit a eucalyptus tree full of oil down the canyon from me. Big charred pieces of black were falling on me now—that was arundo cane, which carried light and far. I could hear the heavy thumping of the Sikorskys dropping veils of water onto the brush. I kept spraying the perimeter of my mother's huge bougainvillea vine, tangled along the perimeter and reaching into the windbreak like a solid wall of bright red, filled with millions of tiny white stars. The ashes rocked and swayed in the wind. But I wasn't scared yet, at least for myself. Easy to jump on the Harley and get back out on all the back trails Manny and I knew so well from when we were kids. Like the one to Bee Canyon. It was my dad and the Vargas brothers I worried about—I didn't want them to have heart attacks, trying to save horses or Mrs. Dottie's house.

Ruby, the caretaker, drove the old lady's ancient Buick Riviera down to the market once a week. Ruby was sixty-five, born in Yorba Linda. She cleaned and cooked and did everything for Mrs. Dottie. Neither of them had ever married or had kids—that's why they got along. If the fire crew banged on the heavy wooden door with the wrought-iron crosses, Mrs. Dottie would probably talk shit before she and Ruby got into the truck with my dad and the horses and headed for the hills, like they said to do.

Manny and the others would be here. I knew it.

The last time I wrote the names on the gravestones, Manny and I were twenty. Just before we went into the CHP academy. Every October, before Día de los Muertos, we'd go to Home Depot. Manny and I couldn't believe other guys bought spray paint to tag the walls, and we bought waterproof paint markers.

"We're taggin the damn cemetery, homes," Manny laughed, but he wasn't tagging anything. Manny could fix any car engine, paint any motorcycle. But his handwriting was shit. Mine was perfect.

His father said, "Shut up and pull them weeds, mijo. From the roots. Don't be lazy."

My father said, "Spell it right, Johnny. Be careful." That was how they always talked to us, even though we thought we were men.

In the polished rectangles, I made letters in Old English. Fancy as I could. Indian people with no last names. MARIA JUANA. FRANCISCO. LUISA. ANTONIO. Then Mexican people. My mother's grandmother. MAGDALENA ANZA ROMERO. My mother's mother. MARIA MAGDALENA ANZA ROMERO. And my mother. LILIANA MARIA ANZA ROMERO FRIAS.

Manny's dad moved them out to San Bernardino when we were sixteen. He started a carburetor and custom shop in Rialto. Bobby Carter Sr., who used to come help my dad butcher the steers, worked at Stater Bros. market in San Bernardino, and he got Manny a job there, too. We had just gotten our licenses. I didn't make any new friends at Santa Ana High School. I played baseball one more year, hung out with my primo Tony and his friends, but mostly I just waited to get back to the ranch.

On the weekends, Manny would drive up the canyon in his old Cougar, and we'd work on the truck my dad gave me, the Chevy Cheyenne, in the barn. Then we'd drive out to San Bernardino to see our friends. Grief Embers Jr., a tall Black guy who played center field, and Bobby Carter Jr., who'd come out a few times with his dad. He was a shorter dude with dark brown hair in a buzz cut who played second base. Manny couldn't run for shit, his torso was so long and his legs were so short, but he was a hell of a catcher.

The four of us hung out at Bobby Carter's yard, because his dad had a half-ton smoker, a full ice chest of beer, and a barn, too. Manny and I started working on cars all weekend, for cash. Bobby Carter Jr. had learned to butcher, and they sold meat for big fiestas and quinceañeras. The summer after we graduated from high school, we all got motorcycles.

Six of us. We called ourselves Free Riders. Manny and me, my primo Tony, Grief and Bobby, and a guy named Reynaldo Rodrigue we met at a gym. Then Manny decided we should take the test for California Highway Patrol. He talked us into it. He kept saying, "We all got bikes, man, we're hella good riders. Orale pues, we can make money ridin! Let's go CHP! I met this dude in Corona, he's been CHP for five years and he makes big dinero. We can ride all day, meet some firme girls when they're speeding."

On this last part, he put his arm around me and threw me to

the ground. "Think about it, homes, hundreds of them, all sizes and ages. Because you need a woman."

I was the only one still living with my father. I had never left Fuego Canyon.

Bobby Carter and I had Indian bikes. We were the fastest, the most skilled at the runs on the practice course we made way out in Yucca Valley, in the desert. We'd ride all day and half the night, drink beer, and sleep on the ground. Bobby was the one who named us Free Riders, after that song from 1973. *The mountain is high, the valley is low, and you're confused, on which way to go . . .*

FREE RIDE looked good on our jackets. Manny's girl Lena and Grief's girl Larette sewed all the embroidery on the back, and Bobby's girl Trish got the jackets from the Levi's store where she worked back then. We didn't have the money for leather. We had black Levi's denim, and a big patch with the sun, and a dude with a big Zapata mustache on a Harley. Really it was Cheech Marin because we loved him. Larette made the design into a transfer and then she and Lena sewed all the colors beautiful.

We had been riding together for about a year. Bobby and I painted our bikes dark cherry candy flake, and we chromed the engines. The guy who sold us the Indians was an old white dude in San Bernardino, and he kept asking if we had Indian blood. He said to me, "You're just Mexican, though." Bobby rolled his eyes and said, "You want the money or not?" Grief's and Bobby's people came from California—Cahuilla and Serrano. Manny had Purépecha from Michoacán. Reynaldo from the gym—he said he was from the Wild Tchoupitoulas people in New Orleans—the people that hid slaves when they ran away.

I had my mother's Yuma blood, and my dad's people from thousands of years ago in Jalisco. I didn't have to say shit to that old gabacho with his long blond beard in a braid.

Grief and Manny had Harleys. Shovelheads. They knew a guy in Fontana who sold Harleys for cheap. A former Hells Angel—scary white guy Bobby's father knew who loved T-bone steaks.

My primo Tony only lasted six months in Free Riders. He hated motorcycles. He never even took the CHP test. He said my friends were stupid pendejos, and he got a job installing underground cable all over southern California. He'd work in places like Santa Clarita and Torrance for weeks at a time, sleeping in motels with other guys on the job. He made serious money.

Reynaldo didn't really want to be a cop, either, but passed the test and came to the academy. He made fun of the whole thing. He loved women. He wanted to learn capoeira and dance samba, he was obsessed with Brazil and the beach culture. He said he'd go to Rio one day. Now he's a big Instagram star and he runs a famous capoeira studio in Venice. Famous actors and athletes work out with him. But back in 1999, Rey rode borrowed motorcycles—he lived with cousins and aunts and uncles, we never knew where he was staying. He never had a home, and we did. He was *born* shady, Grief's girl Larette used to say, and he slept with every girl he met. Even one of Larette's cousins, and then he got his ass kicked when he never called her back.

In 1999, five of us went up to West Sacramento. People say California Highway Patrol is the toughest academy in the nation for cops. Twenty-seven weeks. They broke us down in basic training just like the Marines, yelling in our faces and behind our ears, where you feel the spit tickle that place you wish a woman would kiss you. They made us run for miles, which was bad for Manny with his short legs. Do sit-ups and push-ups in the big gym, which Reynaldo was really good at, but I hated. I remember Grief said, "I get it, man, we gotta get broken down as humans to get built back up as cops. But some of these motherfuckers hate us."

Sergeant Michael Miller Sr. hated us all. "Inland Empire assholes—don't you guys have brain damage from birth? Wait, Frías is from the OC. How the hell is he the best shot at the range?"

He singled out Grief and Bobby, because they'd been friends so long they had a secret language. One night in the cafeteria he heard Grief say, "Himes, this ain't the pandu right here, and this meat do *not* require the hatchet."

Miller said, "What the hell is that supposed to mean? Heims? Are you suggesting I'm a German Nazi and you want to kill me? With a *hatchet*? I will fuck you both up right now."

Bobby held up his hands, because he was the half-white one, and said, "No, Sergeant, sir, that's just how we talk sometimes."

"Well, what the fuck did you say?"

Bobby looked at Grief. He said, "Himes is, like, our version of homeboy. We got tired of people saying homes, and we used to get—"

High. Grief couldn't say high. He said, "Lit up, like we had some beer, and we'd say high and homes, and it was himes."

Bobby said, "The pad was for home, and the Ponderosa was because we had ranches around us, so it was the pandu. And my dad's a butcher, and we always took the hatchet to the good meat. Like the ribs and the rack of lamb."

Sergeant Miller hated them even more after that. Because that all sounded so good. I never forgot the sergeant interrogating me about the exam, telling me he was from Indiana. LaGrange. Indian killers.

His son, Michael Miller Jr., was in the same recruitment class as us. He started fucking with us, too, after that time in the cafeteria. Miller Junior wasn't from Indiana. He was born in Huntington Beach. He hung out with skinhead surfers, and he kept saying that if he saw us back in SoCal, they'd kick ass on mongrels like us.

I remember Grief in the barracks one night: "But that's everything, man—if you're in a gang, if you're on a football team, if you go Army or Marines, shit, if you're in some families that's how it works. You gotta be nothing so you can be them. Only them."

Manny said, "Yeah, you're good at that cause Larette already broke you, man, she made you her show pony. You trot with them big-ass size thirteens up high when your girl tells you to!"

We all laughed because it was true. I'd never seen someone love a woman like Grief loved Larette. She made him sing to her all the time, in front of us. Songs from the musicals she did in theater class. She'd make him sing *The Wiz* and *My Fair Lady* and we'd bust up.

We only got to go home one time, in May, for three days. Manny said we should party with Larette and Lena and the girls in their nursing school class. "Bikers and nurses? That shit is hilarious. Bobby can get the meat, and we can get the cervezas. Pues, we can charge, like, ten bucks, fool! We gotta find a park."

We had the party a few miles up the river from here, at Anza Narrows. Where Juan Bautista de Anza and his people built a wooden bridge and crossed the river. I didn't say anything that day, about my mom's people, because that would have been weird, but I stood next to the plaque up there on the bluff above the river, looking down at the water. Horses and cows had drowned, the water was so wide back then. Now there was a big railroad bridge with cement arches covered with spray-paint graffiti.

"Free Riders and Fine Angels," Manny kept shouting, holding up his beer. He'd made a flyer with our logo and then some sexy nurse costume from, like, Halloween, and his girl Lena got mad because she said that was a fucking stereotype, that nurses were giving CPR and suturing wounds on stupid-ass fools who got cut and shot, but he told her that was sexy, too, and started kissing her, and she stopped shoving him around the park. About a hundred people came, all of us but also a lot of other guys who heard about the food, and a bunch of women. Bobby's girl Trish was dressed up because she said she had to go to work at the mall. Her hair was twisted up in a long roll, and she kept pulling on these slivers of gold highlights around her face like a model. She was really beautiful, but she never liked us—she sat apart, with her Virginia Slims cigarettes, watching Bobby grill the meat.

Larette and her cousin Merry had on tight sundresses and black sunglasses, their long curly hair down their backs. Merry lived in LA, and she already had a nursing job lined up at County/USC Hospital. She'd bought a new car, a little Corolla.

Reynaldo showed up with a girl named Matelasse. She was shy, really young, maybe seventeen. She had on jeans, and her thumbnails were black at the edges, I saw when she held out her paper plate for meat and beans and rice. Larette was serving gumbo from a big electric cooker on the picnic table, and Reynaldo said, "Look at that andouille! Girl, you made it like New Orleans."

Larette gave him the evil eye. But Reynaldo said, "That's how I met my girl here—her uncle makes the best gumbo I ever had, way out in the orange groves."

She looked embarrassed, and then I knew it was citrus rime darkening her thumbs—just like mine always. I offered her a Tecate and she nodded. I sat next to her on a folding chair and said, "Valencias or navels?"

She grinned. "Both. With my grandpa and my mom. We're, like, the last two groves on our street." Her eyes weren't green, or gray, or brown. They were some combination like rain clouds. No makeup, her cheeks turning a little red under the brown when I teased her about Reynaldo never shutting up. "His dad was in the military," she said. "I don't think he remembers his mom. She was from Tijuana."

"You been to Mexico?" I said, watching Reynaldo do his weird capoeria moves on the grass. His linen pants and shirt white, like a woman's. All these wooden bead necklaces. He'd had to cut off his hair for academy, like the rest of us, but he had long dreads before that.

"No," she said. "Are you from Mexico?"

I shook my head. "Santa Ana." I was darker than Reynaldo or her. "Never even seen the border," I said. I stood up.

Her eyes got full of tears, and she said, "I'm sorry." Before I could say anything, Reynaldo came up behind me and put ice down my collar. He said, "Leave my girl alone, Officer. Look at you, the only one with a natural law enforcement stance, man, when we're just kickin it."

Then Manny said, "Who the hell is that?"

Two big trucks pulled up in the parking lot. Michael Miller Jr. and three other guys. White guys wearing T-shirts and jeans and Doc Martens. Huntington Beach. They said, "Party, huh? Rodrigue told us about it. He came to the beach and was trying to learn to surf. Showed us some Brazilian workout shit."

Reynaldo lifted his chin at them and went down to the blanket he'd put under a sycamore tree, with Matelasse. She wouldn't look at me.

I realized I was already a cop—every single person I saw now, there were five or six things to remember in case I had to describe them to myself. Or somebody else.

Miller Junior and his friends walked over to the smoker, stood in front of Bobby and Grief. Bobby said, "Plenty of food. Fraternal brothers and all that shit. Come on."

The four guys actually sat at a picnic table with us for half an hour. But they kept fucking with us. Manny tried—"Hey, man, carne asada and Tecate, eh?"

Miller Jr. said, "We drink American beer."

"So do we, homes, there's Coors in the cooler."

"We call it T-bone," one of Miller's friends said.

Grief said, "So put the bone back in it, man."

We could tell they wanted to fight someone. But it wasn't Grief. I figured it out after a few more minutes. They wanted Reynaldo Rodrigue. Miller kept looking over at him, lying next to his girl on the blanket.

And when Reynaldo and Matelasse finally came back up the hill, Miller said, "So you're a fuckin Black hippie? What's with all the jewelry? You a faggot? This your fake girlfriend?"

Reynaldo—the worst judge of anybody for faces. He laughed.

One of the skinheads said, "Stay the fuck outta Huntington Beach. *Bro*."

Reynaldo still didn't get it. He said, "Cause I was too good at surfing, right? I caught that one big-ass wave! Man, I love all that. Surfing, running, jamming to the music. I'm gonna buy a house at the beach someday, man, leave all this smog behind."

Miller stood up and said, "You good at boxing? Cause that's what we're gonna do now. Next week up in Sacramento is fight club."

Reynaldo froze up, but he was still smiling, like behind his teeth he was thinking what to do. You can't run. You can never run. Me and Manny and Grief moved behind Reynaldo. Bobby stayed by the smoker in case one of them went for something to burn somebody with.

And the women must have melted back because I don't remember any sounds. I just remember Miller taking two steps and punching Reynaldo in the face. But Reynaldo ducked graceful as a dancer, one of his moves, ducking and twisting so the punch went up over his temple through the air. He contorted his body to kick Miller, but they both fell on the ground, and Miller was a lot heavier. Reynaldo was hurting when he got up, and Miller went for his face with a right hook. Reynaldo didn't hold up his hands. He didn't fight like that.

But me and Manny did. I knew Manny would stand tough on those short legs and pound the shit out of Miller's friend, and he did. He got the first guy low in the ribs, kept working the abdomen like we learned. Manny's fists were like cement.

I looked at Miller like I was roping a steer. Went for his legs. Took him out. I hoped Grief would move Reynaldo out of the way. I got up and waited for Miller to stand up and fight me. He threw the right again, and I slanted it off with my fists. Then he said, "Fuckin wetback, you can't beat me. You're not smart enough."

I did what Luis Padilla taught me and Manny in his boxing club, up by old Chavez Ravine. I didn't have to think. Automatic. Three punches. Right to the temple, left up under the chin to make him show his throat, and—

If I hit him in the throat and he died, that was the end for me. I pulled back my fist on the third punch. Shoved him in the chest so he could fall and his friends could pick him up.

We all stood there panting like dogs. Miller said, "You really fucked up now. Fritos."

But I knew better. He'd never tell anyone at the academy that I'd beaten him, or let him go. Especially not his father.

Merry had a first-aid kit in her new car. She and Lena and some girl from their nursing class named Yvette Rojas laid out the antiseptic and bandages on the picnic table, while most of the strangers at the party drifted off to the parking lot and left. The sun was going down. Merry and Yvette took care of my cuts at the picnic table, leaned in close to me with the antiseptic and bandages. "I don't know why y'all want to be cops," Merry said softly to me. "Grief is the kindest man in the world. Look at today. Nurses, we're trying to fix the world."

"So are we," I said, staring down into the willows along the river.

"Different kind of fixing, baby," Merry said. The cuts stung. She backed away.

Yvette Rojas leaned in. She put on the last bandage and said, "Pues ya que. Look at you. A cop looking vato and shit." She whispered, "Come on, I can kiss it and make it better, papi chulo."

She had an apartment with another one of the nurses, near the college, and I stayed there for the rest of the night, and the morning. She made coffee and gave me aspirin in the morning, even went down the street and bought menudo at a place called Tony's Market. It was floating with hominy and little pennies of fat. It was good. We stayed in bed all day.

But she never called me back. I tried for two months. Manny shrugged. "Lena said Yvette moved to San Fernando. She met some dude who owns a cement company."

By the end of the year, Manny married Lena, Grief married Larette, Bobby married Trish. Merry met a guy in LA, had a son named Tenerife, and her son was her life after they broke up. Reynaldo married Matelasse, and they had two boys. I'd see them when we all got together at Bobby Carter's, for Fourth of July or Labor Day. Her boys had epic hair, like baby Bob Marleys but with gray-gold eyes, like hers.

Reynaldo left her and moved to Venice, just last year. He loved the beach more than her and his sons. Stupid cabrón.

The wind was blowing the right way now, back from the east—right for us in the canyon, wrong for the freeway and the other side of the hills, and I stood there hosing down the Vargas brothers' house, but looking at the three cement steps where Manny used to sit, where we used to crack pistachios. I heard the motorcycles coming down the back trail from the east, where the guys must have gotten off at Green River Road and gone up the fire roads. The engines were loud, even through the wind, those badass engines growling like only Harleys and Indians when you add the glasspacks and customize them so everyone in the damn world can hear you coming, with your brothers.

SAN LUIS REY

Turns out you can measure the days like this: 150 sandwich-size baggies in a box. Two boys. Joachim and Antonio. Fourth grade and second grade. One sandwich for each boy, each school day. Five days a week. Chips in another baggie because it's cheaper to buy the big bag. Four Oreos times two boys. Two more baggies each because Joachim doesn't like Doritos dust on his Oreos. Orange and black. Not cool.

Antonio doesn't care about color mixing. But he hates peanut butter on his sandwiches. He only eats ham. Thin sliced. Sixty-nine cents a package on sale. I can do that.

Too much math for me, to figure out how fast these damn weeks go by, when the boys are at school and I'm at work. Sometimes I make a lunch for me. I like the little cups of mandarin oranges in juice. I hate lunch meat. I loved deviled ham, with the tiny devil on the can, but my sons won't touch it. So sometimes I eat Buddig ham that has a nasty rainbow sheen.

Except when life pisses me off and I go with Dawna to the taqueria. We smell like Conroy's—carnations and roses and ferns, and the stems that get slimy strong when they've been sitting in water and dye. People want green carnations for St. Patrick's Day, yellow for Easter, blue for Fourth of July, and black carnations for Halloween. Today two Instagram moms came in and made me touch up the black with spray paint, and then add some gold glitter.

Dawna and I go to El Ojo de Agua. My aunt Glorette died in the alley behind this taqueria. Someone killed her. Glorette was my mother's cousin. Every time I come into El Ojo de Agua, I think about her sitting here, to keep out of the cold. She used to work that alley, where someone killed her. And one night, when my mother was drunk, she said, "I miss her every day, and I never said nothing nice to her."

My mother still lives in the orange groves. When I take the boys out there on Sundays, she'll sit with them for a few minutes, up at my uncle Enrique's house, but she won't even look at me. She hates my face so much she'll leave while I'm in the kitchen.

The women who own the taqueria are from Oaxaca. Araceli and Serafina. The first time we went in there they spoke Spanish to me. People usually think I'm Mexican. Dawna's blond, but she learned Spanish in high school, and I took French. So she tells them I only habla specific foods. Carne asada tacos. Horchata—my favorite drink in the world.

Serafina today. She smiles and squints at my Conroy's name tag. Usually she doesn't talk but she says, "Matelasse? What is that mean?"

A Louisiana word. Slavery word. No way to explain it easily to someone from California or Mexico, so I always smile and shrug. She hands me two carne asada tacos. Dawna says, "Qué linda," pointing at Serafina's earrings, and the woman says, "Gracias." She has gold edging on two teeth—like gilt picture frames.

Soon as I get to the table, my phone rings. Unknown number. Gotta be Reynaldo. Dawna's in the bathroom. Reynaldo says, "I wanted to see what the boys are planning to costume for Halloween. Our American version of Carnaval, or as close as we can get to letting go in this country." He always talks to me like we're on some stupid diversity panel, because he can't talk like we used to love each other.

"They'll be boys with candy," I say. My tacos are like two little birds sleeping close together. Getting cold. Shit.

He says, "Well, I almost forgot it was tomorrow. Every day feels like Halloween here, with the performance aspect of people on the beach in Venice."

Says the word every time he calls. Venice. He lives in a "charming, perceptively restored but fully modernized cottage, steps from the beach, with a remarkably roomy mirrored studio where an old carriage house once stood." That's what some architecture magazine called "the capoeira compound."

"Mm-hmm," I say, because I'm past hungry. "I gotta go."

The horchata is cold and sweet. I didn't find out what my name meant until I was ten. My mother was probably drunk when she named me. She said she used to hear the word when she was small, visiting in Louisiana. She thought it was a pretty woman people talked about. "I wasn't payin no attention," she said.

But on my tenth birthday, my grandmother told me, "When I make ten, like you, they put me work in the matelasse. On the old plantation. Call it Seven Oaks. Big pile of sugar cane, when they cut it. Look." She showed me an old snapshot, six kids sitting on a huge raft of green stalks. "We pile it up, so them cane don't freeze in winter. They pull it out next year. All you do, dig a ditch and lay that cane in there like bones. That new cane grow up from the joints, yeah. Like magic."

She smiled at me. "That you. Matelasse. We keep you warm all winter. Then you grow. Like magic."

But my mother didn't think so.

My phone rang again, just before we closed. Larette. She said, "Girl, there's a big fire out there in the canyons by Johnny's old house. His dad's place. Grief and Bobby and Manny went out there on the motorcycles, to help him. You could never tell them not to go—those four are tighter than ticks."

Yeah, I thought. Reynaldo never did thank them when Johnny and the others saved his ass. But Reynaldo never got along with other men. Just women.

Larette said, "I'm coming to get you in the morning. Tomorrow's your day off, right? Lena gave me five boxes of KFC from her job and Bobby's daughter Ivy just dropped off a box of steaks. We gotta get them some food and help Johnny clean up."

A wildfire? "They got it out? They're sleeping out there?" I said.

"You can't tell these men a damn thing," Larette said, and then, I heard it, she remembered, and she said, "Sorry, Matelasse. You know what I mean."

She meant she still wasn't used to Reynaldo being gone. She and Grief were the perfect couple, and Manny and Lena loved each other to death. Bobby's wife Trish had left him years ago. But everyone kept forgetting that Reynaldo was gone, because I didn't talk about it.

I said, "Come get me at dawn. I can't ask my mom to watch the boys, but my uncle will."

★　★　★

I knew Reynaldo would call the boys that night. Eight o'clock. I was just sitting. Watching *Diners, Drive-Ins and Dives*. My feet up. My toes like ten little piggies that shoulda been gone to market a long time ago.

He used to call from a damn pay phone. Found one near the beach, thought it was hilarious to tell the boys he was Superman. Noisy as hell. Now he has a burner phone, and first thing I always want to say is, "Gena still checks your cell? So much trust."

He can't be sitting in their living room, which I can visualize because of the damn magazine, because how is he gonna call his not-even-ex-wife and the kids when Gena doesn't know we exist?

I never ask. It's been fourteen months.

"The boys up?" he says.

I never listen. Over the next couple of days Joachim will tell me the four or five things his dad said. When we're in the car, he'll say, "Daddy has a big capoeira festival next week in San Francisco." While we're doing math, he'll say, "Daddy says when you turn your body for this one move, your feet are going like twenty miles an hour."

Antonio never says much of anything. Just, "Daddy talks funny."

I say, "Uh-huh. I think so, too."

Because now Reynaldo's not a brother born in and raised in San Bernardino. He's Rey. No last name. He's from fucking Brazil, he's a capoeira and martial arts master, and he hangs out with men from São Paulo. Not men like Grief and Bobby and Manny and Johnny, even though they saved his ass so many times. Not women like me.

"Matelasse. Seriously. I don't understand why you don't just take a picture of yourself wearing a badass dress, with your beautiful boys, and put in the comments on her Instagram, 'Bitch please, he's married.'"

"Larette. I'm not tryin to get him back. I don't want him now. I just want him to remember he's got kids. I want him to tell her the truth. Not me."

"Shit. Reynaldo wasn't built to tell the truth." Larette put on her seat belt and rolled her eyes. "You're a better person than I am."

I had to laugh. "No, I'm not. You're still a nurse. You get to save people. I just get to make the flower arrangements when they die or when some man's trying to say sorry."

"Damn, girl. That just got dark."

We drove down the 91 toward Santa Ana. Uncle Enrique had been up at dawn, of course, when I brought the boys to him in the orange groves. He was eighty-seven years old, and he'd drink coffee, talk to the photograph of my aunt, who died five years ago, and then be at his workbench in his barn for hours. The boys loved it there, with ancient hammers and plows, smudge pots like one-armed soldiers from the old days.

Larette and I drove in her van. Usually the back was full of baseball stuff for her son, Dante, and Manny's son Manny Three. Today there were boxes of fried chicken and tubs of mashed potatoes and coleslaw from Lena. Tide, Clorox, buckets, rags, and paper towels. Traffic wasn't terrible, because it was six a.m. on Saturday. My one day to sleep in.

The smoke was almost gone, but the air smelled like ashes and soot, like it always does after a fire. We got off on Gypsum Canyon Road. The fire had started on the edge of the freeway and tore up the riverbed, so the big sycamore trees and cottonwoods were burned, and the palm trees that grew like weeds everywhere looked like sad headless worms rising black out of the ground. I remember the first time Johnny said where he lived, when I met him at the party he had with Reynaldo and their friends. "I grew up in Fuego Canyon," he said. "Like fire."

I said without thinking, "Feu. My mom calls it le feu. The fire. In French."

He frowned, and I remember I said, "My mom's from Louisiana. Larette's mom, too."

Now I said to Larette, "Looks like somebody painted the world." There was red fire retardant splashed up on the canyons, covering the boulders and trees. A big plume of red right on the narrow dirt road in front of us, where we turned to go up to Johnny's. ANZA RANCH, the wooden sign read. NO TRESPASSING. But the big iron gate was open.

The ashes were thick as snow all around the van when we drove up the long ranch road lined with pomegranate trees, branches down all along the road bank. I said, "Larette, let me get a few pomegranates. They'll be beautiful in a bouquet. I'm gonna make something for my own house for once."

The red leather balls were dusty with black ash but I put seven of them in my purse. Lucky seven.

I had only been up here once before, when Reynaldo and Grief brought us to ride horses for fun, and I was too scared to get on the pretty palomino horse Johnny's father brought to me. His dad spoke mostly Spanish, but he said, "Jefa. The boss of us. It's a nice horse." I shook my head, and he laughed. His black cowboy hat fell back on his head and I saw where his hair was combed all perfect with something that smelled sweet.

When we got to the turnoff for the ranch houses, I could see where the flames came right to the edge of the land, about fifty feet away, the charred black dried grass stopped in a line perfect like spray paint. Johnny Frías was standing there, holding a cup of coffee, staring at the burned ground. We parked in the dirt next to a carport covered with the biggest bougainvillea I'd ever seen, sprawling all over the house and porch and even into the nearest eucalyptus tree. The red blossoms bright as the sun lit them up. I opened the car window—thousands of red ovals all see-through, like tissue paper. Hardly anyone knew that the flower was only the tiny white star inside, and the red was bracts—leaves, not petals. One of the first things I learned as a florist.

Just like the orange groves where I grew up, there were ten little wooden houses along a dirt lane. In Johnny's father's house, the first one in the row, seven men standing in the kitchen light, in the doorway and front porch, all eating what looked like tacos in foil. The motorcycles were parked under the palm-frond ramada in the yard. There were already stacks of burned tree trunks cut and piled high at the edge of the road. We could hear Grief making everyone laugh, and Larette shook her head, smiling.

She cut off the engine and rolled down her window. The car stereo was still on—she messed with her Spotify until she found what she wanted. Sirens and guitars and drums and then the Ohio Players sang "Fire!" Johnny and Grief came outside.

"Jesus, Larette," Grief said. "I can think of better choices."

They met in high school doing theater. Then they went to San Bernardino Valley College, where she did musicals, and he built the sets. They were crazy. She sang to him all the time and he had to sing back. But he was terrible.

"Fine, baby," she said, and messed with her phone again. Bill Withers. "When you're down, and troubled, and you need a helping hand," she sang along with him, her voice a perfect harmony.

Johnny opened my door and said, "Thanks, Matelasse. My dad's not the best at cleaning on a regular day. Now there's ashes and smoke all over."

"You guys must have been up all night, worried about how

close it was," I said, picking up the pail full of Magic Erasers and bottles of Mr. Clean.

Johnny looked out toward the next canyon, facing west, and he said, "Yeah. But the fire skipped us and went for Bee Canyon. Burned the hell out of that one. All our stock and the barns are okay. The planes dropped retardant everywhere. Looks like blood fell from the sky."

Grief carried in Larette's bucket. "Nah, man, it's fake red. Looks like some woman spilled blusher all over the damn place."

Then Johnny laughed. "I forget you know way too much about makeup."

I started in the tiny kitchen, the little four-burner white stove that must have been bought thirty years ago from Sears, and the flakes of burned tortilla were right there along with the silvery feathers of ash that had blown in around the windowsill. Johnny's mom died when he was small, and her picture watched me from the little altar. The candle had gone out, dark and cold.

Capri Suns. Ten to a box. That's one week. Two boxes for $5. When you're home you better get a glass of water from the Brita pitcher. The boys know. I tell them don't even think about that juice when you're sitting on the couch.

Halloween is over, and then November's gone, no more Thanksgiving centerpieces at work, and Antonio's done with subtraction and Joachim's started on Indians of the Plains.

"They got Indians in Brazil," Joachim tells me when I'm sitting there with my coffee even though it's nine at night and dark as a bruise outside. The pomegranates are still shiny, beautiful red in a bowl on the table—I waxed them and just let them be. No greenery or branches.

I have one more load of wash. Towels and more socks. I only buy two colors. Socks balled up and little-boy funky. White like dirty snowballs and black like charcoal briquettes.

"You're not from Brazil," I tell him. "Don't start."

"Daddy said when he . . ."

"Daddy isn't here."

When we first met, Reynaldo said, "Let's go to Rio. Come on. You hear that bossa nova? That samba? You see how it is there?" He had just shown me his favorite movie. *Black Orpheus*.

I was seventeen, and he was twenty-one. He started coming out to the groves to pick up gumbo from my grandmother and my uncle Enrique. On the weekends they cooked huge pots of gumbo outside over a fire—chicken and seafood—and people came from all over to buy containers of gumbo and rice. Reynaldo worked with my cousin Lafayette on plastering jobs. He bought a lot of gumbo, because his mother was gone and his father didn't cook.

He took me to *Black Orpheus* downtown, at a foreign movie festival. All he talked about was Brazil, how it was a magical place for people like us. Better than America.

We were mutts. Reynaldo was French and Black and Mexican. His mom was from Tijuana, but she died when he was little; his dad was old-school New Orleans, but he'd lived everywhere, being in the Air Force. My grandmother was from Louisiana, and I never knew my grandfather. He was dead. My mother had some of everything in her: Spanish and French and Indian and African.

When I was a kid and I asked about my father, my mother Bettina said, "Do you see that motherfucker? You see him here? That's what he look like. Invisible."

Reynaldo's not invisible. He went to the beach one day without us, drove for two hours because he needed some time alone. Took him about eight hours to find Gena. She's not from Brazil. She's from Redondo. She's a makeup artist for actresses, like Jennifer Aniston and Kate Hudson. Gena's hair is like the long gold raffia we tie around flower arrangements. Her butt's like two halves of a cantaloupe. She wore a thong in their photo shoot, for their new fitness studio website. Every day she and Reynaldo run five miles on the beach and lift weights. Then they do two fucking hours of yoga. I haven't had two hours in a row to do something my whole fucking life.

Then Reynaldo does two hours of capoeira workouts, and Gena's assistant records him for their studio. I've seen his YouTube videos. Sometimes he looks like a man flying in circles through the air. Sometimes a lizard contorting on the ground. They go to festivals all over California, Nevada, even New York, and he performs with guys from São Paulo and Rio. They all have one name. Like Pelé.

Now he has only one name. Rey.

Dawna pulled up the website one day at work, back in July when I was freaking out because the boys went to Venice for one night. "Dynamic duo bringing Rio lifestyle and dance to Venice!" He taught the boys some capoeira, they slept on mats at the studio and ate Brazilian food they bought at a cool restaurant. Because Gena was in New York. She has no idea that we are alive, or that Reynaldo Rodrigue was born in San Bernardino.

The second week of August he came here and took them to the movies. *Fast and Furious*. That's the last time he saw them.

"Plains Indians used every part of the buffalo," Joachim reads to me now from his book. "Even the hoofs and tail."

"Hooves," I say, looking at his dirty fingernails, thinking I have to get in there with an old toothbrush, and he smiles and puts his foot up on my knee.

"Hoof," he says. "After Christmas we're gonna learn California

Indians and then we have to make a mission," he says. "We have to make it ourselves and you're not supposed to help. Cause some parents do the whole thing."

I said, "I know."

"Wait, you made one?" He looks up from his book.

"Yeah. I made one in fourth grade." I'm already thinking about the choices I'm gonna let him have for the roof: uncooked lasagna noodles, painted red like tile, or cardboard torn down to the corrugation part, painted red. That's one thing I have. Spray paint.

I'd already heard two dads talking at the school holiday concert about their kids' mission projects. "The San Juan Capistrano disaster of 2017," one of them laughed. "My wife made me test seven shades of red paint for the tile. The plaster dried way too fast and it cracked."

I remember my mother yelling when she saw my mission, back when I was nine. I remember the smell of beer, the swarm of ants, and wishing I had a father to help me make the roof.

I haven't gone out but four times. I went out to Chili's with a man who came to fix the dryer. He was from Sears. Mark. He wanted a new wife, real bad. I went out twice with a guy who came into Conroy's for flowers for his mother. DeMontre. A lawyer. His suit was dark, dark blue, like the best delphiniums. He had some octopus hands. When he asked for a third date, I found him on Facebook and realized the flowers were for his wife. Slick. Very slick.

The fourth time, I met a man named Warren at the gas station, and he said I had the most beautiful feet he'd ever seen. We went to Starbucks. He wanted me to come to his house and touch him with my feet. I took my café au lait home and made sure he didn't follow me.

✳   ✳   ✳

In January, an envelope comes in the mail. It's nobody's birthday. The card has an elephant wearing a necklace of flowers. Inside it says, "Happy 2020. Everyone is a God to someone." Okay. But three new hundred-dollar bills are inside, hidden in plain paper. Who sends money in the mail? Jesus.

At the counter the next day, I'm sorting through the ferns and the eucalyptus stems, thinking that the elephant is wearing a garland of big marigolds.

Dawna says, "You okay?"

She's been here for ten years. I've been here for seven.

She pulls some purple ribbon, and when she measures it with her arm out, the little curtain of fat hangs down. Batwings, she jokes about it. Impossible to get rid of it at her age, and she's not gonna stop eating enchiladas. Her husband hasn't touched her for two years. He stays home and does website design, so he picks up their two girls from school, and I can leave by four most days.

"I'm fine," I say. I pull out the foam circle for a funeral wreath.

"You know what bothers me most about Pornhub?" she says, because we're alone in the store. She wraps the ribbon around one of the cheap glass vases. "Not just that he's in his office for hours every night and I'm watching Disney Channel with the kids. His favorite porn isn't even real women. It's those Japanese cartoons. Whatever they're called. Teenage girls."

"And you can't take away the computer," I say. "Like you could with a kid."

Dawna shakes her head. "I can't believe how much money he made last year." She moves around the vase. "But I don't want to quit here. In case—you know. He leaves."

"Yeah," I say. I start with the ferns on the wreath.

Reynaldo asked me to marry him while he was in the police academy, for the Highway Patrol. We went to a big party near the Santa Ana River. I went with my cousins Merry and Larette. Her aunt Pearl was from Houma, Louisiana, and they knew my mom. Merry and Larette were in nursing school, and I was tired of working the orange groves. I had just registered for nursing school, but I was scared. I didn't think I was cut out for blood and people screaming, and Merry said to me at the party, "Girl, it ain't all blood every day. We already did some hours at the hospital. You might get the babies. They're hilarious, all the newborns. There's nothing like holding a newborn in the ICU—you're the whole damn world."

Reynaldo said he'd make big money with CHP. He'd been gone for three months, living at the academy way up in Sacramento. We were all dancing under this big white tent they put up, drinking Corona, eating ribs and carnitas and hot links.

Then Reynaldo and I went down to the trees and lay on a blanket. When we used to lie in the back of my cousin's truck, Reynaldo and me in the orange groves where you could hear coyotes calling each other near the river, I'd put my thumbs on his collarbone and my fingernails over his shoulder to pull him down. Not digging in to hurt him. Just pricking him, and he would shiver like crazy. Like I had electricity.

That night at the Anza party, we were down in the trees, on a blanket, and Reynaldo gave me a ring. A little tiny diamond from Zales. I was looking at it, worried he bought it stolen. Then some white guys showed up, and Reynaldo went up the hill. It wasn't but five minutes and he was on the ground, fighting one of them, and Johnny Frías stepped in and almost killed the other man.

Reynaldo never went back to the academy. He said he'd wasn't cut out for cop. He did plastering work with his dad after we got married. After I had the boys, he was always restless, even more obsessed with martial arts, with samba and Brazil, with movies. He'd gone to so many art movies at that theater downtown that the manager hired him to work projection. He saw movies from France, Italy, Japan. But it was *City of God* and *Black Orpheus* that he watched over and over. He worked nights and I worked days.

There were four of us women from the party who had boys. Merry had a son, Tenerife; Larette had a boy named Dante; Lena had Manny Three. Merry and Larette became nurses, and they teased me for working at Conroy's, where all the flowers came from before they died in the hospital rooms. "You kind of in the medical profession, girl," Merry would laugh when we got together in LA; we took the boys to see Tenerife play basketball at a big tournament. He was much older than our boys, fourteen and tall as a redwood, with a goofy smile and tiny mustache. About six hairs on each side, Merry laughed.

She and I told our sons they had Houma Indian blood, and the blood of the Cherokee and Creek peoples who had been slaves and then freedmen, so they'd have trouble growing big mustaches. "Yeah, none of the men like Sitting Bull and Crazy Horse in the history books have beards," Tenerife said. He was a cool teenager— Joaquin and Antonio thought he was a god, with his big hands and perfect braids.

I remember that weekend because when we got home, I had to cook spaghetti for dinner. Cheese. We had no meat. I had no money, and Reynaldo didn't even come in that night. At dawn, he said, "Hey, you're getting thick and bitchy. Bad combination for a sister. You need to take a dance class."

I threw a pan full of cold pasta water at him. The drops caught like milk in his long dreads. My mother always called him snakehead.

Whenever I took the boys to the groves, my mother would be sitting on the porch, feet swollen up from her diabetes, grumpy and hot and her hands black from citrus rind. The star-shaped scar on her cheekbone got paler every year. Only one time, when the boys were inside eating, she spoke to me. She said, "Why you picked that Reynaldo fool? He don't know what he want."

Like it was my fault. Like when she used to say, "Stop axing me about your father. Do you see his sorry ass right now?"

When I was fifteen, I yelled at her once, "My father wasn't invisible when you two were in bed, right?" and she slapped me so hard I had a buzz in that hollow next to my ear. A humming for days, like a bee had gone inside.

The parent letter from Joachim's teacher reads: *Our field trip is February 10. We moved up the time for our special outing to Mission San Luis Rey! We will be taking a long bus ride and need parent volunteers!*

"Normally we go to San Juan Capistrano," she tells me the week before, when I pick up Joachim after school. "But that one's so touristy and crowded. I have a good friend who works at San Luis Rey and she'll give us a special tour. We need four parent chaperones and Joachim volunteered you! He told me you love missions!"

I take such a big breath that I can feel my collarbone move. "He says that because my grandmother had a drawing I made of San Juan Capistrano with colored pencils. Hanging in her living room." The only kid without a mission on the display day. I drew all night. The picture was acceptable by the rules. But the teacher gave me a C. Lack of effort.

"Well, I wanted to give you the opportunity!" she says, both palms up like she's holding globes in front of the board. She's nice—she's about fifty, with pink cheeks that I see for the first time are powdery blooms of blush, like pollen.

"I'll be here."

"Great! We bring our own lunches, all right?"

February is crazy at Conroy's. Valentine's Day. We have a ton of orders. What the hell am I supposed to say to Dawna and Mr. Singh, the owner?

On February 2nd, I still can't figure out how to ask. Dawna and I are doing the big orders first. I have a wide jade-green bowl, low and long, for a "Congratulations on the 2020 Chamber Award!"

Start with four brown willow stems, twist them into the sponge. Delphiniums. Not the dark dark ones—like DeMontre's suit. Blue blue—royal blue. Some white larkspur. I'm doing the filler—white spider chrysanthemums, baby's breath—when my cell rings. Dawna says, "Uh-oh. Can't be good." Only the school calls my cell during work.

Reynaldo says, "I need to talk to you."

"Not now."

"Matelasse. Please."

I pull out some lavender scabiosa, little lacy puffs. I put him on speaker, on my ancient flip phone. "Talk."

Dawna looks at me and I roll my eyes. She rolls hers back.

"I'm finally going to Brazil."

"The motherland, huh?" I wipe my hands on my apron.

"Matelasse. Everybody has a dream."

But my chest turns into a sponge now—green block of foam when we jam it into glass. "Well, you're a nightmare, *Reynaldo*. A fuckin fake."

"Why do you always start cursing whenever we talk?"

Dawna's laughing silently now, so hard her glasses go crooked. No one is in the store—it's only 9:40. I bundle a cloud of baby's breath and then put it down. "You know why? Because all day I have to be so goddamn nice and polite at work and the minute I leave I have to pick up the boys and be polite to their teachers and then I sure can't be cussin at home. So teach me some fuckin Brazilian cusswords and I will cuss out your sorry San Bernardino country ass like that, okay?"

"Portuguese," he says, real soft. "They speak Portuguese. Just listen."

The store is so quiet. Dawna is adjusting a vase of long-stemmed red roses.

"I had to get a visa," he says. I hear a siren go past somewhere near him. Like a ribbon. I give up on the arrangement and hold the phone. "That means I had to get a passport and everything."

"You did?"

"I don't have any papers," he says.

"Oh, a dog with no papers?"

"Listen to me! I haven't had a birth certificate or Social Security card for years. Nothing. My dad lost all our stuff one year when we moved. You know we moved about twenty times. He was never one for paperwork. You're aware of that."

He sounds all stiff and formal to me. His words. The way he cuts them off. I say, "Gena has a visa?"

"Yes. She has a passport. She travels all the time."

"Where was she born?" Her fancy athleisurewear, leggings, and sports bra in the magazine, her square brown stomach. Her hair gold and brown, stylized waves around her shoulders.

"Redondo. Her passport's good for six more years. Till she's fifty."

"What?" I can't believe this. "She's forty-four? Seven years older than me?"

"I—"

Dawna's shaking her head, and the bell rings over the door.

"Oh, no," I say. "No, no, no, no. You did *not* just say that."

Mrs. Walther comes inside. Her glasses are sideways teardrops.

She's eighty-two. Every Friday she comes in a few minutes before ten. Her hair always smells of fresh spray, and I used to imagine her life—weekly salon, same auburn curls like beautiful shells arranged on her skull. Same number of curlers. I tried to count once, when she bent her head to write the check. She picks up four bouquets for the altar at her church.

"No," I say, and Dawna slants her head toward the stockroom.

It's dark in here, sharp smell of willow wood. I stand next to the big metal frames for the funeral arrangements. Reynaldo says, "I don't want to talk about Gena."

I say, "Neither do I. So finish up."

"I got a passport and a visa. They say I was born in Brazil. In Rio."

"What? You lied?"

"It's easy to get whatever you need in LA. A Guatemalan guy told me about this place where you can get anything." Now he sounds all proud. "I took a new picture. I look completely Rio."

I am surrounded by red roses. Reynaldo is telling me he is not even the same human I used to sleep beside. Wait—how would he explain this to the boys? Tell them they were half-Brazilian or half-straight-up liar?

Out in front, Mrs. Walther says, "Oh, these look lovely, as always. You two girls do such a nice job every week. You never fail to impress."

"I have to go," I say to Reynaldo, and I close the phone. I like smelling her hair, and next Mrs. Walther will turn to me and say, "Now let's get these beauties to the car."

I look at their YouTube channel, and their Instagram, that night in the kitchen. "We met on the beach in Venice," Gena says. "It was karma." All the photos. Reynaldo's skin glows in the sun. Like the copper-gold spray we have for eucalyptus and willow stems. He is beautiful, with his dreads pulled back into a ponytail, his red seed necklaces and black beads in layers around his neck.

The boys are sleeping. Their forks are in the sink. Antonio still uses the small fork with Paddington Bear on it. Reynaldo didn't call to tell them about Brazil. I can't believe it.

He calls the next day when I'm at work.

"I can't talk now."

"You can't cuss now."

I nod at Dawna, since she's writing an order for a customer, and she says, "Matelasse, can you get some glads from the back?"

In the storeroom I say, "Fuck you, Reynaldo. You picked someone that old?"

"She's younger than that," he says. "In real life. And I don't want any more kids." I hear cars passing behind him, and I feel a hot mix of wanting to hurt him—cut off his dreads with these heavy scissors—and wanting to feel sorry for him, sneaking around like a little kid, mailing me an elephant card, standing outside somewhere.

"Any *more* kids?" I say, real quiet. "You don't have any kids now."

The foam crumbs are like snow under my feet. He does have kids. Forever.

"I had my tubes tied after Antonio, remember?" I say. "Cause you were freaked out."

He's silent. Just the cars. Maybe a bus.

Tubes tied. I hate saying that. Like some damn shoelaces. Didn't feel like that.

He says, "It hurts me to talk to you."

The cash register beeps. The funeral wreaths stacked like doughnuts for the Jolly Green Giant.

"We're leaving Sunday," he says. "I can't tell the boys. They might get nervous. I'll tell them about it when I come back."

"What if you don't come back?"

"Stop being so negative."

Suddenly he's clipped and fine. Because it's my fault. "Shit, it's dangerous in Brazil. I see the news."

"It's dangerous here in America for a Black man," he says. "Stop bringing negativity all the time. Please."

"*Please?* Do they say *Negro-please* in Brazil? Like we do *out here*?" It's so strange to push a button and hear nothing. You can't bang down some big old black receiver like my mother always did, when I was small and she was pissed at a man.

Joachim begs that night. "Three other moms are coming," he says. "Christian's mom, and Cheyenne's, and Haley's. Mrs. Thatcher said you're the fourth. She said you were excited to come."

"Well, I have to figure out what to do about Antonio, because that's a long bus ride, and he'll probably get out of school before we get back, so don't—"

"Call Uncle Enrique." He doesn't mention my mother.

"It's harvest time—he's working in the groves."

"Call Dad and see—"

"Very funny. Hilarious." I look at the refrigerator. Reynaldo's on that plane. But I shouldn't have said it like that. My son's eyes go blank for a few seconds.

He goes into the other room, and I cuss at myself. Shit. But he comes back with the parent letter again. "Mom. The bus comes back right when school gets out. Please."

✳ ✳ ✳

I call Mr. Singh at six a.m. and lie. Tell him I'm sick. But when Dawna calls me at seven thirty and we're in the parking lot, I start crying. "Honey," she says. "Everyone gets sick. I'll be fine here. I'm used to being alone. Just get some rest." She knows.

Antonio says all quavery, "Are you sure the bus comes back before school is over?" and I hug him so hard his bones move a little. He goes off to the second-grade room, biting his lips.

I sit with Joachim on the bus. It's eight and I'm already starving. At work, now I have my second cup of coffee and a samosa from Mrs. Singh. But our paper-bag lunches are on our laps. Peanut butter and jelly. Doritos. Oreos. Hell, I want my Doritos right now.

Two blond moms up in the front row, talking nonstop about remodeling their kitchens. One seriously highlighted mom sitting with Mrs. Thatcher, telling her how smart her daughter is, working the teacher like it's already time for college applications. We are three rows back. Two kid heads in each seat. Curly and spike-waxed and two kids almost bald, their hair is cut so short. Two little blond girls just behind their moms. Hair straight like curtains, swaying in the air from the open window.

Joachim says, "You still listen to Dad's music?"

"You heard me?" I've been playing the old Astrud Gilberto and Antônio Carlos Jobim CDs late at night. Last month I redid my bedroom, put up glittery curtains, pale green, from Target, and covered the headboard in apricot satin. Took down the heavy cotton drapes with Afro-Brazilian designs and the wooden carvings.

Joachim says, "Yeah. Dad says I'm old enough for a cell phone. He's getting me one. He says we can speak in Portuguese so I can learn. He's taking me to Brazil this summer. Not Rio cause that's where everybody goes. He's checking out Bahia."

"Uh-huh." We're quiet down Old Highway 215, where Uncle

Enrique always brought crateloads of oranges to Perris and Temecula. Then we get on the 15 toward San Diego, and the wind roars loud. Finally we take Pala Road, winding down through avocado groves. We see the mission. It's not a fancy flower-covered place, like Capistrano. San Luis Rey is dark, set alone on a knoll. Austere. A man once asked me to make an austere arrangement for his father.

I used to cry after confession, when I first slept with Reynaldo. I was only seventeen. I thought the purposeful wasting of seed, the only way he would do it, was a sin we could never erase. We didn't have Joachim until Reynaldo said he was ready to be a father.

"Dad told me we can go to Bahia in June. Antonio's not old enough. He has to wait." The bus pulls into the mission parking lot, and the swaying makes me sick.

My son whispers, "He's full of crap."

"Joachim!" I say.

"Dad's full of crap." My son leans toward me and the bus lurches into a hole. His elbow knocks against the metal bar of the seat in front of us, so hard his bones sound hollow.

"You been eating your lunch?" I say.

He rolls his eyes. "Mom." He rubs his elbow.

"Is it your funny bone?"

"It's not funny." He leans close again. The other students stand up like mushrooms after a rain. He whispers all hoarse to me, "Dad says you can travel inside your mind, and you can make yourself a citizen of the world. That's bullshit."

In the shade of the outside mission wall, Mrs. Thatcher puts us into groups. I have Ricky, José, Jesús, Dakota, and my son. We stand in a tight little circle waiting while Mrs. Thatcher goes to find the guide. Joachim says, "Mom, put on your name tag."

"Mrs. Rodrigue." Jesús reads my tag, his voice soft. "Are you from Mexico?"

My skin is light brown, my hair is long and held back in a bun, and my eyes are the color of root beer. I smile at him. "I'm from here," I say. "Born in Rio Seco, California." Should I ask? Does he want me to? "What about you, Jesús?"

"Born in San Bernardino, California." He grins and ducks his head. The grooves from his comb are precise as lines on an old LP. "During open house you were looking at my paper. You said, *Jesus Dreams of Peace*. Like it was church."

"No, she didn't!" Joachim is pissed.

"Yeah, I did," I say, smiling. "But now I'll call you Jesús the Spanish way."

Five boys, their feet raising dust, their shoulders moving to feel the space. Smell of fruit snacks on their skin—the little packets my boys eat all day. Three boxes a week.

Jesús says, "My mom was born in Tijuana. She told me I could wave at the border today." He turns to look out past the trees.

"That's south," I tell him, and point toward Mexico. From here, it's only thirty miles or so.

Jesús says, "She came here fifteen years ago."

I wave with him, and then he looks embarrassed. I say, "My mom was born much further away than that. Tijuana used to be California anyway. Let's head out, guys."

The other moms smile vaguely at me and then move away. The blond moms keep their groups of girls together. They probably think I speak Spanish. I could order them food. I could teach them a few words in Portuguese. Tristeza. Astrud sings about it.

Corcovado. The quiet stars. Me sitting out on the steps at night and staring up in the dark sky. Saudade.

We follow the guide for an hour, and then we break off into our groups to find all the places on our scavenger hunt packets, and answer questions for ten points each.

"Where is the pepper tree in the courtyard originally from?"

"How old is it?"

Of course it's the first Brazilian pepper tree brought to California, by Father Lasuén. The boys crouch down and write. Of course I've been seeing pepper trees like green feathery clouds all my life, all over Rio Seco, pink spicy berries we used for ammunition.

The plaster walls are so thick and cool that the pathways make me shiver. "I want to make this mission," Joachim says. "I like the bell tower."

"I'm making San Juan Capistrano," Dakota says. "My mom already bought the swallows and the Indians and the padres from Michaels."

"Me, too," Jesús says. "My mom bought Capistrano, too."

"What?" I say, and Joachim frowns at me.

"The kits, Mom. Remember we saw them?"

He's right. We went to Michaels last year and saw the big bin full of mission kits, the Indian men and women and padres, small humans plastic-wrapped, hanging on racks above. With axes and pots and barrels. Joachim's embarrassed at my lack of preparation. The berries under our feet are papery and crackling. What if some government official decides Reynaldo has to stay, because they think he's a Brazilian citizen? What if he can't come back? Shit. Shit.

We walk through the cemetery. The names are all Irish or Spanish. The boys sit on benches and write answers to who's buried here, and I stand in the arched entry in the ancient wall. I'm so hungry I think I'll pass out.

"You don't have a name tag," a man says.

He's leaning against the outside of the wall, looking out over the mission grounds. He has a long black ponytail held with six black rubber bands. It looks like bamboo.

My name tag is gone. Only some adhesive mist left on my shirt. "Just a mom," I say. I know I sound like a bitch.

All he does is nod. "Where you from?"

"Rio Seco."

He nods again. He has on a perfect white button-down shirt and black jeans. He has a stomach. But his face is all beautiful brown cheekbones and black eyes with long lashes. Like a girl's. He slants his head. "You Indian? Mexican?"

It just comes out. He's not a customer. He's a damn stranger. "You nosy?"

Now he smiles and unfolds his arms. "Just curious. Your hair looks like—"

"Like I was in a hurry," I say. It's in a big loose bun. Who in the hell tries to pick up a woman at a damn mission?

The boys' voices float through the entryway. They're looking for me.

He lifts his chin, waves, and walks toward what seems like the edge of the property, stops at a small sign, and looks up into the sky. Then his legs disappear—he walks down some hidden stairway and vanishes into a huge hole. I don't see a pit on my packet.

Back in the main courtyard, we get our groups settled on the grass for lunch. But I stand up. "I need a break," I say.

Joachim hisses, "Mom. Chaperones don't get to take a break."

The other three groups of kids are sitting on the lawn near the roses. The moms are perched on the low wall like birds. They're talking yoga class, PTA. The blond moms have made the high-lighted mom feel bad somehow. You can tell by how she's sitting.

I say, "You know what? I do get to take a break. Tell Mrs. Thatcher I need to use the ladies' room, but I have all boys, okay?"

"You already went," he says.

I give him a look. "You the restroom police? Tell her to hang out with you guys for fifteen minutes. Fifteen whole minutes."

I go back through the cemetery and look out the archway. Was there a giant pit near the parking lot? What was down there? A silver mine?

In fourth grade, I made my mission out of sugar cubes, like my friend Tara. Uncle Enrique bought me ten boxes of sugar cubes, some glue, some wood, and a big piece of cardboard. I made little metal crosses from nails for my cemetery. My mission glittered in the kitchen light. Not Capistrano because I didn't have swallows. I made a little sign that said Santa Barbara because that sounded beautiful. I painted the cardboard roof with red food coloring, mixed with pink nail polish I found on the bathroom sink. When my mother came home, she lost her shit, because I'd wasted her nail polish. She woke me up. Yelling. She'd spilled beer on the bell tower and she saw the first ants marching into the melting sugar. "Sugar? You out your goddamn mind?" She hated ants more than anything. They were everywhere in the orange groves, but they came to our house constantly because of the empty beer cans and tequila bottles on the back porch.

She made me carry the mission up to Uncle Enrique's. It was after midnight. I was so scared, walking up the dirt lane, and the ir-rigation water came on in a big spray from the cistern along the grove road. He watered at night because of the heat. The rest of my mission dissolved on the wet cardboard and dripped onto my chest. All the cubes I'd glued so carefully. I would get an F.

"Ain't nothin fair in life," my mother used to say. "You might as well find out now. Life will fuck with you every time."

She used to tell Reynaldo that all the time, when we got married. When my mother saw him wearing linen pants and sandals, when he'd named Joachim, she brought this bowl of nuts over to our apartment. The big brown crinkly ones. She said, "Brazil nuts. We don't be eatin em, cause they so damn expensive. I used to see them at this rich white lady's house around Christmas. When we went to rehang the drapes from the dry cleaners. She call them nigger toes. Right in front of us."

"This isn't Louisiana," he said to her, and my mother laughed.

"That was here in California, baby," she said. "Don't matter where you are. You think what you think, and other people think what they think. Life gon fuck with you, Reynaldo Rodrigue. Nothin else to it."

I want those Doritos now. Even that damn Capri Sun. Joachim packed it. Berry Cooler, he said. But I walk out of the cemetery and across the parking lot. I hear someone singing. Not English words. Not Spanish. The dirt path leads to a low ruined wall of adobe brick, and past that wide stone stairs leading down into something like an amphitheater. Stone channels hold musty water, smelling like roots, and a stone gargoyle spits water into a little pool. The guide didn't mention this place. Maybe it's not part of the mission. Behind me, kid voices drift up out of the courtyard like confetti going back into the air.

What am I doing? I have about five minutes left before someone notices I'm gone. Someone besides Joachim.

He's sitting on the step just above the water. I sit two steps up from him. Seven rubber bands. Not six. His hair is long and black and straight as mine.

"So what is this place?" I say. He stops singing, but he doesn't look up at me. Fuck it. I don't do this. Talk to strangers.

And this dude doesn't answer me. Shit. Of course. I'm thirty-six years old. Men want girls twenty-six, twenty-seven. Except Reynaldo.

I stand up and a rock falls down the steps. The man turns. He has an iPod in his ears, the white wires like little reins around his chin, and he's crying. Not bawling like a kid, but tears shine in two lines down his face.

He takes out the earbuds. "Hey."

I nod. "You okay?"

He turns and rests his arm on his leg. His black jeans dusty at the knee. "My three times great-grandmother's birthday. Today's the day someone wrote down, anyway, when the Spanish brought her here. She washed clothes down there. The men dug all the zanjas and made the bricks and built this place, and they ran the water from the river through there—" He points to the channels. "The women made soap with ashes and beef tallow. Washed all the soldier's clothes so the dudes could whip her people in the morning. Then the women washed out all the blood the next day." He looked back at me. "You're gonna make a mission."

"With my son," I say.

He nods. "Fourth grade. My moms said hell no, we weren't making a mission about the padres who killed my people, so my teacher said I could write a report. I wrote about wanting to play for the San Diego Chargers. I lived down the road, in Oceanside. All my friends were Samoan. I was gonna be the first Pala pro foot-ball player, even though everybody thought I was Samoan. I always told them I was Luiseño, Serrano, and Cahuilla people. Look at my hair—no waves here." He wipes his face with his sleeve, and grins. "It was pretty funny. My teacher got mad. She said I had to report on a mission, and I said it was my mission to play linebacker for the Chargers."

He's hilarious and smart. Like Joachim. I have to smile, too. "If my son does this place, I have to come up with something for that blue dome." I shade my eyes and look up at the bell tower. Maybe a small plastic champagne glass. A wedding favor. Upside down bowl. Paint it with—pale blue nail polish. I will fucking buy the perfect blue Essie bottle for Joachim.

He doesn't ask why my husband wouldn't construct the bell tower. He looks down at the greenish water and mumbles, "Nigger women."

My scalp goes cold and prickled. I say, "Excuse me? What the hell did you just say? Did you call me the n-word?"

He whips his head around. "What? Shit, no! No. *Digger* women. That's what they called Indians. Her and her sisters. My aunts have a picture of them, and some anthropologist wrote a caption. *Digger Women at San Luis Rey.*"

Now I feel like I'll pass out, smelling the wet damp in the stone stairs. So hungry. The women here hungry. My grandmere telling me one night how a man on the sugar cane plantation called her never by name, only nigger woman. Bring that water. Bring them hoe. Her voice in the dark. They don't do like that in California, she said.

He says, "They called her Domenica. She walked up and down here hundreds of times, so I come see it on her birthday. My moms never came here, not once. She said this was not her country." He has big gnarled hands like hard work, but designer jeans.

Then he says, "Yeah, she's not buried here. My mom and Domenica are buried on the rez at Pala, and now we got the casino, so they're laughing. I work nights, so sometimes I come down here during the day. I figure they all see me here." He stands up and the back of his jeans are dusted like a saddle. He's a big guy, wide shoulders like pads under his shirt. "They call this the lavandería. Plenty of blood ran down these stairs. You could tell that to the nice guide lady." He pulls out a card.

James Martinez. "Your last name is Spanish."

He grins again. "My mom married a guy from Torres-Martinez Reservation in Coachella. My dad's people are in the desert."

Casino operations. Restaurant manager, his card says.

"You should come over to the casino for dinner sometime. My treat."

"I have kids," I say.

"No shit, you're on a field trip. Unless the teacher rented you." He laughed. "Don't your kids eat?"

I start laughing, too. I can't help it. "Two boys. They eat all day and night."

"I got two girls. But they're twenty and twenty-two. I've been separated for a couple years. Working nights didn't help." He looks back down to the gargoyle. "They never come into the restaurant, because they're in college. Up at Stanford." Then he stops, like he's out of breath. "You don't have a card?"

"From Conroy's?" I try not to suck my teeth like my mother does. I say, "Matelasse Rodrigue," and put out my hand. His palm is big as a pancake. "I'm part Houma."

He tilts his head to the side like a little kid. "Houma?"

"My fifteen minutes are up," I say. "I gotta go rescue Jesús. I like him. He dreams of peace. And my son will be pissed off." I look at the worn-smooth place where the women rubbed cloth against rock. "Houma Indians. Near the Mississippi River, in Louisiana. A

Houma man married my three times great-grandmother. She was a slave. Don't ask me about my name yet."

"Matelasse?"

"You have a pen?" He has one of those beautiful leather messenger bags. I write my cell number on his card, and give it back to him.

That heat edging around my heart. The heart is a muscle. Use it or lose it.

He walks up the stairs with me. "I'm getting divorced." There. I'm going to have to say it all the time now. Ugly word. Not pretty like fado or tristeza or even piranha. I always thought piranha was a cool word. "Yeah. My husband is on a trip to—" I have no idea where Bahia is. Not even close. "He's headed down the Amazon, in Brazil. Goddamn piranhas all around his boat."

I start laughing, and James Martinez looks at me like I'm crazy. "Or maybe those little fish they have in the rivers down there—you know, the ones they always talk about that swim up your—when you pee? They say that's a pain worse than childbirth."

"You're scaring me now," he says, but he's grinning again. He hands me another card, and I head toward the kid-voices rising too loud. I'm in trouble. All that sugar kicking in. James Martinez says, "Give me a call," and I hold up his card with my first two fingers, hold it up high like it's the message in the plastic pitchfork we use for bouquets. Then I put it in my back pocket, so he can see me keeping it.

Joachim and Jesús are in the cemetery. Joachim isn't crying, because he's so mad the tears are all built up around his eyes and even his forehead. His whole face looks swollen up in fury like I haven't seen since Antonio broke his little Transformer guys. Joachim hardly ever gets mad. But he runs toward me and says, "You can't do that! Moms don't get to just walk around like that!"

"Hi, Mrs. Rodrigue," Jesús says. "We were looking for you."

I try to be cool. "I hope you weren't looking in the ladies' bathroom."

But Joachim isn't going for it. "Mom!" He grabs my arm and pulls me toward the courtyard. "Everybody's waiting." His voice is desperate. His throat is shaky with those tears.

I can't believe it. I can't hold his hand because he's too old, and my eyes are filling up, too, so I put my fingers on his shoulder, hot T-shirt cloth, and say, "I'm right here. I just took a walk."

The other moms are standing with their groups, busy not looking at me. Easy to see they've been talking about my lack of responsibility. Lunch was that fast? Mrs. Thatcher smiles, her lips sealed under a new coat of lipstick. I get my group together and she says quietly, "Joachim insisted that he go get you, and normally I would never let a student leave his group, but Jesús volunteered to accompany him, so we made an exception. We need to get back on the bus early because of the traffic."

When did moms have to be perfect? Who passed that fucking law?

I eat one Dorito while we're walking through the parking lot to the bus. At the door, Mrs. Thatcher turns and says to us all, "You all have your packets. There are two word games about the mission, and one place for you to write a paragraph. You can finish these on the bus or when we get back."

Lavandería. Digger. Domenica. She knelt where we sat. His wrist strong and wide when his hand brushed against mine.

✳　✳　✳

The bus enters the freeway with a long whine. Joachim doesn't speak to me for a long time. Finally he says, "I don't know which mission I want to make. We have to look at the packet again." Then he falls asleep in minutes, and so do most of the other kids. Their heads are thrown back, mouths open like baby birds to the sky.

Joachim's head falls onto my shoulder, his sweaty hair plastered to his forehead, black curls like a thousand tornados under my fingers. I'm going to have to tell him that his father's gone for good, even if Reynaldo does come back to LA. I have to tell Antonio, too.

My mother had been drunk the whole week when our missions were due. I don't remember what I said to her about the fathers of my friends who were helping make their missions.

My mother had wavy hair she pulled tight in a bun, the baby hairs like intricate lace plastered to her forehead with Vaseline. Her cheeks were so pink, with a few freckles. If she put on makeup, it filled in the white puckered scar.

Only once did my grandmother ever tell me what happened. My mother had disappeared for a week. I was fourteen. I thought I was smart, and said, "Maybe she'll get a matching scar."

My grandmother's voice came in the dark from the porch. "Pinkie ring. He hit her with a diamond pinkie ring. I hate that word, pinkie, cause my finger's brown. All of em."

Then she said, "He come out here to show off his Cadillac. Call hisself want to see the oranges. Say he like a drive to the country. My cousin Pearl bring him here, cause she miss me. She live in LA with this fat rich man and she don't like him. Me and Pearl made gumbo up there at Enrique house, and we come back down here and your mama cryin, her face got blood all on it. Shirt tore. Enrique pull out his gun, but that man Dryan pull out a knife so fast and got it on Pearl neck. They get in the Cadillac and I never see my cousin again, me."

Until then, all I knew was my father could be some fool right here in Rio Seco, or some fool in LA. But it took me a long time to figure out the ring. This dude Dryan had to have backhanded my mother, with the pinkie ring. To make the scar there on her face. She was fifteen. And I cried a long time for her. Just that one night.

My phone rings. I don't know the number. The other moms are talking, and Mrs. Thatcher is nodding off. It's funny to see her head swing forward and then swing back up. She's been on a hundred field trips, I think. Still patient and kind.

"Hello?" I whisper.

"I'm not stalking you." James Martinez. "I wanted to see if you gave me a fake number."

"I don't do fake stuff."

"You're on the bus."

Joachim moves against my shoulder, his mouth still open. Doritos dust on his cheek. I brush it away. "No shit," I whisper.

"So what mission did you make in fourth grade?"

I see it on my uncle Enrique's wall, even now. I stayed up all night, after the sugar and food coloring melted onto my arms. I drew every roof tile and all the archways and the bricks, even the fountain, from the photo I had in my book. I had the little pencil sharpener and bird wings of curled shaving all around me in the morning.

"None of your business," I whisper.

"I wanted to say my wife didn't leave because I'm a jerk," he says.

"Okay."

"Can I talk? I know you can't talk." I can barely hear him over the noise of the engine and the rushing wind. "Look," he says. "I grew up on the rez, and my grandma's house didn't even have electricity or running water until I was about ten. Now we have all this money. My wife met somebody from Barona about three years ago. Another reservation. She moved down there and she works at that casino." He does something with the phone, something noisy, and then he says, "I can't believe you saw me cry."

"I can't come to dinner with you right now," I whisper. "Maybe not for a month. Maybe two. If that's okay."

The bus is motoring down the freeway past groves of avocado trees on the steep hillsides. Joachim jerks his head up like he knows he's been sleeping, and his eyes open wide. I can tell he doesn't know where he is for a minute, and I close the phone very quietly and hold it on my leg. I can't take Joachim's hand, like when he was little, so I just put my fingers on top of his and he doesn't move his hand away. He takes a big waking-up breath and frowns, looking out the window at the dark cliffs rushing past us.

Then coronavirus came. Reynaldo had barely made it back from Brazil before everything closed down. Joachim didn't even make a mission in April. There was no school by then. I had to take the boys to Uncle Enrique every morning, and my brother Alfonso, who had never been the best student, helped them with their classes online.

Dawna and I made funeral wreaths. Over and over and over. No hospital bouquets. I would stand in the stockroom and cry for an hour, with my hands on those fucking green sponges dry as sand.

It isn't until June 23rd that I go out for coffee, with James. We sit there for three hours, in the parking lot outside a Denny's, drinking in go-cups, and we have to get a Grand Slam breakfast for lunch, and more coffee. The boys are with Uncle Enrique, but I don't show James their pictures yet. We talk about stupid shit that happened to us when we were kids, and my face hurts from laughing when I get home. Those muscles hadn't been used for a long time either.

It isn't until July 15th that we go out for dinner, not at the Pala casino restaurant but at the Fantasy Springs casino in Indio, where his cousin is the hotel manager. The boys are with Reynaldo for two days. And Gena. He finally told her about his real life, showed her photos of the boys, and she thought they'd be great on Instagram. Shit, I thought, cute little brown mascots for her. But they wanted to try capoeira, with their dad. She'd probably get ten thousand new followers from the three of them together. The perfect father.

I'm worried that Gena will say something stupid, hurt their feelings, but I know they'll call me on the new cell phone Reynaldo got them, for this weekend.

We are in bed. At a vacation rental. I bought new underwear at Target. I haven't told anyone where I am. No one. I am thirty-seven years old and James is the second man I have ever slept with, and I am terrified. Sitting up against the fancy plush headboard, we each have a shot of rum. He thinks it's funny that I won't touch tequila.

His chest and arms are so much wider than Reynaldo's. I can't touch his collarbone. I'm afraid to put my face behind his ear. Not yet. But when he lifts himself up from me, and his hair falls onto my shoulders, I put my fingers up under his arms, those pectorals, the muscles thick. My thumbs at the edge of his collarbone. He says, "Damn, that tickles!" and just about crushes me when he starts laughing and falls onto his side.

Of course my phone rings then. Kids have extra-sense powers

for when you're having a good time. That's when they get strep throat or break a finger.

It isn't the boys. It's Merry. I say, "Girl, you—"

She says, "Matelasse. They shot him. I'm at the hospital."

"What?"

"Tenerife." Then she can't even talk, she's sobbing so hard. "He's shot. Larette didn't answer her phone. Go get her. Please. And come. County/USC. He's downstairs. My son is downstairs in surgery."

I put down the phone, and James stares up at the ceiling. "That a preplanned exit call? From your girlfriend?"

I can't say anything. I can't move. The sweat and wet on my chest and thighs cold in the air-conditioning. All the time we are terrified, for our boys. My sons are still so little. Tenerife is sixteen now. Tall and beautiful and a nationally ranked baller. He doesn't even have a car.

"Guys have a wingman," James says. "I always imagine women have an ERT. Emergency Rescue Technician."

Is he mad? Even when he's being funny? I don't know him at all. I turn my back to the bed, to put on my bra. My shirt.

"A real emergency," I say. "My cousin. Her son's been shot."

He sits up. "By who?"

"I don't even know. She lives in LA."

He gathers his hair and takes one of the six elastic bands from his wrist. The same as me, with my one black band. He looks at me and says, "That's almost a hundred miles from here. I'll drive you there."

ANGEL WINGS

Matelasse, is that you? When you get here?

You got Larette?

Larette.

I can't do this.

Yeah, in my uniform, because I was working NICU when they called my cell. Now I'm down here in ICU and they call me Mom. Like we call the ones at work. We're working on him, Mom. Why don't you go get some coffee?

I can't do this.

When they called me, all I could think of was chicken. Because I didn't really understand what happened. How he was shot. They said he was at the drive-thru window of Jack in the Box, and you know my son didn't like Jack. He always wanted good chicken. Wingstop or KFC.

All those chickens that died for him. Because I would always see Aunt Opal's yard, remember, Larette? Down in Houma? They took us to Louisiana that summer. I was ten. You were, eight, right? Aunt Opal was my mama's sister. She made us go out in the yard with her and get the chicken every time. She said we were too California and she would put some country in us. Remember we had to wring that bird around like a toy and the neck would stretch all long like a swan? The feathers were everywhere.

Subway Burger King Flame Broiler KFC Popeyes. Matelasse, you know them boys eat wherever they can find after tournaments. You know how everybody thinks they're lazy and they don't study. Those boys were practicing every single night all summer, or playing in a summer league tournament. Remember you brought Joachim and Antonio to see him play last week—how he had his summer school homework up there in the bleachers and the other boys would tease him? And Coach Renard would say, Now you better not play like some honors white boy.

Because he was taking AP bio in the summer.

*

COMMENTS (42)

Merryjordan24@gmail.com: They told me not to read the comments. My friends and my son's coach. My son plays for Above the Rim with Coach Wesley Renard. They said they would take the iPad away so I wouldn't read the comments. But you are writing that he is a gangbanger and of course he got shot and you have all read his name in the newspaper for a little glory during basketball season. He met Kobe and Kawhi and took pictures with them. Kawhi is his idol. He wears his hair like Kawhi. He was recruited everywhere and you have seen his name for three-point records. Tenerife Jordan. My son.

DuckHunt22@aol.com: What a ghetto name.

Merryjordan24@gmail.com   mailto:DuckHunt9@aol.com: That's what you wrote?

grammarpolice@yahoo.com: Keep it civil, people.

DuckHunt22@aol.com: I am. He had his civil rights. He was free to eat wherever he wanted. Jack in the Box. He was free to be a gangbanger. He was free to participate in an attempted robbery and he is getting free healthcare right now on our taxes because of welfare and he is free to recover or die.

Merryjordan24@gmail.com: You don't know anything about him. Or me. I can't believe you would write this about a human. A boy.

Homeofthebrave1067@sbcglobal.net: Believe what I see, ma'am. He was reaching toward what appeared to be a weapon. The officer had no choice.

Merryjordan24@gmail.com: Right here, in the paper, I could look at his name, just his last name and the points in the scorebox, while I was on lunch hour. You all would like the story better if I didn't have a job. Welfare queen. I work in the Neonatal Unit at USC Hospital. I see this article and a picture of my son's face and a story and under that you wrote lies. I wish I couldn't see what you think. You all thought it before. All the time. But I didn't have to know. Even when you came in the hospital with your wife I wouldn't know. Even when I held your baby. If your baby or your grandbaby came early, I held him. I would rather not know what is in your head.

＊

Larette. You brought burritos? They said I could eat in here. Two of the RNs know me from Neonatal. Never thought we'd be in ICU.

I told him he couldn't get a tattoo, remember? Nowhere on his body. Not to honor his grandmere when she passed last year—he wanted her name *Felonise* and a Bible verse. He picked out "You are a lamp unto my feet." He said Kawhi had Bible verses. I told him she would have hated that. I said, "You don't need to do no RIP or Memory Of, cause your grandmere wasn't like that. She was old school. You're just supposed to remember her."

Larette. Look at him.

Only starter on the team didn't have a tattoo. So beautiful with his arms all clean. Even the white kids have ink now. Whole pages on their chests. Tribal stuff on their arms.

I said, "Just remember her—think about her and keep it to yourself."

"That's it?" he said. Like it wasn't enough.

His name has been in the paper every day. Three days. In the comments they call him *a good shoot*.

I had to look.

Larette? It's getting late. I can sleep here. They let me sleep in the room or in the nurses' rest area. But who's taking care of your son? Dante has Little League, right? Then you're missing his game.

Remember when we were all in nursing school and we went to Neonatal for training? You remember the first time you held a white baby? First time I ever held a white baby, I had been working Neonatal four days, but we had five Latino babies and two Black babies. Then we got a white preemie and the skin was so many colors. Mottled, they call it. Cream and red and purple and even green where she had a bruise from the IV.

Tenerife must have been about two. His skin so dark and perfect it was like the word on the Dove bar—*enrobed*. And when I rubbed baby oil into his arms, when he was seven and started playing ball, he would sweat on the court at the park and the sun was on his back and it was a rainbow. Like when the oil floats on rainwater and you see all the colors. Like a butterfly wing—his back. The shoulder blades. They call them angel wings.

The first bullet went in the top of his left biceps because he was reaching down to the ground for that phone. The second bullet went into the left side of his chest.

Tavares?

When did you get here? I took something last night so I could sleep. Larette gave it to me.

I don't know. A Vicodin.

Here. Sit on the chair. I'll stand.

Yeah. I knew you would come. But you can't sleep in here. She wouldn't like it. Your wife. She won't even like it that we're here together.

You drove the whole way? You didn't sleep New Orleans to LA?

When I tell you what happened, you can't say a word. Not a damn word. Not about why was it so late. Or three of them in the car. Nothing.

Deontre was driving his mom's Navigator. Damaris was in the front seat. Tenerife was in the back.

They went to Jack because they were hungry, Tavares. Don't even start with me. They were starving. The tournament went late and they played the last game at seven thirty, and they didn't get out of the gym until eleven. They were hungry. I was at work. They went to Jack because it was closest to the gym.

You stay here with him. I'll go down to the car and sleep. Larette and Matelasse been bringing me food. I haven't left. Because he might wake up.

You bring coffee? Tavares? Where's the cream?

I don't want to look at the footage, Tavares. No. I'm not playing.

I'll sit out here with you for a while but he might wake up.

No. I don't want to see it.

I remember when my grandmama was dying and we just sat in the waiting room for two days and talked. That one little TV up there and you were watching the Lakers. It was November. Put down your damn phone. I don't care if it went viral. Don't show me how.

LAPD is doing an investigation. You remember Johnny Frías? The guy I met way back in 1999 when we were all in nursing school and Grief was trying to be Highway Patrol? We were at a party, when you were living in New Orleans. Johnny Frías had a fight with this cop, Miller. Now Miller's a sergeant for LAPD, and he was training this rookie—I'm not gonna say his name, Tavares. No. Miller kept yelling *Gun Gun Gun*, to the new cop. The rookie was twenty-four. The young one shot Tenerife. He thought—

Yeah. The phone.

It doesn't matter that someone recorded it.

It doesn't matter that everyone in America can see it. I don't give a damn.

If you say I shouldn't have let them ride three to a car, I will never speak to you again.

You the reporter? Is that a cameraman?

It's Mrs. Jordan. Not Ms.

Yes, there is a Mr. Jordan. Tavares Jordan. Yeah, the same last name as his. Tenerife Jordan. Our son. You'd like the story better if we weren't married. We aren't married now. But we were. Long time ago.

I have about fifteen minutes. I have to get back to my son's room.

You need to get that camera outta here until Mr. Jordan comes. I am not doing this alone.

Then you better wait.

No. You cannot have baby photos. No.

Yes, we'll answer some questions now. But don't ask me why he was at the drive-thru. He was hungry. All humans get hungry. You get hungry. You never been to the drive-thru at eleven p.m.? You don't get off work real late and hit Jack in the Box in that news van? What kind of car do you drive? Nissan Altima? You think if your son was in the back seat he'd get shot while you were buying a cheeseburger?

You got enough for your story today? Because I have to go back upstairs. Now.

✳

COMMENTS (267)

> **Merryjordan24@gmail.com:** No, his father is not in jail. We got married when I was 21 and I had my son after

that. We got divorced. You are probably divorced or you wouldn't be sitting here at 2 am writing comments about my son. I am sitting beside a hospital bed. Are you drinking coffee or Red Bull or vodka? Because you all sound crazy.

truthtellerjames@gmail.com: Don't run from the cops dirtbag and you wont get shot. Every time. It's never the officer's fault according to the cousin and the welfare mom.

DuckHunt22@aol.com: He wasn't running. But don't hide behind tinted windows in the back seat of a big SUV and claim you didn't see the officer right? Why were they out so late anyway? Banger time.

rickroberto@ucla.edu: HE'S A BALLER. I JUST SAW HIM PLAY THAT NIGHT

DuckHunt22@aol.com: Good shoot. He would have probably robbed somebody later that night, and law enforcement prevented that. I don't care what his family says.

baller4life99@gmail.com: MY HOMIE TENERIFE YOU A STAR

DuckHunt22@aol.com: See they called him homie because he was a gang bager

grammarpolice@yahoo.com: PLEASE SPELL THINGS CORRECTLY IF YOU'RE GOING TO COMMENT. MY JOB IS NEVER DONE.

DuckHunt22@aol.com: You see their names? Hilarious. And they were riding in a Navigator so tell me they're just poor neglected kids from the ghetto.

rickroberto@ucla.edu: THEY WERE ABOVE THE RIM AND THEY WERE BALLIN.

DuckHunt22@aol.com: Come on. That's as ghetto as it gets. Who gave them the Navigator? Some scout?

*

You from the sports section? *LA Times*?

You wanted me to feed him. Every coach and scout and all you reporters come to the games, you got a job because of him. I have a job because people have babies and those babies stay in Neonatal and I keep them alive. All those chickens died for my son. I washed a thousand socks. All those T-shirts. Nike Summer League and all the MaxPreps tournaments. Above the Rim Invitational. All those shirts and shorts at every camp, all those colleges giving him shirts, every tournament they get a shirt. Socks. So many socks it looks like puppets fighting when they're all tied together in the dryer.

He got to be six-six and it was decided. Like I didn't have any say.

Did you know Ralph Sampson never wanted to play ball? He liked to sew.

You the reporter. You should know who Ralph Sampson is. Google it yourself. He played ball long time ago.

Yeah. Be a better story if I was fourteen when I had my son. But I was twenty-two. I had my AA in nursing.

You asking me if he got money from a coach? Seriously? That fucking phone wasn't even new. It was a 6.

I hear medical students all the time in the hospital cafeteria. Fellowships, stipends, scholarships, research grants. They can get money. A professor can give them money. He can marry one of those young girls in his class. One of my patients was twenty-two, she went on an anthropology trip to Peru to study how people fish and she and the professor fell in love. They got married. He can buy her a diamond ring and there's no NCAA to say shit.

You never write about that. Nobody can even give Tenerife or his friends a ride. But you all are asking why they were in a Navigator.

You the fifth reporter to ask me if Tavares and I were married. Do you hear yourself?

Are you married? Do you eat fast food at night? Do you wear a ball cap? No, no—do you bet fantasy league basketball? You bet March Madness in your office pool at the *Times*?

You the second one to find out Tavares went to jail. For a year. You got a car seat? Of course not. You don't have a baby.

When we first had Tenerife we didn't have a car seat. And I knew better, cause I worked at the hospital. But Tavares was hard-headed and drove to the store and let his cousin Chess hold the baby. They went three blocks. But he got pulled over for a cracked windshield, and then no car seat: $358. Then it went to warrant, and he rode to work with Chess, and Chess had a warrant for gun possession, and there was a .38 in the glove compartment.

Nobody has gloves.

Oh, I'm not supposed to laugh?

I was at work. Tavares couldn't get me on the phone.

A year in county jail over a car seat and broken window glass. When he got out, he didn't want to be in LA. He wanted to be somewhere far away. New Orleans. But I had my job in Neonatal then. I loved those babies. He told me, I got a prior now. And you got an attitude. I'm gonna bounce.

You work for a newspaper. How many times have you moved? Do you have a cracked windshield? Oh—you don't get pulled over.

You take an Uber.

Larette? That you? It's dark in here. I know. I took two of the Vicodin. My head hurts.

I've been awake forever. Listening to the ventilator. You know how hard it is to come off a ventilator. I don't know how Tenerife's gonna get his lungs back in shape for basketball. I don't know how his shoulder's gonna work again.

Don't say that.

We do this all the time. You and me. But when it's your own child . . .

Damaris's mom called me. She said the cops kept yelling at them. You got priors? You got priors? That's what Damaris said the cops kept yelling at them, when they were in the drive-thru. Shit, Larette. I don't want to see it in my head.

And Tenerife was in the back seat, and the cops couldn't see him cause of the window tint, and then when he opened the door his cell phone fell out and they thought it was a gun.

Black phone. I hate that thing. How many people died over a damn phone?

Remember we used to talk about our mamas breaking the receiver cause they slammed it down so hard on a man? Them old black phones. And we had those cheap purple cordless phones from Target. You couldn't leave your yard while you were on them.

Didn't nobody die cause of them phones.

Larette. Look at him. It's been seven days. He's shrinking. No. No, don't tell me that. No. He's shrinking. His legs. Look at his face. His lips. His braids all messed up.

I spend my shift with the babies upstairs and they're skin and bones, the little preemies, and I check all those tubes, and the mamas are reaching in with their gloves and you can see them plump up. Their legs and arms and then their faces. Like magic but it's all that liquid going inside.

All these tubes in him. Breathing.

*　*　*

Is it Wednesday? Thursday? Eight days?

Larette. Please. I need two more. The Vicodin or Percocet. Doesn't matter. I just need to stop thinking and sleep. I can sleep in the chair. Just stay with him while I go to the cafeteria for some tea.

All I can see is how narrow the drive-thru is and how it's full of exhaust and grease and the window where the air blows out and how they couldn't move, couldn't go backward or forward cause there were five LAPD cars and how Tenerife must have been trying to call me. Trying—

Larette. Just give me two more, for tomorrow. I know I should eat. But he's so thin and it's been eight days.

You would lay in the bed and your feet touched the end and you said I had to get a longer bed. You would shoot the ball at the ceiling. A hundred times. Muscle memory. Your muscles remember, baby. Doesn't matter about now. Your arms know. Dream about it.

You didn't even want to play ball at first. You loved all the baller jewelry and hats and shoes. You designed shoes out of clay. Drew shoes all the time. Then you got tall.

At night I would look at you sleeping and you were like the scarecrow in *The Wizard of Oz*.

He watched that movie at your house, Larette. You showed those boys all the musicals. Told em to sit down and shut up and see something amazing. And they were so scared of you they did. Cause even Grief was scared of you.

Grief. That man is so in love with you even after all these years. I always thought I'd find somebody like Grief. But I had Tenerife. I didn't want any man to change my son's life. Tell him what he couldn't do.

You know what? When Tenerife was sleeping, his left hand would be on his heart, and his right arm all stretched out on the sheet. Like the scarecrow introducing himself. Telling Dorothy go that way. That way.

You again? Oh, it's been ten days and the *LA Times* wants an update?

No. Oh, hell no. I am not giving you what you want. You want some story about he was a promising young athlete in the wrong place at the wrong time. But that's bullshit. How is Jack the wrong place? They wanted food! The cashier tripped out and thought they might rob her because it was midnight?

The wrong time? They shot free throws for three hours that night in the gym!

I am not telling you that wrong place story, so you need to take your microphone and your camera outta here before I get my ex-husband to break em both.

Fuck you. I know exactly what you want to say. My uncle used to say, Fuck you and the horse you rode in on. Fuck you and the news van you rode here on. You are gonna try and put it on my son.

Tavares. Get her outta my face. Tavares!

She's talking bout whose car were they ridin in and why didn't we move out of South Central and why were they out so late. No. No! Ask her why she doesn't have to move outta Los Feliz or Studio City or wherever she lives. Ask her how come we always have to move.

Johnny. They sent you? No. Uh-uh.

If you came because of the old days you can sit down. If you came because you're a cop, you can go.

No. I don't want to hear it.

Are you a friend first or a cop first?

You can't be both. Not right now.

Yea, I see you not in uniform. I been wearing the same clothes for days because I can move around the hospital. Larette brought me my other uniform.

You all were Free Riders and we were the Angels. Nurses supposed to be angels. But shit, Johnny. Not now.

You know Miller hates us. He hated us back at the party all those years ago. I don't want to hear it. If you want to sit here, shut up and just sit.

He can hear us.

I know Tenerife loved seeing you on your CHP bike.

Close the door.

Larette. Remember the party at Anza Crossing, by the river? I was the only one already engaged. You all were just falling in love back then.

I remember you and me wore dresses. Those halter dresses.

Remember that old white dude rock song Johnny and Grief loved? Where they took their name? Free Ride. The mountain is high, the valley is low, and you're confused on which way to go, so come on girl. Something like that. Give me your hand, and we'll ride into the promised land.

Like the Bible but with all those guitars.

Damaris is from the Bible. It's a woman's name but his mama didn't think of it like that. She thought it was beautiful.

Remember that last tournament, you and Matelasse brought your boys? I remember the roster from some Orange County team. All Joshua and Jeremiah and Jonah. From the Bible. And a kid named Dresden.

I was in the bathroom and these two moms came in, I don't

know how they didn't see my feet in the stall but they were pissed because we had just beat them in the final game, whupped on them, and this mom said, "Oh, my, god, all those ghetto names on that team. What are those women thinking?"

I came out the stall and she looked away. Like they do. Had her mom jeans on and her team jersey. I had come straight from church, remember, Larette? She saw my dress and heels, like I was headed out to the club.

I washed my hands and I said to her, "Damaris is in the Bible. Dante is from *The Inferno*. But Dresden is a place we bombed the hell out of in Germany. What are *you* thinking?"

I didn't say anything about my son.

I wouldn't tell her Tenerife is a city in the Canary Islands. I saw a picture of it when I was ten, and I imagined I was going there. Tavares loved the way it sounded next to his own name. My baby baller, he used to say when I was holding Tenerife after he was born. Look at them little-ass feet.

Remember we went to Wingstop? I treated them to Wingstop cause they won. I cracked up listening to them. I fed six ballers and your boy Dante that night. Larette, them boys ate fifty-two wings. I had a Coke.

Who do you write for? ESPN? They were riding in Santa Claus's Navigator. My son didn't have a car. NCAA says nobody can give him anything except me, and I couldn't pay for a car.

You wanted me to say that to you? You feel better now?

He had made up his mind to sign with Arizona. I was scared because it was so white.

You didn't ask me about Tide and Clorox and how many nights I sat up by that damn dryer waiting on the last socks?

You never had kids? How old are you? Thirty-six?

Oh. Not yet. Yeah. You got it all planned out.

I'm thirty-eight. My child is in a coma. Matelasse. Can you get the door for him?

✳

COMMENTS (964)

> **DuckHunt22@aol.com:** I don't care what everyone else says. It was a good shoot. Look at the pics. Banger braids and a red hat.

✳

I know it's just these few men and they might not even live in California, they just sit there and type things into their computers. But they hate us, Matelasse.

Good shoot? Like my child is an antelope?

The braids.

Today I saw what she wrote. The first reporter. Quiet but articulate, according to the college coaches recruiting him. Hesitant to shoot sometimes. But a team player.

She listed his grades. He always had grades. He just didn't tell people because he said it was none of their business. He had a 3.69. He thought that was funny.

She wrote articulate. And I kept thinking there's another part always goes before that.

Clean-cut.

Banger braids and a red hat.

I redid his braids every Sunday. He did a summer camp with

Kawhi Leonard in seventh grade, and he loved Kawhi. Kawhi is from here.

I remember asking a white mom when we played a tournament up in Ventura. Her boy had blond hair and brown hair stuck up like porcupine spikes, but shiny as metal. I wanted to touch it. She told me she used wax, but by the time he was ten, her son could do it himself. His name was Dakota. I remember.

The coaches, white men and brothers—with them bald heads, they wax their heads.

You braid their hair? Joachim and Antonio? Don't cry, Matelasse. They got all that hair like Reynaldo. You gonna be scared, too.

Nobody can braid their own hair. Every Sunday I sat him down and we watched whatever game was on—football, basketball, even tennis—and I redid his braids after he washed his hair. Whatever pattern he wanted. This summer the ends hung down just to the bones on top of his shoulders.

On Saturday morning I hotcombed my hair. On Sunday afternoon I did Tenerife's. I always felt lucky—I had him for three hours, no matter what, sitting on the floor right in front of me. He couldn't move. I had him. I didn't let those girls do it—they were always telling him they wanted to braid his hair, to get him and Damaris and Deontre come over so they could get a baller.

Larette. How long you been here?

I know. I took three of them.

They help me sleep. I can't sleep. I keep seeing him.

Remember? We told him since he was twelve. I was always at work. Shit. I could never drive them. Three's a gang. Don't matter if it's your cousins or your teammates. Three's a gang. To them. Take two cars. Get a ride with somebody's mama.

But never go four. Never.

I even had Tavares call him from New Orleans. He said, Same way down there, Pops? Tavares told him, No, New Orleans got its own crazy, but I came up in LA. Stop jokin around, he said. I ain't playin. Never go three or four in one car. Wait for your coach.

Tavares came to watch him last year. He came for two weeks of Christmas tournaments. UCLA and USC looking at Tenerife. But he wanted Arizona. When Tavares said, "Boy, I woulda killed to go to UCLA," Tenerife said, "Then you shoulda played better. You shoulda took your own advice."

Larette. Don't tell me don't cry. Three of em in the car. His braids.

All my fault.

✳

COMMENTS (1024)

He was there to entertain you. Even if he played the piano or he was a doctor you all would say You don't play ball with all that height? You're probably a natural! That's a shame. That's what you would say. I know you think I shouldn't be articulate enough to type back to you. But I type all night at Neonatal. I type names. I have to spell the names right. The names of all your babies. Blood pressures and heart rates and jaundice counts and APGAR. He was in the gym for the past ten years of my life. He did his homework in the gym. You want me to say he came home and went out to the driveway to shoot hoops until after midnight or what-ever but that is for entertainment. For your story. He didn't. He was in love. He texted some girl half the night. I never

met her. She lived in Arizona. He met her when he got recruited. I think he was going to Arizona because he was in
love. With a girl named Kelli. He was wearing a red Arizona hat from their coach. He was on TV two times. When
they played for CIF state semifinals. You all yelled and hollered at him Shoot Shoot Shoot the damn ball! In a bar or
a restaurant because I have seen him on the TV there. The
coaches were yelling and his father probably yelled when
he watched the DVD. You yell at him like you know him.
Like he owes you because you have money on the game. Or
just because you can see he should shoot. You say SHOOT
SHOOT SHOOT. That kills me.

*

Larette. If you saw him.

If you saw him. The ones at work, I can hold them in my hand.
But his feet off the end of the bed. All the IVs. It's been twelve days.

That's why I called you. You must be at work. I don't want to
tell you like this but the neurologist and the attending came in just
now. His. His. His brain is dead. They asked if I would consent to
the DNR and unhook the machines. Me and Tavares have to sign.
I didn't call him yet. I can't.

You have to tell Tavares. He has to unhook the machines. I can't
do it. I know other mothers are stronger. I can't.

Even the neurologist was crying. He said Tenerife's heart is so
good. So strong.

I can't. They asked me about organ donation and I can't.

Call Tavares and tell him to come to the hospital.

* * *

Tavares. I'm writing this on a prescription pad. Go to my house. Take all the letters from all the universities. He had 37 letters. In a box on his bed. And his team jerseys. The T-shirts from Arizona and the other schools. I folded them. You better wear them sometimes. If I see you don't wear them, I will haunt your ass.

You have to do it. The DNR. Be right here when he goes. I can't. I want to be waiting for him.

Matelasse and Larette. You are my sisters. I'm writing this here in his room but I will be in my car. You know where I park.

My Aunt Opal down in Houma told me one time after my mama died she was the last branch on the tree cause we had left for LA. Tenerife was my only branch.

You know how easy it was for me to get what I needed from the nursing station. I just took one capsule from each bottle until I had enough. Nobody to blame.

He never opened his eyes. He never got to see me again. He was calling me. I know it. I just want to be with my son. He's the only one to make me laugh like he did. I know you two are coming all the way to LA with chicken because that's how you do. I know you drove from San Bernardino, two hours on a Wednesday night. I'm sorry. But we see them die in here and they're so small. If you saw him. My baby. His feet.

PART II

RIBS, MUSCLE, BONE

I was eight when my father brought home the long piece of butcher paper. I sat on the kitchen floor with my crayons. He laid out the paper, put a mixing bowl on one end and a soup pot on the other end, and measured the piece with his magic metal tape. *Ten feet!* he said. Then he held out the tape to me and I touched the button and the metal slithered back inside, like a snake's tongue returning to his mouth. The year before, there had been a rattlesnake in the yard behind the metal shed where my father kept his tools—he cut off the head with a machete attached to a hoe. The thing he used to get avocados off the tree. He taught me to catch the avocados in a wash basket lined with a blanket. *Fuertes*, he always said. *Better than Hass any day.* Long and smooth skinned, like big green teardrops on the dusty tree.

That night my mother stood in the doorway between the kitchen and the hallway. My father was leaving for work, like he always did. The sun had gone down. It was summer, and he left when the night sky was purple. *Ten feet. All yours. Your pictures, whatever you draw, that's gonna be ten feet of art. No one else can draw a single damn thing on there. Not even one flower.* Then he left for work at Stater Bros. Market. He turned around like every night, one hand on the doorknob, and said to my mother, "What do you want me to bring home, Trish?" and my mother said, "Stop calling me Trish. I told you I'm going with Patricia now."

"What do you want, Patricia?" my father said, grinning.

My mother said, "Nothing. I never want another piece of meat in my life. Never. Not a roast or steak or even one stupid rib. I want salad and dessert three times a day, okay?"

I remember that night. After his truck went down the driveway, and my mother went into their bedroom, I laid down on the butcher paper. I drew pies with the cuts in them like feathers. Inside the slits you could see purple for boysenberry, red for cherry, but I had no gold for apple. I drew an ice cream sundae with a cherry on top, but the red crayon was dull. Not shiny. *Maraschino*, my father always said. *That's from Dalmatia, same place where the fire dogs first come from.* My mother's purse was on the table. I found red nail polish. The perfect cherry. For pistachio ice cream, the best green was the one eye shadow in the little black pot, and for the strawberry there was blush in the compact with the mirror. I remember that I lay on my back when I was done, looking in the little mirror. Our bathroom mirror was little, so high up I never got close enough to see my face.

Maybe the compact was the first time I saw my own eyes. Brown with spokes of black inside like wagon wheels. My mother's eyes were blue with specks of yellow like cornflakes. Then she came out of her bedroom, wearing her robe. I remember that she bit her lips so hard they disappeared into her mouth, and then she shook her head. She said, "Ivy. You had to use the Lancôme eye shadow. The best I had. Not the Cover Girl."

"It's a triple scoop. Like at Dairy Queen." I know I rolled the compact across the wooden floor, and it stopped like a wheel at the wall.

"But I can't eat any of this." My mother put everything back into her purse, stooped to get the compact from the floor, and zipped the purse shut. She wiped her eyes. Then I knew she'd been crying in their room. I froze on my back, imagining I was a fig beetle stranded on the sidewalk, waiting to see how angry my mother was. She never hit me—she only broke things she hated, like my father's weird beer mugs from old bars. Once she even went out to stick a knife in the tires of his motorcycle because he'd been gone all weekend for a ride with his friends.

I waited and my mother didn't move. I imagined my belly iridescent and green under my T-shirt. I still have the T-shirt I wore that night. Pioneer Pirates. From second grade. The principal said Pirates were too violent. So now it was Pioneer Panthers. My father said, *Well, that's stupid, because Pioneers killed everything they didn't like. And Panthers? That's not violent? Jesus, they're idiots. You better keep that shirt. I was a Pioneer Pirate at that school. Jesus.*

My mother said, *Yeah. Five-mile radius in Rialto. For your whole life. And stop taking Jesus name in vain. Jesus would tell you to take better care of your family. There's nothing wrong with money.*

I thought she meant she didn't want Jesus in my father's veins. I looked at his arms—the veins were under his skin and ran up from his wrists like brown leather cords. My mother's veins were little green rivers beside her eyes. Two on each side.

That night, my mother did what she always did then, when she was tired of me and my father. She turned on the TV. My mother

TiVo'd all the services from Crystal Cathedral. My father knew she was obsessed with the Crystal Cathedral, but he didn't know that for the last four Sundays, when he worked a double shift because Sunday was when everyone bought their meat, my mother had been taking me all the way to Garden Grove, to the Crystal Cathedral. Then we went to lunch at a fancy restaurant named Benihana, with Carter Pierce.

My mother started to sing along with the choir on TV, under her breath. The forks clinked in the old cast-iron sink. It sounded like hail. Had hail once hit the roof at Crystal Cathedral—a gray day? A softer tapping. The church was all glass. We had been there four times. Three sunny Sundays. One cloudy Sunday where water or ice tapped at the glass.

I was ten when my father told me he thought my mother would leave. He waited until she was gone to the mall. She had quit being a nurse years ago. She got a job at the Clinique counter, at Nordstrom in Fashion Island. In Newport Beach. She drove an hour and a half to get there, from Rialto. Then she started making extra money doing makeup for weddings at the beach.

Our house was small. Two bedrooms, kitchen, and dining room. The little archway into the living room at the front. There were four tall narrow windows that looked out at the eucalyptus trees and the long dirt driveway. My father's great-grandfather built the house in 1859. Those numbers were scratched into the big wood beam over the front porch. My father said his great-grandfather used to sit every night facing the windows so he could see if robbers came up on horses. The Old Cucamonga Road was near the end of our driveway. Now it was Old Route 66.

It was September. We were sitting on the floor playing Chinese checkers. It had been 105 for three days in a row. My father said, "July and August, it's okay to be hot. But by September, the earth is tired, man. No dew. Everything feels worse. Everyone's grumpy. You gotta give your mom a break."

"She has plenty of breaks." I'd been to Fashion Island. It was huge. The week before, my mother had taken me to work with her, because I had a fever. I sat on all the benches near Nordstrom, and the air was freezing, smelling of coffee, chocolate, perfume, and, somehow, leather from the shoes. Cowhide. Alligator. Crocodile. My mother hated meat but she loved skin. I wanted to sleep so bad. My mother had two breaks, and she bought me tea from the fancy bakery, but I hated the mall.

Three shadows darted on the wooden floor beside the metal checkerboard. Lizards. I had never seen them climb the window screens. They hung upside down. I went close but they didn't move. I saw the fringe of their toes. Their blue throats. Their black and cream checked sides like my mother's new coat. She called it houndstooth. I couldn't figure out why that would work, since dogs' teeth were pointy.

My dad said, "You paid that much for a coat, in September? Wool, Trish? Where the hell are you gonna wear that, when it's so hot?" and my mother just smiled.

The lizard undersides were creamy pale, shiny as concealer. "I guess they can feel the AC on their bellies," my father said now. "First time I ever seen that, and you know I been here all my thirty-one years. Used to be nothing out here but citrus and chickens. Now all the new houses and sidewalks and streets make it hotter. Look at those dudes!"

Western lizards, they were called. They navigated the screens all afternoon, and finally they ran down the door frame one last time and disappeared. My father said, "Ivy. It looks to me like she's going to move to Newport Beach. She's got a place to wear that coat. Cold and foggy at the beach. But it's not you she's leaving, okay? It's me." He turned on the Dodger game and went into the kitchen. He got out a package of meat. He'd go outside and grill tri-tip. His favorite. He loved it cold for two days after that, sliced it pink and sprinkled with salt and cracked pepper.

"You sound like a bad TV show," I said. I imitated what people always said on shows—*It's not you, it's me.* I got out my homework. I wasn't going to cry. Not in front of him.

"There aren't any good TV shows," he said. "Just sports. We had a good summer. Lotta baseball, right?"

I heard him go out the back door, slap of the screen. He always made sure the spring-loaded arm shut it fast to keep out flies. I went to the kitchen window and watched my dad. I was sad for me, because I knew my mother would never lie on the floor with me again, never play checkers or let me eat ice cream at midnight. I wished she wasn't so disappointed in how I looked. She said I thought I was a boy, because we were surrounded by guys, and she'd had it. "There's a big difference between boys, guys, and men," she said to me.

That summer, I'd played baseball every week in the park and rec league with Dante Embers and Manny Delgado. Our fathers were best friends before we were all born. I watched my father put orange wood chips into his smaller grill—I was the only girl. All his friends had boys, except Johnny Frías, who was a cop and never got married.

The big smoker and grill stood at the edge of the cement patio. My father and his friends had built a huge ramada when I was very small—I remember the hammering and laughing and all the beer. Then all of us kids—Dante, Manny, a kid named Tenerife who lived in LA, two little boys Joachim and Antonio—we went all around the place picking up palm fronds knocked off the trees by the big winds. The men told us to pile them up, and then they layered the fronds all along the roof of the ramada. We had shade for two years, until the rain and heat made the fronds fall apart. When they started to shed and drop gray strings and particles of bark onto the tables, my father climbed up and took them off. Then we collected new fronds, because the Santa Ana winds blew them down every year.

My mother hated the ramada. She said it was full of insects and dirt. My father always laughed and said a tarp would hold way more water and bugs. My mother always said a tarp was the last thing she had in mind. She wanted a whole new house. A garden with a big marble gazebo and fountain, like in her *Coast* magazines. Somewhere not in Rialto.

She was leaving my father for Carter Pierce. A man who wore suits and a gold watch and always had a cloth in his Mercedes to brush the dust off his fancy Italian shoes.

She hated everything that summer. The backyard full after our baseball games, when my father and Grief and Manny Sr. laid out the meat and tortillas and grilled corn on the cob, and then they turned on the TV my father kept outside, to watch the Dodgers. Manny Sr. would always shout, "Bobby's right—meat and Modelo make Wednesday work! Órale pues, Frías, you gotta leave first, so you can't say shit about us driving, homes." Johnny Frías would shake his head and roll his eyes. He looked different from the dads—he was the most tanned, dark brown, and his face was like a mask sometimes when he watched us playing ball. No smile wrinkles on his cheeks, only pale lines on his temples from his CHP sunglasses.

My mother would come in late because it took so long to drive from Fashion Island, and I would be playing pickle with the boys in the back. We had two acres of orange and lemon trees, avocados, what used to be a corral for horses, and a windmill. Tenerife and his mom came sometimes from LA—he was eleven, and he was playing basketball. He was really tall, but he'd play baseball with us. "I can always see where you live cause of the windmill," he told me. "It looks crazy sticking up in the air like that. Like some old western."

His mother's name was Merry, and she'd holler that he couldn't play pickle, or he'd hurt his knee and miss games. My mother liked Merry—her hair and makeup were always perfect, and she wore dresses and beautiful leather sandals. "Cause I'm still a nurse, girl, and I gotta wear that uniform every day, so when it's my day off, I go like Beyoncé."

But most nights it was just the fathers and sons, and a lot of noise, and my mother would close the bedroom door.

"I trust Carter, he's leased a beautiful place for us and I haven't even seen it," she said on the phone the next night to her friend from work. My dad had left for Stater Bros. "The driveway here is dirt—need I say more? It's not even Spanish Colonial, it's early San Bernardino pioneer prison."

My father was wrong. She was leaving us and the house. We were like furniture. From Kmart.

Her friend Denise worked the MAC counter. I waited until my mother hung up. I said, "We live in Rialto. San Bernardino is two blocks east." My father said that all the time.

My mother looked at me. I was doing my homework in the living room. The front windows were full of sunset, because the house faced southwest. The front square of grass was green, like a blanket laid out just to the porch. My mother's face was still made up from work. Her eye shadow was gold and deep bronze, and it made the specks floating in her blue eyes look like real gold flake in a painting. When you were really close, you could see the lip liner making her mouth perfect. She said, "I know, Ivy. He tells everyone that. He told me that when I first met him. I was with Larette and Merry in nursing school, but I had already decided I wasn't going to wipe up blood all day, and then here's your dad, a butcher." I could see her eyes getting shiny with tears. "We laughed for a week about that."

My mother sat on the couch beside me and put her hands on top of her head. Right hand and then left, like she was trying to cover a hole. That was what she did so she never cried. Even when I got a huge cut on my leg in the orange grove and we could see the bone, and she said, "The scar!!!" she put her hands like that, so she wouldn't wreck her face. Because the good makeup was so expensive.

"Baseline Avenue. The first street that ran from San Bernardino all the way to LA. I know," she said. "Here we are at the heart of history. Ivy, history is dusty and old, and some people care and some people don't. I love you but I can't live here anymore. It's too hot, and I like new things. You like new things. I just brought you five new outfits for fifth grade, right? No more Pioneer T-shirts. It took me forever to pick out those clothes on sale. And next week I'm taking you to a salon to get an actual haircut."

I waited until she was done. Then I said, "What's a lease?"

My mother smiled and shook her head. "It's an agreement, for a year. You're coming to see the new house in a few weeks. From our living room window you can see the ocean."

The next night was Monday. My father's night off. She told him she was moving to Newport Beach, and that in October I would spend Saturday and Sundays there. I was in bed, and they were on the porch, so I had left my window open, and it was like they were in the room with me. My mother said, "He doesn't sell pork chops and steaks, Bobby. He sells houses. Giant houses with kitchens with more square footage than this whole place. Pools. Not sheds."

"Then why does he want you? He needs a constant supply of moisturizer?"

"He says I'm more valuable than you'll ever figure out. Because all you know is $6.99 a pound."

"Slick. Very slick." I heard my father open a beer. "And Pierce is good to Ivy? You're not gonna see her for a month?"

"He says the house isn't childproof yet and we have to get it ready for her."

"Childproof! She's ten! I mean, shit, I don't want her there anyway. I want her here. But what the hell does he have to childproof? She can handle a machete and a baseball bat. She doesn't need a baby gate on the stairs."

My mother said, "He has thousands of dollars' worth of art. Vases and statues."

"She's gonna tackle a fucking statue?"

"You're cursing. That's why you can't handle church."

"Crystal Cathedral isn't church. It's something else. Look at how you got what you wanted."

"Church is about what you want—for your soul and your life and your—"

That was the first time I heard my father's voice go low and silver. Like a knife. "Fucking shut up. Sing that fucking song somewhere else."

She did. She took one suitcase. That was it. I heard the wheels clacking on the wooden floor. She left me a card with roses and angels. She had written: *Ivy, my love, I can't wait to see you on Saturday and Sunday. Those will be our special days. I am putting together your new bedroom in our new house. I found a beautiful comforter set at Macy's. Love, Mom.*

When I was twelve and had to get my first bras, my father took me to Target, pointed to the Women's sign, and told me to ask a woman for help. He went to the housewares section so he could make fun of the knives.

I couldn't find a salesperson. There was only a young guy in that section, putting together a clothes rack. I panicked and grabbed five bras all in different sizes and went to the fitting room and an older woman looked bored and handed me a plastic tag for the door—five items. That lady was wearing a Target shirt and her chest was like a bookshelf halfway down to her stomach.

I shut the door and took off my tank top and tried on the bras like my friend Marisol said—hook them in front and then turn the whole thing around and pull it up over your boobs—but everything got twisted so I just picked two of the smallest—32A—and left the rest on the bench and then walked fast out of the dressing room and left the 5 tag on the counter where the woman was gone. My father was wandering around at the edge of Women's like he wasn't a pervert. When we left, I looked at the vases in the Home Decor section and thought it would be funny to buy one for my mother and Carter.

I had been to their house eleven times. Saturday morning to Sunday night. Many weekends they were gone. My mother would call on Thursday night to say they were going out of town for a real estate trip to Texas or Arizona, and she would see me next weekend. But the eleven times I'd slept there, in the white bedroom with the roses and ivy comforter and shams, when I closed my eyes I saw the statues downstairs. The great room, my mother said. White marble floor and black marble shelves in the walls and white figures inside them. Niches. Vases on all the tables.

I didn't tackle the statues or throw baseballs at the vases. We went to lunch. Always. Carter Pierce looked like Pierce Brosnan. Tanned. Hair with comb marks. White teeth. We ate salad with one protein. Salmon or seared tuna.

"That house is only leased, Trish," my father said to her one night when she came to pick me up. "It wasn't hard to have Johnny Frías look him up." Johnny Frías could look people up. "Carter Pierce. Real name Timothy MacDonald. Little Timmy born in Madison County, Iowa. Winterset. Birthplace of John Wayne. In 1969, Trish. He's fuckin forty-three years old. Timmy got his real estate license in 2010. Leased that home in 2018."

But my mother just laughed. She was driving a new car. A Lexus. "Everything is leased. This car is leased, Bobby. Everyone else reinvents themselves and makes a new life. Just not you. Or apparently anybody else from San Bernardino." My mother was now Patricia, in Newport Beach. She wore dresses with geometric patterns, and heels. Her eyebrows were perfect. She wore only Lancôme makeup, and her perfume was Chanel, which smelled to me like shimmering pale green.

All my father said was, "Trish—a Lexus is a boring-ass car. I thought you had some imagination. Or class."

She drove away so fast the dust rose up all the way to the top of the eucalyptus trees. I remember that.

One night my father drank a lot of Tecate, and grilled a lot of tri-tip with Grief. Grief was an animal control officer. He and Dante and Dante's mom Larette lived about a mile away. My father and

Grief were going to be CHP way back when, but they changed their minds. My father got his job at the butcher counter, and Grief bought ribs, steaks, and hot links from my dad every week. Every Easter, my father made Larette a whole roasted rack of lamb, with decorations on the bones, and she would sing to it, because she loved musicals.

They made fun of Carter Pierce. Grief said, "I love these white dudes named Tanner. Hunter. Miller. Wright. Like that makes them sound rich. Those are just trade titles, man. We had this discussion before, Bobby Carter Jr."

My father laughed. "I know. My great-grandpa the carter. On the fucking wagon coming out here to California."

Grief said, "Well, the first Grief sure as shit didn't want to walk across the country behind the Mormon wagons. If California decided to ever talk about when slavery was fine with them." He finished his beer. "San Bernardino was happy to have Grief Embers and Biddy Mason raise cattle and plant wheat out here. Not free."

I sat on the porch steps watching them. My father with his hands big as frying pans from cutting all those bones and cartilage and tree branches. His black hair feathery around his ears. The Carter who drove the wagon met a woman named María Juana when she sold him pine needle baskets. She was a Serrano woman from the San Bernardino mountains. They got married. Grief's grandfather married a Spanish-Apache woman named Apollonia, from Agua Mansa. Grief with his curly hair in a long braid down his back, and his mustache black and straight around his mouth, and I always wondered how hair could be different coming from the same skull.

I had been to Crystal Cathedral the week before, and I saw all the bald heads in the rows. Almost all white. Men and boys—you could see their lives and their genes and their ages in their heads. Big folds of skull skin at the back on some guys. Their heads scarred from getting hit or even from bug bites. We were in church forever.

I knew I would never leave my father. Even if someday my mother and Carter asked me to, I would never move to Newport Beach. I had Mexican Coke in a bottle, the good stuff, and two tacos on my lap. My dad's salsa. His avocados from our tree. My father and his friend were laughing. My father said, "I don't give a shit what fucking computers they invent or what houses they build. Everybody has to eat meat and the only way to get a steak is for me to cut up a fucking cow and wrap the pieces in butcher paper. Every damn day. I see their eyes when I'm wrapping up that big brisket or roast and they think I'm a fucking god. This one lady cried first time she came in. She was from Sudan. Like her husband was one of those Lost Boys. She watched me put this rack of lamb together and she started crying."

He looked over at me. I knew staying wouldn't make my life easier. He'd be scared of the Women's section his whole life. People always say a butcher will cut off a finger. But when I was seventeen, he taught me to drive, and I drove his truck along the old sandy roads where the vineyards used to be in Cucamonga. I kept drifting off the edge of the shoulder. He was still so nervous by the time he got to work, he cut off part of the soft edge of his left hand, below the little finger. A wedge of palm. It took forever to heal. And then the scar pulled his fingers into a claw.

A few months later, we went to Los Angeles for the memorial service for Tenerife and his mom, Merry. The caskets were beside each other. Tenerife was only nine months older than me, but he was so tall. His hair was in braids that fell away from his face onto the blue satin pillow. Merry looked beautiful, like a small Beyoncé, with her hair loose. She always said she had to wear it in a bun when she was at work, so she let it be free when she wasn't a nurse. I remembered that.

My mother didn't come to the church. She and Carter were in Houston all week, for a national real estate convention. She said they couldn't cancel.

All the other mothers were there—Dante's mom Larette, Manny's mom Lena, Mrs. Rodrigue and her boys Joachim and Antonio. Johnny Frías wasn't there. Tenerife had been shot by a cop.

Tenerife's dad was named Tavares, and my dad used to hang out with him way back in the day. So my dad hosted a memorial barbecue after the funeral, for all of us. Tavares was tall, with a full beard, and he was wearing Tenerife's favorite Kawhi Leonard jersey. It was the last week of August. Hot but the light was gold in the backyard, coming through the palm fronds on the ramada like millions of silver needles on our feet. My father and Manny Delgado had the smoker going, ribs and burgers, hot links and cut-up chicken, and when Tenerife's dad saw the chicken he started crying, because he said Tenerife ate chicken every day of his life. He cried so hard, telling us how Merry used to count the chicken wings and thighs from one week of Tenerife eating and she wrote it on the refrigerator: 23. LeBron's number. Then Larette and Matelasse were crying.

The whole backyard was full of people. I kept bringing out more paper plates, getting rid of the empty bottles, checking the ice chests. When we were all little kids, my father bought us soda in bottles so we could click necks, like grown-ups with their beer, but we had Fanta or Coke. He told us, "You gotta greet your friends with a bottle, man. Only way to be a human."

I went into the kitchen for more napkins, and Matelasse and

Larette came out of the bathroom. They had cried off their makeup, and they had put more on, but their eyes were red. I thought of my mother, and then Larette said, "Oh, look at you with all those dishes, Ivy, you're the woman of the house." She hugged me very hard. She smelled like cherry Jergens. She had changed from her nursing scrubs, because she came straight from the hospital.

When she let go, I went over to the sink and washed out one of the bowls that had tortilla chips. Some salsa had gotten spilled inside. I was going to leave for college in two weeks. But only to San Diego—to study engineering. Ninety miles away—I could be home in two hours if my father needed me.

I didn't want to be a woman who got left, or a mother whose son died. Merry's face had been perfect in her casket, because she didn't die of cancer or something long and terrible. She took her own life. I kept seeing her like that. Her hands crossed over her heart. That's how I slept, every night. I always had.

When I went back outside, there was a super handsome guy that looked like an actor, with dreads tied back in a leather cord, wooden bead necklaces, and a long white shirt. Joachim and Antonio ran over and grabbed his waist. It had to be their dad. And behind him was Johnny Frías. Johnny wasn't in his cop uniform; he was wearing jeans and a Dodgers jersey, but Tenerife's dad knew who he was.

"Get out of here," Tavares yelled. "What the fuck are you doing? You know that sergeant, right? Miller? He's the one got my son shot! I saw the video a thousand times, I saw his face and he wanted them dead!"

"Tavares," Johnny Frías said. "I loved Merry and your son from the first day I met them way back at the river. I just wanted to—"

But Tavares stood up and dropped his plate on the dirt. He shouted, "Grief, tell this man to take his ass away. He ain't got a wife or a kid so he don't know shit!"

Johnny Frías held up his hands and said, "I'm sorry, Tavares, and—"

Then Tavares started crying like I never saw someone cry before. His whole face twisted and his mouth open to breathe, and he was shouting, "No! I had to do it, man! I had to tell them to turn off the fuckin machines! Poor Merry couldn't do it and shit—"

He put his hands inside his hair, like he was trying to keep his brain from falling out. I couldn't move, no one moved. He sobbed, "Nothin worse in the whole gotdamn world than tellin a fuckin stranger to turn off the machine and you hold your son till he stop breathin." He took out his phone from his pocket, and yelled, "For a fuckin cell phone!" He threw it into the eucalyptus trees. And then he took five steps real fast and punched Johnny Frías in the face. His right hand and then his left.

My father ran over there, dropped his tongs in the dirt, and got between them. He was standing there, one hand on each guy's chest, and the part of his palm he lost to the knife, because of me, made that hand smaller when he pushed Johnny Frías back. My father said, "Not yet, man, not yet." My father's face was covered with sweat, and it looked like smoke was rising off his hair, and he looked up at the palm fronds to shake the salt water out of his eyes without letting go of their shirts.

My father helped me move to San Diego, with his old truck. My dorm room—he could barely look at the walls. A few days later, he had a heart attack in the freezer at the store, on a Sunday morning. It was September, the day before Labor Day, so I could imagine him joking that he was working harder than ever cutting up meat for people to celebrate they had a day off. He'd called me the day before, said it had been 108, 107, 110 degrees for six days. My father couldn't text. His fingers and hands couldn't work the phone screen.

It was 111 degrees that Sunday. He'd gone from the hot truck cab to the icy cold of the butcher area, put on his sweatshirt with the hood up, then his long butcher coat, and fell on the cement floor.

Mrs. Trujillo saw him go down. She was waiting for him to cut beef for fajitas. She hollered at the other women lined up at the counter, and busted into the swinging door and got down on her knees in her church dress to give my father CPR. She's seventy-two. Mrs. DeFrance is eighty-four, and she did chest compressions until the EMT guys came. Mrs. DeFrance bought a pot roast every Sunday, no matter how hot it was, because that was her husband's favorite meal, and even though she buried him five years ago, she made it with carrots and potatoes and celery, for him.

Larette met me at the hospital. She had been beside my father the whole time, in ICU. He was going to have bypass surgery. "All four ventricles blocked. Cholesterol, Ivy," she said to me. "All that meat." But she was smiling. "He's gonna be okay. But he's gonna have to eat some damn salad." Then she whispered to me, "This year was too much, Ivy. People die of broken hearts. It's an actual medical condition. Look at Merry. But not this time. Not with your dad. We're not gonna let that happen."

It had taken me three hours to drive home. The whole waiting room was full of women—Mrs. Espinoza still wearing her lace mantilla from church, Mrs. Trujillo with blood from the butcher floor on the knees of her thick support hose, Mrs. DeFrance with her silver hair and glasses and pink cheeks, Magdalena Delgado. My friend from elementary school, Rafaela Venegas, who worked at the market now with my father. And ladies I didn't even know, who talked to my father every week at the meat counter. These were the women who loved him, after my mother left us.

THE LYRIDS,
THE ETA AQUARIIDS,
THE PERSEIDS

ROUTE 66 AND THE CAJON PASS

APRIL 22, 2020: THE LYRIDS

Dante was supposed to keep a quarantine journal. Manny and Montrell had texted him *Fuck That! A diary is for girls!!* Dante laughed, but he still tried to write in the extra notebook his mother had brought from Rite Aid when school stopped back in March.

He was alone for at least four hours a day now, mostly at night, since his mother had to stay in an RV somebody had donated for nurses to live near the hospital because she couldn't come home or she'd bring the virus to him and his father. He imagined it coating her, the people coughing and the respirators that she said pushed clouds of droplets into the air by the beds. The emergency room full of mist carrying the virus they always showed on TV like stupid blue and red rubber toys floating around. There were five trailers now parked on a dead-end street. His mother's had a Dodgers flag in the window. He and his father had left a bag with clean clothes for her, at the curb.

No one touched her old Honda Accord. She called it the plague wagon. Dante could only ride in his father's truck—the '59 Apache Manny Delgado's dad had started restoring last year. Mr. Delgado put in a new engine, but the truck was still painted with black primer.

The animals had started taking over the earth all around San Bernardino, Rialto, and Fontana. Dante's father worked extra shifts, too, trying to catch raccoons that had colonized empty stores, possums that had twelve babies inside someone's locked-up beauty salon. A huge male bobcat came up from the Santa Ana River and walked right down Riverside Avenue in Colton, into a warehouse where the workers freaked out and called Animal Control. His dad had shot the bobcat with a tranquilizer gun, where it was hiding in a big pile of empty boxes. He took the bobcat up to Lytle Creek and left it there in a canyon, waiting in the county truck until he could see the cat wake up and walk into the brush. "Like a drunk dude trying to maintain his dignity," his father said. "You know. Kinda slantwise. But proud."

He showed Dante a picture on his phone—the most beautiful animal Dante had ever seen. Long legs and faint spots and soft triangle ears standing straight up, a tuft of black hair at the top. Dante's mom came home that night, after she showered and disinfected at the RV. She said to his father, "Grief! You caught that? Look at those ears—like he put mascara on the edge of the fur to make himself even prettier."

His mother cooked a huge pot of rice and beans and made a whole roasted chicken in the oven. She sat at the table and ate with them. She had one day off. She was a little like her old self. She got out her coupon box and took out the expired ones. She looked at his father and said, "I can see that bobcat walking straight down Route 66. Right?"

His father looked surprised. She'd been crying for an hour before dinner, in their bedroom. He said, "Right past the Wigwam Motel."

One of the first songs she'd ever taught Dante, something she made his father sing all the time when Dante was little: *Get your kicks on Route 66 . . . Flagstaff, Arizona, don't forget Winona, Kingman, Barstow, San Bern-ar-di-no . . .*

Dante looked at her swollen eyes. It felt like she'd been gone for a year, and crying for that long. Last summer, she'd been in LA all the time, staying with Tenerife's mom after he got shot. Tenerife's mom died, just before he did. Dante's mother had stayed in bed for a week after that. She wouldn't move.

Then in fall, his dad's best friend Bobby Carter had a heart attack, so she stayed in ICU at St. Bernardine's with him, because he didn't have a wife. Now she was gone all the time because of the virus. Every time she left, Dante thought she wouldn't come back.

"I know it's a hazard of the job, everyone's been dying around me for years, but this—this shit is too much," she said. It looked like she had pinkeye. She hated pinkeye.

The year 2020 sucked. Dante hadn't been to school for weeks. He couldn't even go to Manny's to play baseball in their yard. The baseball diamond was closed, the park was closed, everything had yellow police tape around it. Every day, Dante finished his homework in two hours. He talked to Manny on the phone. No eighth-grade graduation. No stupid school dance. No Little League.

Nothing to do but walk around the empty road. Minerva Court was a dead end. Dante's house was on the last hundred yards of dirt where the land opened up to scrub and the arroyo along the 215 freeway, where it then headed up the Cajon Pass and went through the San Bernardino Mountains to Barstow, and on to Las

Vegas. The only other houses were the two small wooden bungalows where Mrs. Baptiste and Mrs. Jimerson used to live. They were sisters, eighty-five and eighty-seven, and they had both died in March. Coronavirus. Now the windows were boarded up, because they had no family who wanted to live in the dusty little houses so far out in the fields, where Lily John had built the first house. She was his father's great-grandmother, who came out to San Bernardino with the Mormons in their wagons. Not because she wanted to. She was a slave, in 1851, and they walked thousands of miles behind the wagons. When she was free, she built this house. Once, his father said, she shot a horse thief. A white man. She buried him under the windmill.

Dante always thought his father was joking. But maybe not.

"We're the last ones on Minerva Court," his father said. "At least it's not hard to quarantine. But hell, I wish we could go to Bobby's for barbecue."

The closest house was half a mile west, Uncle Perry's. Dante used to have to walk to Uncle Perry's for a ride to school, if his parents worked overtime. Dante complained once, and his father said, "Lily John walked 1,989 miles. I measured it on Google maps. That was a hella walk, so stop belly achin. What my grampa used to say? Quit your belly achin."

Dante used to wonder, Was the belly aching because the person was hungry, or sick?

On April 1, Dante had made the meteor schedule. For the last three years, he'd tried to watch the Perseids and the Leonids, because his father had told him a story about his grandfather, Grief John Embers, watching the stars at night. He loved the Perseids in August, and it was dark enough out here in the old Mormon land to see every meteor streaking across the sky. And back in 1966, his father said, Grief John had seen the Leonids, a historic meteor shower that sent thousands of shooting stars so bright the whole night lit up. Grief John had been out here in the yard, the horses stamping their feet in the corral, nervous at the silver sky, his father said. Nothing like it before.

When they started distance learning, his favorite teacher Mr. Matsuno had assigned them one original project for science. He emailed the class: *Choose something you love to observe and journal for three months, since we have no school until fall. It can be an orange tree, a sunflower, a dandelion. It can be butterflies, ants, birds, lizards. It can be your little sister or brother. It can be your dog. Anything that moves or grows, in these hard times.*

Dante had typed the meteor schedule. He emailed it to Mr. Matsuno: *For the last three years, I couldn't see very many meteors in August or November. There was too much smog in August. There was too much city light in November. But now it is reported less smog because of the virus, so the viewing of the Lyrids on April 22 should be optimal.*

Mr. Matsuno had emailed him: *That is a great idea, for a potential astronomer. Anything optimal in 2020 would be welcome. I look forward to seeing your report.*

Tonight was the Lyrids. For the last ten days, Dante had been looking up the predictions on different stargazing websites. No moon, so the meteors would be more visible, more intense. Sometimes the Lyrids were disappointing, people reported for the last few years, but tonight, because the world had stopped, there would be less pollution, less light from cars and trucks. More dark.

The only problem was he had to be outside from about two a.m. to four thirty, for the peak of the shower, and the temperature had shot up to ninety-four degrees so Manny had asked him to come over to swim in his backyard. It was illegal, but they had spent three hours in the pool, staying six feet apart, their masks wet and sticking to their faces like spiderwebs, making sure not to yell so neighbors wouldn't hear them. It was the first time they'd been together in weeks. Manny's mom worked at KFC—she brought a bucket of crispy and all the sides, and they ate after they swam. Then she gave Dante a clean mask, told him to get all the way in the back of their big van, and she brought him home.

His dad set the alarm for one a.m. He woke Dante and they went outside to lie on the blankets in the truck bed, parked in the backyard. The moon really was gone, and the sky was blue-black. Dante had his laptop, but the internet was bad so far from the house, and he couldn't check in on what other stargazers around the world were seeing. So he and his father just lay back and stared up at the sky. It was so quiet, even fewer trucks on the grade from the Cajon Pass. Only the sirens every ten minutes or so, from all around San Bernardino—east and west, threading through the night like lassos. His father had taught him to lasso the hitching post in front of the house, way back when he was six, and Dante kept seeing the rope fly again and again in his mind. Corona cases.

He woke up when his father nudged him and said, "Son. The sun. Comin up now."

Dante sat up fast. "I missed the whole thing?"

His father said, "You were out, man. Smelled like chlorine and all. I poked you about twenty times and all you said was No No No. That's how it is when you ain't swam for a while."

The sky wasn't blue but a kind of white, which meant it would be hot again—the sun was just a silver blur at the edge of Mt. San Gorgonio. Dante thought he might cry. He had nothing to report.

But his father said, "I recorded what I could on my phone. You can take a look. Come on—I gotta get some coffee on."

Dante closed all the curtains in his bedroom and looked at the twenty minutes of video his father had shot. Lucky his dad had a new phone, bought so he could FaceTime with his mom. The screen was black and crisp, and seven meteors shot long trails across the sky, scribbles of white and even one with a tail. Dante looked up hundreds of photos and videos other people had taken, around the world. They said the Lyrids left pink and green at the very end of the tail, if you were lucky enough to catch it.

But he only had one handful of sky. He wouldn't mess up next time.

He wrote his report truthfully, because his father always told him not to lie. He said that this Lyrid shower was the best in years, and that he estimated thirty-two meteors per hour had gone past the earth during the twenty minutes his father had recorded. He wrote about the darkness, but he kept seeing the stupid coronavirus floating everywhere. The ugliest red spherical planet-resembling shit he had to see a hundred times a day on TV.

Mr. Matsuno wrote: *Honesty makes for better science. Research should never exaggerate, imagine, or falsify results. I kept up with the Lyrids last night, too, for the first time. You should borrow some binoculars. They make stargazing better, if you don't have a telescope. It's too bad all the observatories are closed.*

Manny laughed when Dante called him to say what happened. Manny was writing every day about his mother's corn, tomatoes, cucumbers, and squash. "My mom says it's hilarious hearing on the news how all the white people are growing gardens now because of the virus. She says Mexicans been doing that forever so big deal." He measured her plants with his dad's tape measure and counted the blossoms that would be vegetables. "Except pinche tomatoes are fruits. Whatever. My mom said all the rich people are learning to make bread. She said she was making fifty tortillas every morning when she was seven."

Dante said, "I could try to catch some bugs. Or a scorpion or tarantula. But my mom hates those. I remember when I was little and my dad said tarantulas were animals, not insects. I bet Mr. Matsuno would like that."

He could have written pages about the day his father took him up to Lytle Creek and showed him the world. He remembered everything. He was seven. It was November, because the tumbleweeds were blue-green then, big as hippos rising from the earth just down the ravine.

"Right here," his father told Dante, his arm sweeping the horizon of the San Bernardino Mountains, the Cajon Pass, the sandy flats and eucalyptus windbreaks and deep arroyos. "Eucalyptus isn't from here, it's from Australia, and those trees burn like a motherfucker, so you and Manny never mess around with matches, and never even hang out in all that bark when it falls. Sycamore and cottonwood are indigenous. Like your great-great-grandpa. They belong here. See that palm tree? The fat short one? That's indigenous. The really tall ones all along the streets, the ones everybody thinks are true California? Shit, no, those are imported, too."

Then his father said, "Here's the important part, son. I mean it. All this here"—and his father pointed to the cities below—"Fontana, Rialto, San Bernardino, all this, right here you have predators and vermin and scavengers. Your mom doesn't want me scaring you. But that's my job. You got scorpions, tarantulas, black widows, brown recluse spiders, and centipedes. All those will bite or sting you. So watch the woodpile and the fences. You got rattle-snakes, especially out by the windmill. They hung out back there when I was little." He pointed to the arroyo. "You got coyotes, bobcats, feral dogs. You're still little. All those things will try to eat you."

Dante could see the teeth in his leg. He was sure they would go for his leg.

His father said, "But, dude, even raccoons will fight you. They'll kick your ass." He pointed to the east. "Over by Box Springs, there are wild burros. Kick the shit out of you. Bite you with them big burro teeth. When your uncle Perry got the deputy job, he got bit by a damn burro and I had to go help him out."

Then his father had pointed to the freeway, and the edge of San Bernardino. Green city trees and billboards in the distance. "You got two kinds of humans might come up on you. Assholes and knuckleheads. Assholes want to hurt you. Not eat you—just hurt you. Maybe kill you—for no reason, but they will do it. Gun or knife or rock or car, Dante. Wearing the wrong color. Being the wrong color. You gotta watch humans just as hard."

"What about the other ones?"

"Knuckleheads are just stupid. You gotta learn to tell the differ-ence fast."

Dante and Manny had learned fast, how to tell the difference.

May 5 was the Eta Aquariids.

He even practiced on May 1, taking an old cot out of the barn where his father's great-grandmother used to keep horses. He brushed off the dust, set up the cot in the center of the yard, and lay there at one a.m. He wasn't afraid, because his father's bed-room window was open and he could hear the radio playing softly.

Art Laboe and killer oldies. The Stylistics' high voices like angels. The fan droning, the only way his father could sleep now that it was so hot, he said. He couldn't cool off. His mother hadn't been home for six days, because there was a surge in cases.

But on May 2 his father started to cough hard. He'd said earlier that it was the wind, dust blowing down the pass. Dante heard the sound like a file rasping away on wood. His father's lungs. He listened to the constant sirens in the distance. He heard his father's radio playing Al Green. Then he heard a crash.

He ran inside. His father was crawling down the hallway in his Lakers shorts, back shining with sweat, his head down like a horse seeking water. "It's so hot," he whispered, and then his father fell onto his elbows, his head swinging. He crawled another foot, and then he fell onto his side against the wall.

Dante grabbed his phone and called his mother. "Dad's got it! Mom! He just fell down. Mom!" Dante was crying. "You need to come! The ambulance will never find us. That's what you always say—they take forever to get out here."

"I'm coming, baby," she said. "Put a mask on and cover your whole face. Go to your room."

"No!"

Dante wet a towel and put it over his father's back. He sat with his back against the hallway wall, his hoodie tied over his mask. Only his eyes uncovered. Fuck corona if it attacked his eyes. Fuck this fucking shit.

His father's cheek was smashed to the wooden floor, his hair was glittered with sweat, and he whispered, "I'm okay. I'm okay. I'm okay, son. Just give me a minute to catch my breath."

★   ★   ★

Tyrone, his father's friend, was an EMT. He got there in eleven minutes, from St. Bernardine's. "I got him, I got him, Dante, chill, just sit right there on the couch. Sit down. Chill." Tyrone and the other EMT wore white spacesuits, and their voices came like monsters from behind the masks. They lifted up his father and put him on a gurney and rolled him outside. Then Tyrone came running back in and said, "You can't come, little man, you can't. I know your mom's trying to get off shift. You're what—twelve?"

"Thirteen in August."

"Yeah, well, I can't leave you here but we gotta go. Call your friend Manny. From baseball."

Tyrone ran back to the ambulance and the tires crunched over the sand and the siren spooled out again, erasing every other sound. Lassos of red lit up the living room and then were gone. His father's fan and little radio were like insects in the back bedroom, tiny and hidden in the dark.

He slept in a girl's bedroom for five weeks. At Bobby Carter's house. Ivy's old bedroom. She was in college. But on the wall she had some drawings she must have made when she was little. Ten pieces of butcher paper, with pie and candy and cake. They were in wooden frames that looked homemade. One foot square, all around the room.

Dante had to stay inside, with the door closed, for three weeks. Bobby was a master butcher, and he had to go to work every night at seven. People were going crazy for meat. He left a dinner plate covered with foil outside the bedroom door at six p.m. every day. Ribs and potatoes, steak and rice, hamburgers and fries, on a wooden orange crate. He left a little cooler with ice, filled with bottles of Mexican Coke—the good stuff. It was hot as shit inside Bobby's old house, but Dante told his mother on the phone, "We're used to hot as shit, right, Mom? Our house is even older than Bobby's."

"Don't cuss, son," she'd say.

"Whatever. Bobby eats oatmeal every morning cause of his heart. Cause you told him to."

"I'm happy to hear that."

"Mom. I miss Cap'n Crunch. And Honeycomb." He couldn't help the tears. He wouldn't say it. He wouldn't be a baby. So he said, "I miss the fuckin coupon box. For real."

"I know," his mother said, and he could hear she was crying, too. "I know. It's not forever."

It felt longer than forever. Dante slept for hours and hours. The Wi-Fi in the bedroom was shit. Dante watched stuff on his phone. Every day he talked to Manny about three times.

That night, when the ambulance took his father, he called Manny. Manny answered, "Whappen, fool?"

But Mr. Delgado came on the phone and said, "Mijo, you're like my son but I can't bring you here. I can't. Pues, Manny's mom has diabetes, you know, and Manny's got asthma. But we got you. Bobby Carter's comin, okay?"

Half an hour later, a super loud old engine rumbled outside, and someone honked at his father's driveway. Dante got into Bobby's truck with a duffel bag.

Bobby said, "Man, I got new heart valves, so I'm not worried. I already saw heaven and they didn't want me there. Come on, Dante, stick your head out the window and get some air, cause quarantine is a bitch."

★   ★   ★

Every day, his mother FaceTimed from his father's room. Dante held the phone up, both thumbs framing his parents. They both wore masks and shields, so they couldn't say anything, they just sat there looking at him and nodding sometimes.

On May 14, Dante said, "I missed the stars for my school project. No more meteor showers until July. Then school's over. I'll probably get an F."

His mother's eyes huge and dark above her mask; his father weak, his hair in a cap, an oxygen tube taped to his nostrils.

Dante said, "Fuck the stars. Nobody cares."

"Dante," his mother said. He could hear that word, muffled under her mask.

Shame like a splinter in his ribs. He could feel it. He said, "Sorry, Mom. Bobby got me a lizard, in a big jar, with a screen on the top. I'm writing in my journal about that."

His father nodded. Maybe one inch. His eyes were closed. But he said one word. His mother leaned closer. Then she lifted up and he could see from her eyes she was grinning. "He said, *Unfortunate*, baby. That's good!"

Dante nodded back, before his throat could fill up with heat.

His father's favorite word was *unfortunate*. Back when they still had baseball, Dante struck out one night and his father said, "Unfortunate inning, man. Not a single moment of luck."

Manny's mom always brought snacks—KFC popcorn nuggets. She said to Dante's mother, "New eye shadow, no?"

"An unfortunate selection," his father said.

His mother folded her arms and glared at his father. "I had a coupon for Revlon," his mother said. "Magnificent Metallics. Two for 99 cents."

Dante looked at his mother's eyelids. Not gold—kind of dull yellow, like bee pollen.

"Looks like eight days after the fight," his father joked. "Like you got punched in both eyes."

But then he must have remembered Johnny Frías, getting punched by Tenerife's dad after the funeral. Johnny's eye had seven different colors. His cheekbone was broken, so his eye dragged down a little, like he was sad. His father rubbed his own cheek.

Manny's mother said, "You never get mad at him, Larette? Afortunado."

Manny's father said, "Órale pues, Grief and Larette both work with death all the time, man, and they're always happy. That shit is crazy." He held out the box of chicken for the boys.

"I'm not dead," Dante's mother said. "So I'm always happy."

"My clients don't always end up dead. Not every time," Dante's father said. "And someday Dante's gonna hit a homer."

"You work with death all day, Mami," Manny said. "The chickens are hella dead when you fry em."

Manny's mother sighed. "Pues ya que."

"Grief!" his father's friend Tyrone shouted that night, when he walked up to see his son Montrell play. Tyrone was on break—wearing his EMT uniform. "You ain't sang yet? Larette ain't made you sing tonight?"

They all loved the story: In high school, Larette was so pretty that after Grief had built every set for theater, he followed her to San Bernardino Valley College, where he built sets for all their shows, too. Larette tested him on lyrics to each song she sang, in every musical. *Carmen Jones. The Wiz. Grease.*

But to torture him in front of Tyrone or Manny's parents or his uncle, she always picked *The Sound of Music.* It was just familiar enough that they'd all recognize something to laugh at. Grief was required to sing two answering verses of whatever Larette chose, and everyone would fall out laughing on the bleachers.

That night, his mother wanted payback for his comment about the gold eye shadow. She smiled sweetly and sang her favorite eleven notes. The eleven notes of a few of her favorite things. *"Pieces of chicken all coated in batter . . ."*

Grief rolled his eyes. *"My son will hit a home run with a . . . clatter?"*

She shook her head. "That was terrible."

Dante lay in bed that night after Bobby Carter left. Someone always came to sleep in the living room, so Dante wouldn't be alone. He would hear them talking to Bobby, hear the door shut, and they would holler at him through the bedroom door. "Dante! Johnny Frías here. I'm on the couch, man, okay? Don't worry. I left you some doughnuts. From a friend. Apple fritters." He came three nights a week.

Manny's aunt Helena came four nights a week. She already had the virus, way back in March. The first time, she hollered at the door, "Dante, mijo? It's Helena. Remember me? I used to work hospice with your mom, back in the day. Oh, my God, we used to sing all the time. I miss Larette. I'm right here, mijo." He remembered her big laugh and long hair in a bun so big it looked like a new tire on her head. Helena never got married. She watched TV all night, really loud, and he could hear her laughing at her shows. She left him shrimp burritos.

He kept track on his phone how many days it had been. Twenty-eight.

He lay in Ivy's bed, with the yellow sheets. His mother used to make his father sing all the songs from *The Sound of Music*. Especially "Edelweiss" and "My Favorite Things," because he had to change all the lyrics to something new, and he could do it with those songs.

Just a few months ago, at Christmas, the tumbleweeds were huge in the yard. "Tumbleweeds are the edelweiss of our cul-de-sac," his mother had joked.

"Mormons didn't speak German or French," his father said. "This ain't no cul-de-sac. It's calle culo. We're at the ass end of the road."

"Grief, no cussing," his mother said. That night tumbleweeds flew out of the corral, carried so high that two were caught in the fake palm trees across the road, the cell phone towers. The golden balls there for weeks, like giant holiday ornaments.

On Christmas morning, his mother sat on his father's lap and they looked out the window, and he sang tenderly as the hatchet-faced Captain von Trapp: *"Tumbleweed, tumbleweed, every winter you beat me. Big and brown, prickly and round, you will always defeat me."*

On May 27, Dante was writing about the lizard. Three times, he had gone out into the yard when he was alone, collecting insects. Bobby Carter left mealworms in a small container, next to Dante's dinner, and a note that said, "Make sure you eat the right one! Hahaha."

Western blue-throated fringe-toed lizard. The jar was big—an old pickle jar from the barn. Maybe fifty years old. Dante laid it sideways, so the lizard had more room to run. The lizard spent time hanging on the screen, upside down, tongue flicking out. It was hella hot. But Mr. Matsuno liked Dante's lizard journal. He wrote: *Interesting food choices. My mother and I fed mealworms to that same species, in 1984. I tried ants, sowbugs, and earthworms, just as you have.*

In the morning, his mother FaceTimed him. His father had been walking down the hallway, very slowly, and the nurses were cheering. When Dante's phone rang that night, he thought it was her.

"Son," his father said. The word clear, no mask, but like it came up from his feet, his throat was so raw from the cough. "Son. She's sick now."

His mother was in the ICU for ten days. He saw nothing. No one sent him photos of her.

He stayed at Bobby Carter's for two more weeks. His father was released, but he didn't want Dante to come home yet. The house hadn't been cleaned. What if the virus lingered on everything, his hair, his clothes?

His father FaceTimed him every day, for half an hour, from the hospital parking lot. He sat in the truck. As close as he could get to her.

He wore no mask. He told Dante, "I'm the only motherfucker in the parking lot ain't gotta wear a mask. Cause I got cleared by the County Health Department. I can't give this shit to you, or get it again."

Dante said nothing. Helena had made him put out the bedsheets again, and his towels, and she had washed everything and folded it and put it back in the basket by his door.

"She's getting better," his father said. "Her fever's down. She's not on a ventilator." His father looked up at the sky. "I can't believe we gotta know all the words from your mom's work now. Intubation and ventilator and oxygen saturation and all that shit."

"Dad. Don't cuss."

"That was unfortunate," his father said, and smiled. His eyes were still sunk into deep dark wells. Worse than a raccoon. "She'll be home soon. We'll all be home soon."

She came home on June 10. The Delgados came to the house with Dante and his father. They cleaned everything, the dust sitting inches thick on the wooden floors by the doorsills and window-sills, the white cast-iron sink sifted with tiny sand dunes from the constant wind of spring and early summer.

Dante dusted the beautiful wooden box that held his mother's coupons, hundreds of them arranged alphabetically in compart-ments that used to hold Lily John's sewing supplies. His father had given her the cedar box, flowers and garlands carved on the top, when they got married. The first Grief made the box in Utah, be-fore they walked across the desert.

They washed windows and washed bedding, wiped down the walls and mopped the floors, and Dante sprayed with the hose all the porch pillars of white stone, the cement steps and the sidewalk lined with rocks, until they were bright and clean.

His mother came home in a wheelchair. His father pushed it, singing the old O'Jays song his mother loved. *"Here we go, climbing the stairway to heaven . . ."* Dante and Manny rolled their eyes. That heaven was about sex. Dante's parents could barely walk. He whis-pered to Manny, "Shut up, man, don't say shit. You do, I'm finna knock you out."

Then his mother stood up, shaky, and reached for the coupon box. "Grief!" she said. "You probably let all these expire."

He said, "Woman, how the hell would I buy Charmin and Tide Pods, Clorox and Bounty? All your favorite things? That shit been gone from the store for months!" Everyone laughed for a long time.

His parents slept for about a week. Dante made them pancakes and eggs and bacon. Bobby dropped off pork chops and Dante fried them in a pan. His mother had taught him to cook long ago.

They all watched TV for another week. And then his parents went back to work.

The days spun by, pointless and hot. For a week, southern California would be not locked down, and people would go out, swim and drink and party, and then would come another spike of deaths. Lockdown again. There was a short time of unofficial Little League, and he and Manny and Montrell played baseball in the city park. In late July came the word that there would be no school in fall, only online learning, to begin August 8.

His mother looked like herself again, when she was home. Her skin not gray but golden brown, because she lifted her face to the sun in the yard when she had a few hours off. She conditioned her hair with a cap, and combed out her curls, and then joked she had to cover her face and put a cap on her hair as soon as she got to the hospital. "Ten of us now," she told his father. "Julissa just got it. I know you and I don't have to mask up, technically, at home, but we have no idea when it's gonna mutate. Viruses are much more adaptable than we are."

They both wore masks to work. Dante still wore the black bandanna mask when he was anywhere except Minerva Court.

The Delta Aquariids came on July 28th, and Dante didn't even go outside. It was hot, and he didn't care. The whole street was dark, since all the wiring for streetlights had been stolen the week before, and he still didn't care. "No moon, no lights, that should be a good show," his father said. "We could sit outside in the truck bed."

Dante shook his head. He'd never have Mr. Matsuno again. Eighth grade was over. No school in the fall. Freshman year online with a grip of strangers. He and his father watched Dodger reruns. LA versus the Yankees, from 2018.

When his mother came home, she said, "It's like the neighborhood is a black velvet painting and there's no subject. So dark. Who the heck is still stealing metal, Grief?"

"Pandemic doesn't stop people from smoking meth," his father said.

Three weeks ago, metal thieves took the bleachers from the park. Every single piece of aluminum. They took the copper wire from the park lights. No more baseball games.

Johnny Frías said, "That pisses me off. I'm gonna find out who's buying bleachers and melting them down. Who doesn't call the cops when some pendejo shows up to sell bleachers?"

"Like the walking *dead*," Tyrone said. "They come out at *night*. Our little fake season's over now, fellas. Park ain't got no money to replace lights."

Dante figured he'd watch the Perseids. He was bored to death. That's how people said it. To death.

His mother was back at the RV again, for two weeks at least, because the corona spiked in August. His father had extra shifts because the animals came out in the heat, in the deserted streets and yards. A black bear punctured a big inflatable pool, in San Bernardino. Two coyotes drinking from someone's fountain. A whole family of skunks, five babies, living in a garage where no one had taken out the car in weeks. They sprayed some dude's BMW and the man tried to shoot them. He shot up his own car, and when Grief showed up in the Animal Control truck, he had to call the cops.

On August 12, his father was at work all afternoon. Dante scheduled the whole year of meteor showers, because his mother said the damn virus would keep coming back, she knew it, and it was up to him to learn what he loved. Science, math, and art, he decided. He could do all three with the meteors.

At 1:40 a.m., he had just gotten settled into the bed of his father's truck, parked on the shoulder of the street. He'd stayed up until eleven thirty waiting for his father, and then had fallen asleep for an hour. The show was supposed to peak from two a.m. to after three, and he figured he could lie back on the blankets and stare straight up into the sky. With no streetlights, it was blacker than a thousand midnights, like his dad always said.

He listened to the constant sirens, and the long whine and downshift of semitrucks heading down the Cajon Pass into San Bernardino. When he was little, listening in bed, he imagined the trucks like dinosaurs farting their way down the grade.

Last night there had been a few early meteors, amazingly fast streaks across the sky, one that looked like it ripped the black in half it was so long. Tonight was peak, hundreds of shooting stars per hour. He was wearing his black hoodie, holding the new binoculars. Utter darkness, like people called it. Not total. One blogger wrote about the Perseids, "Try to find a place where utter darkness can be achieved. That usually isn't possible in southern California."

But it was here, because all the streetlight wiring was gone. Dante turned the binoculars on the land behind his house. Black acres of sandy field, the corral where his grandfather's horses and the bull named Coalmine used to live. Then the arroyo, and the foothills.

The front door, thirty feet away down the long cement path bordered with river rock, past the old plow and stone water trough. The ancient redwood shingles on the house had darkened to tight black scales. The first time Manny's dad picked up Dante for baseball practice, way back when Dante was seven, Mr. Delgado put his hand on the side of the porch and said to Dante's father, "Damn, Grief, these shingles aren't even painted, homes!"

Dante's father said, "Linseed oil and turpentine, man, my greatgrandpa brushed that shit on back in 1889. Sinks in permanent."

"I already had to repaint my stucco, man, after a year."

"You got a new house," his father had laughed. "Me—I relax. No chores. I watch *Saturday Night Fever*. *Wizard of Oz*. *Hairspray*. Whatever Larette wants to see."

Manny Jr. waited until they were hitting grounders to say, "Your dad watches some weird shit. My dad just watches sports."

His mother had painted the river rock along the pathway. Bright white, like huge pearls in the dark. The front window's original glass all wavery—like black Saran wrap.

It hadn't been ten minutes when he heard the shitty little white Ford Ranger truck laboring up Baseline Avenue toward his street. The same truck as last night. The downshift as it turned onto the narrow dirt-covered road. He recognized the whiny old engine. The two meth heads. They had checked out the cell towers at the dead end last night.

The three fake palm trees held the cell towers, and two real palm trees grew inside the fenced locked enclosure the Verizon workers had built. These two guys were coming back to steal the copper wire.

They hadn't seen him last night, when he'd been on the porch recording the early meteors. Dante hadn't thought the men would come back so fast. Tonight he'd left his phone in the coupon box, filed under *P*. Pepperidge Farm, Pantene, Pillsbury, and Pampers— his mother always bought diapers with coupons, on sale, to donate to new moms at the hospital.

No blue light, no screens. You were supposed to let your eyes adjust to night dark for forty-five minutes before a meteor shower.

The truck got closer and closer. No headlights. Dante's father kept saying he would put up a solar porch light. He said Lily John used to sit up with her kerosene lantern watching for cattle rustlers.

These guys in the raggedy white Ranger were copper rustlers. Had to be. He'd seen their truck bed last night. Torn-off freeway guardrails stacked like dirty gray rib bones. Brass fittings from irrigation systems, poking up like beaked bird heads. These were the kind of speed freaks who stole bleachers. They stole catalytic converters. Manny's father was pissed off last week because someone stole the catalytic converters off seven trucks, right in the driveways on his block.

They couldn't steal last night because they had no room left in the truck bed—they'd reversed down the dirt road and gone away.

His father always said, "You can't be sitting outside in the truck unless I'm home, Dante."

Last night his father looked like shit again. Dante was worried. His father hadn't been sleeping at all since his mother was at the RV again. The black pouches under his father's eyes were like greasepaint on a football player.

Probably 1:50 now. The schedule of the stars never varied. This was why his mother loved to hear about his project. She said it helped to think the stars would never disappear, no matter what the idiots did on earth.

Dante was sweating hard. It was still about ninety degrees, even now. Nothing moved but the Ford Ranger, creeping toward him.

Dante didn't want to go inside. They weren't predators. They were vermin. Scavengers. They'd be fast. It was so dark they'd never notice him.

He lowered the binoculars and then his upper body back down the metal grooves of his father's truck bed, between the two toolboxes bolted in on each side. Now he could see only what he'd come out here to see: the sky.

The truck idled silently past him. The men probably thought the Apache was abandoned, because it was still primer black, and the house was dark. But he worried they'd hear the swamp coolers working overtime loud, which meant someone lived here.

Assholes or knuckleheads—Dante couldn't tell yet. A thread of cigarette smoke hung in the air. One guy said, "Don't fuck up, Carlos. Pull the wire. I'll be back. I'm gettin that marker off the old sign we passed."

The historic marker on Baseline. The brass plaque. The Mormons.

Carlos said, "It's fuckin boring with no radio. We should play some Metallica, man. *Exit light, enter night.* Gonna bring the night right now."

"Shut up, Carlos." The man put the truck in reverse and went back down the street, so slowly Dante could hear rocks pop softly off the bald treads. He lay still. He kept his eyes closed. Mouth closed. No white showing, in case Carlos glanced into the truck bed. He'd see a pile of work tarps, that's all. The truck was too old for a catalytic converter.

Carlos rustled through the oleander bushes growing around the fence and started clipping the chain link. His tool belt clanked every time he moved. Bolt cutters pinging on each diamond of chain link, and then a more silvery ping on the strands of barbed wire. Pliers and wire cutters and hammer probably on his belt. His boots silent on the sand. Then Dante heard the thud of each boot on the metal rungs of the cell tower.

Verizon had put up the towers in 2015. "Fake-ass palm trees," his father said about the three cell towers. "How you gonna put up something so expensive and advertise it to thieves?"

"Who the hell designed those pinche trees?" Manny's dad said. "Must have been some cabrón from back East. We don't have fuckin coconuts out here!"

"An unfortunate mix," his father said. "Those panels look like flat green bananas."

Dante had said, "And they don't blow in the wind. So weird."

Now Carlos coughed a few times, way up in the sky. Dante didn't move. Last winter, during a big Santa Ana, the wind was so strong that even the metal fronds moved a little, like they were dignified and reserved—superior in their stiffness to the wild tossing and crashing of the real fronds on the real trees.

Suddenly flapping wings burst out of the real palm trees, and Dante jumped. That was where the owl lived, the one who dropped rabbit heads onto the street.

"Fuckin birds," Carlos said, loud like he was trying to keep himself company. He must have made it to the top. In the total darkness of his hoodie, Dante imagined himself blind, hearing as someone who couldn't see. The white truck droning like a pissed-off wasp toward Baseline Avenue. Baseline and Meridian. The beginning of southern California, where some old white man had laid out the streets that went all the way to LA and Hollywood and Santa Monica.

He heard the white truck stop. Then the tiny sound of a chisel or hammer carried in the silence. Brass plaque. Speed freaks took everything.

He breathed shallow, getting pissed, wishing this dude Carlos would hurry up. The meteors wouldn't wait. The peak was only an hour.

A sound of metal pried open, like the screech of a blue jay. A mockingbird started up for a minute, and then stopped abruptly. Mockingbirds fought epic song battles, starting near midnight, lasting until dawn, the birds delirious and high, repeating the same notes over and over, from the two tall palms with shaggy fronds perfect for nests. They could mimic car alarms, coyotes, and other birds like sparrows and blue jays.

Fucking Carlos. Fucking bird. Tears slid sideways hot into Dante's ears. Shit. Shiny on his face. Like torture not to wipe them away. He couldn't move.

What if she didn't come back again? What if tonight was when some random human got a different mutation of the virus, a brand-new variant? What if the human had been somewhere else in the world and then he came to San Bernardino and got sick, and Dante's mother was the nurse he coughed on and one miniscule droplet flew under her mask? Miniscule was the word she taught him. Like one particle of fog.

The explosion was loud as fireworks but more personal. Contained somehow. Damp and muffled for one second, and then *Boom*. Dante opened his eyes. The shower of sparks splayed out like a huge Roman candle attached to the pole—a burst of light curving, floating, and then disappeared.

Carlos sailed out from the metal tower like he was not a human. A bulk of cloth, heavy and soft. He didn't land like a tackle at football practice—no plastic pads on his shoulders to make that hard crack. He landed like the sewing dummy his mother had used to make costumes.

Carlos made no second sound. He was burned. Maybe that

made his whole body instantly softer. Dante felt vomit rising in his belly. Then came soft noise. About four feet away—Carlos had landed near the Apache. Hissing—breathing or skin or something else? Was he alive? Shit. Dante was afraid to raise up and look. The smell was so strong and sweet and terrible that he pushed the strings of his hoodie into his mouth and sucked hard, to keep from throwing up. One last whisper of a settle. Close by. An exhalation. The strings tasted of Tide. Don't cry. Don't.

Then the silence was complete. Carlos had knocked out the power to the whole area.

The three swamp coolers attached to the windows of the living room, his parents' bedroom, and his own room—all went quiet as if stunned to be given a break. The house would be an oven in about ten minutes. Fifteen at most. Unbearable.

But if he could get out of the truck bed and make it to the house now, he could tell his dad. Then he heard the white truck snarl to life and start speeding back here. Dante slid his hoodie off and breathed hard, covered with sweat, his eyes stinging. He stumbled, trying to get out from under the folded tarps. He got out the big cop flashlight Johnny Frías had given him back at Bobby's house.

Dante crawled to the tailgate and turned on the flashlight, training it on the dark heap. A human burnt to lava. Black and red. Black shiny as obsidian through the holes in the jacket. Blacker than any skin. Red not shiny. Red like posters in science class of the body. The back of his head red. The sheath of muscle over his skull exposed. No glisten. Smoked.

The flashlight fell from his hand to the ground, and he threw up over the tailgate. Cap'n Crunch he'd eaten at midnight. Quivering puddle next to the black boots. Saliva dripped from his mouth, and he threw up again, heaving and heaving.

The swamp coolers dripped condensation onto the sand around the house. He could jump out of the truck bed and run inside before the other guy got here. He put his leg up over the tailgate, and just then a breeze sent the smell into his face. He threw up again and again, green liquid onto the old chrome bumper. What did his mother call it? Bile. *You got nothing but bile left, baby. It's okay.*

Dizzy and fire behind his eyelids. The Ranger skidded fast around the corner. Dante thought he would pass out, fall right beside Carlos. He lay back in the truck bed, shaking uncontrollably, pulling the hood back up over his head, swallowing the acid scouring his throat.

His father would come. He could hear his mother saying *Sing. Sing if you're scared, baby.* How Dante sang inside his head when gangsters came up on him and Manny and Montrell at the mall or at school, shoving them around, showing the guns tucked into their jeans. How he had when they stood at Tenerife's coffin, and Merry's, and his mother fell on the floor crying.

His father would sing, *Raindrops on roses and whiskers on kittens. Modelo and Dove bars and hell no on mittens.*

But the smell of Carlos had jumped into his mouth. He heaved again and threw up bile under the left toolbox. The white truck skidded into the oleander bushes. Shit. *Carlos.* The name was already imprinted in his brain. Under the muscles of scalp.

Fuck Fuck Fuck Fuck. The other guy said it loud, like a woodpecker in the silence. He walked closer to Carlos. So tall Dante could see the upper half of him. He heard a knee joint crack. The dude bending toward Carlos's body. Asshole or knucklehead? *Fuck*, he said one more time.

Then a sigh. A sigh from the ground. Carlos. Was that a breath? Or the skin releasing a breath? Carlos was alive inside the crust of black skin? Dante shivered, clenched his jaw shut.

The tall guy picked up Dante's flashlight. Clicked it on, then off. He said it one more time. *Fuck.* Then he started walking back toward the truck.

Dante couldn't believe it. He was leaving Carlos? No. Hell no. His friend who might be alive, or a dead body right here by his father's truck? If Carlos wasn't dead, Dante's father would have to call an ambulance and the cops, and if Carlos was dead by the time they came, it would be him and his dad—two Black guys sitting by a dead man. The deputies might start shooting at them, in the dark.

His father always said, "Don't ever put yourself in the situation where you get shot behind a stranger, Dante."

Dante raised up, got on his knees, and said, "You finna pack him up, right?"

The man turned and shone the flashlight on Dante. He pulled a gun from his waistband with the other hand. He walked back toward Dante, holding both straight ahead like he had six-shooters in *Gunsmoke.* Black shiny forehead over a black bandanna. "The fuck did you say?" Wiry white-dude voice.

Green bile in Dante's throat. "You fin-na pack-him-up," he said clearly. "Your friend."

"Speak English, bro. You saw what happened?" The man's ears were pink. The fingers around the gun were pink. The black on his face was blacking. Like in football. Damn—this was a white guy.

"How I'm not gon see what happened and he fell right here?"

"What the fuck are you doin out here? At fuckin two a.m.?"

"Perseids, man."

"I told you to speak English. *Bro.*" He waved the gun at Dante.

Meteors, Dante thought. No. I'm not telling you. I am not your bro. His mother used to say after a stranger got happy—I am not your *girl*, and I am not planning to *go* anywhere. The gun. Barrel like one nostril of the bull Uncle Perry once kept in the corral. Bull named Coalmine.

The man said, "Stand up. Hands up, too. I will fuckin shoot you. Why are you out here?"

Dante stood. He lifted his hands. Distinctly. Each word careful. "Meteors. Shooting stars. Tonight."

"Are you messing with me? Don't mess with me right now. You a gangbanger? You got a fuckin piece? Hand it out here. Slow."

"No gun." Dante lifted his hands higher.

Not a knucklehead. Predator. This man would kill him. His truck engine clicked and clicked. Overhot. The swamp coolers on Dante's house ticked and dripped. His father had to come now.

The wind blew down the pass again, pushed the smell of Carlos straight toward them. The asshole dropped to one knee, let the flashlight fall. He pulled the bandanna down, gasping. His face cleaved in half. White lips open like a fish. This asshole had put on blackface so if anyone saw him, they'd report a Black man.

He rested the hand with the gun on his thigh and panted. The hot wind rustled the oleander. "Whose truck is this? You're not old enough to drive." The man panted. "What are you doing out here?"

"I live here."

"Who the fuck still lives out here?" The guy didn't take his eyes off Dante's face. "This is Mormon land."

Congratulations—he read the historical marker before he stole it. Dante said, "My dad's people came out with the Mormons."

"Bullshit. Mormons didn't let in Blacks." He waved the gun toward the house. Like the pistol was an extension of his finger. "Your gangbanger friends in there?"

"No."

"Who lives there?"

"Me and my dad."

"Where's your dad?"

Dante hesitated. He listened to the coolers ticking. "At work."

"He left you alone?"

"He works night security."

"Where's your mom?"

Dante said, "None of your fuckin business."

The guy murmured, "Yeah, she ran away, who the fuck wants to live out here?"

Dante's eyes stung. "I'm thirteen. Legal to be home."

The man spoke casually again, as if still talking to himself. "Your house doesn't even look Black."

Dante threw his head back and stared at the sky. He saw the beginning of the Perseids. Scribbles of silver. Less than a second to linger. Dissipate. Ash.

Then he said, "Fuck you, man. Even the wood is black on my house."

The guy turned the gun back on him. "Fuck you. It looks like a cowboy house."

"Actually it is." How long was meth head attention span? Would he shoot when he got bored? Fuck it. "What should be out in the yard, man?" Dante said. "Watermelons? Statue of Eazy-E? You finna shoot me?"

The guy rubbed his hand across his mouth and looked toward the Cajon Pass. He wanted to be on the freeway now. The bandanna hung around his neck like he was a fake train robber. Speed scabs like big black sow bugs on his jaw. When he squinted, his front teeth showed, big and creamy and square like Rice Chex. Not like meth mouth.

"*Finna?* What the fuck is that?"

This dude was so high. "Finna. You finna find out if you don't go."

The man made up his mind. He came toward Dante and said, "You finna whatever the fuck it is. Pick him up and take him in the house." He lifted the gun to Dante's face.

One more minute. Please. His father would wake up because it was so hot. No cooler. No fan by the bed. No clock radio playing Art Laboe, because his father couldn't sleep without his mother breathing, needed old-school R&B love songs to mask the singing coyotes and mockingbirds that made him cry. His father wasn't sure she was coming back either. The hills and trees alive with the sound of her music. Right now sweat dripping into his dad's eyes even if they were closed. Salt. Stinging. Wake up wake up wake up.

"Now." The man took two more steps toward Dante.

"Time for you to hat up, man," Dante said, staring straight into the nostril of the gun. He waited for his father. He spoke his father's language. *Man, you and Manny need to hat up right now because I'm tired of feedin you crumbsnatchers. Even with coupons, right, Larette? How can y'all eat so much cereal she gotta file em under General Mills? The whole corporation! All that Cap'n Crunch.*

The vomit drying into a yellow cow patty next to Carlos's boots.

Dante propped his hands on the tailgate and closed his eyes. He swung his legs over and hopped to the ground, as he had hundreds of times when his father delivered him and Manny to the ballpark. He waited for the sound of the gun. For the bullet in his spine. The soft sand under his Jordans. The same sand where Lily's horses used to stand when they drank at the old trough.

Dante closed his eyes. He bent and touched Carlos's boots. He put his fingers around the black heels.

The man said, "Turn him over. You're a weird fuckin kid. You should be watchin TV in your fuckin house like a normal kid."

Dante pulled on the boots. Two inches. He gagged.

"Turn him over!"

Carlos. Not heavy. Speed freak. His blood not liquid now? The bile rose green in Dante's throat. He pulled the boots a few inches, onto the old pitted asphalt, and the body sighed. Carlos sighed. Dante dropped the boots. Carlos's back, onyx skin under ragged holes in the green jacket burnt to shreds, rose and fell. Carlos was breathing. Dante backed away.

The guy lowered his gun and walked toward Carlos. Dante's father stepped out from the side of the house and fired the rifle from there. Thirty feet. The tranquilizer dart hit the man in the shoulder blade. Something flew from the man's mouth and landed in the sand. He dropped the gun and the flashlight and fell to his knees, contorted and trying to reach the dart in his back.

Dante ran over to the gun. Fingerprints. He slid a fat splinter of dried palm frond into the trigger, carried the gun to his father. He picked up the flashlight and trained it onto the other thing in the dirt. Top teeth—a pink-and-white clamshell.

"Fuck," the guy shouted, bent over rocking, clutching at the dart in his back. He couldn't reach it, the blood bright red drops on his shirt. "You—" he said.

Dante's father walked close, crouched near the guy, and said, "Call me that word. Say it, man. Say it and I'll shoot you in the nuts, man, just to hear you scream. I will tranquilize your scrotum." His father's hair glistened with sweat in the distant starlight, his T-shirt wet and transparent over his chest. The pouches under his eyes triangular. Like viper heads. Poison is a triangle shape, he always said.

"I'm so damn tired I would love to shoot you," he said softly. "Call me that. Do it."

His father had gotten home at midnight, after hours of looking for the mother of five puppies he found near the freeway. He figured the mother dog had been hit by a car, and he'd crawled through oleander and weeds, following her blood by the banks of the freeway until he found her. "Broken back leg," he told Dante. "Musta been half-dead and she tried to crawl back. I had to look forever. Half–pit bull, half-Lab, maybe. I found her near the Muscoy exit."

His father had been asleep for only two hours when the power went out. His eyes were slitted and golden.

"Are you fuckin serious?" the man moaned. He was crumpling, fading.

His father kept his crouch near the man and said softly, almost tenderly, "Shut your punk ass up. You know how hard it is for me not to shoot the next dart into your eye? You made my son touch that guy. You put death in his head." The knot of bandanna over the white man's neck. "Oh, you a fake Crip? You know how hard it is for me not to kill you now and bury your ass under the corral?"

"Dad. The other one's not dead. He's alive," Dante said.

"Damn." His father winced. He got up and looked at Carlos in the flashlight beam. The skull. The mouth open. "Get your phone and call Uncle Perry. He probably heard my rifle. Then call nine-one-one. Tell them we need an ambulance, tell them it's Grief and ask if Tyrone's on duty. Then call Johnny Frías and tell him to ride out here fast. So we got two cops on our side when the rest of them come. So they don't shoot us first and ask questions later."

The white man drooled into the dirt now. He was out. An animal taken down.

Dante started to walk up the path to the house, light from the sieve of the sky on the white stones. He looked up at the Perseids. One second. Two. A meteor shot across the eastern sky over the mountains, leaving a trail. Sparkling white lingered and then dissipated.

His father whistled absentmindedly. Five notes. *Snowflakes on mittens*. Dante fell onto the cement and cried tearing sobs. Blown sand cutting into his cheek. His father crouched beside him and held his shoulders. His father whispered, "Get your phone from the coupon box, son. She'll come home. She'll be home tomorrow."

Dante couldn't move. He felt hollow. "But she's in the ER tonight. She has to take care of an asshole like him. He probably has the virus."

"Dante. She called me while I was looking for the dog. She's okay for tonight. She's in the trailer now." His father helped him stand up, and he pointed to the sky. "Hurry up before the damn ambulance gets here and lights everything up. Go lay down in the backyard and look up at the sky. I got this. And hey—the Leonids are coming in November. Your mom can sit out here with us then. It's gotta be over by that time. She told me she can't wait to see the stars. With you."

TODOS MRS. BUNNY

On Monday, May 25, 2020, Ximena opened the Michael Kors messenger bag and put inside her notebook, an extra T-shirt in case she had to clean the oven or refrigerator or move something from the garage, and the cherry lip balm and menthol cough drops that helped when she couldn't breathe because of Mrs. Bunny's smoke. She put her ID in her bra. All weekend, she'd kept the book about painters and paintings inside the bag, so Elpidia couldn't tease her about it. Art. Hockney and Klee and Rothko. Ximena had read it in the Silverado on Saturday night, to keep Rodolfo company.

Now she could recognize them. The two paintings upstairs.

She'd been working for Mrs. Bunny since September 9, 2019. For Christmas, Mrs. Bunny had given Ximena a Michael Kors clutch purse. To clutch meant to hold in the hand. Ximena gave it to Elpidia, who cared about purses. But Mrs. Bunny had noticed the first day Ximena didn't carry it. In March of this year, when the corona got bad, she gave Ximena the black leather messenger bag, and said, "This is worth as much as a week's cash, X. Take it. I don't want you to quit. Don't quit."

Mrs. Bunny would never say please. But Ximena liked that about her. Her cousin Fidelia never said please either.

Mrs. Bunny kept twenty purses on their own shelf in the shoe closet. Dooney & Bourke. Kate Spade. Elpidia wanted them all. There were two crates of older purses in the garage. Mrs. Bunny said, "You can't be rich with a shitty purse and crap shoes. Seriously, X. That's what people look at. Put on Jimmy Choo or Manolo and you're gold."

Elpidia knew all the bags. Cross-body, clutch, tote, hobo bag. But she didn't care about where the words came from. Ximena sat every day in Mrs. Bunny's kitchen writing words, while Mrs. Bunny napped after lunch. Hobo. A tramp. Tramp meant walk. Hobo and tramp meant a homeless, in the old days. These purses were in the magazines at Mrs. Bunny's. Tote. She hadn't found that word yet.

Message. Messenger. This morning, she put the bag on the bed, by Elpidia's feet in the covers. "Give me the phone," she said to Elpidia, in English.

"Not yet."

In the kitchen, Ximena packed two enchiladas from last night into a plastic container. Every day she packed her lunch. Enchiladas or a burrito, because she hated Mrs. Bunny's salads. Back in the bedroom, she held out her hand for her go-phone. In case of emergency. The whole world was an emergency. She shouldn't even be working. All the other housekeepers had been let go. But Mrs. Bunny said she couldn't survive without Ximena. At the end of March, she'd offered Ximena double pay. Not $450 per week, but $1,000.

Mrs. Bunny had lived in quarantine for years anyway. Uncle

Epifanio said it was too much money to lose, since the others weren't working now.

Last night, on the phone, Ximena whispered to her cousin that she was saving money for them both. Fidelia said, "What, like a few hundred dollars can help us now?"

Ximena couldn't tell her how much money she had.

Then Fidelia said, "There's not gonna be College of the Desert for you. And no UCLA for me. No high school. No graduation. Nothing's coming back for a long time."

"That's not true," Ximena said.

"You don't know the science," Fidelia said. "Your old white lady just wants you there if she dies. So her body won't decompose with ants and flies."

"Fidelia!"

"I have to go." Fidelia cut off the FaceTime and disappeared.

She missed Fidelia every day. The first notebook was still in the Prowler. No one lived there now. No one had crossed since corona.

Ximena had bought herself ten new notebooks, at Rite Aid. They were the notebooks used by Harriet the Spy. One of Fidelia's favorite books when she was small. Ximena had read part of it online at Mrs. Bunny's house, on her phone. Every day, Ximena wrote words and sentences in the sections she had divided in the notebooks. She had five gel pens.

There was one dresser in the bedroom she shared with Elpidia and the twins; they each had a single drawer. There was one small closet; they each had twelve inches of hanger space. Yesika and Yesenia had measured the old wooden rod, and Epifanio, their father, had glued on plastic dividers. Since Ximena didn't care about clothes, she let Elpidia have half of her space. Every day, Elpidia had to wear the landscaper uniform, faded jeans and a khaki shirt, so the minute she got home, she wanted to wear dresses, or tight leggings and long shirts, and her black leather ankle boots, and the Michael Kors purse.

Ximena had three pairs of black Forever 21 jeans, three black T-shirts, and three black blouses. She had the white sneakers she wore with her uniform, and one pair of brown ankle boots. She wouldn't spend her money on anything else.

The money she took from her pay, before she gave the rest to Uncle Epifanio, was rolled tightly into a thin tube. Twenty-eight $50 bills. Two weeks after she had started working for Mrs. Bunny, the woman paid her in cash every week, and said, "I know you have to give all this to your dad. But there's one extra bill in here for you. Hide it. Someday you'll need it. Everyone woman needs a stash. Trust me."

Mrs. Bunny had been drunk one Monday morning, last month, searching in the freezer for ice. She said she'd fallen in the bath-room Sunday night and hurt her face. She said to Ximena, "Men are stupid assholes. They keep their drug money in the freezer. You know that, X? They keep fucking ten thousand bucks in bags in a fucking ice cream tub. Like cops don't know that. They keep twenty thousand bucks in a dirty sock in a clothes hamper. Don't ever do that. Keep your stash someplace nobody would guess." She looked at her phone. "Nadie lo sabe," she said. Mrs. Bunny loved her Google translate.

Ximena had found Mrs. Bunny's stash of money back in Sep-tember. The fourth time she did the laundry.

Now she tied the black bandanna face covering loosely around her neck. She'd fasten it tightly when she got to the sidewalk. The virus was everywhere—on the fences and store counters and bus seats, at the market. But no one here had it. Her uncles always had enough food and supplies for a month—for the earthquake. And no one took the bus since they had the trucks. They didn't stop at

7-Eleven for coffee anymore; only Moises and Tomás bought gas, and they wore gloves and masks, and touched no one at home until they washed.

It was 6:15 a.m. Ximena still wasn't used to the sound a single car or truck made on the freeway, screaming past, now that there was no traffic. No heavy rumbling of cars and trucks in the slow lane only thirty feet away from the bedroom. No honking horns or brief snatches of music when the cars stopped and people had their windows open and their songs rolled right into her window for a few minutes before they moved away. The court was one block of cottages, ending at a high concrete wall where the 101 hummed above, in the sky. The Hollywood Freeway. To the east was the 5. The Golden State. Yesika had told her, "Say 'The.' Don't say 'Number.' Ever."

The smell of coffee from the kitchen was strong now. Elpidia was still in the double bed they shared, checking how many followers she had gained overnight on Instagram.

Elpidia said in Mixtec, "I saw on Facebook last night Carlos got engaged to some ugly girl. In Coachella."

Ximena rubbed her eyes. "That was fast."

"But you did take him away from me," Elpidia said.

"ICE took you away," Ximena said.

Across the narrow channel between the two double beds in the room, one of the twins poked her head up from her sheets and said, "Shut up, whatever you're saying."

Yesika. She had remnants of gold eye shadow around her lashes. Yesenia always wore green. Yesika wore reddish lip gloss. Yesenia wore pink. That was how they tried to make sure people could tell them apart. It worked for all the women in the apartment court, but the men paid no attention to makeup. So Yesika wore red leather ankle boots, and Yesenia wore dark blue.

The twins were Ximena's cousins. They didn't speak Mixtec. They were born here, in Los Angeles. They spoke Spanish and perfect English. Like Fidelia. No matter how long Ximena studied, no matter how many words she wrote in her notebooks, her English would never be like theirs.

Elpidia held up the phone toward Yesika and said in English, "Look. The Insta. Marti. She dress. She look a cow. I have so many followers. She never get DMs all night."

And Yesenia said, "Is that the one with that dude Carlos you met like, once? Shut up! You're pathetic. Any dog has a million followers."

"An ugly poodle with his tongue sticking out has ten million followers," Yesika said. "I *cannot* with you. You are way too extra for morning."

They had no school. They were fourteen.

But their mother, Flor, shouted from the kitchen for all the girls to eat. The trucks were almost ready. And the twins had to teach.

Ximena got her earrings from the one thing that was hers alone: a tiny delicate mahogany bedside table with black marble top, given to her by Mrs. Bunny one day in the garage, where all the dark things stayed. On the small round top was the photo of Ximena's mother, taken when she was ten, braids wrapped around her head like a crown, her skirt held wide in each hand for a dance in the zócalo. Liliana. Back in San Cristóbal.

Beside her in a small gold frame was Esteban. Last August, when she and Elpidia and Rodolfo had arrived here in Hollywood, Ximena stayed in the bed. Crying. Flor brought atole in a coffee cup for Ximena that night. Steaming and cinnamon flecked. Flor sat on the edge of the bed and handed her a small snapshot.

Her brother. The last time she saw him he was floating in the water, moving further and further away.

The frame fit into her palm. He was in his tiny white suit for baptism. Flor whispered for a long time into Ximena's hair, that Ximena's mother sent the photo before she left for California, so many years ago. Flor had believed she would see his face again, last summer, when she knew they were crossing.

"Keep him here beside you. He can watch over you from above."

Now Elpidia said, "Look, four hundred eighty-nine likes. Pues, I post at midnight. Only morning now."

"Time for you to go," Yesika said, pulling on her jeans. "Please shut up and go. Put your stupid bathing suit away. It's pathetic."

The red bikini top Elpidia had worn last night, in the tiny corner of the bedroom where Ximena took her photo, was twisted on the bed. Elpidia had done her hair and makeup, arranged small palm fronds across her stomach and behind her head like a green sun ray. She had bought a cheap black satin sheet over at Dollar Tree. For the photos, she taped it to the wall. The twins had taught Elpidia about Instagram and TikTok, what to post, what to say, how to arrange things, but now they hated hearing her. Last night was red. Her lipstick and bathing suit matched perfectly. The caption was *Canela*.

Ximena had no social media. She didn't want strangers to see her. Like Mrs. Bunny said, "Humans only care about what they can get from you."

Ximena said to Elpidia, "Five minutes."

She braided her hair in the small pink-tiled bathroom. Once, these apartments were where Hollywood women lived, back in 1930, Uncle Epifanio said.

He was sitting at the kitchen table. He studied them impassively, as every day. Three brothers—Emiliano, Eufemio, and Epifanio. Epifanio was the oldest. He'd come to California first. His cheeks wide, his lips flat and motionless, three small moles like flecks of charcoal beside his left eye. His hair thick and black, his neck powerful, his body short and wide in the dark green work shirt and pants with the name tag sewn to the pocket. JOSE. "José is a good name for them to say," he told Ximena. "They call everyone José. They can pay José."

He said to his twins, "Time for school." The smallest edge of a smile when Yesika rolled her eyes. They took the tortillas rolled around scrambled eggs and chorizo, and Yesenia grabbed her backpack with lessons for the kids.

"The school of Yesenia starts so early," Flor said in Mixtec. "She hates it."

Her aunt and uncle spoke Mixtec to her and Elpidia, and to the older people in the apartments. But the twins wouldn't say a word.

Ximena followed them down the cement walkway that led through the center of the court. Five small stucco cottages sat on each side of the walkway. Each had one bedroom, a kitchen, and a living room with a bed that came out of the wall. Murphy beds. Irish beds, Yesika joked. The first time Ximena walked down the line of doors, she shivered, thinking of the cottages at Seven Palms. Each one exactly the same.

But at Uncle Epifanio's rancho, each house had been painted a different color. Pink. Yellow. Turquoise. Lime. Roses sprawled over the wrought-iron fence. New corn grew along every block wall, and sugar cane like purple bones against the garage at the back; old Jesús, who must have been ninety, already sat in front of the wooden garage door, in his white plastic chair, drinking coffee. He kept everything watered. Chickens argued under the bougainvillea. Her uncles had replicated everything they could of home. Ermelinda made moles, amarillo or negro or verde, every day; Jesús grew the strange fruits of California—loquats and boysenberries—but also bananas and sugar cane and avocados. Uncle Eufemio's wife had died three years ago; he lived in the last house, white with blue trim, and Rodolfo slept on the Murphy bed there. Eufemio's three sons—Ulises, Moises, and Tomás—each lived with their wives and children in cottages—dark blue, apricot, and lilac.

Strollers and Big Wheels and soccer balls were everywhere in the small yards. The twins did a lot of recess. Strange word—recess meant playtime outside.

When they reached Queta's house, the kids were laughing at *Dora the Explorer* on the television. Yesika and Yesenia went inside the open front door. Ten kids inside, all sitting on the floor.

Ximena waited to see the baby.

Queta held him in front of her, one hand on his belly, while she closed the door. Every morning he threw his arms and legs out in a frantic dance, all four limbs hitting his mother while he tried to launch himself into the air. "When they are ten months, they always try to fly," Queta said, shaking her head.

When she walked beside Queta, for only a few minutes, smelling the baby named Alex, his damp hair, the milk lingering in the folds of his neck, she let herself think that if her baby had lived, it would be two months old. She could have told her uncles that she had been with a man at home, in San Cristóbal. They could have believed her or not. She could be holding a baby who soon would try every day to fly, even if his or her blood was that of a rapist. A killer. A man not Mexican. An American animal. Coyote.

Alex hit his mother in the face with the back of his fat tiny hand, and Ximena grabbed his fingers. He grinned, with two teeth like white pebbles in his swimming gums.

Then Ximena would think about the baby girl from Seven Palms, her fists lavender and cold. She was ten months old. If she was alive. Who had taken her from the hospital in Indio? Who would ever tell Dr. Don? Fidelia still had the note, but she had never mentioned the baby again.

Queta took her child quickly across the sidewalk to Ermelinda's house—she watched the two babies in the court. Then she and Ximena hurried toward the front gate, the trucks and the van warming up, sending steam into the dawn sunlight.

No one could see the court from the street, because a morning glory vine tangled over the top of the heavy wrought iron gate at the entrance. Back in August, when she and Elpidia and Rodolfo arrived, Epifanio pointed to the wild profusion of blue trumpet blossoms. He said, "That is why people think an old white woman lives here still. Flowers no one trims."

The gate was halfway open. Ulises sat in the black Chevy Silverado, his Dodgers cap pulled low, his blue bandanna tight around his face, watching the street, his phone in the cupholder on the dashboard. All day he sat in the truck, guarding the rancho. At night, Rodolfo sat for four hours, dreaming about his own truck, his phone in his hand.

Rodolfo never complained. He said raccoons and possums walked across the sidewalk, even onto the truck, and stared at him. Owls sat on tree branches and stared at him. The neighborhood was all industrial now, except for the apartment court. Trucks came and went at all hours, taking boxes of things to people inside their houses.

Rodolfo grabbed the phone from Elpidia and said in Mixtec, "You'll get in trouble." He handed it to Ximena.

There was only one go-phone for each job location. Less chance of tracing anyone. Eufemio had a phone for the palm tree crew; Moises had a phone for the median crew that worked the long wide avenues in Encino; Ulises had his phone in the Silverado; and Ximena, because she worked alone at Mrs. Bunny's, had her own phone.

Elpidia hated it. Even this morning, when Ximena rubbed her eyes and said she had a headache, Elpidia said angrily, "Why? You don't do anything hard. You sit around and eat your lunch. I have to work so hard and you get a phone."

Ximena couldn't tell her how hard it was to take care of Mrs. Bunny, since she was scared of every sound, angry about something invisible, all the while appearing to inhabit someone else's body.

The palm tree crew got into one truck, and the median crew got into the other. White trucks with king cabs. Four people on each crew. SUNSET GARDENING SERVICES painted on the doors, with a yellow sun sliding into blue water, and two tiny green palms at the edge. Ulises had painted them. Epifanio said the first way to look undocumented was to have a dirty, small, old truck with equipment rattling around and no name.

Twenty years ago, Epifanio had been the gardener and handyman at Rose Garden Apartments; when the old lady who owned them, and lived in the front apartment, died, she left the place to him. Her name had been Rose Friedman. Epifanio took down the sign, put in a heavy gate, and let the vines grow wild over the entrance.

If police or ICE stopped them, the trucks looked more official, more American. Everyone was wearing uniform shirts, as if an American owned the company. Epifanio told them to say, "I work for Sunset Corporation. Rose Friedman." They practiced again and again.

Ximena got into the white van, doors painted with SUNSET HOUSEKEEPING SERVICES and the same yellow sun. Before the virus, Epifanio used to drop off Queta, Marisol, and Dolores at the Magic Castle Hotel, in Hollywood. Now he drove only Ximena.

The radio was on 97.5. The Spanish was fast for Ximena. A song about Michoacán.

Her uncle drove east on Sunset, facing the sunrise, then onto Vermont, in Los Feliz. Up into the hills, to the winding narrow Dundee Drive, the van laboring uphill. He stopped at the gate, metal bars perfect white and glossy. On Fridays, Epifanio came here for four hours. He covered any rust spots with new paint. He trimmed the trees, checked the sprinklers, painted white things white and black things black.

Ximena pushed the Ring that hung on the side of the gate. The gate slid open. Mrs. Bunny sometimes didn't say anything. Ximena walked the quarter mile up the cement driveway shaded by huge cypress trees pointing at the sky like black candles. Ten on each side. The silence was broken only by birds and lawnmowers. All humans inside, except the trucks and vans of UPS, Amazon, FedEx, and the plain white vans leaving boxes at the curb.

Every morning, she felt how strange it was to leave the court, past the smaller kids riding Big Wheels, and women talking to each other from the steps, and then to walk up this hill through stripes of shadow and sun toward the one human she spent all day watching.

She had gotten this job for herself. The fourth day in Los Angeles, she approached her uncle at dawn, where he sat outside the apartment, drinking his coffee. She handed him the ID cards and medication bottle. Uncle Emiliano had told his brother about the baby, and ICE, why the three of them came to Hollywood. But no one else knew, except Flor. Not Elpidia, or Rodolfo.

That day back in August, her uncle had driven the women to the Magic Castle Hotel, and then he looked up Dundee Drive on Google Maps. "Los Feliz," he said dryly. "The Happys. Marisol used to work in a house here."

He parked outside the gate, watching the house. Her uncle said, "She has no gardener. You can see the weeds in the cracks between the gate and the sidewalk. You can see the trees covering the driveway." He got out and walked partway up the street, came back, and said, "You can see the house from there. A big house. They have money."

The gate slid open, creaking, and a long white car came racing down the driveway, stopped abruptly when the old woman with silver hair who was driving saw the van. She honked four times, and Emiliano drove up the narrow street as if he hadn't been looking at her gate.

"A vieja," he said. "You don't want to work for her."

Ximena thought about Seven Palms. Cleaning six cottages. Queta and the others cleaned twenty rooms every day. Maybe this was a kind old woman whose niece or daughter or granddaughter had been at Seven Palms.

And abandoned a baby. At least, Ximena should deliver the small embroidered pouch to her.

The next day, Flor washed and ironed the uniform from Seven Palms. HOUSEKEEPING stitched in black above the pocket.

Emiliano pushed the Ring doorbell beside the rusted black gate. A man's deep eerie electronic voice came through the speaker.

"No deliveries scheduled today. Get lost. I will call LAPD."

Her uncle held up the license with the blond girl. "We are look for Barbara Goldman. We have a purse."

There was silence and a click. The gate slid open, into the dark bushes on either side.

On this long driveway where Ximena walked now, the van had brushed against branches that thumped green at the windows. A tunnel of soft darkness. Then a circle of cement driveway, and overgrown bushes and vines everywhere on the big white house. Like a church, with an arched doorway and black wrought-iron balconies below the windows. The heavy wooden door was open.

A woman was there, wearing a white robe, with a dark green oxygen tank at her side. She waited until Ximena and her uncle got within ten feet. Then they saw the black gun at the end of her wide sleeve. "Give it to me," she said. She wore a turban, like an old lady in a telenovela from long ago.

She looked at the tiny purse. She took the orange bottle. Ximena knew it said Dr. Donald Sanderson. "Where did you find this?" the old woman said to Ximena.

Luz had said those words countless times. "Coachella," Ximena said.

"The fucking music festival?"

Ximena thought quickly. Fidelia said to listen to the first part of the word. Música. She said, "No. From a doctor." She couldn't think of the word for Seven Palms. She looked at the small mouth of the gun, and then at the woman's lipstick mouth.

The woman lowered the gun. Pointed at the uniform. "You're a nurse?"

Ximena looked away, at the white roses. Not at the boobs, in the silk robe. Had this woman left the baby on the bed? She was too old. It had to be her daughter. Maybe a niece.

The woman said, "Did you see her? Angel?"

Ximena nodded. She thought hard about how Fidelia said it. I see her. I saw her. I know her. I knew her.

"I saw her. Angel."

"How do I know you're not lying? What did she look like?"

Ximena took a deep breath. She looked into the woman's eyes. One blue. One blue on top and a disc of green on the bottom. She held her breath. She'd seen an eye like that before. The baby from Seven Palms. But this woman was old as an abuela.

"Who sent you here?" the woman said, lifting the gun.

"She have a bee. On her—" Ximena touched her own left shoulder. "And a—conejo." What had Fidelia called it? "Rabbit. Here." She touched her right shoulder. The woman took a huge breath and then nodded.

Epifanio said in Mixtec, "Tell her you want to work here. Tell her I can trim the trees."

"You do it."

"You say it. She is afraid of me."

The woman said, "Don't do that. Don't talk whatever you're saying. That's not even Spanish. I know Spanish. What the fuck do you want? Did you come here for money? Cause I'm betting you're illegal. If I'm illegal and Angel's illegal, you're illegal, too, so what the fuck do you want?"

Fidelia said to listen for a long time while Americans spoke, to figure out what kind of people they were, before you let them know you understood English, and could answer. But Ximena didn't have a long time to listen, not with the gun pointed at Epifanio. She said, "No nurse. I am housekeeping. I want a job. He want a job."

The woman held the medication bottle tightly. Her face was covered with heavy foundation, nearly bronze. Her eyebrows drawn black. Her lips thick with dark pink lipstick. "A uniform. I like that. Classy. Look, I'm seventy-one years old and I'm fucking tired. It's a fucking mess in here. I can use you." She lifted her chin at Epifanio. "Leave her here. Come back at five. Push the Ring. I'll pay a hundred dollars a day in cash if she lasts. If she keeps her mouth shut. You can come do the yard on Friday mornings eight to twelve. Only then. I don't want to see you. I hate the sound of blowers. I mean it. I need all the trees done, everything cleaned up. But if you bring anybody else, or you come here at night, I'll shoot you. Not your daughter here. You."

Then she covered the gun with her sleeve and went back inside. Epifanio nodded. Ximena followed her through the huge arch of doorway.

Inside, Mrs. Bunny had held up the medication bottle and said, "What did she look like? This girl? When you saw her? This pharmacy is in Indio."

Ximena said, "Red hair. She come to Seven Palms. For—" She couldn't say it. Boobs? Boobs that didn't work? If this was Mrs. Bunny's daughter, how would Ximena just begin with the baby? "To see a doctor. Dr. Don."

Mrs. Bunny shook her head, said "Fucking Percocet." She threw the bottle in the trash, then got it back out. She didn't say anything else. Nothing about a baby. She slammed the orange bottle onto the black stone counter and said, "Take this outside to the garage. Find a shovel. Smash it and bury it by the fence. And then find some white spray paint. All these oxygen tanks are the ugliest fucking green. I want them white." She typed something on her phone, then looked up. "Blanco. Comprende?"

Ximena had never seen the gun again. But she knew where it was.

This morning, the heavy wooden door was closed. Six days a week, at eight a.m., Mrs. Bunny always opened the door in her thick white cotton robe, her head in the white silk turban. Then she went back upstairs. Today was Monday. The circle drive was empty, as every day. Only the white Cadillac, parked just in front of the garage doors. The garage was full of black crates with white labels. The car was always outside. On Fridays, Mrs. Bunny took it to the car wash.

The yard was spotless, now that her uncle came. The white brick planter in the center of the circle had only white roses, black large stones beneath them. The vines trailing over the wrought-iron balconies were white jasmine, their star flowers fading now in May. At the edges of the yard, the electric fence was covered by hedges of dark oleander, with white blooms. No yellow. No pink. No red.

No sound from the upstairs window. No television or music. She called up, "Mrs. Bunny. I am here. It is Monday."

Ximena's day off was Sunday. There had been an accident on a Saturday night in February. X had found Mrs. Bunny that Monday. Afterward, Mrs. Bunny had given her three keys. Ximena had used them only once since, on March 18. The day after LA went into lockdown.

A soft thumping against the upstairs window. Like a bird banging its head against the glass.

Now Ximena used her keys to open the deadbolt, then the second deadbolt. A new spiderweb between the two wrought-iron bars of the tiny window in the door.

Silence inside. In the kitchen, all the white cupboard doors closed, but on the long black marble counter, a crazy amount of color. Four empty bottles of Bombay Sapphire, the most beautiful blue. On the white wooden table with silver edges in the kitchen, five empty green bottles. Tonic water. Wine.

It had been blue bottles during the accident in February. The empty glasses would be upstairs.

Cocktail glasses. Why the tail of a cock? She missed Esteban, like the sudden fierce pinch he would give her elbow when they were small, in the forest, when he saw a bird's tail feathers gleaming. Quiet. Silence in their footsteps. She touched the blue bottle. The black water, the shine of his wet hair. His hand. Sometimes she believed he'd survived the canal. He'd bumped into the next ladder further down. Where would he go in the desert?

Sometimes she believed he had turned himself over and floated all the way to the sea.

Ximena put the Bombay bottles softly into the recycling. Flor loved blue. But Ximena had never taken a single napkin from this house.

She did exactly what she did every day. She made one fried egg and one toast with five strawberries on the side and one coffee. The juice of one tangerine, one grapefruit, and one orange, which she poured into a beautiful thin-glass bubble with gold on the rim. She opened the compartments of the medicine box and chose the right numbers from the list. She put the small white bowl of tablets and capsules, like the colorful droppings of magical animals, on the glass tray, and went up the white-carpeted stairs.

This was the bedroom suite. Sweet. Sweat. No Mixtec word for suite, because it was French. A French word to Spanish and English—a series of connected rooms inside a house. A series of connected musical pieces.

Maybe it had once been several rooms, but the entire second floor was the bedroom now. A round white bed the size of a moon, a glossy round white table with one white chair where Mrs. Bunny ate her breakfast, and all the walls that were not windows were white sliding doors. A giant walk-in closet for clothes and the smaller closet for shoes, a long white daybed with white pillows. The glass dressing table and the glass chair with the spoon back.

The glass chair was worth $12,500. Ximena had seen it in the *Vogue* on the table downstairs.

No other bedrooms were needed. Ximena had never seen another human inside this house since she began working for Mrs. Bunny. No animals, either. No small dog or fish or bird. Once, on the sliding glass doors at the back patio, which she sprayed with Windex and wiped every day, she had found a blue-throated lizard with a checkered back, but she escorted it outside with the broom.

Mrs. Bunny was not sitting at the dressing table. Not good. She put on her makeup before she did anything else. The white carpet was covered with clothes and shoes. Black dresses and white shirts. Black shoes. The closet doors were open and things were off hangers. The television was not on. The bed had not been slept in. There were two meal containers from Trader Joe's, half-eaten things, on the white table. Six glasses.

Ximena put down the breakfast tray. Silence.

The two paintings on the wall above Mrs. Bunny's bed were large squares of color. They were each worth a million dollars.

The only colors upstairs were those: droplets and threads and smears of paint on the canvas; the medications in the bowl; and the lipsticks, blush, eye shadows on the dressing table. The perfume bottle was gold.

Every morning, at nine, Mrs. Bunny ate breakfast in her bedroom. She would already have on her makeup. She would eat in bed, talk on the phone for two hours or so, then adjust the white-blond swirl of her hair, put on more makeup and perfume at her dressing table, and drink a second cup of coffee. She loved that cup, thin white china with a gold G, and that strong black coffee, more than anything. She would say, "X, the first cup—yeah. But the second cup—heaven. Nothing in the day is a good as that, X. Not until Tanqueray Time."

Then Mrs. Bunny would open the doors of the white closet containing the big-screen television, built into the wall facing the bed, and choose a morning movie.

Every morning, Ximena would take the breakfast dishes downstairs to the kitchen, and begin the daily tasks. The first day, Mrs. Bunny had shown her everything. "Todos las días," she told Ximena, "lo mismo." Then she ran out of Spanish. "Make it like we were never here. Never. *Nada*. No, that's nothing. Shit." Mrs. Bunny put her phone on Google translate and said it two times. *"Never here.* Clean like that."

Mrs. Bunny stayed up very late every night, watching television. She took her first nap at two p.m. Then, in the kitchen, Ximena would sit at the table and write in her notebooks.

Mrs. Bunny left only on Friday. Today was Monday.

Ximena said, "Mrs. Bunny."

The egg trembled a little on the plate. There was the sound of water running in the tub. This never happened. Mrs. Bunny always took a shower. The oxygen tanks were gone from their place near the bed.

"X."

"Mrs. Bunny."

"X. I need help. But the door is locked."

Ximena pushed against the bathroom door. Heavy wood, also painted white. She could smell alcohol, water, smoke.

"X. There's a fucking skeleton key. When Angel was little she would always try and open this door with the skeleton key. You know, like bones? Shit. What's the fucking word for bones? There's a big ass metal key. Like for a castle. In the drawer by the back door."

Ximena said, "Yes."

She went downstairs and found the drawer. Stupid word for a

key. Bones. Huesos. A metal ring with big blackened keys like in a children's book. Like for a castle. Back upstairs, she tried three. The fourth opened the bathroom door.

Mrs. Bunny was inside the giant built-in white marble bathtub. Ximena had never seen it used. The walls were dripping with water. The candles were out. The four oxygen tanks were lined up against the wall, near the tub, but she did not have her tube in her nose. Her cigarettes were gone. The ends of them inside one of the cocktail glasses on the bathroom floor, near the tub. She was not naked. She was in her silk pajamas, under the water. Her face had no makeup, her hair was many colors, and she held up her hands. Mrs. Bunny was missing the end of her middle finger, on her left hand—an absence she had never spoken about. Today, on each palm—two deep red burns. Perfect circles.

"Look. I can't get out of here. All I could do was add hot water about a million fucking times." She narrowed her eyes at Ximena. "You remember the deal, right? Kneetonosebasis. This is a oneoff."

Ximena tried to memorize the words.

"Three things, X. Yeah, I peed in here, and then I drained the fucking tub and ran new water. Twice. Yeah, the bathtub is the safest place if it's a hurricane or gunfight, okay? Yeah, you've seen me like this twice now, so you get it. This time it was Angel. Get me the fuck out of here."

Ximena pulled a stack of thick white towels out of the cupboard, where she put them every day. Where was the gun? The gun would be in here somewhere.

The first week, when Mrs. Bunny said, "Look, X, everything in my house is kneetonose, okay? Strict kneetonose and all you kneetonose I'm not gonna shoot you, because you're never gonna scare me or surprise me. Endofstory."

Ximena wrapped towels around Mrs. Bunny's thin shoulders

and pulled her up out of the water. Mrs. Bunny leaned hard onto her, and lifted out one leg. Then the other. She said, "Close your fucking eyes," and stripped off the pajamas. Ximena could feel the water through her pants legs. Mrs. Bunny said, "Throw them away. Silk. Fucking ruined."

She was wrapped in the towels, shivering. Her face was covered with pale freckles, flecks of gold in her pink skin, and the lines of white scars around her nose, which was flat and a little crooked. Her eyebrows were invisible. Without the wig, her hair was not white-blond. It was red and brown and black in a long stripe down the center of her skull. Her skin unlined. Ximena had known for months that Mrs. Bunny was not seventy-one.

Her fingers were wrinkled and fat as terrible grubs. She held on to Ximena's arm. She said, "I gotta sleep, X."

Ximena brought the thick cotton robe. Mrs. Bunny shivered. She looked at her palms. She said, "I laughed when he was doing it, because I couldn't feel a fucking thing. I had to work so hard when I was little I can't feel shit in my hands." Then she looked up at Ximena. "My hands looked like an old lady, so I figured my face could match. It's worked for years."

Ximena tried to follow. Match. Not the fire. Old lady.

He was doing it. A man. The man who had burned her couldn't have been here. Mrs. Bunny would never let anyone inside. She had left. She had gone somewhere on Saturday night or Sunday. Like February.

Mrs. Bunny lay in the bed in her robe, shivering. She ate one toast and took her pills with the orange juice. She turned on the television to the Hallmark Channel and went to sleep, the bedspread pulled up over her head like a rebozo, only her face showing. The round white satin pillow under her cheek.

Ximena was trembling. Monday was big laundry. Everything

off the bed. She was afraid to pick up the clothes, to stay in the room. She put the soaked towels in the basket and went downstairs to the laundry room.

Every day, she washed the towels, the two bathrobes, and the bath mat, dried them all, and put them back exactly as they had been in the upstairs bathroom. As every day, she poured in the liquid All and a half cup of the lime-scented liquid to make the towels smell fresh. She closed the lid and waited until the machine clicked and the waterfall began. Her favorite sound in this house. All. Todos.

Then she opened the center box of powder All detergent. No one had disturbed it. Like new snow. When it snowed in the mountains in Oaxaca, her grandmother took her to sit beside the perfect light drifts and wait for the first birds to etch their trails. Her grandmother said that was the most beautiful writing in the world. Messages sent to the gods.

If anyone came here, they came at night, after Ximena was gone. But she didn't think so. The day in February, Mrs. Bunny had been naked, sleeping on the floor. The bedroom was like an oven. The air-conditioning had broken. But Mrs. Bunny wouldn't call anyone. Ximena knew she'd never let a workman come inside.

Once, a repairman came for the refrigerator, which meant Mrs. Bunny must have called him, but when he came in his truck up the driveway and then stood outside the front door, Mrs. Bunny looked down from her bedroom window and shook her head. She told Ximena, "No, not now." Ximena opened the door and said, "No, not now."

The landline downstairs in the kitchen rang many times and he left his voice, but Mrs. Bunny only turned the dial inside the refrigerator. Sometimes the juice was frozen to slush and sometimes it was not. Sometimes the strawberries were hard as stones and sometimes they were not.

Mrs. Bunny had the Ring on her phone. Since corona, when the boxes came every day—makeup and shampoo and clothes and shoes and food—she could see the delivery truck and the men who left the packages by the gate. If they pushed the Ring, she said into her phone, "Leave the boxes and get on the road." Her voice was changed to a man's. If strangers pushed the Ring, she said, "Get the fuck off my property."

Twice, a motorcycle policeman came, with a helmet and sunglasses. Mrs. Bunny said into the Ring, "I didn't call the cops. Get your fake YMCA ass out of here." Three times, a Mexican man came, in a green truck. Mrs. Bunny said, "I have a gardener. Get the fuck off my driveway."

But last month, when Ximena went to retrieve the boxes in the cart she would bring up the driveway, that truck was sitting across the narrow street, half parked in a hedge. A green truck with a white stripe. The man got out and talked to her through the gate. Mirror sunglasses. Brown face, no beard or mustache, black hair short and combed back flat and shiny.

"Señorita!" he called. "Señorita!" He said something in Spanish. ICE. He looked like ICE. Don't run, Uncle Epifanio always said. Run means fear and guilt. Walk. She turned, feeling the cement under her white sneaker, and walked up the driveway as if he were only a stray animal. But inside she was quivering. She heard the electronic voice say, "Get the fuck away from my mailbox. I'm calling LAPD right now."

When she was halfway up the driveway, the loud truck moved away from the gate.

Mrs. Bunny looked at the Ring video footage for the whole morning. The man had been sitting there for two hours, reading something and looking at the driveway. "Who is this loser?" Mrs. Bunny said once. "What the hell?"

⋆ ⋆ ⋆

Ximena put the halves of the different fruits into the trash and washed the dishes. She kept looking out the glass back door at the yard. The electric fence inside the oleander bushes. The bushes were poison. The fence would kill someone. But who had burned Mrs. Bunny? For what reason?

She couldn't use the voice text on her go-phone, or Mrs. Bunny might hear and think she was telling someone. Ximena took all the glass bottles out to the recycling bin behind the garage. Near the electric fence that sent a strange minor hum through the hedges, she hesitated. Some of the words didn't translate at all into Mixtec or Spanish. She said slowly into the phone for Fidelia, "She say kneetonose bases. She is hurt. Somebody is hurt her. She say oneoff. Text me. I know you have school zoom."

Fidelia texted back immediately. *No internet today. The wind. Need to know basis? Like only what she tells you. Like secrets. Oneoff means it only happens one time. No more. Are you ok? Vieja loca shit! You better tell Tio Epifanio.*

Ximena whispered, "Yes. I am okay." Then she thought hard about her cousin's impatience. Fidelia's anger about corona. No school. No college. "Do not ghost me. I miss you."

Fidelia responded again. *Call Tio Epifanio.*

She didn't say I miss you, too. Fidelia hated the word *too*. Back in the Prowler, she told Ximena, "Love you too, miss you too, that shit means you don't. Not at all."

She slipped the phone into her apron pocket. She closed the trash bin. The wind was bending the tops of the huge dark cypress trees along the driveway. She hated it here sometimes. Alone in the crazy of Mrs. Bunny, or crowded in the bedroom with the girls. She didn't miss Oaxaca as much now as she missed Mecca. Sitting in the plastic chairs under the date palms. The sound the fronds made in the breeze. Sitting with her notebook at the small white table in the Prowler with Fidelia. Inez would bring a stack of galletas María, put the plate precisely between them. Soda—manzana for Fidelia, tamarindo for Ximena.

She didn't want to tell her uncle the truth about Mrs. Bunny. Four more days this week. One thousand dollars. If she lasted two more weeks, she would tell her uncle she wanted to go back to Mecca. Elpidia could stay here. Ximena would even work in the fields. At night, she could study with Fidelia, at her own table.

The rest of the day was quiet. It felt like Friday.

Every Friday at nine a.m., Mrs. Bunny called a woman named Anne-Marie, the phone on speaker, propped against the mirror. She would say, "Anne-Marie, it's lunchtime in New York." The woman would say, "I transferred the specified amount. Have a pleasant weekend, Mrs. Goldman. We miss your husband very much."

On Fridays, Mrs. Bunny took the car down the hill to get her hair and nails done, to go to the doctor, and to buy clothes and food. She was gone for six hours. During that time, Uncle Epifanio trimmed the hedges into perfect circles and squares along the edges of the white walls of the house. With a ladder, he carefully trimmed the bottoms of the cypress trees. He said one day she would have to call a man with a crane. He ate in his truck, and washed his hands at the hose, and peed into a hedge far from the house.

But since la corona, Mrs. Bunny hadn't left the house. Sixty-seven days. Until last night, when someone burned her hands.

Mrs. Bunny kept sleeping. Ximena didn't have to make the lunch salad with the ten vegetables. She ate her enchiladas. She folded the dried towels and bath mats and put them back in the laundry closet at the top of the stairs. She opened the door, to hear Mrs. Bunny breathing.

In the living room, as every day, she vacuumed. There was a white sofa, a white leather chair, another painting on the big wall, a glass table, and the black marble fireplace. Only three things stood on the mantel. She dusted them every day.

First the silver box that held Mr. Bunny's ashes. He had been a rich man. He sold fur coats to women. Then he collected paintings. He was dead.

Then the silver frame that held Mrs. Bunny's favorite photo. Like the Noir filter on the camera that Elpidia used once for her Instagram post. Mr. Bunny in a black suit, his black hair combed straight up and back, gleaming and shiny as Uncle Epifanio's. He was old, his throat wobbly above the tie, his eyebrows thick and lifted. Mrs. Bunny stood beside him in a white dress, strapless, her collarbones with a dark hollow at the center, and her red lipstick so dark it looked black here, her lips full and flat, her dimple a gray shadow, and the black dot beside her bottom lip. Her white-blond hair in two curves around her face and the ends flipped up like a frayed broom. A diamond necklace like the movies around her throat.

The other silver frame held a photo of Mr. and Mrs. Bunny standing near a horse. A girl on the horse, her hair braided with a white ribbon, her shirt creamy, a dimple on her left cheek, like her mother. The horse white with dark feet and tail, nostrils like black caves. Angel. Her boots black and shined; a black dot on her neck.

This was the girl from Seven Palms. How had she left a baby on that big white bed? How had she not brought the baby here, to Mrs. Bunny's big white bed?

Every day Ximena thought she should tell Mrs. Bunny about the baby. She said this once, to her uncle Epifanio, in the morning before anyone woke up. He sat watching the sky lighten above the tile roofs of the old apartments. He said, "You touched that baby. If you tell anyone, you are a criminal. They will arrest you. Deport you. If that woman doesn't shoot you."

"Why are you not afraid she'll shoot me now?"

He lifted his chin and moved his face toward Ximena like a turtle. Slow. Imperious. Mildly impatient. "She looked at me. She knows I am not what she thinks. I know she is not what she thinks."

Epifanio's gun was inside a tall flowered pot for umbrellas. Right by the front door. He and Flor slept in the Murphy bed a few feet from the front door. Emiliano and Jesús had guns in their bedrooms. Ulises had a handgun in an old wooden birdhouse attached to the tree two feet from his truck window. If the police came, they would never look there. But if someone tried to rob the rancho, which had happened two years ago when gang members wearing black hooded jackets rushed the trucks on a Friday afternoon, payday, as they pulled into the gate, yelling in Spanish to give them the money, holding guns on Queta, Moises, and Eufemio, this time there would be a fight.

Rodolfo had told Ximena about the guns. Ximena herself knew about the money, hidden in twenty different places all over the rancho. Flor had told her. "If the earthquake kills half of us, the other half can find the money."

Every woman needs her own stash, Mrs. Bunny said. You can't trust anyone. Ximena held the photo. Had Angel been here last night, even though there wasn't a trace of another smell? Ximena couldn't imagine Mrs. Bunny pregnant, or giving birth. Maybe Angel was a hallucination. One Monday, when Mrs. Bunny had drunk from the beautiful Bombay Sapphire bottle all afternoon, she held the photo of the three of them, and said to Ximena, "No padre." She put her finger on Mr. Bunny's small chest. "Not the padre."

Her husband. Not a priest? Not a father.

Then she said, her face private and terrible, her eyes red, "The padre was el Diablo. I know that word. Right? Diablo." She said the word slowly. "I sleep with el Diablo."

A father who was a devil.

Mr. Bunny's bones were larger pieces of gray and black in the dust of his flesh. Ximena had looked inside the box, once, on a Friday. Bones didn't burn completely. Her grandfather and everyone else buried in wooden boxes at the church in San Cristóbal were not even bones now—they had been eaten and carried away by the insects underground. When the police found her mother's body inside the car, in the flooded wash of the river outside Oaxaca City, she had been buried by mud and rocks for years. Abuela had to pay someone to bring back a box containing bones.

Ximena didn't think every day now about the bones of the baby buried inside the cement tower. The Mecca earth so dry and sandy and hot. She'd never tell anyone about the coyote. It didn't matter now. In her apron pocket, the phone buzzed with a text. *Coffee. Toast.*

She made the French press coffee. She toasted two pieces of the white bread. Butter only. She took it upstairs on the tray.

Mrs. Bunny was sitting at the white table, dressed in soft white pants, a white blouse with sheer long sleeves, and black sandals. She had put on all her makeup. And her hair was the usual silvery blond called Ash. It was a twisted bun on top of her head, with a white headband around her forehead.

Ximena took out the Windex and paper towels. She cleaned the drops of dark foundation from the glass dressing table, the spill of blue eye shadow. A set of drawers against the wall contained all the makeup and lotions. Mrs. Bunny might be the only woman in California who covered her face every morning, adjusted her wig, and attached her oxygen tank to her nose, just to look like a sexy grandmother.

"Yeah. A new wig." Mrs. Bunny took the coffee cup. "That's how I got in trouble Saturday. I went down to a wig store in Hollywood. And another place I should never have gone back to. But look, X. You're going to stay here tonight. Call your dad."

Ximena said, "I don't stay all night. The rules."

Mrs. Bunny said calmly, "The rules changed last night. There was a Mexican guy. He called when I was with Angel. FaceTime. He said he wants some money. He said he knows where I live, and he knows where my pretty little maid lives. I guess he's seen your dad's van."

The man in the green truck? With the mirrored sunglasses? Ximena couldn't breathe. All these months she'd been afraid of the virus—people said you would try to take in air and it felt like a man was sitting on your chest. She felt the coyote in the garage, sitting on her, crushing her face into the floor. "Who he is? The man?"

Mrs. Bunny said, "I only saw her face on his phone. He's an asshole. Speaks Spanish and English. Cowboy shirt. That's it. She—" For the first time, Mrs. Bunny's backbone melted. She never sat anything but straight like a queen in her chairs and on her bed, up here in this second story. She had never come downstairs while Ximena was here, after the first day.

"She met him at some bar. I haven't seen her for two years. But you're staying here. She's my kid. You're his kid. Your dad's. So call him now and tell him you're staying here where it's safe inside the fence. Unless he's got a helicopter, this asshole can't get to us. But your dad should keep an eye out wherever you live. At your house. I hope your mom has a dog."

Ximena sat on the floor. She had never sat on the glass chair or the bed or the white leather couch. She looked at Mrs. Bunny's ankles.

Mrs. Bunny said, "Look. X. You think he did this to me?" She held up her palms. The burns were black-edged holes inside the curl of her hands. "I'll tell you the truth. He kept calling last night telling me what he'd do to me if I didn't give him the money, and I lit a cigarette and did this to myself on his fucking FaceTime. I told him if I could do that to myself what the fuck would I do to him? And I hung up." But tears edged out of her eyes, and ran fast off the heavy foundation on her cheeks. She grabbed a tissue.

Ximena took the coffee cup with its heavy pink stain of lipstick, and the white plate. She told herself what Fidelia said when she panicked on a test. Breathe in count four, breathe out count seven. Not a sound.

She went downstairs. She voice texted her uncle. *I have to stay here tonight. Mrs. Bunny is sick. Maybe the virus. I cannot come home until tomorrow.*

He texted back. *No.*

Yes. It is ok. I am not sick. She is in her room. Upstairs.

No. I am coming.

Ximena said into her phone, *The gate is locked. The fence is on. I am sleep on the couch. I will see you tomorrow. She can call ICE. Do not come here.*

Because no matter what Mrs. Bunny said, or how much money she gave Ximena, she could always call ICE if she wanted to. Ximena never forgot that.

Until midnight, Mrs. Bunny talked on the phone to someone. Not speakerphone like usual, propped against her pillow. Just her own voice, low and unceasing.

Ximena had gotten sheets and a blanket from the linen cupboard. She lay on the couch downstairs, listening to the mockingbird. She breathed. She opened her phone and looked at Elpidia's

Instagram to distract herself. She would post for her cousin, who would be as angry as Uncle Epifanio that Ximena hadn't come home. With the phone.

Back in August, on their first night sharing the double bed in Hollywood, Elpidia was so angry that she'd poked holes into Ximena's back with a safety pin from her uniform. "You cost me Carlos," she cried near Ximena's ear. "I only got one night with him. He would have married me."

Ximena felt the blood welling up from the holes. Five pricks. But she was afraid to move, because they would smear the sheets, and she didn't know yet whether Flor had a temper. In the morning, Yesika's old T-shirt stuck to Ximena's back as if the five small black dots were buttons fastened to her skin.

They gave Elpidia a long-sleeved khaki shirt and told her to get in the palm tree truck. She complained bitterly. She wore a hat, gloves, and covered her face with sunscreen. But after the first month, she lost weight, and her face changed. No more baby fat—all hollows and lips and big eyes. On Sundays, she and Ximena went to Goodwill, to Dollar Tree, and at night, Elpidia transformed herself into @oaxacaliprincess.

Yesika and Yesenia showed Elpidia hundreds of Instagrams, how to crop out everything but her face and body, and only two accessories—a flower, a necklace, a fake tattoo, a diamond glued to her body. Ximena took all the photos on the phone—she was good with angles and lighting now. But it was stupid and dangerous—the phone tracked them. Ads popped up for everything they spoke about—as if watchful gods were in the bedroom. Their uncle would be furious if he found out.

At night, on Ximena's phone, Elpidia posted her photos and read every DM sent to her by every lonely man. She smiled and read some aloud to Ximena from her pillow. "I don't want to meet them. I just want them to see how beautiful I am," she whispered. But the phone knew East Hollywood as their location, and Ximena said, "ICE will find us. Google knows our address. It hears us."

Elpidia shrugged. "No one can find us here. Not at this stupid rancho. Like a jail."

Ximena scrolled through photos from two nights ago, which they hadn't used yet. Elpidia had dressed in a blue bathing suit from Savers, one she'd worn before, but she did her hair differently and put on dark blue lipstick. She made Ximena take the photo in front of the bedroom mirror, only her back showing, the temporary tattoo of a sunflower at the center of her spine, and the edge of her hair and cheeks and lips from where she looked around to her own butt. Her arms were toned and muscled now, her hair long and glossy, ending just before the tattoo.

Ximena closed her eyes and listened. Mrs. Bunny's voice rolled on, not agitated. The mockingbird—he would stop singing if someone tried to drive up. The fence was on.

She had taken thirty-six photos of Elpidia in the blue. She edited the best one carefully. Vivid blue. Sunflower sharp. What would Elpidia write? *Me&You*. Boys loved that. She posted it. Elpidia had 4,289 followers. Last night's post had 597 likes, 36 DMs. Yesika would see this one within seconds.

The twins had their own secret Instagram. Their photo was from the back, their long hair braided together into a single thick twine with ribbons and flowers, like a beautiful vine to their waists. They were @amortrenzas. They loved only each other. Their photos were only their boots, alongside each other; their hands, on the sidewalk, with rings; their knees, in lacy skirts; their faces, with matching makeup and earrings. They had 12,362 followers.

She left the phone under the couch pillow. She was afraid to turn it off. All the buzzing while strangers sent hearts to her cousin would help her stay awake.

She could hear a single cricket outside the front window. "People say they sing, but they rub their legs together," Fidelia said. "Thank god, not the grasshoppers." The grasshoppers of Los Angeles were gray monsters with razor legs and terrifying skulls that hit Ximena in the face when they flew from the roses.

She had no idea whether she should be afraid. Her notebook was on the glass coffee table beside her. She lit the white jasmine candle and peered at the pages. Suite. Sweat. Sweet. Class. Classy. With Class. In Class. Pedicure. Manicure.

She saw the silk pajamas sticking to Mrs. Bunny's legs in the bathtub. Calves. Cows. Calf. Thigh. Ankle. Knee. Heel. Don't give me the bread heel. Chicken—thigh or drumstick. Not a real drumstick.

Palm trees. Palm fronds. Hearts of palm in the salad. The palm of your hand. Burned.

She closed her eyes. The room was dark but for the moonlight coming in one slice through the heavy drapes. When she was small, her grandmother had talked about a woman who had lost a child. She said a lost child was like the moon. Always in the sky—even new, even in daylight, a sliver like the edge of a scythe blade. Never not there.

She heard a terrible ringing. The landline in the kitchen. Voices shouted into the message machine. Mrs. Bunny ran downstairs. Ximena jumped up from the couch and stared.

"Pick up, Mom! Pick up!"

"Pick up the fucking phone or I kill her, cabrona. You old bitch! Answer the phone!"

Mrs. Bunny was wearing the same white pants and a bra. No shirt. The white silk turban on her head, which she wore only while applying her makeup. Never to leave the house.

She had put foundation only on her forehead. It was as if a cloud had landed there, golden and smudged. Her cheeks and her chest were like a mosaic of gold and brown and beige. Her skin was transparent above her breasts, every green and blue vein branched out into her shoulders as if her heart was a tree. Ximena caught her breath at the thought of red blood turned cool by the time it reached the arms.

She said, "Come up here, X. Now."

On the bedroom television were people gathered in front of buildings, lining up, shouting. Upper lips lifted and teeth showing. More like anger than fear. No pieces of building lying in the street, but there were broken windows. Where was this? The earth had not shaken.

"Hackers. The whole system is going down. I let my phone die last night, I guess." She looked out the big bedroom window. "Coffee."

While Ximena made the coffee in the kitchen, she heard the landline ring again. Shouting. Mrs. Bunny came down the stairs with thick makeup smeared across only her nose, cheeks and forehead, two slashes of thick red lipstick, the turban tilted on her head, a white blouse buttoned wrong, and a white silk flow half hiding the wrinkles on her pants. Her purse clutched tight to her chest. She had no eyebrows. She went out the front door without speaking to Ximena. She didn't have her air in the tank, or a mask on. Ximena ran upstairs to get both, but Mrs. Bunny had started the Cadillac. The long white car roared around the circle driveway. A flutter of white dangled from the driver's door.

Mrs. Bunny had twenty-seven flows. Ximena had counted them. Long sheer vests, mesh sweaters, shimmery pieces of fabric that hung past her knees. She'd turn at the mirror and say, "A flow makes any outfit look classy. It gives you a long line."

She'd slammed the big car door on her favorite flow—white silk long sleeves, past her hands so no one could see her missing finger. Tiny black embroidered blossoms. Mrs. Bunny swerved and then roared down the driveway.

The earth had not shaken. If the earth shook on a Friday, the only day Mrs. Bunny left the house, Ximena's instructions were to take down the two paintings in the bedroom, wrap them in white sheets, take them outside far from anything that could fall on them, and sit beside them until Mrs. Bunny, and no one else, came home.

She looked down at her phone. It was 10:57. How had they slept so long? The television went silent, the refrigerator ceased humming. The only sound was the mockingbird. He trilled like a car alarm, barked like a dog, screeched like tires, and then broke into a long melodious song that must have belonged to another bird. Ximena shivered, thinking of Rodolfo whistling the notes back at Seven Palms, to tell them ICE was coming. Right now, Elpidia and Rodolfo might be as far as San Fernando, or Encino.

But Uncle Epifanio could be on his way here.

In the laundry room, she opened the cupboard where she kept her messenger bag. If she had to run down the hill, toward Hollywood, someone might try to grab it. She took out her California ID card, her money—three bills every day, for safety, a one, five, and ten. She put them into the left cup of her bra. The three boxes of All detergent smelled strong. She could take some of Mrs. Bunny's money now. If Mrs. Bunny didn't come back, and the power didn't come back, she'd take $100 and walk home.

Uncle Epifanio had told everyone that when the earth shook, they were to stay exactly where they were. He would come for them. Never walk away. Never. I will find you. Or your body.

The uncles would find everyone, no matter where they were. And Ximena wondered at night, when the earth shook a little, whether they would shove away the bodies of strangers.

Ximena went upstairs to look at the paintings. Should she take them down now? She had just gotten out white sheets when she heard the powerful engine of the Eldorado returning up the driveway.

She stood hidden in the heavy drapes by the bedroom window. The Cadillac came slowly up the hill, stopping and starting, hesitating and then surging forward as if Mrs. Bunny had never navigated the incline. Mrs. Bunny always drove fast and smooth. Once she had knocked her radio off the dresser when a loud song came on. "'Slow Ride.' I hate this song. I drive fast. Always have."

The car lurched forward once more like a leashed dog. Then it stopped in the circle at the top of the drive. But Mrs. Bunny's car door didn't open. She never wanted Ximena to come outside and open the door. She liked to open it herself, come inside with her purse, and then Ximena could get the bags.

She'd been to Trader Joe's? In that crowd of people? She hadn't worn a mask. What if she had the corona? What if she were drunk?

Suddenly the whine of another car labored up the driveway. Small and blue. It emerged from the line of cypress and circled to block in Mrs. Bunny's car. Headlights to headlights. A man got out and stalked toward Mrs. Bunny's window to bang his hand flat on the glass. He hit the window three times. "Fuck!" he shouted. "Angel! You fuckin bitch!"

When the driver's door opened, that white hair was not Mrs. Bunny's. It was yellower, thick and dry as yucca fiber swirled onto the skull. Another old woman, Ximena thought, until the man grabbed the back of the hair and tilted up the face, and from the high window Ximena saw the black eyeliner and red lipstick on the young woman's face before he kissed her roughly for a long time.

Mrs. Bunny must be dead. These two people had stolen her car. Ximena faded herself further into the drapes. She had to run. But the man was shouting again, and she made herself look out the window. He held the elbow of the yucca-haired woman. Her blouse was pulled off both shoulders. Tattoos covering her back in a floral hedge. A bee? A rabbit? His fingers dug in and he spun her around. "Do it, mamacita."

The young woman opened the passenger door, and Mrs. Bunny's thin arm appeared in her fingers. She pulled hard. She said, "Ándale, bitch."

Ximena ran down the stairs to the laundry room. She grabbed the box of All and ran back up to the bedroom. The front door slammed open. Mrs. Bunny kept the black gun under a round white satin pillow that lay flat, touching the headboard.

They shouted downstairs. "The money! Where's the money, old bitch?" Something broke in the kitchen. Glasses and bottles. Then they came upstairs. Mrs. Bunny had not spoken. From inside the smaller closet, Ximena smelled the leather of the many shoes. The musky odor of pantyhose even though she had washed them.

The man slammed open the sliding mirrored door of the big closet, tore at the clothes and shouted, "Fuck! You said fur coats!"

Then his black pointy-toe boots stopped at the crack of light near Ximena's knees. She hadn't been able to completely close the doors from the inside, holding the detergent and the gun.

He slammed the door open. He wore a black pearl-snap shirt. He was pale as Luz, and he called her terrible names in Spanish, which she understood. She was on her knees. She didn't move. He shouted long instructional sentences in Spanish, which she didn't understand. His teeth were edged with gold.

The first coyote had screamed at her in the same Spanish, on the Mexican side of the border at Mexicali, four teeth lined with gold like tiny gilt-framed portraits in his open mouth. The first coyote had shouted for her to swim, for her brother to swim. Fuckin indios! Swim! The swift waters of the All-American Canal had shoved her sideways, as if snakes roped her legs, and then she remembered the dogs in the river back at San Cristóbal, heads up, snouts in the air, legs furious below. She lifted her face to the night and kicked. But Esteban went under. Ten feet away, he rose, his T-shirt filled with air like bread. His hair glistening in the flashlight beams of the coyotes. Then his hand, sliding away. Then nothing.

Ximena had scrabbled for the other side of the sloped cement wall. A metal ladder slammed into her shoulder and she twisted for it. On the other side, the second coyote waited until she made the top rung, gasping, and then he grabbed her by the hair, pulled her over the side, and threw her to the earth so hot it burned her shoulder blades, even though it was night. Then he kicked her onto her stomach, and the sand filled her mouth.

Now this man took a step over the closet threshold. His boot. "Puta! Give me the pistola, fuckin culera." She knew these words. She could smell him. Ximena shot him in the left foot. Straight down. That way, she didn't have to look up at his teeth.

He fell sideways, like a corn stalk. He screamed like a pig, voice high. And from behind, Mrs. Bunny hit him in the head with her oxygen tank.

He lay with a trickle of blood coming from the back of his skull, where the tank had smashed bone. A river of blood pulsed out of the hole in the top of his black boot. Red on the white carpet. Mrs. Bunny whispered, "Angel!"

Angel put both hands on her head and looked at the chandelier above her. Mrs. Bunny backed toward the bed, and Angel helped her sit down. Mrs. Bunny tried to breathe—the thickened hiss and gasp at the base of her throat. Ximena crawled around the man and stood up. She wheeled the other canister of air close, hooked up the tube, and Mrs. Bunny draped the plastic at her nostrils.

Then Ximena handed Mrs. Bunny the box of All. Todos. Under a thick layer of detergent, Mrs. Bunny kept paper money rolled tight as flautas, tied with twine, and encased in Ziploc baggies. When Ximena found the stash, she thought it might be a test. While the sheets and towels swirled in the machine, she had counted the money in one baggie, counted the baggies, estimated the total, and slid them all back under the detergent. She shook the box gently to settle it. Her fingers felt slick as small fish under the faucet when she washed off the residue of soap.

Angel stared at her. The black dot at the left side of her throat was larger than in the picture with the horse. Ximena was almost afraid to look at the boobs under her peasant blouse, the black bra under white cotton. The tattoo of the rabbit was now surrounded by flowers—roses and vines and strange tendrils along her shoulders. The bee held up gloves—into sunflowers.

The baby was her baby. The tiny lips. The fingers.

Ximena crouched down and held on to the side of the mattress, so she wouldn't fall. Mrs. Bunny breathed again and said, "You did good, X. Come on. You're fine."

Angel went into the bathroom and came out with a white towel, which she wrapped around the man's boot. Ximena grabbed the bottle of spray cleaner from the dressing table and bent near the blood on the carpet, but Mrs. Bunny said, "No. We have to go. Vamos."

Angel tied the towel around the man's boot with the thin satin belt from the white dressing gown hanging on the door. The man's mouth hung open and his eyes stayed closed. Ximena looked into the gold recesses of his teeth. Was he American? Americans never had gold teeth in front. Did they have them in the back?

Was he breathing?

Angel wrapped another thick towel around his face and head and tied it with the thick cotton belt from the white bathrobe. She gestured to Ximena. Ximena took the feet.

He didn't move.

They carried the man down the stairs, out the front door, and laid him on the hot concrete for a moment. Angel opened the trunk of the Cadillac, and they lifted him inside. The lid slammed down tight and square.

Ximena looked into Angel's face. How old was she? The fine freckled skin she had glimpsed at Seven Palms was covered now with heavy foundation. A bruise deep blue on her cheek. Her eye-liner slanted up in jaunty black tails. But on her forehead, three deep lines etched into the skin over each eyebrow. She raised her brows now and Ximena saw how the lines had gotten there. Her throat was marked with bruises of green and yellow.

"What?" Angel said. "What the fuck are you looking at?"

Mrs. Bunny called now from the front door. "X! The other Klee."

She had made herself older again. Wide-legged white pants and a white jacket with the gold entwined C's. Chanel. She had put the wig on, and the rest of her foundation, and her lipstick. Gold shadow and black lines on her eyelids, brown on her brows. She held one painting from her bedroom, like a small door under her left arm, and the oxygen cart handle in her right hand. She had loaded the canister herself. But she pointed back upstairs.

Ximena stood on the bed to get the painting from the wall. Mrs. Bunny had put the box of All on the dressing table. Ximena picked it up. At the linen closet, her hands trembling, she got two more clean sheets from the stack. In the laundry room, her messenger bag.

In the driveway, she took the black gun from her apron pocket, handed it to Angel, and got in the back seat of the Cadillac, with the paintings on the floor.

Mrs. Bunny drove down the alternating stripes of light from the cypress. Flash and dark and flash and dark. Her canister in the special holder between the seats. The man was inches from Ximena's back, in the trunk.

She had shot him in the foot. That wouldn't kill him. Mrs. Bunny had killed him.

"Three years," Mrs. Bunny said.

"I know," Angel said, looking out the window.

"Where the hell were you?"

"I can't tell you. Just like you couldn't tell me."

"Angel."

"Phoenix. Palm Springs."

"With him?"

"No."

In the bright sudden light at the end of the driveway, Mrs. Bunny's cheeks were deeply cross-hatched. The skin on the backs of her hands so thin that as she gripped the white leather steering wheel, those four small bones showed like the structure under batwings.

As the gate slid open, Mrs. Bunny looked both ways on the winding narrow street. She didn't notice the green truck with the white stripe on the door. Parked halfway in the hedge across the street. The brown man in the driver's seat. His mirrored sunglasses.

Then Angel spoke softly. "Mom," she said. "Mommy."

Ximena closed her eyes. The way they said the words here, in Los Angeles. Mom. Mommy.

Mrs. Bunny drove fast down the winding Dundee Drive. The green truck followed. This man was ICE, or he was another criminal who knew the man in the trunk.

From her wallet, Ximena took out the yellow Post-it where Uncle Epifanio had written the address of home. She reached forward to tap Angel on the shoulder. But she stopped. The huge pink flower on her left shoulder blade. Angel had left the baby girl wearing a pink dress. On that bed. For Don. She's yours. You feed her. Would Angel tell her mother?

Ximena touched the yellow throat of the pink flower. Angel jumped as if burned. Her hair was so dry it looked baked onto her head, in snakes of curls. Her forearms had purple scars everywhere, and the new red marks from the fingers of the man in the trunk.

Ximena pictured the bones of his feet. The five bones at the top, where she had shot him. She looked at the bones of Mrs. Bunny's hands turning the wheel. She had to get out of this car.

Angel said the address out loud, and Mrs. Bunny said, "Hollywood? Sunset Boulevard? Shit."

Down two more hills, on the wide avenue, the street was full of cars, honking and stopped. Masked people were lined up in front of ATMs. They argued on the sidewalks. Their arms were moving, gesticulating, waving, or pointing. Phones held in one hand. No one was bent over, concentrating. The money. The money was gone. The phones were dead.

"Fucking China," Angel said. "Whoever."

Mrs. Bunny pointed to Angel's arms. "That wasn't China," she said.

The red lights were all blinking on the big street. Mrs. Bunny swerved the car to a small street, then another one, and drove west. Ximena knew it was west because the sun was slightly in front of them. It was lunchtime.

She could walk home. The man in the truck could be calling police, or calling his friends. Epifanio said, "Los Feliz has small mountains. Santa Monica is the west. We are in the center. You could walk if you had to, after the earthquake. Find Sunset Boulevard and keep walking west. Never put the address in your phone. Never."

Mrs. Bunny drove as if she knew exactly where she was going. She honked her horn, went into the bus lane, and all the while spoke long quiet sentences to her daughter, who was crying. Mrs. Bunny did not sound angry, or sad. She told a story about Hollywood. That word over and over. And Your Father.

Mrs. Bunny swerved around corners and roared forward in the big car, then stopped fast, until Ximena felt so sick she pressed her head against the window. After a long time, she saw the Botánica Esperanza y Caridad.

Ximena leaned forward and said, "Here."

Mrs. Bunny stopped abruptly, and the oxygen canister rattled in the holder. They were never to give a different address to Americans or let anyone see the entrance to the court. Mrs. Bunny didn't care. She said something to Angel, who looked into the back seat. She pointed to Ximena's apron. Ximena took it off, and Angel pointed to the two paintings wrapped in the sheets. Ximena hesitated, and Angel looked at her mother, then drew her finger in a line from the apron to the paintings.

Ximena wrapped her apron over the white sheets, then put three flowered Trader Joe's reusable bags on top. Mrs. Bunny said nothing. She was looking straight ahead. Then she slanted her fist backward over the seat, and dropped two rolls of money like a pair of green cigarettes into Ximena's lap.

One roll had ten $100 bills. There were one hundred rolls in the box of All.

Cars were honking loudly at the stopped Cadillac. "Adios," Angel said softly.

Would she tell her mother about the baby? Would they go to Seven Palms? Would a woman like that—how old was she?—forget the baby completely?

Ximena put the money in the right cup of her bra. She stepped onto the street, stepped quickly to the sidewalk. The Cadillac rolled slowly away. She put on her bandanna mask. She didn't move until the green truck had passed her. The man with the sunglasses didn't look at her. He watched the Eldorado.

She walked the wrong way for four blocks, just in case he had criminal friends watching her. There were people everywhere on the sidewalk, some in masks, some not. She had no sweater, no apron—just the white uniform that said HOUSEKEEPING.

She had kept the house. The feel of the gun. The smell of it. She had no job now. She would explain to her uncle that Mrs. Bunny had disappeared. Ximena would ask him to take her to Mecca. There was no reason to stay here. She could hide the rolls of money until corona was gone, and the College of the Desert was open. Fidelia said in California, anyone could go to community college. Anyone.

She turned around and began to walk back. Finally she saw the shiny black truck with the big tires. Ulises in his Silverado. Parked along the depression in the sidewalk in front of the gate. Usually playing games on his phone, while he watched, or making fun of girls and their Instagrams. But now he grinned at her, from the window, and said in Mixtec, "They did it. The Russians. Or North Koreans." He laughed. "Not the Mexicans. They can stop hating on us."

"Did what?"

"Broke the system. The internet is down. Banks are hacked. Somebody wants to shut America down again." He looked at her messenger bag. "You walked? You were supposed to stay there."

"She gave me a ride. Last day."

"What happened to your knees?" He frowned.

Blood. "She cut herself. I had to clean the floor."

He unlocked the gate and let her in. She slid through and walked down the court.

In the hiding places, the uncles had bills of each denomination because they said after the earthquake, they would need one and five and ten and twenty, to buy gas and propane and maybe meat. They had five-gallon containers of water in each apartment.

Uncle Eufemio and Epifanio sat in chairs in front of the first house, watching her approach. Eufemio's shoulder wrapped with bandages soaked in alcohol and herbs. She'd forgotten a heavy fall of palm bark had hit him the day before—his shoulder nearly broken. His hands were folded over his wide square belly. They waited for Ximena to tell them why she hadn't stayed as instructed. But she did not speak.

She turned into her doorway and went to her room. She took off her uniform, spattered with blood around the knees, and pushed the pants and shirt into the tiny closet. The apron had caught most of the blood, and now it was guarding the paintings in the car.

She moved through the narrow channel between the two

double beds and the dressers. She got into the cool empty bed where Elpidia usually took up room.

On the windowsill, she kept one china cup with the thinnest gold rim, which Mrs. Bunny had given her. She kept a single short stem of flowers there. The tiny white stars inside the red blossoms of bougainvillea, like a secret held inside each flower. Back in January, one evening the sun had gone down so early that she sat near Mrs. Bunny's gate and white moths had come to drink nectar from the blossoms of a silver cactus.

Her grandmother said if you could find one small piece of beauty every day you would live. No matter what. Even a coffee bean with a dimple. She handed the bean to Ximena. "Like your cheek," she said to Ximena.

If she could never see her grandmother again, never see Esteban, she wanted Fidelia. For a sister. She closed her eyes now, hearing sirens, the helicopters overhead; smelling the fresh-scent detergent-dusted bills between her breasts; seeing the back of Mrs. Bunny's neck where the flesh was still unmarked, sloping down into the collar of the white Chanel knit jacket with faint gold thread woven into the fabric. Mrs. Bunny had her daughter back.

She saw her brother laughing, the summer before they left, in the field of corn, calling her to come see the grasshoppers, his palm over the opening of the coffee can filled with so many small leapings.

ELDORADO

Last year, in August, I couldn't go to work when I had the black eye. When you're a cop, you're always supposed to be breaking up fights, keeping people from killing each other, but your face has to look respectable, like you haven't gotten your ass kicked. On *Gunsmoke*, all those cowboys and criminals punching each other in the face at the Long Branch, they hit each other with chairs and knocked each other out, but Matt Dillon never walked around with a black eye for weeks.

Tavares had a hell of a fist. He took out everything about his son on my face.

My sergeant told me to take three weeks off because I had so much sick time. I went to the doctor. One of my orbital bones was broken. My skull like the calavera, but no sugar to make it sparkle. My left eye sagging above my cheekbone, and the doctor said the swelling was so bad he couldn't tell yet whether he could fix it.

I went back to Bobby Carter's place. He and Manny and Grief were there, drinking beer. Grief said, "If you had a kid, you'da known better. You shouldn't have come. He lost his boy. And his first love. Shit, Johnny, Miller trained that rookie? Did Miller know we knew Tenerife?"

I shook my head. "He didn't know. Miller said he saw a black object. Weapon. He started yelling *Gun Gun Gun*." I looked up at the ramada. "Rookie quit the job and went to live with his mom in Oklahoma. Miller's still a sergeant."

Grief threw his beer bottle at one of the old eucalyptus trees. Shatter that always sounded sweet though it was never anything but mean. He shouted, "That's bullshit! That works all the time now. Phone's always a gun! What the hell am I supposed to tell Dante?"

Then he took a bucket and went away from us, picked up the glass on the ground, but his shoulders were shaking. Manny said to me, "You better go, homes. Not yet."

I looked at Manny. "Remember Luis Padilla? When we went to his gym? That's how I almost killed Miller. Back at Anza Crossing. You think I don't do that fucking Jenga game in my head, mano? If Miller was dead, I'd be in jail for life. But Tenerife and Merry would be alive. Maybe. That's the kind of shit I get to consider while I'm on the bike and now I'm at home on the couch. I got nada. Not a fucking thing."

I drove the truck from Rialto all the way to Echo Park. The old gym on Sunset Boulevard near Alvarado was closed now. The virus.

I sat in front of the wrought-iron door. Back then, Luis Padilla told us, "You want to kill some pendejo, you don't need a gun. Guns are for cowards, man. Three punches. Not the damn jaw, man. Órale pues, you want him not breathing? You see how boxers keep their chin down? To protect the throat. Hit a man in his right temple and you get his eye and his brain. Two seconds and he's not thinking as good. Then lift up his chin with your left. Then go for the throat with your right. He ain't breathing after that, homes." Then he surprised us. "But you'll be breathing in prison. Cause you'll be a killer. So don't do that shit by accident. Fight the body, right here. And don't forget what somebody might do to you."

I used to think all the time, what if I hadn't had the service gun when I went up to Bee Canyon? Could I have killed the guy with three punches? He was vicious and he had a knife. I didn't know Reynaldo's capoeira kicks, like somebody in a movie, to get rid of the knife. But everything in my life had started with that one bullet.

I took Sunset up to Vermont and drove into Los Feliz. Dundee Drive. The black gate. A white van with a sunset decal—SUNSET HOUSEKEEPING—stopped there. The small girl with the long trenza and white uniform came out of the gate. She stared right at me. Her face like my mother's in her high school portrait. Big black eyes. Tilted up to match her cheekbones.

Viejo driving. He didn't even look at me. He went slow, turning around at the top of the street. I got out and pushed the Ring and the distorted deep electric man's voice said, "Get the fuck off my property. I don't need a gardener. I will call LAPD. Go."

I drove down the Golden State Freeway to Santa Ana. I went to Samana Som's doughnut shop. He said, "Johnny Frías. What happen to you?"

"I got punched," I told him. Som never looked any different. Short, wide, his face the same brown as mine, never wrinkled or changed. His daughter dead in my arms, the deer bleeding, still alive, making sounds I had never heard before. Chhoua. Wetsuit on the Volkswagen seat.

One day a few years ago he brought out a map and put it on

the counter. He waited till we were alone in the shop, which almost never happened. He said, "Johnny. She keep this in her room when she in high school. Look at these wave." She'd marked the Pacific Ocean, off the coast of southern California, then past Hawaii, where the water turned into South China Sea, and then Bay of Thailand, where the waves washed up onto the shores of Cambodia.

She'd been headed to the beach and maybe thinking about the water like that, about her dad leaving on a boat and ending up in a refugee camp. Her grandmother. The photo of flowers in pots at the doorway of the wooden shelter. The dimes on her mother's wrist. Now all three women buried in the cemetery in Santa Ana.

Samana Som took the map back without a word. Suddenly I heard Melt Olson say, *Out of the blue, she says that*. Never out of the green, or orange, or brown. Out of the blue.

Samana Som said now, "You go see your dad?" I nodded back. He filled a pink box with my father's favorite buttermilk bars and the basic round glazed me and the Vargas brothers liked. I put two twenties into his tip jar.

I drove up the ranch road. My eye felt like it was jelly that would fall out of my skull. My dad said, "Mijo, you crashed the bike?"

I shook my head and sat on the new redwood chair. Still gold and pink. A family made them every year, sold them off a truck all over Orange County. Romany people. Their grandmother used to come here.

No rope. I looked at my dad. He sighed.

"Johnny. You never fight. You went to the wrong bar? MAGAs? Borrachos, pues?"

He got a piece of steak from the old Frigidaire. Seriously, like a cartoon. A big porterhouse flopping over his hand. Why the hell was a steak full of blood and muscle and fat supposed to heal a black eye that was blood and thin eyelid skin and a hole in the head?

I told him about the Jack in the Box, Miller ordering the boys out onto their knees but it was the drive-thru and there was no room to move. The black phone falling out and Tenerife bending to pick it up.

"Diablo. The phone," he said.

"Papi," I said. "Ya sabes, there'd be something else. They got you all back in the day for a hoe or a machete."

He looked up into the bougainvillea and said, "Sí. The pruning knife for lemons. Benny Hernández. They shot him in Placentia. 1971."

While the black eye turned purple, green, and then yellow, I helped my father clear more burned wood from last year's fire. We chain-sawed the charred sycamore trunks and stacked the big pieces for him to decide what to do with it later. Sometimes he liked to make benches to set in the groves, or near the corral. The pomegranate trees hadn't burned—the orange blossoms lining the ranch road up to Mrs. Dottie's house. We ended up pruning the trees at the edge of her big garden, and she came outside to watch us. The tiniest old lady, but stocky in the chest in her work dress, and boots on her feet. She watered the pots of geraniums and roses she had on the tile patio. She lifted her chin at us and went inside.

We waited until we got in the truck to bust up laughing. We would take her baskets of red balls like ornaments at Christmas, and she'd give my father a single hundred-dollar bill. I watched him open his battered thermos, and I realized how much help my father needed, once he had me for ten days.

He had trained the palomino pony and named her Chispa. But he called her Jefecita. She was bossy. I rode Mano, and my father rode Chispa. We checked on the cattle in the heat, on the stock tanks and the ground-squirrel holes and gopher mounds. We waited quiet in the dusk with the old .22 rifles and when the go-phers poked up their heads from the holes we shot them. At night we sat under the palm-frond ramada, and we drank some tequila a guy brought up the canyon to sell. He made it from agave he grew in his back yard in Santa Ana. It tasted like iron.

Then one day, Ramón came to the barn and told me someone had stolen the quad runner from up by the stock tank. "Pues, the cabrón probably run out of gas," he said. "You got the eyes for tracking."

He and I took the horses out along the fire road that branched to the west of the ranch. Mano was glad to be on a trail again, the cottonwoods turning gold, the air clean. But we got to the charred area where the fire had burned last year—blackened palm trees with the brown mesh of new growth edging out. The tracks led across the foothills and dropped down into Bee Canyon.

When a fire raged through old brush, people reported bodies—fresh bodies, at the base of a cliff, or in a cleft between boulders, or even under a fallen tree. I'd seen those reports, of found humans un-covered by flame. But it was the water drops I'd worried about last year—and I never had the nerve to come here alone. We hadn't had any real rain since the fire. I led Mano up the sandy wash and into the canyon, Ramón's horse behind me snorting at something—he must have smelled coyote, or bobcat. There was always water here, a trickle from the old spring at the top of the canyon, near where the bee boxes had fallen apart now. We rounded the big boulder, scrawled with graffiti—marijuana leaves, dicks, Fuck 2020—and the smell of damp sand and willow leaves rose toward me.

The quad was sitting like a squat, patient dinosaur under the big sycamore tree I'd forgotten—its pale branches so low to the earth that someone had lined up ten cans of Bud on the flattest part.

"Pinche puto," Ramón said, getting down from his horse, handing me the reins, and looking at the quad. But nothing was damaged—just dirty. What was it about this canyon and childlike phantoms? I looked up at the ridge where he'd stood up with his stuffed dog, the slope bare and new grass poking up like green whiskers in the black. Ramón had the keys—he poured in the quart of gas he'd carried in his backpack and started up the quad. He lifted his chin to me, and I lifted my hand. He went first, and I waited awhile to let the dust settle and the sound recede, for the horses.

For myself. I sat on Mano, while he and Jefa searched for weeds coming up, their lips so delicate on the sand, and I stared at the tumble of boulders stretching ten feet, at the other side of the wash. More stones had caught in the pile I had made on the grave over the years, washing down from the bluff. There was absolute silence, only the huffing of the horses, and the smallest trickle of water dripping further up, hidden. I didn't feel anything. No fear of a spirit, no evil lingering in the sycamores. Mano jerked his head to the right. Nothing here. He was ready to go. He turned that shining neck to head down toward home, and my leg followed his lead, and so did Jefa. We trotted out into the lowering sun.

The next day, my phone rang over and over while I was trying to cut back some of the bougainvillea covering the roof. I didn't want rats getting comfortable up there. When I got down off the ladder, and listened to the voicemail, it was Esme Portillo. *I'm sorry, you probably don't remember me, but you helped me with an accident, and I kept your report, and I called the station today to find you. The lady, she was really nice. Dianne. She gave me your number. I know that's not how CHP works but I really needed your help.*

I hadn't slept until three a.m., like I was on my old shift. On the old couch, finally the birds woke me up in the morning, hundreds of them in the bougainvillea, so loud I had no idea where I was. The sunlight, the birds, the red flowers in the window—I cried for my mom like a little kid, but I couldn't let my dad hear so I wrapped my jacket around my face so hard the Levi's brass buttons left dents in my forehead. Forty years old and crying like a mocoso.

I texted Esme. She gave me her address, in the City of Orange, and I drove down there in the truck. What the hell could I help her with? I parked in front of a new apartment building, all dark colors and wrought-iron balconies. She was waiting in the front. She stood next to an old Shovelhead Harley, and smiled.

She needed to learn how to sit on it and not be afraid, for a photo shoot in front of a bar. Hilarious. It belonged to the art director of the magazine. She hadn't wanted him to see her nervousness. She had the keys.

We drove just a few blocks, to a park, and I showed her how to use the kickstand, to not be afraid of the weight of the bike. I helped her get on and lean back. "I can't reach the handlebars," Esme said. She was wearing another flowery dress, and a crocheted vest, tall black boots to her knees, and a black bolero hat. I wanted to take her and the bike back to my house right then. But I said, "I don't think they want you all hunched over the handlebars like a dude. They probably want you to lean back like that." I had to roll my eyes, and she rolled hers back, and started laughing. Then she got scared when the bike shifted a little.

"What happened to your face?" she said. "I didn't put you for the kind of guy who fights."

"That's why I got hit so hard," I said. "I wasn't fighting."

"Why not?" she asked.

I shook my head. "Not a story for today." Then her phone buzzed, and it was time for her to show up. I drove her to the bar, her hands sliding along my jeans and then my waist, and the director was waiting in front. "Can your boyfriend here hold this light?" he said.

I hung out and watched for two hours. When she was done, and they left, I said, "How the hell were you planning on getting home? With the director?"

She said, "If you didn't call me back, I was gonna call an Uber. You're much sexier."

She came to my place, and she stayed for two days. I kept the curtains all closed, and she laughed and laughed under the sheets, hearing Albert hollering at his sons, hearing Rose's birds singing. No one knew Esme was there, because she didn't have a vehicle. All I had to eat was a pack of tortillas, some eggs and Salvadoran chorizo, and Modelo. That lasted long enough.

Then she left for San Francisco. She had a job for a music video, and a commercial for health insurance. She'd be gone for two weeks.

In the afternoon, I drove. I went to Merry's and Tenerife's graves at Forest Lawn, where all the movie stars and regular people were beside each other in the ground. Merry's mother had been hairdresser to all the famous Black actresses in the 1950s, and she bought three plots back in 1982. For her daughter and her future husband. But Tenerife was the love of Merry's life.

I had nobody except my father, and my mother was the love of his life, and I was his son. But I thought maybe I could bring Esme Portillo to the ranch. I thought maybe she wouldn't trip out on the little house. She might love the bougainvillea.

I could feel the bone in my face heal and stiffen a little, the calcium filling in the crack, but my eye slanted down a little now. All the gangsters had teardrops tattooed in this exact spot, if they'd killed someone. I had killed someone. My whole damn eye was the teardrop.

I went back to work. And on my days off, I drove. I missed the old Indian bike and thought I'd buy one. But I drove the Chevy Cheyenne truck. I'd put a good engine in it long ago. It was like a secret power inside a frame only someone like me and Manny would recognize. We used to joke about it. 1976. Three years before we were born. The Bicentennial of America. 1776.

And my mom would roll her eyes and say, "Independencia."

In March, when the virus came, the freeways were empty, and of course, I knew there would be people like me, who loved the speed and curves of driving empty highways. I patrolled the toll roads through the canyons, the 91 and the 5—I gave out tickets for guys going 97, 103, and one night around nine, James Malcom, thirty-seven, Tustin, going 127 miles per hour in his Lexus on the 5 up from San Juan Capistrano. He was unrepentant. A Melt Olson word. "I'll never be able to do that again, officer," Malcom said, grinning. "Worth every dollar. You ever gone 127?"

I waited five seconds.

He said, "You never had a car go that fast?"

Shit. I said, "I did it in a patrol car. On the course at the academy. Four of us. We all went 127. Every day. For weeks."

I handed him the ticket. I lifted my chin and said, "What a feeling, right?"

By April, Esme had gotten another job in the Bay Area. She told me there was coronavirus up there, too—she was staying with a cousin and didn't want to come back down yet. I drove past her apartment and it was dark; I drove past the bar where she'd sat on the Harley and it was dark.

Manny called me. We hadn't seen much of each other for the first time in our lives. He was laying low, staying in the shop working on cars with the doors closed, scared of corona. But Grief got the virus and it was touch-and-go whether he'd make it. Larette was like a zombie. I went out to stay at Bobby Carter's house and keep an eye on Dante.

It was like having a kid, and not. I could hear Dante in Ivy's old room. I left food for him at the door. I listened to him talk to Manny Three. And I slept on Bobby's couch, thinking of what my son would have looked like, if I had one, with Leti.

I called her one night. She told me she'd call back, and I heard music, a man's voice. She called two days later. She told me she met a guy on Hinge. He was a lawyer. And he'd given her a yellow diamond engagement ring. I hung up, wondering if Dante had heard anything. But he never said anything to me through the door. I figured he hated me.

But Manny came to drop off food, stood six feet from me in Bobby's yard, and said, "Bro, he's a teenager. He don't say shit to nobody. Manny don't want nothing to do with us, pero that's hormones." We faced each other wearing black bandannas, like vaqueros, and he said, "I missed you, homes. These boys ain't got the canyons, right? We had a good time, mano. Soon, my brother."

At the end of May, I had Monday and Tuesday off. I got a call from my friend Louis Lozano, a guy who'd been a rookie with me and now worked for LAPD. "Frías, man, remember you gave me that plate for a 1978 Eldorado and said if I ever got anything on it to let you know?"

"Yeah?"

"This weekend there was an altercation at a liquor store in Hollywood. Some old lady assaulted a lowlife named Arturo Hernandez. Bunny Goldman. She's, like, seventy-one. She hit him in the head with a bottle of—Bombay Sapphire—and took off. When patrol got there, the owner said she had a badass old Cadillac. But Hernandez took off, too. Anyway—I checked out the plates. Two speeding tickets for Morris Goldman, way back in 2005. Nothing since. But that's your El Dog."

Bunny Gunnarson would be about fifty by now. This had to be her mother. The older woman I'd been seeing in the Eldorado.

I had nothing to do but drive, since California was still in lockdown. So I filled up the Cheyenne and headed up the Golden State. If nothing else, I could go to Boyle Heights and get takeout birria for my father.

But at nine a.m., the world went crazy. My phone had no reception. The trick radio said hackers had attacked the infrastructure of Los Angeles County and surrounding areas. Nobody had been physically going to the bank for months, and now they were running to ATMs, gas stations, and convenience stores. People were standing on the freeway shoulder, holding their phones up to the sky and spinning around, trying to get service, like crazy toys.

I was a Mexican guy with sunglasses and an old truck. Nobody would think I had shit, and that was fine with me. I had my gun and my badge in the glove box, and I was wearing my vaquero boots, and I had $200 in twenties, tens, and fives, because that's how my father taught me to roll, in case of an earthquake. The money was not in my wallet. It was in a slit of the truck bench seat by my right hand, covered with silver duct tape.

On Dundee, I parked across the street because someone in quarantine had finally trimmed the oleanders at the edge of the road. The gates. The big old cypress trees like knives cutting the sky.

Silence. These people were rich. They were all in their houses talking to their stockbrokers and lawyers. They didn't have to go down to an ATM and cry. Why would this rich old lady be at a liquor store with Arturo Hernandez?

Then the Eldorado came roaring down the long driveway right through those cypress trees. The gate opened up. I thought she'd hit the truck, she was going so fast, but she swung left like a pro and didn't even see me. White hair and big sunglasses, fake brown tan. A white woman in the passenger seat turning sideways yelling at the old lady. Blond hair and a Mexican blouse pulled off her shoulders and a lot of tattoos. What the hell? That couldn't be Bunny Gunnarson.

When they turned I saw the Mexican girl in the back seat, and she saw me. She looked right at my Ray-Bans, like before when I tried to talk to her. She was wearing that white uniform.

They headed down to Vermont in the traffic like an Avengers movie, and then Sunset Boulevard. I stayed one or two cars behind. It took forever to get to Sunset and Poinsettia. Suddenly the car stopped, in the right lane, and the Mexican girl got out of the back seat. She stood in front of a wig shop and a botánica, staring at me when I cruised past real slow in the other lane, and then she started walking fast down the sidewalk.

She still thought I was ICE.

It took four blocks to be able to pass the Eldorado real slow. The older lady turned sideways and threw her cigarette out the window, rested her hand on the door. That left hand. Missing the end of the middle finger. Shit. It was definitely Bunny.

The girl in the passenger seat was arguing with her—like a daughter. Bleached blond hair piled high like Amy Winehouse. Eyeliner like a cat slanted off toward her cheekbones, and red lipstick. The Mexican blouse still off her shoulders, showing a lot of cleavage and big boobs. The tattoos like a garden all along her shoulders.

Bunny. She was twenty-nine in Bee Canyon. She'd be fifty now. Shit—if this was her daughter, where the hell were they going? Why had Bunny turned herself into an old lady for all this time? Did she have a new life, assaulting guys under another name? Like a Black Widow deal?

I slowed, dropping back one car. Did she know the guy from Bee Canyon was dead? Did she think he'd killed me, had stood up bleeding from the chest and stabbed me, had made it to the freeway and a hospital? Did she think he'd been waiting to get behind that gate and kill her, for all these years?

That's all I ever wanted to tell her. *You took off, but he was dead, and no one knows except for a phantom who was like a sad little kid, even though he was a man, and he passed away in a mental hospital. The asshole can't find you and hurt you again.*

She went down Sunset, then Cahuenga. She knew where she was going. The back of Los Angeles. Cahuenga, then Mulholland Drive, then Barham, and we wound down through the Hollywood Hills. All the famous LA names from the movies.

We came out of the hills and turned right onto Forest Lawn Drive. We passed the huge cemetery. Merry and Tenerife. Merry couldn't live in this world without her boy. I'd never wanted to feel that way. About a woman, who'd leave me, get hurt, and take off. Fall in love with someone better. On Hinge or eharmony. Or die— and leave me. Like my father.

He might live to be eighty, but he'd just be waiting to join my mother. He was living on earth for me, and the ranch. I'd never given him a son to ride on Jefa with him, or in the truck cab with the dashboard microwave for his burritos de papas at lunch. Steaming and hot.

From above, Merry watched me follow the Cadillac, Merry and Tenerife, a tall kid who used to throw the baseball with Manny's son and Grief's son in Rialto now and then. My mother and my sisters watched me, too. *What the hell are you doing, mijo?* my mother said. *This pendejada is no good. Go home. Your papi's worried about you.*

I have to tell her he's dead, I told my mother.

We took the Glendale Freeway toward the Pasadena Freeway, so they were headed east now. Bunny Goldman was going toward San Bernardino and the desert.

From the bridge over the huge arroyo that splits LA and Pasadena, I could see three layers of mountains rising out of the mist. The most beautiful thing you could imagine, and no one would be looking at it. They never really looked, even on normal days, because they were fucking tired and trying to get home in traffic going east, or they were looking down at their phones, or talking on their Bluetooth but of course they were only seeing the bumper of the car they were trying not to hit while they were texting or talking. They were definitely not looking west to see the Santa Monica Mountains in the distance, or south to where El Monte and Whittier had their own hills, or behind us, at Chavez Ravine.

The Eldorado sped through Pasadena, Arcadia, and then got onto the 210 heading along the San Bernardino Mountains. To the south of us was Rialto, where Bobby Carter lived right off Baseline, and about three miles further, Grief and Larette lived off Baseline and Meridian. The beginning of all the roads in southern California back in 1860.

Bunny kept going, toward the San Gorgonio Mountains, and then she headed down onto the 10 and we wound through the Badlands. She drove like a Formula One racer in the big old car. I kept her half a mile in front of me. We were on the fucking Christopher

Columbus Transcontinental Highway. The way me and the guys used to come on our bikes, to ride out in Yucca Valley. She had to be headed to Palm Springs.

But Bunny passed the Palm Springs exit doing ninety. She finally got off in Indio and headed out into the serious desert, where there was nothing but gated golf course communities behind big white walls, with Mexican landscapers working the trimmers and blowers on the medians with drought-resistant plants all gray and silver. No sign of panic here. Mexican crews were everywhere, building a new wall of golden granite block, mowing a parking strip, trimming palms and sending down the fronds like daggers into the ground.

A guy was trimming scarlet bougainvillea where we pulled into a long rock-lined driveway with a wrought-iron gate wide open between ten-foot-high, white-painted block walls. Seven Palms: A Desert Spa Experience. But about twenty palms all reaching for the sky, rustling in the wind.

Shit. They were heading to a spa? Massages and facials? I was done. I had to figure out how to turn around, behind the maintenance building, because my old truck stood out here among the Beemers and Range Rovers. The Eldorado parked in the handicapped spot closest to the entry. There was a frontage road behind a huge hedge of eucalyptus, where a service truck loaded with gardening equipment was parked. I pulled up behind the maintenance building and got out, because my legs were tired. No one around. It was hot as hell, the whole place humming with air conditioners so loud the spa sounded like a Star Wars colony ready to lift up off the earth. Time for me to go home. I'd been thinking about birria that morning. Now I wanted it bad.

A woman wearing a pink uniform with LUZ embroidered on the pocket came out of the laundry area and stared at me. She walked toward me, speaking in Spanish, and I held up my hand.

She said, "Ice, no ice today." She thought I was a delivery guy. But then she said, "I am a citizen. We have a deal. No ice today."

She meant ICE. My Ray-Bans. My black T-shirt. My stance.

I shook my head. "I'm not ICE." But she kept coming toward me so I got in the truck and turned around on the hot sand. I headed into the parking lot just as a guy wearing medical scrubs came out walking slow. Brown hair in gelled control off his forehead. Short sideburns. About forty. Right behind him was Bunny, and behind her was her daughter.

Bunny was wearing white pants and a white jacket, designer fancy. Her silver hair in a bun. Gold jewelry. She had a gun on him, through her purse. She was too close behind him, and he walked that zombie pace of people who know they're gonna die.

The doctor got into a black S-Class Mercedes. Brand-new. Bunny in the back seat opposite, and that's how you knew she had the gun. If she got into the front seat, he'd think he could take a swipe at her. She was pointing it and telling him where to go. He pulled out. Vanity plates: DDDSDOC. A dentist? Her daughter got into the Eldorado and followed.

She was kidnapping a dentist. Shit. I reviewed in my head. Attacked by a man she knew in 1999. Lived in the old Excelsior apartment building, then married a rich older man. Morris Goldman. Furrier. Lived in a mansion in Los Feliz. Had money. Had lost her mind this week and hit somebody with a gin bottle. Why the hell would she kidnap a dentist? Had he fucked up her dental implants?

I kept three cars between us. I thought they were going back to LA with this guy. But they went to John F. Kennedy Hospital, in Indio. Bunny and the doctor parked where doctors get to park. The place we always wish we could park. She kept her purse on him and they went inside.

I thought her daughter was trying to find a parking place, but she kept driving around the lot, up and down the rows real slow. The Cadillac like a great white shark moving through the heat. She never stopped. Like the radiator was shark gills, needed movement or it would die.

I parked right by the hospital entrance, watching with my binoculars. And after about an hour, the doctor and Bunny came out slow. The Mercedes came toward me, then the Eldorado, and we headed back toward the freeway.

Still easy to tail them until they swerved off onto the 62, toward Joshua Tree. Two lanes each way, and cars speeding like idiots. CHP heavy, the first I'd seen all day. Two big Chevy Tahoe patrols, pulling over speeders on the mountain curves heading down, and people on the straightaway heading up through the Morongo Valley. Bunny and the doctor kept it at sixty-five. Good boy. Rich people headed to Joshua Tree, and weird van campers, and big RVs, like these people didn't give a shit that there was no money, because they were on vacation. Or maybe they were preppers, heading out into the desert to wait out the apocalypse. Maybe that RV was full of canned goods and guns and ammo.

The Mercedes got off on the exit for Pioneertown, the Cadillac behind, and headed down a long two-lane highway full of dips. I had to keep a distance. We passed Pioneertown, the old fake Western movie set, and then we were out in nowhere again. Rocks and brush and the road dipping and curving, and I came up at the top of a crest and saw a gold caterpillar of dust crawling along toward the mountains on a dirt road. I passed the unmarked road Bunny had taken, turned around and came back, and waited for a few minutes before I followed. The road dipped into dry creekbeds full of sand, and then lifted into another run up at the canyon. Past a wash of boulders, the Eldorado fishtailed from the shoulder to follow me now. I was boxed in the middle. Bunny's daughter was as good as her.

We drove slowly in a row, through rocks jagged and black in some places, and golden red square boulders piled almost like walls in other places, like God had shaped them with a chisel, like my father's friend Diego had been out here for a hundred years sitting on his stool making these rocks in case anyone needed headstones. Shit. This woman could kill me and the dentist. Maybe he stole Bunny's money.

The Mercedes turned down another dirt road. No marking. Another rutted lane washed out a million times by floods, through sand and around rocks, up into a canyon with no name. Or maybe Bunny knew the name. The Cheyenne rattled and shook. Meant for the grove roads my father and the Vargas brothers kept smooth and rolled after rains. Only trees out here were the Joshua trees waving at me like I didn't know shit. Arms up like cops directing traffic. Dr. Seuss cops.

I kept my head up and took my service revolver out of the glove box. The old kind that fell open. Smith & Wesson .40-caliber. Whatever gun Bunny had, it wasn't this. But her daughter might have a weapon, too. I tucked it behind me, in the waistband of my jeans, under my T-shirt. I pulled my black bandanna up to my eyes. They could kill me with corona, too.

We moved along in a cloud of dust so big I didn't even see the little cabin until we went around a curve and the end of the canyon rose up in a wall of rocks and brush and yucca plants spiky and green.

This wasn't hipster Joshua Tree. The cabin was maybe three rooms, the boards so black you knew the wood had been nailed together back in the 1920s. Just a square house with posts in front and a little lip of tin roof. It was almost exactly like our old house in Fuego Canyon.

We all stopped slowly, the Cadillac inches from my back bumper. The dentist got out first, and stood there by his dusty Mercedes, staring at Bunny. She held the gun on him, a black Beretta .380, but she looked at me. Did she recognize my face, after all these years? Had she ever believed I was CHP, back when I was twenty and scared?

She held out her hand and said, "Keys." The dentist threw them to her. Her daughter got out of the Cadillac and stared at the abandoned cabin.

"What the fuck, Mom?" she said.

"My grandfather's house," Bunny said. "Don't go inside yet. Me and this cop are gonna check for snakes." She waved the gun at me.

I got out of the truck. She said, "You can bring your gun. I don't give a shit. I know who you are. I just need to know exactly what you want. You been stalking me for a long time. If you're thinking blackmail—"

I looked at her face. Behind the sunglasses, her left eye would be half green. And I looked back at her daughter. Eyes the dark wine-bottle green of the man in the canyon.

"Weird word, blackmail. Why is it black? Why would it come in the mail? I don't want money," I said. "Give your daughter the gun. I'll help you look for snakes in there."

Bunny actually laughed. "She slept with this asshole," Bunny said, motioning to the dentist. "She can't hold a gun on him yet. She's too young. If he can talk her into driving off in the Cadillac, then they can find their baby together."

"Jesus Christ," the dentist said. "How am I supposed to find this baby if you keep me up here? You don't even know if it's mine."

Bunny laughed. "Oh, we have cell phone service up here now. Don. Rimrock is just across the way. We'll be fine when the dust settles on this shit. So you'll figure out where the baby went. Get in the back seat of your car until I check the house. Unless you want to kill the snakes."

He didn't. He got into the back seat. The windows were tinted.

She waited until Angel had gone around the Cadillac, out of voice range. Then she said to me, "You never know how your kids are gonna turn out. Like you, or like their father. How many kids do you have? You have boys?"

I shook my head.

She nodded toward the cabin. "Come on."

She had a key. For that old house. She shoved the door, and it wouldn't open, so I pushed hard on the top and the bottom and used my shoulder near the lock. The hot dark air that rushed out smelled like reptile, for sure. We both stopped. No movement or rattling. Not yet.

Inside, there were drifts of sand under the windows and near the door. Kitchen was just a hot plate and sink, a tiny refrigerator, and an old chest freezer, like my father's. For the kind of guy who hunted. Table and chairs. A decrepit couch. And books everywhere, on shelves built all around the walls. Paintings and photographs framed and propped up on every top shelf.

"My grandpa had an onyx mine up here in the canyon. Gunnarson. They called him the Swede," she said, taking off her sunglasses. "My mom had me whenever, with some asshole, and she died when I was little. He raised me in here. That's how I learned what's valuable. That's how I could talk to the right men, once I got to LA."

She lifted her chin. Her nose was flat, like a cat's, from being broken. Her makeup was thick as spackle, brown to the edge of her jaw, but her neck was white. Her eyebrows were gone, just drawn on with pencil, like old-school veteranas. Her wig didn't cover the reddish-brown hair at her neck.

"I saved your life. Back in 1999," I said. "He's dead. You seem to be in some kind of disguise."

She shook her head. "You didn't save me. He'd been doing that to me for two days. He had a plan. He would've come down from the high and fell asleep and I'd have taken the fucking car. I was coming out here and he'd never have found me. All you had to do was turn around and go back to wherever you came from that day."

"He might have killed you."

"Assholes like that don't kill their toys. Look. I met Morris Goldman at the Getty. He fell in love and we got married in Vegas. Morris sold fur coats in LA, San Francisco, and Vegas. He was the kindest man I ever knew. But Glen, he was an idiot. I met him at a concert, and he was from fucking Florida. He thought he was Axl Rose."

She looked around at the sad flowered curtains in the two windows. A spatula on the little refrigerator, like a black claw. "Glen knew I was pregnant. Only two months pregnant with Angel. He wanted money or he'd tell Morris. I said Morris had been waiting for a kid all his life. And Glen said no other man was gonna raise his seed. He said he would rape that baby out of me. Took me out to Orange County. He was winding down. Like all speed freaks. He woulda fallen asleep once he drank his tequila. He was always passed out somewhere."

I looked at her fancy jacket and white pants. Her weird face like some old poster of Marilyn Monroe mixed with a grandmother. "None of that makes sense."

"Not to you. But it wasn't your life." She lifted up her gun. "Get out your piece. I meant it about the snakes. Come on."

"Ma'am," I said. "You forgot he had a knife. He woulda killed me."

She shook her head. "You know what? No woman likes to be called ma'am. Not a single fucking woman anywhere. So don't say that shit again."

Then she sighed. "He was always pulling that knife out in some bar, and I never saw him use it. He thought you'd run away, and there you were, being a cop, all righteous and brave. A fucking teenager. Look—twenty years. Who cares? You killed him? Okay. You did whatever you did. I have a plastic surgeon out there who could be my son-in-law but he's already married and I have to check this place for snakes cause Dr. Don is gonna be here for two days. You're not a cop right now. You're—whatever. An accessory." She frowned. "Who thought that shit up? Like a purse or scarf. Anyway. I didn't hear a car start. Go out there and see if the doctor is crying."

She took a broom from the corner of the kitchen and went toward the bedroom door. Her wide leg pants already brown at the hems. The air was a sauna of dust and mice and old paper. The Swede. He had to be the guy in the newspaper photo framed by the door. An old blond guy with a bony face and a black hat, a pick and shovel, and the canyon behind him.

I went outside. Her daughter came around and looked at me. Tattoos. A bumblebee wearing boxing gloves. A bunny. Jessica Rabbit. Sexy with a red dress and her ears folded down like she was listening. "Where's my mom?" she said.

Bunny came back out, her gun in her hand again.

"Mom," her daughter whispered. "He's alive."

Bunny motioned me toward the Eldorado. In the huge trunk was a guy wearing vaquero clothes, roach-killer boot on one foot and a towel black with dried blood around the other foot. His chest and arms wrapped with a blanket and tied with yellow rope. The towel behind his head black with blood, too. His eyes open and furious. He spat at me and said in Spanish, "I'm gonna kill you and those fucking whores, you bastard."

"What'd he say?" Bunny asked me.

"You don't want to know," I said.

Bunny said, "I didn't shoot him. My housekeeper did."

"The girl you dropped off?"

"Yeah. Her name is X."

"X?"

"Yeah. I call her X. I pay her in cash. Her dad's a landscaper. They live in Hollywood. God knows where. She shot him in the foot so he's lost a lot of blood but we wrapped him up. Angel is a home health care aide. She's good at stopping blood." Bunny rolled her eyes. "She went to private school. She had her own fucking horse and riding lessons. Look at her. She's beautiful. And she works at a fucking memory care place."

Angel said, "Old people fall down and get cut up all the time, and they're on, like, warfarin and shit. Blood thinners. They bleed way worse than him."

"Arturo Hernandez," I said, looking down.

He said, "Fuckin culero. I'll kill you."

I looked hard at Bunny. She better not say anything about who I was.

Angel jumped in and said, "I met him at a bar and he had a lot of money. We had a good time for a week and then he started whaling on me. He's got a meth thing going on. This morning we couldn't get any money and he knew my mom lived in a big house up in Los Feliz so he said we were gonna rob her. He fucking broke my little finger to make me take him up there."

"Wait—your finger's broken?" I said.

She held up her left hand. The small finger was smashed and purple, swollen like a tiny eggplant. She shrugged. "Shit, having my boobs done was the worst. And then I had a baby. After that, nothing really hurts like it'd get your attention."

I couldn't believe these women. Pain tolerance like prizefighters.

Bunny said, "Angel. Stop talking. Enough medical diagnosis. Go get your friend. Don't say another fucking word. I mean it."

She shut the trunk on Arturo. She said to me quickly, "She has a kid with that doctor. She left the baby at the spa, and it disappeared. What a fucking stupid plan. I have a granddaughter somewhere. I'm fifty years old. He's gonna find the baby, and he's getting a DNA test, and he's gonna give us a check. Then we're headed out of California." She looked at me hard. "You can't say shit."

This woman—all these years of me remembering her crouched like a wounded animal, the blood spooling from her nostrils, the blood smeared on her legs, the green flies like emeralds landing on his chest. She had a kid with his DNA, and she didn't care. Her daughter was her daughter. Her granddaughter was her granddaughter. She said, "So take Arturo out of my car and put him in your truck and take him somewhere. I don't care where."

And then her face got soft for a minute, because she knew I could say something to Angel. "Don't. Just let the game play out. You should know better by now. You're a fucking cop and you know nothing is ever fair."

Then Bunny said very quiet, her eyes narrowed, "Thanks. Officer. For everything. I mean it. Hasta la vista, baby."

The DD doctor put on his surgical mask and helped me lift Arturo out of the trunk while he spat at us and kicked the shit out of Don's ribs and once in his crotch, until I got the horse ropes from my truck around him. His other foot was like a black bowling ball. He'd been hit in the back of the head, and the blood was matted in his hair. We put him in the truck bed, and Don backed away and pulled off his mask and threw up on the sand. I wanted to say, "Don't you cut women's chests open all day?" but then he'd know I knew. Pretty sure he figured I was some Mexican handyman working for Mrs. Bunny.

Don tried the doors of his car. Locked again. He walked back up toward the open door of the cabin, and sat down on a rock near the porch post, his head in his hands, his shoes still covered in those green booties. Another dude who slept with too many women.

I got a cover out of the area behind the Cheyenne truck bench, for when we used to haul hay. I said to Arturo, "¿A dónde te llevo?"

"Al infierno. The fuck you care, moreno?"

He was a short guy. Güero. Mustache like my dad's, sparse and fringy around his mouth. I said, "I'm not heading to hell. I'm gonna take you to Indio. Drop you off at the hospital."

He tried to spit up at me again, but he didn't have any spit left. I couldn't believe he was still alive. I tied down the cover on the truck bed. He'd have plenty of air. But it was gonna be pretty rough on this dirt road.

I went slow, like a kid learning to drive. Jackrabbits the size of dogs crossing the road ahead of me, and hawks spinning in the air. We made it past two more CHP Tahoes on the 62, going down nice and easy, four miles under the speed limit. Just a Mexican dude in an old truck full of tools from where he'd been working on some rich LA dude's weekend house. I retraced my way back to JFK Hospital in Indio, where I didn't want my license plates on a security camera, so I drove back behind the physical plant area and lifted the tarp and grabbed Arturo fast by the ropes at his chest, like a calf my father and I had to move quickly, and threw him into the back of a linen delivery truck that said Angelica. Two trucks with their back doors open, stacked with towels. Hospitals were crazy busy from corona. Someone would find him fast.

I was still a murderer. Still a fucking idiot. No different than before.

I had saved a stranger, but I hadn't. None of that mattered. I'd saved myself, because I didn't believe Bunny about the knife. Glen hated Mexicans. Maybe she knew nothing about that before, but I could still hear him. *Fucking wetback.* He'd have enjoyed stabbing me. Kicking me. Leaving me for the coyotes and then the beetles.

Bunny wanted her grandchild. She would do anything for this baby. Her line.

I drove onto the old Grapefruit Boulevard. My dad and Manny's brought us to the Indio Date Festival when we were little. Camel races and ostrich races, dates like brown roaches all lined up in boxes but they tasted like sugar and paper on our teeth. I drove south down the boulevard, thousands of palm trees in the distance where all the dates grew, and I remembered my dad talking for a long time to a woman who told us their names. Medjool. Deglet Noor. She was beautiful, working at the fair stand where we bought a box, and she'd packed it herself. She and her two sisters were lining up the dates in perfect rows in the boxes, and I remembered thinking that my father would fall in love, and that my mother had stood in the cold of the citrus packing house in Placentia, and I pulled his arm hard and dragged him away.

Soledad. Her name tag said SOLEDAD RAMIREZ.

What if my father had married her, and had more kids? What if I'd talked Leti into marrying me? What if I let Esme Portillo change me into somebody else? Good story—met some beautiful girl after a fender bender and we got married. I was a fucking self-ish bastard. Chicken to have somebody leave me.

I drove south, past Mecca and Thermal and Oasis, the sandy earth covered with creosote bushes and smoke trees wherever there were no aisles of palm trees. Miles of green fields, with workers throwing watermelons and cantaloupe up onto trucks. A legion of women like Pharaohs wearing white headdresses walked out of the rows of grapevines that stretched forever like green veins toward the purple Mecca Hills. The Salton Sea glittered blue beside me. I had never seen it. I had never been this far south.

I drove through Calipatria, where my father had come to pick cotton one summer when he was seven and his dad needed money. Hernán Frías. My grandfather. His wife, Ermelinda. They died the year before I was born, in a truck accident coming down here to Coachella to work.

I got to Calexico. The border. Calexico and Mexicali. Where my people had crossed hundreds of years ago, before there was a border. Before those names existed.

I got three tacos de pollo from a cart, and drove to the edge of a housing development to stand by the Cheyenne and eat the tacos, drink fresh horchata like my mother used to make, and stare at the border. There was the All-American Canal, a wide and swift river that made a boundary to the east. The new sections of the pinche fucking wall, metal panels about twenty feet high, leaning like a ramp toward the south. The guy who sold me the tacos had laughed and told me, "You feel that big wind yesterday, bro? It blew the wall down! Huff and puff! Right by my house. It fell into the trees on the Mexicali side! My friends said there are guys waiting for tonight so they can pick it up and cut it into scrap. Sell that in the morning."

His house must be pretty close to here, I thought, looking at the wall, the houses and buildings right on the other side. He could joke around with his friends through the cracks.

My mother's people rode their horses up through this desert, with the Spanish priests. My father's people rode horses in Jalisco, and then they came in the back of a wagon, when the Californios wanted men to build the corrals and tan the hides and braid the lariats, shovel the manure and brand the cattle with burning irons. Vaqueros. "El Dorado!" I remembered hearing that in the movies. "The city of gold. The Spanish thought it was here."

I put on my Dodgers cap and got back in the truck. I had one more place to go, back home, and I'd better get there before it got too dark.

Melt Olson and his brother Bum were in the garage, in La Habra, sitting in lawn chairs with the door open. Cooler at their feet. It was almost seven p.m. Ocaso.

I parked on the street. I had only been here once. When Melt retired.

He lifted his hand. Like old guys did. He wore an Angels cap. I walked up the slope of the driveway, the ranch house from 1963 he used to tell me about, the diamond-paned windows he hated washing once a month for the wife. The garage perfectly ordered, shovels and rakes hung on the wall, tools on a pegboard, and a Craftsman rolling red tool cart. Melt said, "Well, look what the cat drug in! We survived coronavirus out here, Johnny! Beer and the old radio. We got baseball out here. The wives stayed in there."

He pointed to what must have been the kitchen. A window and old-school curtains printed with sunflowers. His brother grinned.

"What did they do?" I asked.

Melt looked as surprised as I'd ever seen him. He said, "The wives? Well, I don't know. Whatever they wanted to."

"Them two sisters known each other long before they known us," Bum said.

"Wait—two sisters married two brothers?" I laughed. "And you guys think Mexicans love their families."

Melt said, "Well, it was just after the Dust Bowl. I was eighteen. Bum, were you twenty yet?"

Bum shook his head. "Nope. Not yet. We were all out here working the oranges. Their mother showed up and didn't have a pot to piss in. One truck and six girls. Said they snuck into California because nobody wanted Okies."

I rolled my eyes. "Yeah. Nobody ever wants people to pick fruit here."

"Grab a chair, Johnny," Melt said.

But I looked at Bum. He was the tough customer, like Melt used to say. Bum didn't play. He lifted his chin. "Yep," he said. "Take a load off." He bent forward, opened the cooler, and tossed me a Coors Light.

We were quiet for a minute. The dark blue started collecting in the old ash trees along Melt's sidewalk. I could hear laughing in the kitchen. Melt said, "I never seen a rookie work so hard, Bum. He was obsessed with cars. Wanted to know every make and model, so's he never had to hesitate to call something in. And shoot—he could shoot way better than me. I never cared for the handgun. We grew up with the twenty-two, back in Texas. Shot when we were five and six, right, Bum?"

"Rabbits and snakes and quail," Bum said.

So I told them about Bee Canyon. The whole thing. Starting with the gophers, and the Smith & Wesson. Ending with the pick. The phantom. The grave.

"Well, I'll be. I remember that guy. Throwing rocks like a little kid. He eluded us for six months. You helped the trackers catch him. That tracker, he was from Texas."

Melt didn't say a thing about the dead man. I waited. He had taught me to wait.

He drank half of another beer. Then he said, "Ain't a canyon in America don't have a skeleton. Think about it. We used to talk about them Westerns. Dead men buried everywhere on the Plains. In the desert. Women and kids, too. No marker."

"This was different," I said.

"You can bet your Sunday socks it was different. But you were the law."

"No, I was a stupid kid. A rookie."

"You identified yourself. You had a badge."

"Not on me."

"It's always on you," Melt said, and finished the beer. "Might as well be sewn into your skin. Like a dog chip."

Bum laughed. "That's the truth. And he woulda stuck you like a steer. A steer with a dog chip."

"Maybe. Maybe not."

"His choice." Melt shrugged. "Then he'da had to kill her, too, the woman. And the little hobo. He coulda kilt you all and buried you without a care. Gone on his merry way."

Unrepentant. I looked into the garage at the tools. "We're never supposed to take the law into our own hands."

"Yeah. But we do," Melt said. He pointed at his chest, in the button-up sport shirt.

"You did?"

"Anaheim. 1972. One a those old motels on Katella, near Disneyland. Some guy from Oregon had been holed up for three days with his wife and baby, drunk and pissed, had beat the shit out of her. The motel manager called us."

"You killed him?"

"He come at me with a beer bottle. I shot him. Then his wife hit me with a lamp. Broke my nose. Third time." He looked at his brother. "Bum broke it the first two times."

"He died?"

Melt sucked his teeth. He said, "I got him in the left lung. He was in a coma two weeks, had two surgeries. Cost the county a lot of money, my sergeant kept telling me. Then he woke up, and they shipped him back up to Corvallis. He ended up robbing a bank. Somebody else shot him."

"Mine was different," I said.

"If you want it to be," he said. Then he scratched his neck. "She gonna tell anyone?"

"No."

"Blackmail you? For what? Your truck? Some of your dad's cattle?" He shrugged again. "Been a hell of a year already. She wants to stay away from LA and the virus, she's got her kid, and she wants her grandkid. All her business."

Bum said, "Let women do what they're gonna do. We do what we always do."

These two old men. Thick silver hair combed back off their foreheads with whatever product white guys used. No glasses. Their blue eyes just as sharp as ever, even if they were a little red from the beer. Their wrists and hands thick and powerful as my father's. Just as brown.

Melt said, "What I always told you we do. Wait. Ten seconds. Ten years. The world figures out what it wants to do."

I drank another beer, and we sat there for a while. But I had to say it. "The world is fucked up, though." I told them about Tenerife, and Merry, and Tavares. Showed them the scars around my eye socket. I finally told Melt about Anza Crossing, Sergeant Miller, and Michael Miller Jr. Now Junior was Sergeant Miller, too.

Melt rubbed his chin for a long time. He said, "Them Millers. Always talking about Indiana, but they don't go back there. Always saying they hate California, and here they are. Father and son in Huntington Beach. Big glass house and they can hear the waves, but born with all the grievance in the world. They do damage like two feral dogs out there. You just have to wait until their time is up."

"That's not enough," I said.

"That's all we got," Melt said. We looked into the sky, tangerine haze at the horizon. "What did your dad say, when you told him about Bee Canyon? He musta told you the same thing."

I got up from the lawn chair, stiff from all the driving, from hauling Arturo up, and twice, from where he'd grazed my knee with his unbloody boot. "I never told him," I said. "Never told anyone until now. Never will."

I shook their hands, both of them, even though we weren't supposed to touch each other. I saw a face in the kitchen curtains. A woman with silver glasses and silver hair. Then I walked down the driveway in the dark and got into my truck.

PART III

MECCA

INTERSTATE 10 AND LAND BEFORE ROADS

I looked at him sleeping. His hair was longer than mine, straighter than mine, blacker than mine. Taken out of the six black elastic bands last night.

The way he did it was graceful, sliding them out of his hair. Totally different story for taking my hair out of the big messy bun that was all I ever wore now. This morning James held the elastics in his wide palm and looked up at me and grinned, and then he said, "You only got the one rubber band holding up all that hair?"

I had to smile back. "Women know how to make a structure," I told him. I reached deep inside my hair and undid the four twists I had made before I put in the single big elastic, and my hair fell down around my shoulders. I never sat naked on a bed and felt my own hair tickling my own skin. Not these days. "Look at all those colors," he said, touching one of the curls down near my collarbone. "Copper and gold and brown and black."

"August and a long corona summer," I said. "I had to play a lotta baseball games in San Bernardino. There wasn't any Little League, so me and the other parents got teams together and played with our kids. The outfield will give you highlights."

He shook his head. "Nope. Not if you're Indian. You can be out in the desert your whole life and never even go inside to sleep in summer. But your hair's still gonna be black. Even here." He pointed at his belly.

I wasn't trying to point at my belly. I had pulled the sheet around me to cover my legs and everything up to my waist.

He said, "Of course, there's a whole takeout container of steak from Brazil in the refrigerator right there. The steak you refused to eat." And then he laughed so hard his big wide shoulders shook, too. "Matelasse. What the hell?"

I shrugged. I didn't want to hear about how they carved meat in Brazil. Hell, no.

James slept deep now. But I was awake because I could hear my phone vibrating from the coffee table in the living room part of the hotel room. Luxury suite. He managed the steakhouse restaurant at the casino, and he'd booked this luxury suite for two nights for us. I had four days off. August is the slowest month at Conroy's. No holidays. California had opened back up, but we had only five regular church orders, two wedding anniversaries. Funerals. Just funeral wreaths. Forever. Dawna said she could handle those. I hadn't had four days off for two years. Yesterday afternoon, driving down the freeway toward Pala, I hadn't told anyone where I was going. Not Dawna. Not Reynaldo, who had the boys in Venice with him, for three days.

On the freeway, with my new little suitcase from Marshalls on the seat beside me, I thought, "What if I die? Nobody'll know where I am."

Now it was still dark in the suite on the top floor of the casino hotel, but I could see that black light turning to dark blue in the long skinny gap where the curtains hadn't closed all the way. Must be five a.m. Sunrise. Who the hell would be calling me now? The sound wasn't texts coming in. It was ringing.

Only two people would call, instead of text. My mother, who hadn't called me in years, who had no idea where I was, because she wouldn't give a damn. Or Reynaldo. But why would he be up this early? Gena was at a resort in Italy doing a yoga retreat and beauty week for famous people at some private beach. That's why he had the boys visit. Because she didn't really want to see his kids. Hadn't turned out great for her brand—people wanted her and Rey on YouTube, not two skinny boys who refused to smile. Jesus.

Then the phone went quiet. The suite was humming, kind of, refrigerator and air conditioner and the whole big-ass building. I'd never spent the night up so high. And James was snoring a little, like big guys do. My brother Alfonso used to snore, when we were in high school and he started lifting weights and got big to play football. James and my brother both had those big arms and chests going a little soft now, and hearing his breath rattle out through his throat, I was thinking about all the air that could fit into their bodies, compared to mine.

My mother used to snore like a linebacker. "She built like a linebacker on the top, and a sprinter on the bottom," some guy said once, when I was a teenager, and she was drunk, dancing in the dust at her thirtieth birthday party in the yard in front of our tiny house.

I was thirty-eight. Last night James said into my throat, "You're the most beautiful woman I can imagine. Remember how much shit you talked when I first saw you? At San Luis Rey? You were standing by that wall in the sun. Damn. You were so fine."

"You can stop now," I said. "You got what you wanted."

"Damn," he said again. "I didn't think this would ever happen again. Not how you've been rolling since we met."

He was the most patient man I'd ever met. Back in February of last year, when I gave him my number, we didn't think it would be like this. We spent the one night together, in July, and then Merry's son was shot, and we gathered at the hospital. I didn't see James again until last week, when the boys had a baseball sleepover with Manny Delgado and his son—they slept outside because of coronavirus. James and I went to Oceanside, walked on the beach, drank Modelo Negras, and when I picked up the boys the next day, Joachim sniffed my arm and said, "You had beer!" like it was a huge betrayal. That was because of my mother.

We spent one night in a vacation rental in Oceanside. We moved the bed to the sliding glass doors and kept them open all night, sleeping to the sound of crashing waves. He joked that I still hadn't seen his house, on the reservation, and he still hadn't seen mine. I didn't want him to see my tiny two-bedroom house in Rio Seco, full of boy socks and boy homework, my ancient couch, and even worse, my old bed and comforter, which Antonio had divided down the middle with Magic Marker so he and Joachim wouldn't fight over who had more blanket.

Tonight, after he showed me the fancy hotel suite and I put my suitcase on the rack—I'd never been in a hotel with a luggage rack and a safe and a couch—we went down to the steakhouse. He'd been the manager for five years. On the way to his personal table at the back, people spoke to him, their faces lighting up, so I figured he couldn't be a bad boss. He introduced me and people said, "That's a beautiful name." Like they always did. Matelasse. I could never say to strangers what I was named for. Too hard to explain Louisiana, the plantation of my grandmother, the pile of sugar cane saved through winter for next year's planting. I smiled, as I always did.

We could see the whole restaurant, the people who'd been gambling all day. Then he said, "This is what we have now."

And I knew what he meant: my people have a casino, and strangers leave their money here.

He asked if I ate meat, and I said, "Oh, yeah, I grew up eating gumbo on a good day and hot dogs in a bad month." The servers brought long skewers of some kind of charred beef in circles, and they started carving it. James said, "Everyone loves this. Churrasco. Brazilian barbecue. It's traditional in São Paulo."

Then I said, "Well, shit, I changed my mind," and pushed away my plate. I was embarrassed, because I only cussed when I got really mad and caught off guard.

James stroked his goatee like guys do, and said, "So you don't like beef on moral grounds? Or Brazilian food?"

"Sorry," I said. "I didn't mean to be rude."

He nodded. "Do you want to drink tonight? Because I know you didn't really want to last time."

My boys. They'd grown up seeing my mother drunk. But it was three days till I had to pick them up from Reynaldo. I said, "I would drink a beer." I looked at the meat on the plate. "I would eat this meat tomorrow. When I'm not pissed off at Brazil."

He laughed really hard, said, "Well, I'd like to hear that story," and the server put the meat in a to-go container. James got us a six-pack of Modelo Negra and we got into his truck. He had a new black Silverado, with a bundle of white sage hanging from the rearview mirror releasing smoky scent while he drove up into the mountains above Pala.

He put a blanket in the truckbed, and we sat there drinking the beers, our backs against the cab of the truck. I said, "You tell me the rest first."

Our arms beside each other were exactly the same brown. He had no hair on his arms, and I had a little. His belly showed a bit under his white dress shirt when we were sitting. My belly poked out a bit above my jeans.

James said, "My grandmother's grandmother—Domenica? She was Cupeño. Cupa is south of here. They were in Cupa since the beginning of the world."

He pointed to the south, to the high range lit by the moon. "Then an American named Warner got all the land and the springs in 1844—a Mexican land grant. But he lost the land to the former governor of California in 1880. Dude named Downey."

"Like, the city of Downey?" I said.

He nodded. "My mom refused to use fabric softener because of that asshole. He decided to evict them from Cupa. The federal government was supposed to serve them a notice, tell them they had to file a claim to the land. The place they'd been for a thousand years. The notice got lost. Magically. Like *Gunsmoke*, right?" James finished a bottle and rolled it down the truckbed—it clinked against the tailgate. "1903. In spring, and it was still cold. They had to leave, walk all the way up here to Pala. Some of them died on the way. The government said they'd built houses in Pala, but there was nothing. The people lived in old boxcars."

He showed me a photo on his phone. A boxcar at the back of his land, on the reservation. The wooden siding like ribs of a square dinosaur. "We keep it there," he said. "When she left the mission, Domenica raised my grandmother there. I used to spend most of the summer living in there with my grandmother, when I was really little. Hot as hell. We slept outside under the ramada."

His grandmother survived the boxcar. She married a man from

Pala, and had four daughters. One married a man from Morongo Reservation and had six children. One married a man from Soboba and had four children. One married a man from Barona and had four children. One married a man from Torres Martinez Reservation who moved to Pala, and they had James.

"What?" I said. I couldn't believe it. "I have some family out in Mecca. On reservation land."

"Well, shit, we better not be cousins," he said, kind of serious. "I have something like seventy-five cousins."

I said nothing. I wasn't ready to tell him about my uncles who were not my uncles. My crazy drunk mother. I didn't want him to ask about my father.

A rapist. A pinkie ring.

He said, "Brazil." He put down his beer, kissed me for a long time.

Then I calmed down. "What do you think this man is?" I whispered to him.

He looked down at the photo of Reynaldo on my phone. Wearing only white linen drawstring pants, his chest covered with oil or some shit, capoeira pose in front of a perfectly timed wave on the beach. Gena's Instagram.

James squinted. "You mean what he does for a living?"

"No," I said. "His—how the world identifies him."

"He looks like a kind of self-satisfied dude," James finally said. "Like he cares a lot about his hair." He pointed to the dreadlocks caught up in a bun.

"You care a lot about your hair," I said, probably too quick, not thinking. I had smelled a sweet hair wax near his forehead—the hair around his face was smooth and glossy, pulled back tight into the first band.

He laughed and said, "Man, I grew up in Oceanside, playing

football with Samoan dudes, and we all got our hair pomade from this Chicano guy on the team. Mario Mendoza. He gave us Tres Flores so we could keep our hair slick back under the helmets and out of our eyes."

I told him how I met Reynaldo when I was seventeen, how I believed he was the only man I could ever love. How he fell in love with Brazil, and just decided he was someone else.

"With one name?" James said, balancing his bottle on his knee.

"And a woman from Venice," I said. I finished my second beer and rolled it down to the tailgate. The mountains in front of us were the deepest shade of purple, the creosote bushes turned red like fire for a minute just before the sun set. Then even though the day had been hot, the dark dropped the chill on us like some god was breathing out ice from the boulders.

I had driven seventy-two miles from my house to Venice, to drop off the boys. Then I drove seventy-two miles home, which took over two hours, and packed my suitcase and drove forty-two miles to get here, to Pala. I stared at the boulders, the way they glowed creamy in the dark, and James pulled the blanket over me. I fell asleep.

We came back to the hotel room about one a.m., when we both woke up cold. We fell into this big king-sized bed and both took our hair from the bands.

Now my phone was ringing again. Shivering like it was cold on the coffee table. The slice of light was turning to lighter blue. Dawn. Had to be Reynaldo, telling me something about the boys. Cell phones meant a mom could never disappear. My mother had disappeared for two weeks at a time, when my brother Alfonso and I were little. No phone, no nothing. By the second day, we'd walk up to Uncle Enrique's house and sleep there. He'd put us to work in the barn, have us sharpening tools, pruning low orange tree branches. He'd feed us chicken and rice.

I slid carefully out of the bed and put on the hotel robe. I went into the living room area and slid the wooden doors shut. I pushed the button and said, "What?"

My uncle Enrique's deep smoke-filled Louisiana French voice said, "Matelasse. You home?"

I forgot he had my number, too. My heart leapt. Even though she hated me, I felt a shiver—was my mother sick? Dead?

"Why?" I said carefully.

Uncle Enrique said, "You get tickets?"

Seriously? "Tickets for what? A baseball game?" I kept my voice low.

"Ticket from the po-lice for you speed. You get tickets or you clean?"

My uncle was eighty-eight years old. He was the only man who'd ever raised me. I said, "I'm clean. I try not to speed. Why?" I went into the bathroom and closed the door very softly.

He paused. Then he said, "We go out to Mecca, there. You can drive. Sofelia need us work today. Rachelle got a sick baby. They stay tou soule."

All alone. In case the baby had the virus?

I closed my eyes. I smelled of James. I didn't want to drive out to the Coachella Valley. Probably 120 degrees today.

My uncle played his ace. "How many time Sofelia take care you and Alfonso?"

Shit. Once, my brother and I had lived down there in Mecca, with Sofelia and Uncle RC, when our mother had disappeared for three weeks, and nobody knew whether she would bring trouble home. We'd packed dates into boxes, we'd ridden horses on the

Torres Martinez Reservation, and we'd slept outside under the ramada in the heat.

I said, "I'm down in Pala. Take me an hour to get home."

My uncle took in a breath. He was shocked. I never went anywhere except Conroy's, the elementary school, Stater Bros., and maybe Target. He said, "Pala? Them casino? Where your boys? You gamble, there?"

I looked at my face in the hotel mirror. My hair curled at the forehead from sweating. "Little bit," I said softly. I had gambled on a man for the first time since I was seventeen.

How would I wake this man and explain my family in five minutes? Would he think I was lying? Think I didn't want to be there in the bed with him? Didn't want to eat the fucking Brazilian steak? That I hadn't felt last night like I didn't think I would ever get to feel again?

I touched the lowest part of my earlobe. So soft. He had left his lips an inch from my left ear—breathed so softly that a rush of heat collected between my legs—and then he held my earlobe between his teeth so gently that I lost my mind.

Even now I couldn't put my earrings in. I couldn't touch my own skin there—because it made me want to get back in the bed. If I could lie there and touch him to wake him up, just make love one more time and say only that I had to go to work at Conroy's (a bouquet emergency!). But I would never lie to a man. Not after getting lied to my whole life. And James might think I was playing him.

I put the earrings on the bathroom counter. So he would know I was coming back.

James slept like Antonio—on his side, his hands folded up against his chest like praying, the sheet over his ear like a hoodie. I hesitated.

One thing funny about hotels. Motel 6 or this fancy casino. They all had notepads. I wrote, "I'll be right back. I have to help my uncle for about five hours." I stopped. The pen was so small. I wrote a heart and that seemed like not enough. So I filled it in with black ink. Like I was daydreaming in school.

I had to drive an hour back home to pick up Uncle Enrique, who was my great-uncle, because his old truck would never make it to Mecca, to see his brother RC Burns, who wasn't really his brother, because RC's wife Sofelia, who really was married to RC, needed our help. There was no arguing. This was family. Enrique was the closest thing I'd ever had to a grandfather. He'd lived in worse than a boxcar. He'd lived in the woods. In the swamp. In former slave cabins. When he was seven, his mother died in a flood, and Enrique had lived on the riverbank of the Mississippi, sleeping beside the dead animals that floated past all night.

He got in with a duffel bag. I heard a clink. Shit. He had his rifle in there.

My uncle looked at me, his Sunkist ball cap low over his eyes. "Maybe shoot some rabbit, me. Big old jackrabbit out there in the desert."

Even though I was thirty-seven I hesitated for a minute. "You told me you'd never have to eat rabbit again. Buy your chicken from the store."

My uncle nodded, like I should drive. Then he said, "Sofelia say her daughter get rob. Some young fool."

I sighed. "Great." I hadn't been to Mecca in at least three years. I had no idea what we were talking about. But I'd drop my uncle off, stay an hour, and go back to Pala.

I'd still be a secret. And I realized that this was the first time I'd ever done anything like my mother, who never told me anything. Just showed up after a week, like nothing had happened.

I hadn't told my sons about James. After our field trip, Joachim got obsessed with indigenous peoples, and how much of his own blood was African, French, Spanish, and Houma from southern Louisiana. "Everyone thinks we're Mexican anyway," my son said. "And Dad's not from Brazil. He's from San Bernardino. Grandma told me."

This summer, when the boys had to stay with Uncle Enrique during the day, Joachim and I worked on a family tree. He showed it to Jesús, who made a tree of his family—all from Morelia, Michoacán, except for Jesús and his two brothers. Joachim said, "We're from all over the world except Mexico." He put his finger on the empty box for my father. "You could make Grandma tell us where he's from."

He would be twelve soon. His hair was soft curls and waves, and he'd asked me to braid it for the first time. Hints of copper and bronze from summer, just like mine.

I shook my head. "God couldn't make my mother say anything she didn't want to."

Only the eleventh can of Miller High Life, and I made sure my boys and I were never around for that moment anymore.

The heat gauge edged up into danger when my old Jeep Cherokee got past Highway 111, which swerved off toward Palm Springs. There was a long low incline past Desert Hot Springs on the way to Indio, and it was 7:20 a.m. and already ninety-four degrees out-side. The smoke trees were silvery ghosts tethered to the earth, twitching in the hot wind. My uncle lifted his chin now, to squint out from under his ball cap. The mirages of water in the asphalt ahead were big as lakes. Finally said to my uncle, "I can't tell if we have a problem."

He looked over at the dashboard and said, "Radiator. Open all them window and turn on that heater. Tou fort."

All strength, in his Louisiana French. Hot air blasted my face and arms, from inside and outside, until my tank top was drenched in sweat and my eyes burned. It was like being in a small metal hell surrounded by a larger golden hell. The Coachella Valley in August.

I'd already driven 154 miles and hadn't even had time to text James. He had to be awake by now. And he hadn't texted me.

I kept the car at fifty-nine miles per hour, chugging along as if we were creating our own weather system, heat blasting past my sunglasses. My uncle said, "I pay the gas, me." His voice more Louisiana now than when I was a child, like he was stand-ing on an escalator facing the wrong way, traveling back to his childhood—he, my grandmother Claudine, all the old people who still spoke French when I was a child.

My uncle said, "We get to Mecca, me and RC check that radia-tor, there." He was quiet for a rushing minute.

I looked at his huge scarred hands that always seemed to belong to a larger man, resting on his legs. He was always uncomfortable when he wasn't working, even at his age. He said, "Just today and tomorrow. To help Sofelia."

"Nope. Today. But not tomorrow, too," I said. I never talked disrespectfully to him. My sons were going to get away with saying whatever they wanted to me.

I knew what was coming next. "I know. You bought me this Cherokee. But I'm only in Mecca one day."

As we passed Palm Desert and Rancho Mirage, the Cherokee was shuddering like a little kid who's been crying and can't stop. He pointed to a gas station on the next exit, and we stopped.

He bought something and sprayed the AC with it, lifted the hood, and let the radiator steam. I got more coffee, watching him bend under the hood, amazed that he could stand the heat and smell together. He bought this car for me after Reynaldo left and my little Kia broke down. And RC Burns had helped my uncle get to California, had fixed my uncle's truck back in 1945, when it broke down near Calexico.

I stood in front of the liquor aisle, frozen, seeing a woman buying a six-pack of Coors Light. Eight a.m. A white woman with skin darker than mine, her blond hair hanging like tangled spiderwebs below a straw hat, and when she turned, her eyes that muddy bloody red of my mother's in the morning.

My mother was drunk seven days a week. You think she'd take Sunday off, but she hated Sundays the worst. They used to go visit people in LA on Sundays, but she never went after she was sixteen. I knew this. There was someone in LA she never wanted to see. Something terrible had happened to her when she was sixteen: me.

Dawna and I used to joke on the Saturday before Mother's Day, when men came into Conroy's to buy bouquets for two or three different women, all mothers of their kids. "He left behind his seed in several places," Mr. Singh, the franchise owner, would say. His formal joke for those men. They were all races, all ages, but they all had that player smirk, even when they were old.

I knew exactly two things about the man who was my father.

The pinkie ring. And my mother had two times in my life gotten wasted enough to whisper that he was a devil.

Not *the Devil*. A devil. So I grew up thinking there was a tiered system, and my father was not a star. He was a supporting actor devil. Like Steve Buscemi, except I was too dark; or Bernie Mac, except I wasn't dark enough. Every day at Conroy's, I got mistaken for Mexican and people spoke Spanish to me.

My mother used to be peach-skinned and pretty, with reddish hair caught in a braid and baby hairs pasted like lace to her forehead. I'd seen pictures when she was fifteen, at a party. Big chest in a tank top, plump shoulders, long thin legs in her cutoff shorts. Her arms folded, her mouth open, she was definitely talking shit to the camera. I could see why guys liked her.

Now she was shaped like a cobra, wide shoulders and huge breasts she kept in big T-shirts, her belly high and hard from all that beer, and her legs still long and beautiful up under her denim shorts. Her hair was thin and dyed maroon, in a tight bun, her mouth always set straight but looking downcurved because she held her chin up so high. Trying to tell us she was *somebody*. She had me with a minor devil, when she was only sixteen; she had Alfonso with a handsome football player from Pomona, when she was nineteen; and then when she was thirty-nine, she had my twin brothers, Kurtis and Kortez, with a fine fool from San Bernardino. My mother liked all her boys. She just hated me.

While I got my coffee, near the gas station microwave hearing that strong hum when a guy heated up his cheese Danish, I thought: At this point in my life, my mother had more sex than I did. I remembered being in our old kitchen, some aunt saying, "Girl, never stand in front of a microwave! Them rays make you sterile."

I was about ten. Another aunt said, "What?"

"Sterile."

I was confused. *Sterile bandages* on the boxes in the bathroom. *Sterile nipples* on the box of baby bottles.

"So you can't have kids, fool!"

Someone behind us said, "Well, shit then, somebody shoulda parked Bettina up there long time ago. Before she had Mattie and Fonso. She pregnant again!"

Bettina was my mother. They saw me in the doorway, and they bit their lips, and then everyone turned away.

Now I stood holding my gas station coffee. Friday morning. My mother was probably out in San Bernardino with her regular boyfriend. James still hadn't texted me.

I wanted to be back in that cool hotel room, lying beside him. My first time trying to escape. He'd been so deep into sleep he looked dead.

Antonio whispered to me once about Joachim, "When he falls asleep he looks dead."

I said, "Everyone sleep looks dead." When my boys were babies, I always thought they were sleeping close to death. I'd put my face so close to their mouths, to check whether they were breathing, that I thought they'd wake up. But they didn't.

Once my grandmother, who died when I was young, said to me, "You mama, she tuck a tissue in you lil neck. So hot when you born, in July. She see you breathin in that bed cause that tissue go like a lil flag in the wind."

My mother would never have told me that. On Sundays, my boys loved to pick a few oranges because they didn't have to fill crates all day, like we used to. They loved my twin half brothers, who were only fifteen and would throw the football with them. My mother was usually asleep on Sundays, since she partied harder on

Friday and Saturday, after partying normally the rest of the days. But if she was sitting in her chair on the tiny porch, she never looked directly at my face, not even after four beers. She looked somewhere near my left shoulder. She might say, "Smell like them nasty flowers y'all put in them funeral bouquets." She meant stargazer lilies. She might say, "Them boys need a haircut." That meant she was pissed at their thick black curls, and my own dark hair.

Over the years, I'd see that sparkle-shaped indent in my mother's right cheekbone, a diamond of white that never tanned, and when I was sixteen and some girl slapped a guy at school, I jerked hard, knowing my father had backhanded my mother so hard that whatever jewel he wore had imprinted itself into her face forever.

We made it to Indio, on the 10 freeway. While the radiator blew hot in my face, my uncle stared impassively at the desert. Yesterday I'd driven to the very last exit on the 10, for Venice, where my sons were now sleeping while waves sounded across the sand from their dreaming.

I exited on Monroe Street in Indio. The big streets in Coachella Valley were named for presidents. Jackson. Washington. My uncle said, "RC tell me he seen Clinton Street. Name for Bill Clinton. Little dirt road by them polo field."

The polo field was where Coachella, the music festival, took over the desert. Sofelia and RC said people tried to camp all the way out in Mecca, sleeping in vans and cars, and they got so dehydrated they would appear on the tribal land like zombies, begging for water and food, because things were so expensive inside the tents on the polo grounds.

My uncle finished his coffee. His face was like a skull with dark gold paint applied. Like decoupage. My uncle was the scariest man any of us knew.

I turned onto the old two-lane highway, Grapefruit Boulevard, heading south. No matter how hot, how pissed I was starting to feel, the valley was stunning. It had to be one of the most beautiful places in the world. A gorgeous series of layers and colors—the base of golden sand and white dunes, the silver and green ghost trees and smoke trees floating like strange baby's breath, the spears of white yucca, and the green creosote bushes.

The mountains were layers of purple and gold, ridged and rippled all around us. Santa Rosa Range that separated the desert from the ocean and San Diego. The old Cupa was on the other side of that, I realized. We'd have to go tomorrow, me and James.

We left the boulevard and headed east on Polk toward the Mecca Hills, where the wide irrigation canal went south, all the way to the border with Mexico. People died trying to swim across the All-American Canal at the border. People died in the swift water, they died in the desert, they died under the smoke trees, so they could pick grapes and carrots and beets out here in the fields.

We left behind the last scattered houses and then we were in the date gardens, which I always thought were magic. Rows of tall date palms stretched for miles, hallways of silver and gold where we used to run along the trunks. Reynaldo never would come. He wanted us to forget we came from people who worked fields.

It was eight thirty a.m. Maybe in an hour, Joachim and Antonio would be running on the beach in Venice with him, practicing their capoeira moves, Joachim pissed that his dad expected him to pronounce Portuguese words, Antonio just trying to keep up with his older brother.

James had to be awake now. Would he order room service for one? Would he eat breakfast downstairs with everyone he knew?

Would they ask him where I was? I didn't know him well enough to imagine how his face looked while he thought I was playing games.

I stopped at the last intersection on this dirt road. A vast field of watermelons, like green volleyballs, men and women moving down the rows, covered with bandannas like everyone else had been all spring and summer, from the virus. But they had always kept their faces covered, for the dust and pesticides.

My uncle said, "All them row. Me and RC, we pick cotton in Calipatria. 1945."

He had told me this countless times, when Alfonso and I rode with him. "Cotton look like snow out here. We never pick cotton in Louisiana. Cut cane. They laugh at us, cause our finger bleed. Oui, them cotton hurt down in Calipatria."

Now he lit a cigarillo, as if we needed more heat in the car. Blew out the smoke and somehow it didn't hurt my eyes, since they were full of sweat. He said, "People tell us, you go to California, see the movie and the ocean, oui? All we see was cotton. See that same hoe." I knew what he'd say, like every time, at the end. "Calexico, Calipatria, Coachella. How we work up California. Not for RC, none y'all be here."

I knew the legend. I knew I owed RC whatever he needed. But I had a feeling my uncle was keeping something else back—as he always did.

We passed a sign that said TORRES MARTINEZ RESERVATION— TRIBAL LAND, and I turned down the long dirt road that led to Sofelia's allotment. The reservation land was a checkerboard of squares, some of it leased to big agricultural companies where there were crops, some developed into tilapia farms with fish ponds, some leased out for trailer parks, and some of it left as it had been forever, like the first mile of Sofelia's land.

She had eighty acres. Each tribal member, back in 1912, got

160 acres. Sofelia's grandfather had only two children, and each of them had only one child.

In the distance were the Torres Martinez cemetery and chapel. James had said he had family buried out here. I looked down at my phone. Nothing.

I slowed down, the dust rising all around my car, afraid to close the windows, and my uncle's cigarillo smoke, the radiator heat, and the light dust all mingled like layers of one level of hell. At the big windbreak of eucalyptus trees and tamarisk, there was a clearing and two sets of mailboxes I always loved, their silver tongues hanging open. Two roads took off from there.

There was a massive new gate of black wrought-iron bars, about six feet tall, with small crosses at the top. The gate closed off the whole road. A black truck was parked behind it, and a young man watching us. Behind him, to the left, was the entrance to the trailer park that had been there for twenty years. Rancho Palomitas. The first mobile home was ancient, pale green, with an elaborate altar that I'd always loved. A black-robed woman with white stars on her gown, austere and silvery, and only white roses around her feet, and white candles. La Virgen de la Soledad, Sofelia had told me, because the people who lived in the rancho were from Oaxaca, and she was their patron saint. She stood on a stone structure, and near her feet four dogs panted in the shade of the eucalyptus windbreak, their tongues bright pink ribbons spooling out.

The young man got out of his truck. He pointed at a sign beside the gate. Plywood painted white, black letters shaped elegant and clean.

SOVEREIGN NATION

TRIBAL LAND

PRIVATE—NO TRESPASSING

NO ICE

For a minute, I thought the sign was for the zombies from the Coachella music festival, showing up high on LSD, dizzy and dehydrated. I thought it meant, hey, don't be coming here asking for ice because when you bought your tickets online in Oslo or Boston or London you didn't know how hot the real Coachella gets.

But my uncle said, "Call em ICE now. Always got three letter. FBI. CIA. Federal like three letter." He looked at me. "RC said they come all the time now, catch peoples at the market, at the park, in the field. Come here two time last year. Sofelia put that gate."

The young man pulled out his cell phone and called someone.

I shivered, even though it was so hot. I'd seen ICE up close in February. Just before Valentine's Day.

Mr. Singh had miscalculated on what we'd need for Valentine's. "Perhaps 2020 is a year many people fell in love," he said on February 8, because we'd already sold most of the roses and carnations, and more than half of the specialty pink and red flowers like peonies, dahlias, and the custom-bred chocolate orchids I hated. On February 10, he sent Dawna and me to the Flower District in LA, hoping there were flowers left.

Downtown LA was crazy, nowhere to park, vans everywhere. Valentine's Day. Shit. Every year men would come in and grin at me, buy chocolate orchids, show me little chocolate diamond earrings or necklaces, and boxes of chocolate. They'd say, "I get all three, I'm gold, man. I can do whatever I want for six months."

Dawna and I pushed our way into the warehouse where last year we got roses for a huge school fundraiser. We were all the way into the long wet cement corridor banked by buckets and shelves and smelling of every sweetness and stink of mushy stems. Then people began yelling behind us, and in front of us, in the big deliv-

ery area, women were being handcuffed. Black uniforms surged
our way.

Two men came behind us, and one grabbed my arm and moved
me toward the counter where two agents were typing on a laptop.
His grip was hard. I smelled Old Spice deodorant. He had pink
clean jaws and brown eyes and blond military stubble, a vest that
said POLICE and then ICE. He was about my age.

"What citizen are you a country of?" he said, real loud and
slow, and one of the other guys glanced up.

I lost my shit. "Are you *serious*? I was born in San Bernardino.
St. Bernardine's Hospital. Is that American enough for you?"

He jabbed his finger at my Conroy's name tag. "Matelasse
Rodriguez."

I jerked my arm out of his fingers, but he clamped his hand on
my shoulder. I said, "No *z*. Rodrigue." I looked at his vest name
tag. "Chad McDonnell. Were you born in Ireland?"

"What?"

"Where the hell were *you* born?"

He looked mildly surprised, but he recovered fast. "Not rel-
evant."

"It is to me."

The two supervisor guys at the desk just watched him. Like he
was being tested. He glared at them and then at me. "I was born in
Santa Clarita, okay? Let me see your ID."

I handed him my license.

"You left off the *z* here, too," he said, nasty. "Rodrigue." The
two agents typed.

Reynaldo's last name is classic New Orleans. A slave woman
owned by a Spanish man who freed her when she saved his life in
a fever epidemic.

I said, "There's no damn *z*. That's my married name. You want my maiden name?" What the fuck, why did we still call it that? Maiden? My *virgin* name? I said, "St. Clair. After the plantation in Louisiana that owned my mother's ancestors. You cool now?"

He sucked in the sides of his cheeks trying to look hard. Please. "So you're Black."

"I'm fuckin tired. It's nine in the morning. We need to get back to work."

Then he looked over at Dawna, standing awkwardly by the wall by herself. Of course no one jammed her up. Blond hair in shaggy waves around her face, blue eyes and blue eyeliner and navy mascara and plump shoulders in a pale blue top. She'd told me on the way to LA she'd been using dry spray shampoo because she was too tired to wash her hair, and her head felt covered in flour. Dawna said to him, "Yeah, me and Matelasse went to the same high school. Seriously. What the hell?"

Chad McDonnell glared at Dawna—all red cheeks, his Adam's apple poking out of his wide neck like a little secret buddy watching us.

Then a woman was being pulled past me, two little white gardenias tucked into the black braids pinned together at the crown of her head. Fresh. I could smell the flowers. She put those in her hair for someone who worked here with her. Love. She looked at me for a few seconds and an agent shoved her forward.

I turned and stared right into Chad's eyes and said, "So you're Santa Clarita. If you're thirty-five, which you look thirty-five, you went to Hart High. If you played football, my brother's team beat your ass in the CIF quarterfinals. We went to Linda Vista. We beat you 50–14. He was a linebacker. He got four tackles for a loss. Is that enough American information for you? Get your fuckin hand off me."

I walked back to the van and waited by the passenger door.

The pigeon shit on the silver paint was violet and white. Pretty combination.

Dawna drove. We had to get flowers from a wholesaler in El Monte. We didn't say anything for a few hours.

When we got back to Conroy's, I went in the back room. It took me ten minutes to calm down. I kept staring at the funeral wreath stands. We ended up using a lot of those flowers for people who died, not fallen in love. When corona came, the whole world changed.

The gate was closed in the center with three thick metal chains wrapped around the bars. The young man leaned against the black Chevy Silverado facing the road, parked in the shade of a small ramada made of palm fronds layered onto a wooden structure. He was wide shouldered, with black sunglasses and a Raiders jersey. He finished talking on his cell phone, and then he unlocked the chains and let us in.

"Gated community now?" I joked when we drove slowly over the entrance.

He laughed and said, "Sorry, Sofelia didn't tell me you were comin. I remember you."

"Wait—Omar? Rachelle's husband?"

He nodded. "You're Alfonso's sister."

"Yeah," I said. "That's me." Then I saw the worry on his face. "That's your new baby sick?"

He nodded. "Six months. No idea whether they can get the virus or not. Maybe she just has a fever. But Rachelle and her are quarantined."

At the line of metal mailboxes for the rancho, a young woman was putting envelopes to go out on one box. She wore a UCLA

T-shirt, had her hair in a long braid, and she wore glasses. She stared hard at me as I drove near the eucalyptus windbreak that separated the two roads. In front of the pale green trailer, a man about fifty sat outside now on a folding chair, watching us, too. He looked freakishly like my uncle. Same gilt skin darkened by sun, same lines etched around his mouth, same smooth cheekbones. Straw hat instead of a red ball cap.

"RC say he run the trailer park," my uncle said. "Call him Emiliano. He always watchin." Then he said, "Get goin. Tro chaud."

Too hot. The heat poured from the dashboard. I turned down Sofelia's road. Thick black smoke rose into the air, hesitating lazy for a minute, then blown sideways by the breeze.

"What's on fire?" I said.

"RC barbecue," my uncle said.

"For breakfast?" I said. Nothing today made sense.

We entered the clearing that was RC and Sofelia's place. When I was little, there was just one house, but they'd built two more houses, and now all three buildings were arranged in a triangle around the huge yard. Beige stucco with white trim, like big sugar cookies. The giant, ancient mulberry tree shaded the central yard. Three long white vans were parked near the last house, and a few young men were sitting on folding chairs under two blue E-Z Ups, looking at their phones. RC, short and dark-skinned, his bald head glistening, his arms still thick with muscle under his tank top, closed the lids on a long cooker made of three oil drums welded together. A segmented black ant on wrought-iron legs. Boom. Boom. Boom. When the smoke drifted away, RC saw us. He held out both tongs like they were magic wands.

"Don't turn them engine off," my uncle said, getting out.

"Enrique!" RC shouted. "You finally got Matelasse out here!"

The heat still shoved into my face, from the dashboard, and

the cigarillo smoke. I put the Cherokee in park, stepped out onto the drifting sand at the edge of the yard, and the desert furnace swarmed me. Everything went red and black.

It was so noisy I dreamed I was the inside of the engine. I was drowning in heat and dark oil and then a crack-crack-crack. Someone was shooting at me. Tiny bullets that hit me in the forehead and went inside my brain to rest there like kernels of popcorn.

I woke in a dim bedroom, swimming in sweat, a ceiling fan creaking slowly over me like some drunken spinning flower. A loose screw made the rhythmic cracking noise. A swamp cooler roared beside me, facing the bed, the damp air riffling from the metal slats and messing with my eyebrows.

My feet were bare, on top of the dark red comforter. Where were my boys?

I tried to sit up. My head hurt. My tank top soaked. A dresser with a vase of pink silk flowers. Five lilies. The smell of perfumed powder. Jean Naté. Sofelia's room. That was her smell.

I lay back. I couldn't move. My toenails were like rubies.

Yesterday, my feet were tragic. Red polish worn off like rats had been chewing on the edge of each one. When I first got to the casino suite, I'd been trying to hide my feet. James laughed and said, "I don't care about your toes."

He went down to the casino salon and bought red polish. He asked me to lie with my feet up on two pillows, and he painted my toenails. His hands were so big it was like a bear holding a toy.

He said, "I raised two girls, remember? They told me you can touch up three times before you have to go back to the salon."

Then he wouldn't let me move for an hour. We watched *The*

Great British Baking Show. Now he was never going to talk to me again.

Where the hell was my phone? I tried to get up and everything went black again. I needed to call my boys. I wanted to hear their voices.

In the car on the way to Venice last night, Joachim had said, "Are you and Dad divorced?"

"No. We're separated," I told him.

"That's a stupid word," he said, and went outside.

He was right. Separate the white from the yolk when you're cooking. Separate the stargazer lilies from the other flowers because some people hate the smell. Separate the milk from the cream, baby, that's you, cream of the crop, this one fool always said when he came into Conroy's, trying to get my number. I'm allergic to dairy and players, I always told men like that.

I looked at the black enameled dresser. I had slept in this bed when I was ten. Sofelia's wedding portrait was still there, her white dress. She looked exactly like me.

Last night, James had propped himself on one elbow above me and touched the side of my throat. My pulse. He said, "So he left you."

I nodded. "And your wife left you."

"Yup."

"What does that make us?" I said.

"Two people who got left."

I had to text him. Where was my damn phone? Somebody had carried me in here. The little digital clock said 9:23 a.m. I'd been out for about an hour. I smelled the heavy smoke making its way into the house.

I went out into the hallway. The narrow wooden floor polished by bare feet. The gallery of photos I remembered from childhood. Five kids wearing graduation caps. Two boys. Raymond and Ronald. Both of them had died young, Raymond in Afghanistan, Ronald killed by a drunk driver on the Golden State Freeway after a Dodger game. Three girls. Rita, Rosie, Rachelle. Dark red-brown skin, long wavy hair, Sofelia's cheekbones.

My purse was on the bathroom counter. I splashed water on my face, smoothed water onto my hair, and redid my bun. Purple circles like pansies around my eyes. Two missed calls this morning from a number I'd never seen. Spam risk. They left voicemails—probably trying to scare me about fake taxes. I called James.

"Is there something I need to know?" he said, careful. Voices were moving behind him.

"Hey," I said. "I'm in Mecca. Remember I told you I had family here? My uncle needed me to drive him. He doesn't have a license anymore." I looked in the mirror again. Like Ash Wednesday rubbed there around my eyes. "You giving up on me?"

"Not yet. Maybe next week."

He knew I'd laugh. "I'm just hoping we're not cousins," I said. "My uncle who isn't my blood uncle is married to Sofelia Martinez. Are we okay?"

He laughed hard. Pans clanged nearby. "We're okay. She's my dad's cousin."

I said, "I can try to come back to Pala tonight."

"Let me come out there tonight," James said. "I need to visit my dad in the cemetery. I figured since you're gone I'd work. I'm in the restaurant planning lobster orders. And lots of beef from your least favorite nation."

Suddenly I remembered that stupid phrase boys used to say to me. Don't hate the player, hate the game. I didn't hate Brazil. I didn't hate Reynaldo. I hated the game he thought he had to play.

I didn't want this man to think I was playing him. I said, "Can you please come around six? Because I miss you." Then I hung up. I sounded like a fifteen-year-old.

My head hurt. The towel on the rack smelled of a man. Sweat and aftershave and burnt meat. I closed my eyes. Reynaldo and me on a blanket in the orange groves. He was so particular. He'd put candles on the cistern so it looked like a fairy castle, and he played bossa nova on his boombox—"Corcovado"—and his neck was like damp velvet. Nothing else would ever feel like that.

But James and I had been in the hotel bed, and his sideburns were not strips of hair but hundreds of tiny filaments and my eyelashes were caught when he rested his face against mine. No candlelight. Dark. Our bodies were soft. I had two sons. He had two daughters. Disco thumping from the casino club far below us. And my whole body had shaken in a different way from years ago. I couldn't breathe for a long time.

I walked barefoot toward the living room. A toddler boy was sleeping in a playpen, hair plastered by sweat to his forehead, his fingers buried in the mane of a stuffed horse. "Matelasse," someone said.

Rosie was sitting in the corner, wearing a Dodgers blue mask, putting her hair up. She handed me another mask. "Thanks for coming," she said. "Rachelle's baby has this fever. They're locked in the other house. We can't take a chance. She's watching for the virus."

"Gilbert Three?" I asked, leaning into the playpen.

She nodded. Rosie was thirty-four, the youngest daughter. Her husband Gilbert worked security at the Agua Caliente casino in Palm Springs. "Mom told me you fell out. We carried you in here." She grinned. "You pregnant?"

"Very funny," I said. Then I froze. Wait—from when we were together in July? Not from last night. No way. Hilarious.

"Gilbert doesn't have a fever?" I looked into the playpen.

"I can't tell yet," Rachelle said. "Before the stupid virus, we would take him to Target and walk around, get cooled down to-day, right?"

We laughed. That was our default, if the AC went out. Walk around cold-ass Target for an hour, and you only had to buy the kids some candy or one toy each. Thank God. But not now.

"So Reynaldo took off, huh?"

"Yeah."

She looked at her phone. "Mom's waiting in the yard. You gotta go. You're late. They'll be so hungry they're gonna faint. Like you."

"What?"

"You're driving lunches to the fields."

The yard was full of people moving now. The heat had gathered itself in the oleander bushes and tree branches overhead. More like a concentrated stinging on my skin. My face burned. The vans had open back doors like flat wings, three boys loading massive Yeti coolers inside. Another man was working on my car, at the far edge of the clearing, under another E-Z Up.

RC stood at the long grill, tonging meat into a huge foil container on a wooden picnic table. "There go Matelasse," RC said, smiling, tributaries of sweat running down his temples. "Rubbin her eyes like a lil baby even though she grown."

Always joking. I didn't see Uncle Enrique. The young men loading coolers into the vans were Mexican, their faces guarded, glancing at me. Sofelia said, "You okay now?"

Sofelia. She must have been seventy, but looked exactly the same as always, cheekbones like plump little birds rested there, black eyes that tilted upward, and long black hair in a thick braid down her back. She lifted a hand and put the backs of her fingers on my forehead.

I had to smile and shake my head. We couldn't touch each other.

"You're not hot," she said, as if I were a child, not a woman with two boys. And I put my head down and cried into my hands, not her soft shoulder.

She patted my back twice. I felt like Bambi lifting up my face all wet. I wiped off the tears with a paper towel from RC's roll and said, "I was just tired. I drove from Pala to get Uncle Enrique and then out here."

"Pala?" she said, like everyone else. "You gambling now? No wonder you got hot. They keep it cold and dark in there so you'll never leave."

Pretty funny if she'd seen me in the bed with James.

She looked over at the third house, shuttered tight and the AC roaring, and said, "That baby better be okay. I'm praying it's something we used to hate, like hand, foot, and mouth, or roseola. Never thought I'd say that."

Then she said to RC, "Hurry up with that meat." And to me, "You gotta get on the road. It's late. They'll be waiting for you."

He said to her, "Every day, woman." He opened the cooker and smoke erased his face, but he didn't cough. He turned over the last piles of dark charred meat, glistening, hissing. Carne asada. RC put the last of the meat into the foil container. He said, "You remember when we used to tell you me and Enrique ate Vienna sausage and crackers in the cotton field? When I retired from the county road crew, I had me a van service to pick up the workers, but I hated getting up at three to go out to the camps. We had hooked up the trailer park over there, and I figured since they mostly men, they mostly livin alone, they gotta be hungry. So three years ago, we started makin five-dollar dinners. Get em right from the van."

I carried the meat with Sofelia into the second house, where the door was open. Four huge pots, industrial sized stainless steel, steamed on the big stove. Rosie and Rita stood at a long folding metal table lined with plastic clamshell dinner containers, the kind separated into three sections. They spooned Mexican rice into one compartment, pinto beans flecked with chile verde into another. Sofelia tonged meat into the third compartment, laying three corn tortillas over the steaming carne asada, and snapped the lid shut. She stacked fifteen dinners into a huge soft-sided cooler and hung two coolers from my shoulders like I was a Dutch girl carrying milk in a painting. She said, "Take these out to the vans. You gotta go." She brushed back wisps of hair with her wrist. "They start in the field at five when it's this hot. Lunch at ten."

Outside, RC pointed his tongs toward the front van. "You drivin with Josué," he said. I put down the coolers on the metal floor at the open back, and the young kid lifted his chin at me and stacked them near the others. "You girls drive, because you American and speak English. Nobody can bother you. ICE like to take people on Friday, cause nobody see a judge till Monday, and they might be in the field. But Josué and Albert and Gustavo born here in Coachella. They speak Spanish. No tickets."

He wiped his forehead with his bandanna. "ICE ain't came yet for them workers in the field cause they want them lil personal watermelons, what they call em, in the store. We had big old Texas watermelons when you was little, remember? Size of a pig. You all spit them seeds forever. Americans don't want no seeds now. They want one baby watermelon for theyself." He shrugged.

"They ain't tryin to spit." But then he looked into the distance. "You never know, though. Today's Friday. That's why your uncle goin with you. Security. Last week, somebody rob one of the vans. They knew we had cash. Everything crazy this year. I ain't takin no chances."

My uncle walked up and got into the second seat. Fucking duffel bag at his feet. Shit. At least my boys were running on the beach.

We all three wore bandanna masks. My uncle was silent. Josué said two or three words at a time to me. "Turn left. Left again. Go slow. They don't want dust in the field."

Teenagers. Joachim would do this to me pretty soon. I knew it.

Josué was on his phone the whole time. I saw an Instagram. A beautiful girl with massive hair curled over her shoulders, holding little green palm fronds over her red bathing suit. Then he looked up and said, "Over there."

The first stop was a cantaloupe field. I drove onto the frontage road, six blue porta potties standing guard, and down into the shade of an E-Z Up anchored to the sandy ground near the irrigation ditch. The crew was all men, crouched under what looked like a cartoon plane skimming the rows. A harvester with long wings. They threw melons up to the men with crates atop the structure. Gray bowling balls rising up, again and again.

Jesus Christ, their arms must hurt.

Josué said, "Right here."

He laid out the coolers on the tailgate, spoke to the men in Spanish. They knew the drill. Every guy but one bought a lunch. Fourteen. They ate in the shade of cottonwoods around the big cistern, sitting on the ground or on overturned crates, and played music on an iPhone. Tubas and accordions.

Josué hopped up in the passenger seat and handed me the bills rolled into a tight wet cylinder. "If we get stopped you say we're taking all this food to a family party. Anniversary. Friday we say anniversary. Saturday quinceañera. Sunday wedding. Got it?"

"Shit," I said. "Stopped by who?"

"Whoever."

"Who robbed the van last week?" I asked. I glanced back at my uncle, who was watching the men, the field. His eyes never stopped.

Josué shrugged. "Two pendejos. Wearing bandannas like everybody else. They took the money and got in a white Honda." He pointed to the money. "You keep it, like—" He tapped his heart. He meant my bra.

"I'm not putting all those dirty sweaty fives next to my skin!" I said. I was not a 40DD like my mother.

He looked away.

"Shit," I said. He was right. No cop was gonna search my bra. Now the smell of fertilizer was gonna erase James's aftershave. Perfect.

We went east toward the Mecca Hills. Lincoln Street. The vineyards spread out in green-gold rows for miles, like a god had raked a big comb through the world. The smell of grapes cooking in the heat. Flashes of wine, jelly, raisin, different scents in different places. We went up the frontage road like before, past the toilets again, but this time there were three E-Z Ups and women sorting and weighing grapes into crates in the shade thick with sugar and flies.

Josué leaned over and honked the horn three times. More women came out like ghost warriors from the vines. Twenty, thirty women. They were bent under the leaf canopy of each row, and they straightened up and stopped for a second. White caps, full bandanna covering their faces so only their eyes showed, long-sleeved shirts and gloves, sneakers covered with white dust and sand. Clippers in their hands and some of the women had to unhook the fingers of their friends from the handles, they were so coated with juice and dirt. The women bent at plastic tubs of water and washed their hands, then pulled down their bandannas and smiled at me. Lips closed. Chins pale and wrinkled like fingers left in the bath too long.

Two foremen came down the frontage road on golf carts, bandannas trailing like pirates, and Josué opened the van doors.

Three vineyards in a row, all along the hills. One hundred thirteen lunches. Almost all women. "They're better at being under there and cutting the bunches," Josué said. "That's where my mom worked forever. Now she's in the date packinghouse. It's cooler."

He waved to one young woman, and they sat beside each other for a few minutes. She pulled down her bandanna, smiled at Josué, ducked her head, and they talked. Laughed. She had long hair tucked up under a UCLA cap. Delicate hands.

When Josué came back to the van, I said, "Is that your girl?"

"No, that's my girl's cousin. Ximena."

"She goes to UCLA?" I said, chewing on a tortilla from our foil packet on the seat.

"No. My girl gave her the hat. Fidelia. She's going to UCLA. Starting September. Ximena was working in LA until the virus. She came back here. She's saving money for college. She's smart, too."

The foreman came over and said something in Spanish to Josué, handed him the money. Several of the women sat next to each other, and shared one meal on their thighs. One tortilla each. One torn in half. Like me and Dawna cutting one burrito in half at El Ojo de Agua. I knew who they were saving their money for. Their kids. I put the twenties in my bra.

*　*　*

A few blocks away, two trucks wheeled toward us, spraying something onto a field of green rows. Peppers? My window was open, and the pesticide went right through the bandanna and inside my lungs like sickly sweet varnish, coating my throat.

I made it to the next watermelon field, and then threw up into the corner of weeds at the irrigation ditch. Even while I was wiping my mouth, my eyes focused on the single velvet cattail. Plush. Brown. I could put that in a huge arrangement.

Then I thought, No. It can't be. July? Six weeks ago?

I had thrown up with Joachim. Not with Antonio. No.

Josué stood beside me with a cup. My uncle held a tortilla toward me. The men stared, eating under the shade of the harvester, sitting right there in the fucking rows of watermelon because this field had no shade except the machine itself. Josué said, "Sorry, um—"

"Mrs. Rodrigue," I said without thinking.

"Sorry, Mrs. Rodrigue, I forgot you aren't from here. I should have told you to close the window. And you didn't drink enough water. Here. Gatorade."

I made a face. "I hate Gatorade. Hazard of being a soccer mom."

Back at the van, I grabbed some ice and chewed.

"You okay to drive?" Josué said, actually scared. "I don't have a license. I don't have the money for driving class." He was so young. His ball cap said DMHS.

I put my head on the steering wheel for a minute. I'd been driving for two days. That's all. I wasn't ducking back under the grapevines like those women. I turned to rest my left cheek on the horn. "What's on your hat? Department of Messed-Up Homeland Security?"

He smiled, with his eyes crinkling up. First time. "Desert Mirage High School. I'll be a senior if we get to go back to school."

On the way back to Sofelia's, he told me about his web series, *Coachella4Real*. His TikTok. The GoPro camera he used at Coachella during the 2019 music festival to record crazy rich people. "I worked festival security back then," he said. "I got the idea because of these rich blond girls at school. Triplets. Flynn and McClellan and Kildare. Their mom named them after places in Ireland."

"Seriously?" I said. I couldn't imagine some kid in love moaning *McClellan, oh my God you're amazing.*

"Yeah. Listen. They didn't know I recorded them at school." At a stoplight, he played me a video on his phone. Girl voices— guitar-wire sweet and mean. "Oh my God! You're Jee-sus, right?" Pronounced like Christ.

"Yep."

"So this is your little brother? Josh-u-way? Oh my God, so cute. Is that, like, from the Mexican Bible?"

"Yeah," he said on the phone. "Your boys are all Luke and Ezra and Zachariah. Mexicans are Jesús and Josué and Moisés."

The girl laughed very fake. "Adorable! How many in your family? Nine? Ten? There's, like, so many Hernandez!"

"Nope. Only three boys. But my moms had us normal. One at a time. Not from Clomid and some stranger's eggs."

"Fuck you," she said.

"Nah, I'm good. You're too skinny, aye?" Laughter. He swiped on the phone and the voices stopped abruptly.

I imagined the school hallways. "What if they see it and try to sue you or something?"

He snorted. "They think I can barely read. I record all the time. It's on now."

"What?" I looked over at him. "Where is it?"

He pointed to his own chest. The square leather amulet he wore on a short thick cord around his neck. I looked closely. A black shiny lens peering out from a hole edged in leather stitching. "GoPro. Body cam. Like cops. My dad made it. He used to do leather back in Mexico. Belts and purses and shoes."

"You're recording us right now?"

"I record every day." He paused. "I mean, shit goes on my site, aye? I have, like, fourteen thousand followers. Like, in Mexico City and LA and Chicago. I edit on my computer and charge the camera at night. I'm stuck here. For now. But I'm gonna make movies."

Then he turned his head and said, "The Irish triplets have an Instagram. They shoot in Joshua Tree and Coachella. Clothes and makeup and hair. They have, like, 1.2 million followers."

We turned down Sofelia's road. At the gate, Omar let us in, never removing his headphones. Josué pointed to Rancho Palomitas. "They don't speak much Spanish in there. They speak Mixtec. They're from Oaxaca. Except Fidelia. She was born here. She knows three languages."

"Show me her Instagram," I said.

He shook his head. "She doesn't have one. She doesn't care about that shit."

All boys sound the same, when they think a girl might leave them behind. Wistful. Wavery.

I parked the van and went straight to Sofelia in the first house. Dumped all that money out of my shirt onto the coffee table and said, "You need someone with bigger boobs."

She laughed. She was sitting in a recliner with her swollen feet lifted high. Sofelia said, "RC's in the old date blossom shack, waiting for his brother. He's got homemade moonshine out there." Then she touched my filthy hand. "I'm so happy you came."

★   ★   ★

I went with my uncle in the golf cart, because I loved the date blossoms. They were the first flowers that changed my life.

In February, the date palms bloomed, long sweeping sprays of yellow pollen-covered pistils. We always came out in February. We had Monday off—Washington's Birthday. Alfonso and me—our mother didn't want us around that day, and Enrique would pack us into the truck. Sofelia and RC would be in this little shack with the palmeros, Rafael Torres and his son, who'd been working the dates since something like 1920 when the trees were planted by Sofelia's grandmother. The palmeros climbed the wooden ladders nailed to the palm trunks, machetes flashing, and sliced off the male blooms.

It was magic out here, even in the heat. Giant sweeps of golden strands feathered with tiny blooms, four feet long. Like fantastic brooms and the gods could sweep the sky, I thought when I was little. The men loaded them fast on a flatbed truck and carried them faster into the shack, trailing clouds of bees because the pollen smelled so yeasty and mellow and strong the whole earth was scented. That was when I fell in love with flowers and perfume. That's why I still loved working at Conroy's. We'd watch the palmeros taking the male flowers to each female tree, pollinating the female palms for the Deglet Noor dates.

Now, at the old wooden shack, bright blue back then, faded to turquoise today, it would still be beautiful if I didn't think I was going to die of the heat.

RC was asleep on the military cot in the square front room, where workers always rested in the afternoon heat. The wrecked kitchen beyond, where we used to stack the blossoms, at least had the ancient refrigerator humming, and a fan blew over a Coleman cooler filled with ice and Coke and beer.

RC was awake, of course. Every shut eye ain't sleep, as our mother used to say. He said, "Hand me one them Co-Cola, Matelasse."

I did. My uncle said, "I take that rifle, there. But I ain't seen no rats."

RC sat up and grinned. He took a gallon glass bottle of something clear and pale gold, poured it into a Solo cup, and handed it to Enrique. I shook my head. Varnish in my lungs, and maybe something mysterious in my belly. I wasn't going to think about that. Not yet.

I drove back alone through the cathedral of silver fronds, down the aisles that felt like church to me.

We all sat in folding chairs under the ramada covered with last year's fronds, Sofelia and her daughters, even Omar on his break while Josué watched the gate, and we took a covered plate to the silent house where Rachelle said, "I think she's better" through the screened window. We ate the leftover dinners, the meat spicy-black and the rice soaked up with the juices. I wished for a moment that Joachim and Antonio were here, to see this part of their family. Maybe next February. Right now, it was too hot, and not Venice.

It was four, the worst time for the heat, and Sofelia took me inside the house. She and I napped in her king-sized bed, sounds broken into fragments by the roaring window coolers.

"Come with me," Sofelia said when I woke beside her, the smell of her fresh powder. Jean Naté.

She started the golf cart. We drove to the center of her land, where the water cistern was like a castle with a ladder up the side. The wooden top had recently been repaired, because someone had broken it last year. A strange little shrine beside it—two votive candles burned to pools of pink and blue. Like a boy and a girl. Fresh orange marigolds.

We climbed the ladder to stand atop the cistern. Glimpse of blue Salton Sea to the south when we stood atop the cistern. "Look west," she said, breathing hard. "At the base of the mountains."

We could see the Santa Rosa Range, where bighorn sheep still lived. Where her people used to spend summer, looking down at the lake below that filled the whole Coachella Valley. Lines of black, maroon, gold, and brown striped the bottom of the hills, where the water had been at different levels over the centuries. Sofelia said, "I heard you talking to Rita. You said your boys are out in Venice, and you never even walked on that beach. You said you never been anywhere. Matelasse. See those circles up there? Kind of white and beige?"

I squinted. Like broken bracelets flung across the dry slopes at the base of the mountains.

"Fish traps," I said. "I remember. You took us there once."

"Yes," she said. "They built rock walls and then when the water went down they had fish. That was four hundred years ago. My ten times great-grandfather." She turned a few feet and pointed to the top of the old chapel a mile away. "There's the cemetery. You've been there. My mom and dad, my aunts, my sister, everybody gone but me. I never even went to Mexico when they used to go visit our cousins down there. Cahuilla lived everywhere. Mexico and California was all the same land till somebody made up a border. Now they been talking about the wall two years. I never been to San Francisco, never been to Santa Barbara. I'm seventy years old and I never got anywhere either and that's fine. You stayed home. Like me. You're fine."

So I told her a little bit about James, and how we met at San Luis Rey. Sofelia frowned and said, "Wait—my little cousin? I used to beat the crap out of him when he came here."

"That's who I went to see," I said. "At Pala. He's coming down here tonight."

"You and James?" She smiled. "Lord, now I feel old. Help me climb down from here."

Back in the yard, the guys were washing the vans. The coolers were all washed and dried, stacked in the house. Six p.m. Sofelia said, "Rosie, Matelasse, go get the meat and tortillas and gas up for tomorrow. Josué, take the propane tanks and fill up."

"Tomorrow's Saturday," I said.

They all laughed. "Field don't close for the weekend. Not during harvest."

"Shit," I said, and they all laughed again.

I went into the house to wash my face and wet my hair. Rita handed me a clean tank top of hers since mine was soaked through. FANTASY SPRINGS 29 CASINO. She said, "James? From Pala? He's been out here a couple times. He's like, forty-five, right?

"Girl, I'm thirty-seven."

"I forget. You look good."

"When he comes, you better not talk shit," I said, and put up my hair. I tucked in one rogue curl.

The parking lot at Apple Market on Harrison and 66th Avenue was like a little town. People were everywhere, talking at the gas pumps where trucks and vans carried workers who were buying tacos and burritos, talking on the sidewalk while waiting for food orders. Inside the store, two women with name tags—MARIA B and MARIA T—set aside a hundred pounds of meat for Sofelia. Asada, sometimes pork or chorizo. She wouldn't do tilapia because it tasted like mud and RC didn't want fish on his grill. Tonight it was chicken fajita meat.

Back outside, I sat at one of the picnic tables, waiting for Josué. There were ten women in line near the AmeriGas pump, carrying white tanks like little rockets, and Josué was the only guy. Two of the women held a baby on one hip and the propane tank on the other, laughing and talking in Spanish, and I flashed back to when my mom and aunts were hanging up laundry outside, how they all leaned forward and then threw their heads back laughing. Like all the pictures I'd ever seen from other places where women lined up for water or bread, and they put their heads close to gossip.

But Josué pulled out of line and stood in the shade by the market wall, almost out of our sight. He had both arms stretched out, on either side of the girl in the UCLA shirt. What was her name? Fidelia. He leaned close and she whispered right along his neck. You could see it. Love.

Me and James—anyone would be able to see it. Us. That we'd been together. When he got here tonight, I might as well do it. Put my arms around him, from behind, while he sat on the tailgate. Put my legs over his while we had a beer.

Josué kissed her quickly, said one more thing, and then turned around. Wait—where were the propane tanks? He and his girl-friend went to the middle of the line—the other girl, Ximena, she had two tanks beside her. She was tiny and her skin brown, her hair in a long ponytail that stretched like a second spine down her white T-shirt. Josué made all the women laugh—no one was upset that he cut back in. He was in love.

I hadn't even looked at my own phone since I went out to the cistern with Sofelia. I got it out of my bag and saw three missed calls from the same spam number I didn't recognize. Three new voicemails. More fake tax threats?

I played the first. Shit. Joachim.

Early this morning. His voice reedy and high and he was pissed but didn't want to cry: *Mom. We want to come home. I hate Portuguese and Dad says I have to learn ten words a day so we can go to Brazil. I hate this beach. Everybody's weird and Antonio saw a naked guy.*

Second message two hours ago. Joachim. *Mom. Dad got us this phone so we can call him later after we get back home. So he doesn't have to call you. He's outside. He keeps making us watch capoeira stuff on his laptop cause they don't even have a TV. He says they don't believe in TV. Here's Antonio.*

Then my baby boy: *Mom? Can you come get us right now? It's Friday. We could watch* Avengers *and you could make macaroni and cheese. Please?* His shaky long breath was like big wind—he must have his mouth so close to the phone. *I don't like Dad's food. Can you make the macaroni before you come and put it in my lunchbox so I can eat in the car like that time we went to the doctor?*

Then Joachim said, *She's not there. Give me the phone.* One short sob. Like a thorn in my ribs.

Third message. Just their breathing. Then, *She's still not there, Tonio.* One sniffle. A sword to my heart.

Damn. I was a terrible mother.

Mecca to Venice at seven p.m. on a Friday in August? About four hours on the 10 if I was lucky. About three hours to get back home to Rio Seco with them. I could go into the market right now and get Kraft bowls. I would call the boys and tell them I was on my way. We could heat up the bowls with water at a gas station. In fucking Venice.

Josué hopped into the van and said, "We gotta go. Rosie and Rita already got their gas. They're behind us." He put three tanks in our van. The small white truck with the two girls, Fidelia and Ximena, was already gone.

I drove back down Harrison toward Polk, and Josué got texts every few seconds, texting back, his fingers flying. Then he was fidgeting, messing with his leather amulet that wasn't an amulet. He took it off, hung it from the rearview mirror, facing forward. I said, "What, you're doing a TikTok about extreme heat survival now?"

He gave me a fake laugh. I was going to tell Sofelia I had to leave now. I had to get my boys. I said to Josué, "You're up to something, because I have two sons, nine and eleven, and I know when they're up to something. You're what—seventeen? What's going on? You meeting a different girl?"

No laugh this time. He was dead serious. "I got one girl. All I need. But she just stopped texting. Something's weird."

The two vans followed us like big flat-face bulldogs in the rearview. Rosie driving the second, Rita the third. The meat smelled strong and bloody behind me. Sofelia's road was ahead. A long cloud of gold dust hung in the air like a big caterpillar. Fresh dust. Someone had driven just before us. Maybe the white truck. Maybe James was already here. Maybe he would come to Venice with me. He'd driven me all the way to the hospital, the night Merry's son Tenerife had gotten shot. He'd been okay when I didn't say a word for more than an hour.

Shit. Tonight, James might be too scary for Joachim and Antonio. For Reynaldo, too.

There'd be purple verbena along here in winter. Those big mats of color like someone had spilled paint. I could bring the boys in February for Presidents' Day. We could go to the Indio date festival with James. The dust falling on us now made me go slow. Josué said, "Hold up."

Three black SUVs were ranged in a blockade at the gate. Nosed tight like horses trying to drink. Rosie and Rita stopped right behind me. Three vans in a line.

ICE. Josué said, "They want the people in the rancho. Not us. But damn . . ."

"Nope," I said. "Fuck, no. I have to go. *Now*."

An agent dressed in a black T-shirt and black vest came around the SUVs and held up his hand for me to stop. Where the hell would I go? I had five feet in front of me and five feet behind. He started yelling, "Everyone out of the vehicles and don't try to run. There are multiple agents here." Then he yelled some more, in Spanish.

He was a brown-skinned guy with a wide square face and thin lips. When we got out, he kept shouting in Spanish, waving us to walk forward toward the gate. It was like a football formation. Four white and three brown agents, in a row with their big stance, hollering at the line of people ranged on the other side of the gate. Uncle Enrique, RC, Sofelia, Omar, and another kid in a Dodgers jersey who got out of the black Silverado.

AGENT HENRY DIAZ. His name tag. He took my elbow and talked fast and loud in Spanish. I said, "I speak English."

It wasn't like the flower warehouse. The wide-open desert was around us and the sky was above us and the dust had paused like it was deciding where to go. Me, Rita, Rosie, and Josué. They lined us up at the gate, facing our own people. Then the agents realized that was a double line of fuck you.

They hollered past us through the bars, each agent choosing someone, shouting what they always said: "What citizen are you a country of? Take out your ID."

One ID card thrown through the bars into the dirt.

The first agent picked it up and said, "Enrique Antoine. What country are you a citizen of?"

My uncle said, "First one Marie Therese. She come off them boat from Senegal 1760. She five. Don't ax me nothin, no. I the fifth line, me." Then he pointed at me and said, "Grandfille."

"Gronfee? What the fuck is he talking about?" the agent shouted. "Does he speak English?"

RC folded his arms and said, "He speak French cause he born in Louisiana, man. He tellin you his five great-grandma got here 1760, so they citizen before your people was choppin down cherry tree. Here. Take my damn license. My first people was Mustafa and he from Mali. Come to New Orleans in 1799. I did my AncestryDNA, man. You should do yours."

Sofelia said, "My people were here when the world formed. You know this and you know you aren't getting past this gate. This is my land. Sovereign nation. I'm not required to let you in."

"Federal agents have the right to search tribal land in California. Public Law 280."

"Yeah," she said. "I didn't sign that. This is my land and all these people here and everybody else on the land is my family. All my relatives."

That agent was the lead. He was maybe fifty, with that dark shave shadow on his cheeks. He looked back at the other agents and said, "Great. We'll search the vans first for illegal aliens. Harboring and transporting will get you felony convictions."

We stood in the heat while they slammed things out of the vans. Lead dude kept his arms crossed, facing his agents. My uncle in his Sunkist ball cap; RC in his straw cowboy hat; Sofelia's scent of perfume drifting close to me. The sweat slid down my back and collected at that last bone before my butt, and suddenly I was even more pissed. I never even got to get in the spa at our fancy Pala hotel suite. Never got to smell the hotel soap.

Through the gate, I saw something moving, close to the earth. Someone crawled to the other side of the black Silverado and then lifted up and slid through the passenger window. She sat up slowly and peered over the dashboard. Fidelia. She reached out and put a GoPro camera on the truck hood, disappeared back down into the cab. Josué froze beside me. His breathing changed. Love choke. Shit. He was so scared.

Another figure knelt very slowly along the edge of the tamarisk tree windbreak, thick green branches like ferns. White T-shirt. Long black hair. Ximena. She slowly put another small square Go-Pro on a wooden stump facing toward us, and then she melted back into the trees.

The van doors slammed shut. The agents came hustling back to the gate. "What's all that meat for if you're not feeding a trailer park full of illegals?" the youngest one said.

Sofelia laughed. "I forget white people don't have big parties. My husband's birthday tomorrow. A hundred people coming. We don't serve cheese and crackers, okay? Now you all need to go back to wherever you came from because that meat cost money and I have to start cooking."

The agent said, "Very funny. I need everyone else's ID. We'll stand out here all day and night till you open that fucking gate and we search the property."

Then the younger agent beside him said, "Sir, there's a girl hiding in the trees." He had his hand on the butt of his gun. That posture. "She could be armed!"

All six pulled their guns and pointed them at the windbreak.

"Don't move!" the older one shouted through the gate. "Hold up your hands. You have ID on you? What citizen are you a country of?"

"You want my hands up or you want my ID?" It was Fidelia. She stepped out of the windbreak. Her acid drawl as mean as any American teenage girl's. "I have my birth certificate and my driver's license and my UCLA student ID. I was born in JFK Hospital in Indio. I'm pre-law at UCLA so you better have warrants signed by a judge. With a signature. Not typed."

"Oh, you think you're the shit?" the younger agent shouted.

The older agent said, "Diaz. Warrants."

Diaz handed him three pieces of paper. "You let us in and give these two guys up, and we'll be done. Julio Reyes and—" the lead agent stumbled. "X-men-a Lopez."

"For what?" Fidelia said.

"Citations for driving with no insurance, no license. Reyes. For X-mena, theft charges from her employer. Seven Palms Spa."

Sofelia laughed at him. "That's all you got? You're not disrupting our family celebration for cousins who got tickets a long time ago."

He said, "Our helicopter did infrared and you got fifty-five humans living in there."

"Officer, I have fifty-five *first* cousins," Sofelia said. "My mom was one of ten and my dad was one of eleven. Indians, right?" She folded her arms and said, "But the only good Indian is a dead Indian. That's what your people used to say to my people."

The lead agent had had it by now. He said, "Ma'am, if you all don't cooperate and open that fucking gate, I'm gonna call for the helicopter and the armored vehicles."

RC said, "Y'all ain't smashin my vans. Those are my vans, man. I bought them in San Bernardino."

The agents backed up, guns still aimed. I started shaking and had to put my hand on Josué's shoulder so I wouldn't go down to my knees. The dust shivered toward the date palm grove. Suddenly I knew my uncle had that old rifle with the diamond-wire sight not far from him.

The older agent moved his gun to point directly at RC. The darkest human. He said, "Holster your weapons and search these four out here. Get their IDs."

I heard Reynaldo's voice in my head. Hemmed up. That's how he said it, one night when he didn't show up after work and I was furious, when the boys were small. He was taking a night class, and he came home long after midnight. "Cops hemmed me up, man. Had me up against the fence and kept that shotgun right in my back. Said someone got robbed downtown and I fit the description. Ugly black male wearing clothes. They were laughing the whole time."

His face had crumpled, and he'd turned his body sideways so suddenly I flinched. But Reynaldo had never touched me in anger. He kicked out four of the wooden slats of the railing on our little front porch. Boom boom boom boom. It was so fast and graceful. When he straightened up, he said, "Fuck this. No." A month later he took off for the beach.

My boys were waiting for me there. They were probably calling my phone in the van right now. *She's still not there, Tonio. She's not coming back for us.*

I took three steps into the middle of the dust between us and the agents. I said, "No. No no oh *hell* no. I am not the *one* today. I am French and Black and Spanish and Houma. So do the American history on that. I do not have time."

I looked right at the lead agent. "My sons are waiting for me to pick them up in LA. It's gonna take me four damn hours to get there, and they're gonna be scared if I'm late. They are little boys.

Nine and eleven. There is no one else in the fuckin world can pick them up. So right now, all your optics or whatever is between me and my kids."

He kept his face like stone. Like that would scare me.

Oh, but I was half minor devil. And half Bettina. My uncle was watching me.

And a loud truck was speeding up the road behind the vans. It stopped, and more dust flew toward us. A man shouted, "What the hell is going on? This is Torres Martinez land!"

James. He was breathing hard. Moving past the vans. His ironed perfect white shirt. He said, "This is my family here. We'll all file suit. Pala, Pechanga, Agua Caliente, Cabazon, Morongo. We have hundreds of lawyers."

I closed my eyes.

I heard *Corcovado, oh, so lovely*, the song Reynaldo first played for me, in the orange groves. *Saudade*, he said. Do you feel it?

I felt so lonely—that thorn piercing my throat now. I could never talk to Reynaldo again like when we were young. I was too old to know James deep like that, but I wanted to try. I wanted to turn around and run to his truck and burrow into those Egyptian cotton sheets with him. But my sons wanted me.

I was going to get my boys.

I breathed in that sob like Antonio. I said to the lead agent, "I am putting my hand in my purse. You shoot me and the whole world's gonna see it on camera and then God's soldier will have a bullet for you. So here is my hand."

I knew James heard me. He said, "I'm a casino manager, man. I'm on the phone now, with Pala lawyers. ICE has no jurisdiction here."

Sofelia said, "You know the American president tried to buy Fantasy Springs casino? That was funny. He knows my cousin. I have a picture of the president with my cousin right here on my phone. You want me to call him?"

I moved slowly. I took out my pink plastic wallet that Antonio picked out at Hello Kitty for my birthday. I took out my license. I threw the wallet on the ground between us. I held my keys in my fist. I went dark in the head and down on one knee, because I thought of all those years Mr. Singh told Dawna and me, *When you leave work at night hold your keys in your fist with the ends sticking out so you can punch the rapist in the eyes, okay, girls?*

"Matelasse!" James shouted. He could see me kneeling. I couldn't look back at him. Not yet.

The agent said, "We can call air support."

I said, "Like *Gunsmoke*, right? Your dad watch *Gunsmoke*? Cause I always watched it with my uncle Enrique, right there. You'll bring the army for the Indians?"

No one said anything.

"You check my wallet while I go in there and get my fucking car. A 2014 green Cherokee, okay? I will drive back out here and this shit better be done. That fucking gate better be open for me because I am *not* making my sons wait for hours. They're little boys. They want to watch *Finding Dory*." I closed my mouth and trembled down the sob again. "They don't watch *Gunsmoke*. So don't shoot me. Shit. I'm trying not to cuss here."

"Ma'am," the agent said, "you're gonna have to . . ."

I felt the sob rising up again. "They want macaroni and cheese for dinner so no. *Hell* no."

Kraft. And Doritos. My sons wanted fake American cheese dust. They wanted to watch TV with me sitting on the couch between them.

I turned my back on the agent with the gun, and looked right at my uncle Enrique. He lifted his chin about one sliver of one inch. Sofelia held out her arms. Then I put my right foot on the tangle of chains that locked the center of the gate and pulled myself up, holding on to the tiny crosses that were so hot they burned my fingers.

ACKNOWLEDGMENTS

I'm lucky to live around great storytellers who are way better than I am at transfixing listeners in person: Louis Lozano, who began this book on my porch; General RC Sims III and Dwayne Sims, Trent Chatham and Montrell Hamilton, Derrick and Leslie Sims, Teri Andrews, John Sims in the kinship of the driveway on Michael Street; Adolph Martinez, Kim Chanta, Inez Vasquez, Roberto and Dominga Segundo, Mario and Nancy Soria, Monique Veloz and Marcia Bales for fence and porch stories; Ed Hernandez, Rob Joslen and Darren Shipley, Chris Johnson and Diane Howard, Dawna St. Pierre and Mr. Beebe, Rene Lopez, Larry and Mona Perez, Ray and Lilly Allala at the Elks Lodge. Special thanks to Gordon Johnson.

I'm lucky to have Eleanor Jackson in my corner. I'm also lucky to have a true Californian editor extraordinaire in Jackson Howard, and an advocate in Emily Bell, all Golden State, who found *Mecca* a home. Thanks to Rodrigo Corral for the amazing cover; Brian Gittis, Claire Tobin, Sarita Varma, Mitzi Angel, Nancy Elgin, Louise

Collazo, Stephanie Umeda, NaNá V. Stoelzle, Byron Echeverria, and everyone else who helped; Felisha Carrasco for the photos.

I'm lucky to have generous, patient first readers: Jennifer Beals and Tom Jacobson, who made this such a better novel; Gordon Johnson, Alex Espinoza, Helena Maria Viramontes, Viet Thanh Nguyen, Attica Locke, Tod Goldberg, Michael Jaime-Becerra, Holly Robinson, Luis Alberto Urrea, Luis Rodriguez, Michael Connelly, Hector Tobar, Ivy Pochoda, Walter Mosley, Reiko Rizzuto, Kate Anger, and Stewart O'Nan.

Truly lucky for my family: my daughters, Rosette, Delphine, and Gaila; my sons-in-law, Kunmi and Andre; my little Swiss mom, Gabrielle; my Sims family of hundreds; the Chatham/Hamilton family; the Butts, Vargas, Andrews, and Lark kin; the Collins, Aubert, Chandler, and Gainer clans. Lucky for my communities of Eastside, Westside, Northside, Highgrove and Wood Streets; for my longtime home at the University of California, Riverside; for all the librarians at UCR and the Riverside Public Library; for the First United Methodist Church; for Elks Lodge #643 for dancing and darts and stories; for American Legion Post 79 for the car shows; for American Legion Post 289 for the bands; for the Fraternal Order of Eagles San Bernardino for old-school. Thanks to the live radio deejays who keep us working: Marci Wiser at KLOS, and the magnificent Art Laboe, who at ninety-nine still plays dedications of love every night for the world.

I lost my Dad while writing this, and so many others, from Covid, from living hard and loving hard. I'm grateful for the Santa Ana River at the end of my street, whose waters help me remember every evening those we've lost, and all who are still here in the tumbleweeds and cottonwoods.

A NOTE ABOUT THE AUTHOR

Susan Straight is the author of eight novels, including the national bestseller *Highwire Moon*, a finalist for the National Book Award, and *A Million Nightingales*, a finalist for the Los Angeles Times Book Prize, as well as the memoir *In the Country of Women*, named a best book of 2019 by NPR. She is the recipient of the Edgar Award for Best Short Story, the O. Henry Prize, the Lannan Literary Award for Fiction, and a Guggenheim Fellowship, and her stories and essays have been published in *The New Yorker*, *The New York Times*, *The Guardian*, *Granta*, *Harper's Magazine*, and elsewhere. She was born and continues to live with her family in Riverside, California, where she is Distinguished Professor of Creative Writing at the University of California, Riverside.